Meet Phil K Swift. He is one of the cooles
your whole life (at least he thinks so).

Hang out with Phil as he navigates his way through the mean Windy City streets of Chicagoland. He befriends Bboys and Bgirls (breakdancers) along his trek and learns that not every person is nice. Watch him tastefully deal with "big city" gangbangers, bullies, and trash talkers appropriately.

Phil K Swift assembles an incredible break dance crew called the "Neighborhood Street Rockers" who find themselves in a breakdance battle that has more on the line than pride and money; everything is at stake. Can they all make it out of Chicagoland Rink alive?

Other kick-butt things that will happen while you are reading this crazy story:

You will see how Phil went from being a geeky-nerd to a cool and hip-cat just like that.

Find out where and how this underground BBoy scene started (Break Dance scene).

Meet members of his break crew and learn why you might NOT want to use the term "breakdance." **We are BBOYS.**

You will gain an understanding of Breakdance moves.

Phil deals with teen peer pressure situations that can, "really be a punk ice bee-otch." See how he keeps his morals and beliefs right and is able to say "NO," even in the face of tough pressure.

Final warning: Anyone who reads this book will become cool. You may have people hawking you like a "ROCK STAR," don't say I didn't warn you!

THERE ARE TWO VERSIONS OF THIS STORY.
THIS VERSION IS FOR THE MIDDLE GRADES.

PHIL K SWIFT ASSEMBLES AN INCREDIBLE BREAKDANCE CREW

BY

PHILIP KOCHAN

4

Phil K Swift assembles an incredible break-dance crew

ISBN for paperback 978-0-9967425-0-4

ISBN for ebook 978-0-9967425-1-1

Library of Congress Control Number: 2015953193

Published in the United States of America

Coronation Publishing and books
Coronationpublishing.com

This book is dedicated to my beautiful wife Kelly, my wonderful kids; Anthony, Riley, Savannah, Mariah, and SummerWind - The six of you are my world.

Also, I am grateful for loving and ambitious parents that worked hard their whole lives to provide everything I ever needed. Thank you.

I miss my late brother.

Finally to all of you Bboys and Bgirls out there that are keeping it spinning; you are the lifeline to this thing we call Breakin'.

Don't stop the rock rock.

Once a Bboy, always a Bboy.

Once a Bgirl, always a Bgirl.

This is fresh!

Chapter 1

Phil K Swift

I'm not even trying to brag or anything but I am one of the hippest cats that you're ever going to meet in your entire wildest fantasy of a life, for real. I'm not talking smack. I'm just being honest with you. It turns out that I was a part of the original wave of breakers, which is a very big deal you know. In fact, I may as well tell you the whole story and start from the beginning, since I can tell you really give a freakin' Frack about what I'm saying. That's why you looked this way right?

I've got a whole lot of shiznit to drop on you, so listen up B-Boys and B-Girls while I lay it all on you. I'm not going to leave out any of the crazy ice details either, no matter how nuts it sounds. So cover your eyes and plug your ears if you don't think you can hang. What I am about to tell you is not for the goody goodies out there, so if you're one of them you better leave now before you get corrupted. I'm going to take you back to that year it all started for me.

It was 1983 in Chicagoland, more specifically; Downers Grove, Il. I wasn't called Phil K Swift just yet, that came later, but I was still a hip cat, it's just that nobody knew it yet. I was a legend in my own mind. I didn't really fall into any of those clique groups that everybody else at my school was falling into; I wasn't a jock or a burnout or a prep or a nerd – well … maybe I was just getting out of nerdom by the skin of my teeth. I eventually broke away from nerdom but that was after I figured a few things out. I'll tell you about that later on. But as for being a nerd and such, I was a geek in nerds clothing who became a geek in hip cats clothing so I looked different than I felt but deep down inside, I was still a geek. But I became a cool-geek. Are you following me so far?

Well, the more I think about it - I suppose that last year you could have just called me a geek or a nerd, flat out. The hip cat clothing probably wasn't fooling anybody except me. It's not that I had the black plastic watch with the calculator keyboard on the watch face and I wasn't wearing floods or anything. Well, not too often at least –and I certainly wasn't rocking red socks to my knees with green shorts to contrast the blue vinyl Velcro shoes that other geeks were wearing at my school … and proudly I might add. But I didn't start dressing hella-cool until lately. So yeah, I was half freak last year.

I can't claim to have never looked like any of those "total" geeks and freaks but things did drastically changed for me in the 5th grade when Willy Renoir told me, "Hey dude, nice tough skin pants, did mommy pick those out for you?" It was at that moment that I had realized that I had to stop having mommy pick out my clothes.

By 7th grade, I was dressing straight up sharp because rink fashion had become my passion. I'll tell you about the roller rink in a minute.

By 8th grade I ditched the pop bottle thick; brown framed nerd glasses and got myself some contact lenses, which opened up a whole new selection of chicks for me to mess up puppy love with.

Finally by 9th grade I stopped mom from putting a bowl around my head and giving me a giggle worthy haircut. You know the kind, it was very similar to an Amish mans hairdo, all bowl, no style, very Moe from the Three Stooges.

Anyway, I got rid of the hair combed like Moe by having my mom take me to this fancy schmancy ritzy Richie hoity-toity hair salon in Hinsdale that charged 100 dollars for women's haircuts and 50 bucks for young adults. Where they served adults champagne in the waiting room and rich women carried their 5000 dollar dogs around in their 5000 dollar dog purses.

The first time I went there, this cutie, which was the shampoo girl, phone girl, and champagne passer outer all in one, quietly offered me a glass of, "bubbly." She whispered to me, "Would you like some bubbly sir?" and let's just say, she was hotter than Mercury and Venus combined.

"Sure doll face," I said. Heck; I was only 14 years old and the next thing I knew I was sipping sparkling cider, like rich people do, while waiting to get my haircut. To be honest with you, I didn't know what she had meant when she had whispered, "Bubbly." I was pretty naïve back then but she made it sound so cute. But I later figured out that she had given me sparkling apple cider and the adults were drinking champagne.

Anyway, this hair dresser named Penny hooked me up with a "Billy Idol" spiked haircut which was really being odd and rebellious back in the early 1980's. This new super fly hair cut ended up pushing me out of geek-dom and into hip-cat-ness – just like that!

Nowadays you can have a Mohawk with blue hair, nipple piercings with chains that are attached to your nipple and eyebrow piercings and you might not even get stared at. In the early 80's spiked hair was rare on a kid, well for a little while at least, eventually everyone and their little brothers started rockin' 'em though; everyone eventually likes to jump on everyone else's bandwagon. Y'all a bunch of biters – no offense.

It wasn't just the spiky bleached blonde haircut, cool clothes, and contact lenses that snapped me out of geekdom and nerdiness though. I've got some other secrets, so keep listening. BUT -If you turn into a "Mack Daddy" or a "Cool Chick" don't blame me, I told you to cover your eyes before you get corrupted.

For example, the first night that I hung out at the roller rink after my new hip happening hair cut, I had two girls come up to me and ask, "Ohhh hey, can I touch your hair and feel your spikes?" Which come to think of it, I'm not sure if I even said anything to them when they said that; I think I just smiled out of shock. But that's when I first knew that I had really belonged. Some things –

you just never forget. The rock star, messy spiked, bleached blonde hair, and girls hawkin' me was when I knew, I was in- in like Flynn. Maybe I just had more confidence or maybe I did look cooler. I'm not really sure but whatever the reason, it didn't suck when chicks started diggin' me.

Beneath it all though, I was a guy who from time to time liked to read the dictionary for fun to polish up on fancy schmancy words. I was also the dude who had friends that talked about, "freakin' Punk ice Bee-otches that were going to be shown wazup when we knock 'em out da box." And other kinds of shiznit like that that some of my friends talked about when they were talking all tough. And some of my friends – weren't just talk; they walked the walk.

I had some rebellious friends but the thing about me is that I was smart enough to stay away from drugs but I was also dumb enough to almost inhale smoke this one day on the way home from school with these heavy metal burnouts that I was cool with. I'll tell you about that later; Peer pressure can really be a Punk ice Bee-otch, you know? I'm cool with the burnouts though it's just that 420's not my thing. What I am trying to say is; I am the cool dude that didn't have to drink booze or do drugs to be cool. I was just cool. And since we are on the subject of cool, I'll tell you all about it.

I know there's a lot more to being "cool" and "hip" than just thinking you are though. What makes me a hip cat for real though? I've got the groove baby! I listen to hippest of the mix jams, I dress like a stone cold hipster and I hang out at the rink on the weekends where all of the action happens. Oh yeah, the rink – I told you I'd tell you all about it, didn't I?

I went to Suburbanite Roller Rink every weekend night, which turned me from a kid to a cat – a hip cat, in an instant. From the moment you stepped inside the roller rink it was as if you were entering a whole new world of bigger kid secrets and mysterious things that you just couldn't wrap your brain around – and oh yeah, there was skating too.

There are certain things that happened at the rink from time to time that I probably shouldn't be talking about but I'm kind of a blabber mouth to be honest with you. I even tell my P.s almost everything, I put my foot in my mouth all of the time and tell them almost everything on accident. Thing is, I usually end up freakin' 'em out more than I need to be freakin' 'em out. But even though my mouth was as large as a watermelon, I had somehow managed to not tell them about the crazy amounts of French kissing that was going on at the rink, which would have put that place off limits to me. They didn't want me "growing up too fast" I was still their "little boy." I knew if I had told them about the "making out" that I had seen they literally would have freaked out. And not the good kind of freak out, like "Freak Le Chic" freak out, but the bad kind of freak out like: straight jacket, keep your butt home on the weekend's kind of freak out.

Speaking of freaking out, I just thought about something, so I'll tell you more about the rink in a second. There's something I've been dying to tell you about that I freaked out about – and this time it's the good kind of freaked out. This thing I saw on a TV show called, "PM Magazine" did this story about inner city kids from New York that had supposedly hung up their weapons, stopped fighting, and were now duking it out with "break dancing." Although, I would bet that it was just media spin because I'm sure that dancing wasn't really replacing violence in the gang banging neighborhoods. But I'm not going to get into that right now, what I wanted to tell you was, this show was playing clips of people on the ground: twisting, turning, spinning, twirling, and all sorts of cool ice shiznit like that. It was the first time I had ever heard of "Break dancing." Some things you'll just never forget. I instantly fell in love.

After school one day, while I was walking home with my buddy Brock Blazin' we got to talking about this thing called break dancing, which Brock happened to see the same TV show too. I decided to bust out with break dancing right in the middle of the street as we were walking home. I later learned that the move I was doing that day was called "down rock" or "floor rock" but Brock Blazin' was calling it, "Scatting."

That first day we had tried break dancing together, Blazin' kept saying to me while I was breakin', "Yo Phil, that's Swift man, that's Swift."

I got up off of the ground and I said, "That's why they call me Phil K Swift," even though nobody had ever really called me that before because I had just made it up. But that's what I said, and that's how I got my name.

Blazin' and I vowed from that point on to learn other break moves and become the baddest breakers ever. It eventually became our lives.

Chapter 2

What happens at the rink stays at the rink.

Saturday night was here and it was time to go to Suburbanite Roller Rink. I had been going to that rink for a few years but it wasn't until I bought myself a kickin' pair of roller skates at the pro shop and stopped being a "rental mental" that some of the cool cats that were a part of the rinks "in crowd" started talking to me.

Going to the roller rink is all of those things I had told you about earlier, but the thing that really had got me hooked on skating, other than the girls, was the tricks that could be done on skates; like spaghetti legs, crazy legs, and high speed turns. I loved making the loud screech sound as I power slid to stop on the rinks hardwood floor.

Since I'm telling you about the rink, I will let you know about this "In crowd" at the rink. I'm probably telling you about them because some of them kind of annoyed me. I can tell you that I wasn't in the "in crowd" but once I bought my expensive tricked out skates with the Blinger wheels and speed skate bearings along with the 200 dollar skate plates; it got me "IN" with some of the known "cool people," who actually started talking to me once I had cool skates. Which hey, I get it. Who wants to talk to a "rental mental" that skates like a chump? By the way "rental mentals" were the skaters who had to rent skates when they went to the rink.

I suppose anywhere and everywhere there's an "in crowd" and we all want to be "in" but some of these "in people" were just too cool for school, at least so they thought. I mean some of them seemed kind of dorky to me but because some of them had a brother or sister that knew people in this "in crowd" somehow that made them a part of the club too, which gave them the right to act like tough guys.

Once in a while you had to deal with dorks that thought they were cool because they knew the right people. And they knew that if you messed with them, they would have tall back up waiting in the wings to mess you up. I had watched it happen to many rental mentals who didn't quite get that there was an "in crowd" clique at the rink. These new comer rental mentals would mouth off to the wrong person at the wrong time and then BAMM, "Bruno Capone" or "J.D. Soprano." (a couple of cats from this "in crowd") would be surrounding them like flies on shee-ott and start pushing them around. That's why I mostly just kept to my crowd.

I'd usually get to the rink early right when it opened. I wanted to be one of the first ones inside. I didn't want to miss a thing. Even just waiting in the circular shaped lobby was a trip. The entire lobby reeked of girls perfume, dudes cologne, cigarette smoke, and gum. Older teen's jackets smelled as if they had smoked 10 packs of cigarettes just before they had walked inside. I hate cigarettes. Even 420 seemed to be lingering around the yellow lobby once in a while. Heck, I didn't even know what 420 was or what it smelled like until I started going to the rink. The first few times I had smelled it, I just assumed that someone down the street was burning leaves. But I know what it is now – and it's NOT for me.

While waiting to get in, you can totally hear other people's conversations, because of the acoustics in the circular shaped lobby. It's amazing how many teens were concerned about the fact that they may have had too many beans for dinner that night, whose ass itched, or whose feet smelled even after they took a shower. People should really watch what they say in close quarters, dontchya think?

When I started to hear the muffled music playing in the background, it meant the rink DJ was starting to warm it up and get things going and it meant that the cashier would soon be opening up her window to let us pay to skate. That was when everyone in the lobby would start pulling out their cash, which was a perfect time for a young business man to make his pitch. I'll tell you about him.

This one time, my buddy Witold Dee, (he goes by Witty) and I were laying low, just chatting and such, waiting to get in, when this big dude, which I recognized from school came up to me and opened up his jacket all slick like and pulled out some large packages of gum, "Sup dude? Pack of gum for a buck?" he asked while shifting his eyes around with raised eyebrows and a horizontal smile, not even looking at me, even though he was talking to me. I remembered thinking at the time that he had been sprayed by a skunk before he had walked in but the more I think about it now; it was Mary Jane, but like I said, I didn't know all that much about 420 just then. But I always remembered this incident because I would have sworn that he had been sprayed by a skunk. So I'm going to call this my "dude got sprayed by a skunk story" but I may have to revise that later to, "dude is a smoker story."

I think he tried to sell us gum as a decoy because he asked us seconds later, "Or anything else you guys might need?" and the way he had said it with a certain smile, made me think that he had smokes for sale under his dark green trench coat. I had seen enough of this kind of thing in the movies to know.

I told him, "No thanks, bro."

"Nahhh dude," Witty said.

"Did you get sprayed by a skunk?" I asked.

"Yeah, hah-hah, good one" Big Ted said.

Big Ted shifted his eyes from left to right a few times seeking out his next prospect, then quickly swept his way around the lobby hitting up the rest of the unsuspecting soon to be skaters, leaving a waft of what I now know was "smoke" behind.

After Ted walked away, Witty Dee rolled his eyes, and I told him about Big Ted. "He is the dude that has a pair of speakers in his locker at school. In the mornings and in between class periods he plays Vanity Six, "Nasty Girls" over and over again; every time I walk past his locker, it's jamming. That song is a groove," I said while nodding and smiling, as I noticed a couple of girls staring at me.

"I know who you're talking about," Witty said, "I just didn't recognize him at first, he's a loser, he sells all sorts of bull shee-ott."

Big Ted was the kind of guy that would say something to you confidently. But you wouldn't necessarily agree with him or even think the thing he was saying was true. But he would raise his eyebrows up and down a couple of times, show you the whites of his eyes, while nodding, and before you knew it, you'd be nodding with him too. Which made me start to wonder how much gum Big Ted actually sold that tonight? Ted was one of many "types" that had hung out at the rink. But it wasn't just the people that made the rink a big deal. It was the music and the lights. – and oh yeah … the skating.

I still remember how it always took a while for my eyes to adjust as I walked out of the bright yellow lobby, through the turnstiles, and into the dark, humungous, echoing skate rink that was jamming loud disco music with laser lights flashing that begged for my attention right when I walked in.

The funky fresh skate jams blasting from the speakers would always get my groove moving; the place was instant happiness. That place was where kids became teens. Right when you walked into the rink you could feel that something cool was going on.

Anyway, getting back to the Saturday night at the rink that I was about to tell you about, which was the same Saturday just after I had seen that show PM magazine with the break dancers.

"There's something going on" was echoing through the speakers as I sat down and started lacing up my skates. And as usual, I spotted some of the "in crowd" cats walking into the rink, hugging all over each other as if they hadn't seen each other in years - Even though they had just seen each other last week. They were all slobbering all over each other while they looked at everybody else as if they didn't even exist. This is what they always did, every time I went there. I suppose I was a little jealous and I guess I'm telling you this so you can feel it all. I want you to feel as if you were really there, you dig?

After lacing up my skates and watching the "in crowders" beam their "in crowd" eyes around, I started heading over towards the stand up arcade games. Nobody was on the rink hardwood yet. And I usually needed a few minutes to start to feel my skate groove anyway, so I headed on through the carpeted outskirts of the rink and slowly made my way towards the Donkey Kong and Pac Man video games. I passed by a couple teenagers sitting on the benches where you'd expect them to be lacing up their skates but they had other ideas. They had picked a less lit section of benches where the two horn dogs were ramming each other's tongues down each other's throats. I didn't want to eyeball them too much but they were straight up mashing! Old boy had his octopus arms all over the place. I mean some of this stuff was a little gaudy. They didn't seem to be in too big of a hurry to get their skates on. There was definitely something going on just as the song was singing.

"Yo Phil – Sup?" Witty Dee slapped my back and yelled, "Are ya ready for some roller tag dude?"

"I'm just heading to the back of the rink by the arcade games my brother! I'll get you in a game of tag in minute; I'm about to rock out on some Pac man. I'll catch up with you in a few," I told Witold Dee as he gave me a nod and skated off. I knew he was ready to get on the rink and get some roller tag going but I usually started out my night over by the coin ops. I was only going to drop a quarter in the game but since I could rock it like a rocket, that quarter on Pac Man would last me a good hour, put that on the docket. I was a Pac Man champ, you see, and I remember this part of the night because it was the first time that I had broke 200,000 points and I had made it to the key where the ghosts didn't turn blue anymore, even after eating the power pill. Some things you just never forget.

After my game ran out, I heard the DJ playing my jam, "Don't stop till you get enough," by M.J. If Michael Jackson couldn't get you out on the floor, nothing would. It was time to rock, time to roll, time to skate, and get out on the floor. I had been working on my trick skating a lot in those months –in fact, big time! Trick skating to Michael Jackson made me look like a big deal you know.

For those of you who don't know, trick skating is like dancing on skates. Which may not sound all that tough but I guess you would have to see it to understand; it's actually very tough, just ask any girl who hangs out at the rink. Although, I understand how a lot of people may not see it that way. For example, I first started going to the rink in 5th grade. By sixth grade I already had someone that wanted to kick my butt because I told him I liked to go roller skating. I guess it can sound kind of wimpy if it's not explained the right way.

You see, in sixth grade we had pen pals from another school across town with other kids in our same grade. I wrote in my letter to my pen pal about how I liked to go roller skating on the weekends. So he was probably picturing some pansy that skated around some rink with flowers in his hands or something. He wasn't picturing tough tricks, high speed movements on skates, and hot rink chicks, that's for sure.

Our teachers had arranged for both classes to meet one another so we could all meet our pen pals; on the day that our class walked over to our pen pals school, my pen pal didn't show up. All the kids were telling me how lucky I was that he didn't show up because my pen pal named Bucky Munster was going to kick my ass when he saw me because I said I liked roller skating. I was shocked someone wanted to kick my ass over it.

Looking back, I guess I could have told him that when you go to the roller rink there are a lot of girls there, that are dressed cute, and about the "making out" and stuff like that. Because when it came down to it, the rink was really all about the girls. If there were no girls at the rink, I wouldn't have gone there; Aint nothing pansy about that. But I guess it never really occurred to me to write that in a 6th grade pen pal letter. But it also never occurred to me that someone would want to kick my ass because I said I went roller skating.

Anyway back to my trick skating I was telling you about. I had been practicing my crazy legs and spaghetti legs like a madman. I had just figured out how to do spaghetti legs last month. This is a trick you do while you're skating around the rink floor trying to look all hot-cool. You get up on your two front wheels on each skate and start zig zagging your skates in and out in the shape of the letter "C" with the left skate and a backwards "C" shape with the right skate. Kind of like a pattern you'd see in a top loading washing machine at home while your clothes were switching back and forth. You dig?

And of course I had been working on my speed skating and quick maneuvers too; which came in handy when you had a half a dozen buddies on your tail in a game of roller tag out on the rink floor. Yep, I said roller tag, it's not really as juvenile as it sounds, I'll have to tell you about it later. It's actually kind of dangerous sometimes. Wiping out on a hard wood floor can really kill somebody sometimes; so it's not your little brothers game of "tag" is what I'm saying.

So, where were we? Oh yeah, MJ was grooving over the rinks sound system and after doing a quick lap around the rink to see who was there so far, I spotted 2 hotties entering the rink and heading towards the rental skate booth. I took a couple of more laps around and I let them get their skates from the rental shop. I watched from afar; I tried to not be obvious. The next time I skated around I threw a long look their way. I tried to act as if I wasn't looking at them but I also tried to have a "cool face," whatever that was, but I know I tried. Once I saw they had noticed me, I sort of smiled and tried to look like a hot shot and act as if I wasn't looking, so I busted out into some high speed spaghetti legs.

While I was zig zaggin' my blinger wheeled trick skates back and forth I saw one of the girls nudge the other girl as she secretly pointed in my direction. I took another lap around not to look too anxious, but I knew … it was on, it was on like Donkey Kong. The girl was straight up gawkin'.

As I was making my lap around, I thought about the coolest part about those two chicks, other than the fact they were stone cold foxes, they were rental mentals. You know what that means? It meant they were not a part of the infamous rink "in crowd." I wouldn't have to watch my back, just because I was trying to talk to a couple of girls. If they were Rink regular girls – I'd have to watch my back, just for even looking at them. It's funny, something so small like what kind of skates someone wears tells a whole story.

After my lap around, I was ready to make my move, I smoothly exited the disco lighted hardwood rink floor and I made my way to the darker more mysterious carpeted rink outskirts. I felt the carpet slow my skates as I quietly headed towards the benches by the two unknown "rental mental" girls who were just chilling and casually putting their skates on. It's funny; we guys have to move mountains to look all cute but girls … girls can look all cute by just putting a pair of skates on.

On my way over I was thinking about what I was going to say to those girls. The only thing I could come up with was, "HI." But hi is good. Hi is better than saying nothing at all. And Hi is better than saying something stupid. As I was skating over I saw one of the girls nudging the other girl who was previously the nudger. The nudger had become the nudgee. Girls – all they have to do is nudge another girl with their elbow and they look totally cute with their nudging and such. However, we guys; we have to catch lightning in a bottle to look cute. It's just the way it works.

I was looking in their direction without being too obvious, and trying to have a mix of chill and confidence all in one. They both started waving their arms like two people floating on a life raft that had been lost at sea for hours – it's as if they were waving their arms at a passing airplane for dear life. I remembered thinking, wow - these chicks are really trying to get my attention. They must have loved my trick skating.

I started to skate more directly towards them so I could say, 'HI' and find out their names and all. Then out of nowhere. Witty Dee slapped my back red hot hard and yelled in my ear, "You're it!" it was loud enough where I was sure the girls had heard it.

Witty Dee skated off as to not get a tag back.

And I suddenly felt like a kid.

Now I know I told you that playing tag at the rink is not really as juvenile as it sounds but I also realize that when you're trying to look all cool for the girls, playing tag, doesn't exactly accomplish that goal. But really, I'm serious, cutting in and out through the busy rink crowd at high speeds, trying to avoid another high speed skater from tagging you while also trying to fly under the radar from the rink skate guard, who can throw you out of the rink if he catches you skating all crazy, really makes this game a challenge. But I know, it did nothing for the chick magnet factor.

After Witty Dee skated away I continued to head towards the two smokin' hot rental mentals that were still a good hundred feet away. One of the girls was looking at me square in the eyes. She waved me towards her. She was even being more obvious with her waving than she had been a minute ago, which seemed kind of odd since I was obviously heading their way already.

Another Michael Jackson jam began pumping through the woofers and tweeters while the smell of someone's sweet yet awful perfume that reminded me of old lady perfume hit my nose, practically triggering an asthma attack. I muttered, "If I didn't know any better I'd think that someone was wearing my grandmas' perfume." I said randomly, trying to get a laugh, to this group of "in crowders" that was lingering by the lockers, but nobody paid attention to me. I'm sure if I was an "in crowder" everyone would have laughed his or her jack-asses off. When you're popular, every joke you say is funny. But don't get mad or jealous; just become popular. Don't worry, you'll know how by the end of my story.

I coolly and casually skauntered toward the two girls, oh yeah, skauntered it's my own word – I made it up. Skate and saunter merged together. Studying the dictionary in your free time can really have a weird effect on you, you know? The closer I got to this girl, the cuter she got. The disco lights were bouncing off of her curves like snowflakes. Whether a girl has tiny curves or big curves, it makes no difference to me; girl curves are girl curves; girls should never worry about what kind of curves they have.

As I cool-cat-ed-ly inched over towards her I couldn't help wondering why she had this funny look on her face and was still aggressively waving at me, even though I was close enough for her to spit on me. (Well, if she really belted a hocker out. I mean, if she could spit like a guy, then I was a spitting distance from her.) She was acting as if I hadn't even acknowledged her yet or anything. But I had. I had already winked, did the head nod, and hap hazard wave of my own. Plus I was obviously heading her way. Girls can really be a mystery sometimes.

The closer I got to her; I started thinking about how cute her curly brown hair looked in the purplish red disco lights. Her bangs were hanging down hiding her flirty eyes, which made my heart clang that much faster and her midriff shirt showed her belly button – just barely. Yet all I could think about was: why is this pretty-goofy girl still waving at me like someone at a sporting event trying to get the camera man to put them on TV?

I was seconds away from talking to her when she stopped waving. Belly button showing girl smiled big and I was thinking: cool, so far, so good. Then like a bolt of lightning. Bruno from the rinks "In crowd" swooped in from around me and gave the wavy haired girl a big hug. "That was awkward," I said out loud, but only to myself. I kept on skating passed the two girls and Bruno while feeling like a jack ass.

Then I shouted out, "Yo Witty Dee, wait up," but Witty Dee actually was nowhere in sight. He had skated away just after tagging me. I just had to save some face, you know. So I pretended I was waving at him.

I was wondering if the girls had known that I was heading towards them. But it's cool I got it, they were actually flagging someone else down that was behind me; none other than Bruno from the rinks "In crowd." He was one of the dudes at the rink that had lots of "big friends" and he was definitely not someone to mess with. He had too many people to back him up. In fact he was the last person that I'd want to see those girls talking to. As I skated by, I heard one of the girls say something about how her speed skates were getting repaired – and that was that.

It was time to look for Witty Dee or Brock Blazin' because "I was it" and it was time to un-it myself. It was a perfect time to find someone to tag because Harry the rink guard was still helping the mentals get their rentals instead of being out on the rink floor patrolling. Therefore, I didn't have to worry about getting kicked out of the rink for skating all crazy while I hunted down my targets.

You know what? Real quick, I'll tell you about my buddy Blazin' since he was first on my tag list. Brock Blazin' was one of those cats that you would see in a crowded place like a movie theater and he would just grab your attention out of nowhere. The theater could be dark, crazy, loud, and packed and Brock would just stand out. He would grab your eye, for no particular reason. He'd be the big pumped up cat, big smiled and sculpted jaw teen that was laughing his teeth off. I mean, he would be getting all of his body English into his crazy laugh, grinning with his eyes too – and you'd just have to look, he is that captivating. Funny thing about him - whatever he was laughing about probably wasn't even funny to anybody else but him. So when you'd ask him "Wazup?" about all of his laughing. He would then have to explain to you why he was laughing so hard. But his explanation wouldn't make sense, so he'd keep explaining and explaining until you finally laughed too – for no reason, just like him, even though you probably just pretended to laugh to get him off your back, so you could go back to watching the movie again. But that's my buddy Brock Blazin'. Even though it may have been a dark movie theater that you had first met him - you'd remember him if you saw him later, he just stands out, even in the dark. That's exactly why he was the first person on my list to un-it myself.

I scanned the oval rink floor which was slowly becoming filled with skaters and couples, while the carpeted outskirts of the rink were also filled with people: walking, gossiping, and damsels longing to be seen. Or maybe, I was just longing to see them. Many were just chill-axxin' and others were quickly getting their skates on and laced up. There were plenty of lovebirds to go around too. Those two lovebirds I told you about earlier. They were still going at it and talking all of that mushy mush while they stared at each other all starry eyed. I playfully yelled out, "Sup smoochy faces!" while they weren't looking my way. After I had said it, they looked in my direction but I played it off and passed the blame.

I noticed this crowd of dorky looking rental mental guys, one with bucked teeth and another with pants pulled up to his nipples within my path of the lovebirds. While the lovebirds were still staring in my direction, I scolded the dorky gang of guys with my best tough guy impersonation, as if to pass off the blame for that, "smoochy faces" remark. I said, "Y'all should mind your own business" as loud as I could so the lovebirds could hear. I then looked at the lovebirds, coolly nodded, I looked back at the rental mentals, and I shook my head like they were nerds. I kept up my tom foolery by shrugging my shoulders and said, "Kids" as I skated away.

The two lovebirds gave those dorks some dirty looks and then went back to their smoochy smooch. I skated away laughing to myself. I loved doing stuff like that. Truth be told, my buddy Witty Dee taught me this kind of crazy ice shiznit. Witty Dee was always busting someone's chops or blaming someone else for something he had done. Funny thing is - not too long ago, I looked just like those bucked tooth, pop bottle glasses, and pants up to their nipples dorks; the mess-ee had become the messer. I had to mess with them though, even though I felt sort of sorry for them. But not too sorry, I guess. Is it bullying if someone chooses to dress like a dork? The moral to this story is: DON'T DRESS LIKE A DORK!

An animated shadowy figure had caught my eyes from half way across the rink. Someone was flailing about under the bright snack bar lights. It had stuck out like a zit on cheek. I quickly skated my way over on a hunch. Show nuf, it was Blazin'. I skated over to his table; Blazin' was all chillin' like a villain. He was going on and on about how freshy fresh some dudes shoes were, who was also sitting at the table. Blazin' was all foaming at the mouth and filling the snack bar room with echoes of his voice - louder than anything else that was going on in the snack bar. You could feel the eyes glaring at our loud table. Mainly Blazin's uproar.

Blazin's mouth and eyes were filled with energy as he talked loudly about the dudes kicks. I had only caught a glimpse of them, but the more Blazin' went on and on about them, I felt the pressure to agree. I even started thinking quietly to myself, maybe the shoes are really cool and I just didn't know it yet. Maybe I was just not getting it and I should get with it. Heck I even started to want a pair. Brocks salivating, open mouth, and nodding head, made me want a pair. It's funny though, I could barely even see the dudes' shoes because his feet were camped out under the table. Yet I suddenly wanted a pair too. That's the kind of passion Brock Blazin' had. I didn't even have to see the dudes shoes, yet I knew I wanted them.

I started to get the impression that the dude with the "killer kicks" wasn't really that excited about his own shoes; at least the same way Blazin' was excited about them. I could tell the dude was starting to feel the pressure to get a little more excited about his own stinkin' shoes because he started adding to the conversation, "Yeah, umm, my shoes are cool dude, I agree, okay, they're cool, it's all good man …. Chill," he had said sort of annoyed; when the dude told Brock to chill, he really meant shut up.

Blazin' can have that effect on a person.

After talking about that cat's shoes for a million minutes, Brock Blazin' finally asked me, "Yo Swift – have you seen Witty Dee yet?"

"Yeah I caught up with him for a minute. I've just been out there skating and looking around the rink … and there are some chica's up in this jizz-oint tonight my brudda," I said to Blazin', all slick like, since there was a table load of girl's right next to us. It's funny, when girls are around, they can make me talk like a hip cat.

Blazin' continued on, "Have you seen these dudes' kicks yet bro?" he asked me again.

"Yep, they're sharp for sure," I told him, even though I wasn't really sure if I had seen them or not but I wasn't about to make the dude get up from the table and stop eating his pizza, just to show me his darn shoes. If anything the thing that crossed my mind was: why didn't the dude have his skates on yet?

"Yo Brock, I've gotta tell you something but I don't want everyone to hear, come here for a sec," I said. I leaned in all slyly, while positioning my skates for a getaway and then I swiped Blazin's back. "You're it my brother from a different mother, you're it." I quickly skated away into the disco lighted, booming sound system, lovebird haven, gossiping skaters abound – carpeted rink outskirts, and began looking for Witty Dee.

I could hear in the distance, even though the rink speakers were blasting my ears off, "Awe man, you ganked me dude, you ganked me – paybacks are a bee-otch Swift!" I looked back and Blazin' was still sitting at the table. Seconds later, I swear I could still hear Blazin' yelling at me, "That's bunk dude, that's bunk," he was that loud.

I skated passed the lovebirds again and gave 'em a nod, then I saw that Harry the rink guard was done hooking up the initial rush of mentals with their rentals. So I quickened my pace and I caught up to him, I talked with him once in a while. A few girls were huddled around him giving him hugs and kisses and all that stuff which were the perks of being a rink guard. I just waited around a bit, keeping an eye out for Witty and Brock while he talked with the girls and I waited my turn to talk to him. He was a pretty popular cat at the rink. He was a part of that infamous "in crowd" but he was cool to me. Maybe he had to be since he worked there. But either way, he was cool.

Harry was sportin' zipper pants that I had never seen before. They were puffy gray pants with gold zippers running down the sides of his legs with maroon sections of fabric on the inside of the zippered portion; the zipper started at the tapered ankles and extended to the hips, fresh as all heck.

I nodded at Harry a few times, to let him know, I was waiting for him, who half smiled back to acknowledge me. But I understood why he kind of blew me off, he was in the middle of chatting it up with a couple of "in crowd" hotties that were still hugging all over him. You can't blame a guy for giving you the cold shoulder when something like that was going on.

Skate guard Harry and the two girls were finally done talking and exchanging hugs and all of that, so I asked, "Yo Harry I'm not trying to bite your style or anything but you've got to tell me where you got those pants from?"

He smiled and told me, "You can get them at Chess King in Dorktown mall."

I asked him if the zippers on the sides could zip all of the way up and hide the maroon inside if you wanted to, so he started zipping them up and shaking his head yes and then quickly zipped them all the way back down. I knew I sounded like a kid when I had asked it, but I was just too curious not to, so I asked it anyway. After that, I could tell that Harry was done talking to me by the way he had started to skate away as he was unzipping his parachute pants and talking all at once.

Harry skated onto the busy rink floor and I stayed on the outskirts of the rink in the carpeted section where it was more hidden. It was less lit; there were less people, and more shadows, so it was easier to see who was coming at me and who was on the rink floor, which was important when playing roller tag.

"Get down on it," by Kool and the Gang was echoing all throughout my head as I was on the lookout for my mates. I prowled around quietly as I watched the skaters get down to the ground while they were skating. Every time the chorus played, "Get down on it" random skaters throughout the oval shaped rink floor would stick one leg out in front of them and put the other leg simultaneously behind them while pouncing to the floor on the word, "down" and springing back up again by the word "it." There were a good 20 or 30 people, getting "down on it" in unison along with the song. It really looked pretty cool, if you know what I mean. You've really got to see it sometime.

It seemed like forever but I spotted Witty Dee and Brock Blazin' skating together and scheming together. I could tell by their body language that Blazin' must have tagged Witty Dee and they were now trying to find me and nail me. They were teaming up against me, but they didn't know that I was hip to their jive. But because I had been skating in the shadows; you know, laying low like a pro, on the DL like a gazelle. And straight up incognito like a bandito; they had no idea where I was.

My Plan was to stay in the shadows for a bit, at least until "couples skate only." During couples skate - all bets were off; you can't tag anyone during couples skate only. Besides, if I knew Witty Dee and I did. During couples skate only Witty Dee almost always grabbed some mojo (that means; guts or confidence) and would ask some girl to skate. So that would be one less tag opponent to worry about after the couples skate, I figured.

Witty Dee was good like that. He had no fear, any girl was fair game; he didn't care. He'd even ask a rink "in crowd" girl to skate once in a while.

Actually if I've got to tell you the truth, most of the time I'm a big chicken when it comes to asking some random girl that I've never talked to before to skate. Lucky for me, once in a while, some chick would approach me and ask me to skate. Even when I was hideous and nerdy looking, some "okay looking" girl would come ask me to skate. It's not that I thought she was "not so hot" or "just okay" – that's just what my friends had said to me after I had gotten done skating with her. But the way I saw it, a girl was a girl, and that was good enough for me. But ever since I changed my style, things got better, which was cool with me, you see, that's why I've been telling you – it pays to dress cool, have a cool haircut, and be sly on skates with the tricks and such. It really does get you noticed and make you stand out. Who's going to get the chicks? Someone whose standing out or someone whose not?

After a couple of minutes of chillin' like a villain and laying low, one of my jams came on, grooving through the sound system. "Abra Cadabra" reeled me in. That's just one of those songs that even though I knew I was a tag target, I had to take my chances and get out on the floor anyway. You see skating is kind of like dancing on skates, when the music's right; you're just grooving on skates, you dig? So when your jam comes on, you've gotta get out there.

I groovily made my way onto the oval rink floor and busted out with squiggly spaghetti legs right in front of a bench load of girls. I'm quite the show off, most of the time. I really am. I tried to remain a half the rinks oval distance behind my tag mates. Or was it half a distance in front of them? Meanwhile, I was shucking and jiving in and out of skate traffic while mouthing the words to Steve Miller bands jam. Then almost as if time had stopped and had trapped me in awesomeness, I saw off into the distance on the outskirts of the rink where I was just hanging out, not even two minutes ago, the coolest and most amazing thing I had ever seen. I wish I could find a more meaningful way to say it to you, but I can't. Some things you just can't do them any justice by putting them into words, it's just indescribable, if you want to do it proper justice that is, so I won't even try.

I cut right down the middle of the rink floor, while dodging skaters, and avoiding Harry the guard but not caring about my silly little game of tag anymore. I quickly made my way through the swarm of skaters, magically cutting through the maze of people and I made it there. Time unfroze, I felt awesome and fantastic.

Two guys, probably about my age were both wearing red sweatshirts. One guy with a hood, the other guy without, they looked like they might be brothers. The taller of the two had long black hair, a goatee beard (yet he looked young – maybe 15), and black cursive letters on the breast area of his sweatshirt that read, "Poppin G."

The other dude, who had just popped up from the ground, and was the one who had actually caught my eye from across the rink floor, with his fantastically tornadic and whirl winding break dance move, was looking at me and smiling with an: I'm out of breath, sort of smile. He had just rocked 360 degree spins and quick bursts of windmill movements on the ground and I had seen all of it. I saw it from a mile away. His legs were in the shape of the letter V and his body kept spinning continuous back spins to chest spins to back spins again and so on.

Break dancing - I had heard about it not even a week ago from that TV show I had told you about. I had wanted to learn how to do it since last week, but I didn't know anybody else who knew anything about it, other than Blazin' and I. We had been trying to figure it out on our own all week with some moves we had made up but our stuff looked nothing like this cats stuff.

Here I was, smack dab in the middle of a couple of hip cats bustin' out with breakin' and I was hooked. This cat started pacing around in an imaginary circle on the carpet, while making slight eye contact with me, as if he knew that I was watching him. Or maybe he could tell that I had came over out of curiosity for his breakin' and he wanted to make sure I saw it all.

He dove to the floor and started spinning around in complete circles on his chest and back; his legs were stretched out wide in the shape of the letter "V." He was doing a circle within a circle of his own body. Picture a spinning top spinning on top of a record player, you dig?

When he finished, he jumped to his feet fast, kind of rough, but it seemed on purpose. He gave off a friendly smirk to me and then to the rest of the rink but actually at that moment I was among the few people paying attention to him, since most everyone else was skating by that point. He looked back at me and started grinning. In that moment, I knew he was friendly; it was that kind of grin.

He looked over to me and said an out of breath, "hello" or I think he may have even said, "HI Low."

I was next to a ceiling mounted speaker, I could barely hear him. I pointed to my ear as, "Der Komissar" was playing over the speakers and said, "Sup man that was cool – your Break dancing rocked!" I felt like a kid when I had said it, but I didn't care. It did rock.

He smiled wide but he didn't say anything; he just looked at me.

"Where'd you learn that stuff bro?" I asked him.

"I just learned it," he said as he smirked again.

"Wow dude that was awesome! What do you call that?" I asked him.

"Helicopters … some people call them windmills," he said. He was a teen of very few words but very many smiles.

After talking to him for a few minutes I could see that he had some black cursive writing on his sweatshirt that read, "Miguel 2 tough."

I told Miguel, "Hey, well its cool to meet you. My name's Phil K Swift … you can call me Phil." And when I had said it, he had given me the biggest smile ever, to the point where I almost wondered if I had sounded odd or something? - That's how big he had smiled at me.

I didn't usually introduce myself as Phil K Swift but when you're meeting someone named, "Miguel 2 tough" and "Poppin G.," it only seemed right to introduce myself as the cool cat that I was. Miguel smiled so big, it looked like a banana across his mouth when he said, "I'm Miguel and this is my brother Gio."

"Can you teach me how to break dance?" I asked hopefully.

"Sure!" Miguel said. Then he began to go through the steps of how to do helicopters (windmills) with me.

In the middle of hanging out with Miguel and Gio, I heard the DJ get on the mic and say, "Aaaah yeah, couples skate – couples skate only. Grab a girl, grab a guy, couples skate only." At the same time, coming from the rinks skating floor, Witty Dee and Brock Blazin' were heading my way. When they got over by Miguel, Gio, and me they started talking trash about how I was hiding on the carpet because I was afraid of getting tagged and such.

"Ahhh, the scaredy cat is hiding from us," Witty said.

"Chicken," Brock clucked.

But I cut them off and explained to them, "I was out there skating around to my jam, "Abracadabra ..."

Then Witty Dee cut me off and said, "Yeah – you can pull my other leg too, it will disappear!" He obviously thought I was lying.

When Poppin G. busted out into pop lockin', (which is like rhythmic arm dancing, with ticks, and body waves and snaky wrist twists, and stuff, In case you didn't know), that sort of made everyone quiet for a minute while we all watched.

Miguel 2 tough moved to the floor to break again with foot work or "scatting," as Brock had been calling it all week, which finally grabbed Blazin's attention. I mean, it really grabbed him BIG TIME. Blazin' looked at me wide eyed and horse toothed and I told him, "That's the reason I left the rink floor, that's what I was trying to tell you guys, these cats are breakin'!"

Blazin' smiled at me like a teen that had just found a "Playboy" magazine and said, "Whoa dude, that's awesome!"

But Witty Dee seemed less interested in breakin' and told Blazin' and me that he was going to ask a girl to couples skate. – Did I know Witty or what?

Miguel kept helicoptering around, while I watched Witty Dee confidently skate away. He approached this girl that he was checking out last week, but never really said hi or asked her to skate or anything, until now. He approached the girl and switched into his "cute mode." It was weird to watch Witty act nice. I could see him smiling and playing all cute and going in for the arm touch, real quick, yet soft, just to make contact; kind of like a failed attempt at holding her hand. Then he smiled as if he was shy, but he's not. Then he grabbed her hand, motioned cutely with his shoulders, and made her go out on the floor with him for a couples skate.

You could tell that she was just playing hard to get by the way she kept smiling shyly and was willingly creeping closer to the rink floor with him. Witty Dee's a pro but you could also tell that this girl was hoping someone was going to ask her anyway.

The girl Witty had asked, had a buddy, who I was digging – it was one of the girls I had almost said "Hi" to until Bruno cut me off. Now, she was in a conversation with 2 other girls and 2 other guys that were rink regulars, so I left it alone. I sort of checked her out from afar but Blazin' snapped me out of my longing look, when I heard him say, "Yo bro, that's fresh! Your spinning is sweet my man!" Blazin' was giving his compliments to Miguel of course. Then he started looking at me with excited eyes and said, "Did you see those copters Swift? Did you see those copters?"

I nodded and told Brock, "Heck yeah!"

Then Blazin' asked me the same question again out of excitement. Which was typical Blazin'. He would ask me if I just saw something even though he darn well knew that I just saw it. Then he'd ask again. It could go on for hours. When he got pumped, there was no stopping him.

Blazin' and I both started talking to Miguel and Poppin G. about how we wanted to learn how to break. I told them about the entertainment news show that I saw the other night on TV called, "PM magazine."

Miguel cut me off and said, "Yeah, it was kind of phony how they said that gangbangers aren't fighting anymore because of break dancing."

"Yeah, I thought that sounded kind of nuts too," I said.

Miguel continued, "… and they kept calling it break dancing? … I've always called it B-boying or breakin' but whatever. That's what my cousins from New York called it 'breakin'." Then Miguel did a twisting flipping twirl into the air and gravity took him to the ground into helicopters that seemed to have doubled in speed from his last time around.

Blazin' yelled, "That rocked man that rocked!"

Miguel 2 tough kept on breakin' even during the slow couples skate songs as Blazin' and I kept watching with awe.

When "Total eclipse of the heart" stopped playing and the couples skate was over, Witty Dee left the rink floor, skated quickly by us with his "new friend" and said, "This is Muffy, I'll be back in a second," and then they went over by her friends – the "in crowders" where something had really stuck out right away.

As I looked over by Witty and Muffys friends, I saw Bruno giving Witty Dee mean looks. I couldn't tell for sure but it looked like Bruno and Witty Dee were talking about something.

After a bit, Witty Dee skated back over to us and I asked him, "Did Bruno say something to you?"

Witty replied, "Who cares!"

You see, just like I told you, Witty Dee has no fear, even though this dude Bruno was known for picking on people and being a bully and he had a lot of "older" friends, Witty still didn't give a flippin' frog. Then in a flash of thought, I realized that I was Witty Dee's backup if Bruno were to mess with him. I hate having to be someone's backup; I just like having backup, not that I ever want to use it.

Witty Dee asked Blazin' and me, "Do you guys want to join Muffy and her friends and me to go and hang out at the snack shop for some pizza?"

"You want pizza?" I asked Witty with a weird smile.

"Yeah dude, that's what I just said," he said like a tough guy.

"A pizza THEEZ farts," I said while fanning my butt as if I had just farted.

Witty skated away saying, "Ohhh, I see how it is, a wise guy, ehh." He had said it in this "Curly" voice, yet Wittys face had this: you're a friggin' punk sort of smile that told me, he would be getting me back soon. That's the thing about Witty Dee he would always get you back, especially on a burn-joke.

Brock muscled his way into my joke and loudly said, so Witty could hear, "Ohh shiznit, Phil just served you dude. He made you look stupid Witty. STOOO Piddd." I knew Brock was purposely trying to get Witty riled up, because Brock also knew, that old Witty Dee was going to get me back.

I probably would have joined Witty and his "new girl" and such but Blazin' and I were too excited about this thing called breakin', so we skipped the food offer and the females to hang out with our new found friends Miguel and Giovanni.

Witty Dee smoothly grabbed Muffys hand as if he had never even left her side and as if he'd known her for weeks, when in fact he had just met her that night, other than a stare down last week. That's how confident he looked when he grabbed her hand is what I'm screamin'. He was a real pro. He's one of those guys that parents warn their daughters about.

Witty Dee and Muffy smiled and talked to each other as they made their way to the snack shop, when coming as no surprise to me, I saw Bruno looking at the two of them with fire in his eyes. Even though Bruno was at least 100 feet away from me, I swear it looked like he had tightened his teeth together, smashed his hands in anger, and flapped his mouth in what was most likely mean words.

Blazin' and I spent the next couple of hours together with Miguel 2 tough and Poppin G. We chatted it up and learned how to break all night long – we had forgotten all about skating. Before I knew it, time was up and it was time to bounce or as Blazin' liked to say, "Yo, Lets blow this crazy joint Yo!"

I got Miguel 2 tough's number and began to put my skates back on again. I had taken them off a couple of hours ago while Miguel was teaching me how to do helicopters. I didn't quite learn how to do the copters yet but Miguel showed me enough of the moves that I figured I'd be able to learn them at home with some practice.

I knew I was going to have to drag Witty Dee away from his new gal pal because they were looking all cozy ever since they had couples skated. So after tying my skates, I skated over to the snack shop to find Witty Dee. Blazin' told me that he would meet us outside. Blazin's dad was picking us up that night and he didn't want to keep him waiting. But you know, Blazin' was one of those cat's that was always in a big hurry to leave a place, even if we had just got there. I didn't really know for sure if he just didn't want to leave his dad waiting or if he was just in a big hurry for the sake of being in a hurry.

The only reason he had even lasted that long inside of the rink that night was because we were checking out some breakin'. Otherwise, Blazin' would have had us waiting outside in the parking lot a long time ago, for no good reason. Witty Dee and I would always laugh because we'd tell Brock, "You're always in a big hurry to go nowhere, RELAX!"

Blazin' would always say, "Okay, I'll relax, I'll relax" and then I kid you not, one minute later, Blazin' would say, "Hurry up let's go, let's go!" That's just

Blazin' for you. He was always in a big hurry to get somewhere and then he'd always be in a big hurry to leave.

I made my way back onto the rink hardwood floor. I figured I might as well do one last lap around the oval, especially since Rappers Delight was jamming in my ear. I wheeled up onto my front wheels and started zig zaggin' spaghetti legs at a high rate of speed, well as fast as you can go when you're doing that sort of a thing. I wanted to find Witty Dee and get out while the getting was good, you know, before I'd have to end up being Witty Dee's backup or something, if you dig what I'm saying. I really do try to stay out of trouble.

After one quick lap around, I got off the rink floor over by the arcade games and started heading to the snack shop to look for Witty. I almost tripped over two lovebirds in the dimly lit arcade section of the rink. It looked like the same two lovebirds that I had busted out earlier in the night with that "smooch face" comment. They had their legs stretched out and their skates were still on, which made it hard to pass them. They were moving their legs all over the place like spiders, and they had accidentally almost tripped me. That's how busy they were with their serious "make out session." You'd have thought that they were trying to clean peanut butter off of each other's lips, that's how crazy they were kissing is what I'm screamin'. But that's what older teenagers do, you know; they kiss once in a while.

I yelled out again, just like last time, "Wazup smoochy smoochersons" only this time I didn't look away and play it off. I was staring right at them with playful eyes. But I was wrong, it wasn't that other couple of love birds from earlier. It was Witty Dee and Muffy. I skated right up to them and smiled. They both smiled back at me and then went right back at it; kissing the heck out of each other.

I cut them off and said, "Yo Witty Dee, Brock's out in the parking lot already waiting for us."

Witty Dee laughed quietly and said to Muffy, "Our boy Brock ... that dudes always in a Big hurry to go nowhere."

Witty Dee started taking off his skates and said, "I guess I better get going before Brock has a fit."

While I was taking off my skates, I saw Witty Dee say his goodbyes to Muffy, which led to them picking up where they had left off before I told him Brock was outside waiting for us. So I slowly walked towards the front of the rink, since I didn't want to slow his roll, when moments later, Witty Dee yelled in a sarcastic tone, "Wait up dude, are you in a big hurry to go nowhere man?"

Witty Dee and I walked back down the carpeted outskirts of the rink and he sheepishly leaned his mouth towards my ear and said with a boyish giggle, "Dude, it's hard to walk right now because I'm pinching my butt cheeks together because I've got to fart like a madman!"

"Thanks dude but I don't need to know about your fartin' butt," I said with a sideways smirk.

Witty Dee tapped me on the shoulder again and said, "Seriously man, I had to pinch farts the whole time I was kissing her because I didn't want to gas her out, but now I'm going to let it rip!"

"Alright dude I get it, let's just get to our ride and don't get any closer to me with that farting butt of yours," I said.

Witty Dee started chasing me down the corridor while running backwards while he purposely stuck his butt as far out and as far up as he could while yelling, "I'm going to fart on you! I'm going to fart on you," - just to taunt me with his farts, just to mess with me. That's the kind of taunting Witty Dee liked to do, Crazy ice Shiznit like that, no holds barred, no farts barred. He just likes to taunt in any way shape or form. And if that meant chasing someone with his butt sticking out while trying to fart on you, then he'd do it. That's just the kind of taunter Witty Dee was. I'm sure this was a part of my payback for that, "Pizza THEEZ farts" comment I had made earlier too.

When we were kids, there was this time that Witty, just for fun, was chasing me around his backyard trying to spit on me. It was just a game to him. Let's see if I can spit on Phil was his game. He kept chasing me and chasing me with scary goobers and hockers being spat about, when finally I just had to leave his house and walk home. I can still remember him calling me a "sissy" as I was jogging away from his house towards mine. He was the kind of friend that over time had made me tougher.

We quickly walked out of the echoing disco sounds of Suburbanite rink into the bright lights of the circular lobby and Witty kind of calmed down. Well, he was no longer chasing me with his butt. The lobby was quiet, except for someone's grandmother who was waiting for their grandkid.

The doors to the outside were being held open by a chair, to let some fresh air into the rink lobby which come to think of it smelled rather smoky from cigs, most of the time. I could see clearly outside in the parking lot that Blazin' was walking in circles as if something was bothering him. While I was still inside, I made eye contact with Blazin' directly even though we were probably 5o feet away from each other, but as our eyes met, it was confirmed, something was bugging him.

Blazin' tilted his head to the side and moved his eyes in the same direction as to tell me to look to the left as we walked out of the rink. It was clear that he did not want to point but he was definitely trying to tell me something. I was already walking fast because I had just been avoiding Witty's taunting farts, just 5 seconds earlier.

By the time we both were outside in the lot it was even more obvious that something was up, even Witty Dee saw that Blazin' was nervous about something. Witty Dee, under his breath said, "What's up with Brock?"

Blazin' quickly walked over to us, trying to look like he was calm – but he wasn't. Brock whispered loudly, "Bruno just came up to me a couple of minutes ago and told me he's going to kick your butt Witty. He wanted to know where you were. Don't look now, but he's over there," Brock tilted his head in the direction of where Bruno was lurking, "hanging out with JD."

Then, Witty Dee yelled out loudly so everyone in the entire rink parking lot could hear, "Well I'm right freakin' here!" Witty Dee smirked and continued, "Sorry it took so long Brock but I was inside hanging out with this girl Muffy." Just then I thought I saw Bruno and J.D. out of the corner of my eye beginning to trek our way. By happenstance, Blazin's old man had just pulled up in the station wagon and we all piled into the car.

As soon as I closed the door to the car I saw the very blonde – surfer blonde haired, tight lipped Bruno spouting something from his lips. Blazin's old man was coincidentally rolling down his window to get some fresh air - and then it became more clear.

Bruno was shouting, "You're a silly little freak you piece of crap."

"Come back here," Bruno's friend, JD yelled.

"Getting picked up by daddy" Bruno yelled at our car as we drove off. Just because Bruno had a friend that was sixteen and had a drivers license made him think he was a big deal.

"Oh is daddy going to save you guys? Is daddy picking you kiddies up from roller skating," JD said tauntingly. (JD was Bruno's friend with the car.)

Bruno in and of himself wasn't very scary looking, like I said, he looked like a blonde surfer dude in nice clothes who was probably a foot shorter than I was. But nine times out of ten Bruno was hanging with many people that were 3 or 4 years older than he was and no matter how you sliced it, it was not a good idea to mess with him. However, Witty didn't care! He'd mess with anybody.

Blazin's old man chimed in, "Who was that?" obviously he had heard the mean comments coming from Bruno as we were driving off.

Witty Dee laughed, "That's Bruno, he can't handle that his girlfriend broke up with him and that I was couples skating with her," he said and then added, "He's got a lot of older friends here at the rink so he thinks he's tough but he's just a pip squeak and –"

Blazin' cleared his throat and tried to jump into the conversation. You could tell he was getting ready to purposely change the conversation – I could tell by the look in Blazin's eyes that he didn't like Witty Dee's bragging. "Witty" Brock whispered.

"He's just a wanna be tough guy-"Witty said but he finally got cut off by a louder Brock Blazin'.

"How about that breakin' Phil? That was awesome, huh?" Brock said to me while he gave wide eyes aimed at Witty that meant: shut the heck up.

I was glad that Blazin' had changed the topic of the conversation too because what happens at the rink stays at the rink. If you had one nervous parent, before you knew it, you had all of the parents nervous. And nervous parents would keep you home on the weekend.

I helped change the conversation by adding, "Yep, word Brock, word! Miguel had some sweet breakin' moves and Poppin G. seemed like a pretty hip cat too!"

Blazin' replied, "Yep Swifty, we will have to hook up with them mugs and do some break dancing!"

The rest of the ride home Blazin' and I excitedly talked about breakin' with Gio and Miguel and about how we'd have to hook up with them soon, so we could learn how to do those copters. Blazin' and I also made plans to get together at his crib one day next week so we could work on breakin' together. I probably said the word "breakin'" like a million times that car ride home while Witty talked about Muffy and farts the whole ride home.

Chapter 3

This thing called Breakin'

Over the next month Blazin' and I had been hanging tough, almost every day after school and on the weekends too; we had been figuring out break dance moves, acrobatic and gymnastic combinations, and the like. We had both only seen break dancing on TV a couple of times, at the rink last month with Miguel and Gio, and a random kid or two at school, who had rocked out some breakin' moves in the mornings, just before first bell. So we were really just making up our own stuff at first.

Blazin' lived across the way from this cornfield that was in-between our houses. The quickest way to Blazin's house was to cut through my neighbor Miranda's yard that lived directly behind the cornfield. But check this shiznit out, Mirandas dad bought this humungous solar paneled contraption that was smack dab in the middle of their roof. It was the size of an eighteen wheeler parked right on the top of their roof; I swear you could have seen it from an airplane, something right out of the space age. But any given night that I walked home from Brocks, through the cornfield, all I had to do was look for the space aged gizmo to navigate my way through the tall corn stalks; it was my north star. The Solar panels on her roof had nothing to do with anything but when I pictured myself walking to and from Brocks house, that's what I pictured and I wanted you to feel like you were there with me, you dig?

This one night, I hopped Mirandas fence and made haste to Brocks house. I was still in the cornfield but I was close enough to Blazin's that I could see him already working on his moves in the garage. He looked like a shadow in the twilight of his well lit garage, he was working on this move that he had told me about over the phone, just a few minutes beforehand. With each step I took and with each swallow the horizon took of the sun, Blazin' had become more defined as the garage light had put him on showcase.

It was a killer night as all heck with the wind pushing the clouds passed the reddened moon and the smell of burning leaves coming from the backyard of the Lipps house, which had made my cornfield romp feel eerie. The Lipps burned leaves almost every night during the fall, so I knew it was their leaves I smelt.

I could see Blazin's old man's second car in the garage, which Blazin' told me, would be his car once he got his driver's license in a couple of years. It was a 1967 big red boat of a car, Ford something or other. I can't tell you much more, since I'm not really a car buff but I really liked breakin' next to that big 'ol boat of a car though, it added some atmosphere, if you know what I mean?

Blazin' was straight up diving onto the floor and then attempting to bounce right back up. Over the phone Blazin' was calling this move, "The beach ball." The closer I got to Brock's garage, I could see that he was diving to the ground into a spinning movement on his back, and then trying to spring right back up to his feet like a beach ball being spun down onto the ground and then bouncing right back up, hence the name, "beach ball."

"Yo Blazin' Sup my brother from a different mother," I said when I was near his house.

"Sup Swift?" Blazin' excitedly said.

Brock Blazin' had a huge cardboard box from a refrigerator his P's just bought that was taped onto the cemented garage floor to hide the oil stains from our breakin' bodies. "I see that you have finally duct taped the cardboard to the floor … last time I was over, we were swishing, slipping ,and sliding that big piece of cardboard all over the place," I said.

"Yeah, I got tired of the cardboard moving all over the joint," Brock said.

"I've got something to show ya," I said with pride.

"Wazup Swifty?" he said.

I didn't tell Blazin' over the phone I had finally figured out helicopters in my basement the night before. I figured I'd bust out with copters right in front of him, right on the cardboard, next to the big red 67 muscle car. I wanted to surprise him.

I started scampering about with top rocks while playfully looking at Blazin' to make sure I had his attention. Then I started dealing, I just straight up started dizz-ealing. I swiftly twisted and turned some radical revolutions on the fridge box floor while, "The message" by Grand Master Flash and Melle Mel was playing in the background from the boom box. By the way: Top Rockin' kind of looks like tap dancing but more jumpy and playful.

Truth be told about the copters, they started a little clunky and ended a little fast and rough but Blazin' exclaimed, "Yeah Swift, You got 'em buddy, you got 'em, right on man!" He was all pumped, he didn't really care that my intro and exit were a little choppy; after all, I did just figure the things out not even 12 hours ago. All in all it took me a month to get them down. But I finally could rock windmills.

I must have inspired Blazin' because he started playfully top-rockin' around the garage and told me, "Watch this Swift!" He didn't know that I could see him beach balling most of the while I was trekking to his crib through the cornfield. He dove to the ground in a spinning twisting motion, hitting the ground spinning on his back and within a quick second, he propelled back to his feet and landed it.

"Yo dude, that is killa for rilla my nilla," I said. I really was quite amazed, it was like lightning; one quick spinning bounce movement, "Rock those beach balls bro," I added.

Blazin' smiled with excitement at my compliment but he was also excited about what he was going to tell me next, he practically drooled all over the place. He sucked back in the spit that was hanging from his lips, caught his breath, and said, "Yo Phil man, Big Burger is having a break dance contest in Westmont; you know the Burger joint on Cass Ave?" he asked.

"I'm hip bro, I'm hip! I know where you're talking about," I told him as I started to Top Rock dance around.

"Dude, they are having a break dance contest up there – we can come up with some routines, we'll get some matching uniforms, we'll straight up rock the joint, you know Swift, you know?" he said as he looked at me big teethed and wide eyed. He practically made me agree with him by the way he kept shaking his head up and down, until I said yes. Even though I would have agreed with him anyway but I still had no choice. Blazin' was just that excited.

"For show bro, fow show, we'll show what we know, you know. I am in like Flynn. I am so in, it's a sin," I said as Blazin' continued to shake his head with joy and a grin.

Blazin' and I took turns diving onto the cardboard as the mood struck us. And the more I thought about it, the more I wanted to give that Big Burger break dance battle a chance.

I randomly remarked, "Yo Blazin' let's do this thing! Let's enter that Break dance battle!" I said boldly, which made Blazin' grin and top rock around that led to up rocks against each other. If you don't know what "up rockin'" is, I'll tell you. It almost looks like 2 karate students fighting each other, yet dancing at the same time… well, something like that.

Out of the blue Blazin' asked me, "Did you pick up those zipper pants yet? … The ones that Harry the rink guard was rockin'?"

"I had totally forgotten about those," I said. Which was his way of asking me if I wanted to go to the mall.

"Yep, their sweet dude, straight up sharp," he said as he pounced the ground with a beach ball.

"I haven't been up to the mall in a minute and I've been so busy with breakin' every day -after school in my basement and here, that I haven't even bothered to go up to the mall lately. But now that you refreshed my memory about those super sweet swaggerlisious pants, we've got to head up to the mall this weekend," I told Brock.

"Yay, we'll go, bro, no worries," he said.

"We'll check out Chess King and see what kinda clothes they've got on the racks," I said.

"Yay dude, we've got to go to the mall so we can check it out," he said.

"Call me on the weekend and we'll go," I said.

"Yeah dude … no worries," he said.

We spent the next hour developing B-boy routines for the competition at Big Burger, which consisted of synchronized robotic dance moves in between our individual break maneuvers, just to kind of make it all flow together better. We wanted to make our routine flow instead of just randomly taking turns breakin'.

According to my swatch watch, it wasn't all that late yet but Blazin' abruptly said, "All right bro, I'll catch up with you tomorrow." I mean out of nowhere, he was ready to pack it in for the night. In my mind we were just getting started but that's Blazin' for ya, he was always in a big hurry to go nowhere. That boy can change his mood out of nowhere. But it's all good in the hood. I just would have hung out a little longer, that's all I'm saying.

"Peace out my brother from another mother, I'll catch you on the flipside. Hit me up about the mall," I told Blazin' as I slowly exited the garage and into the reddish-orange moonlit night.

Blazin' replied, "I will Swift, later!"

I yelled back at Blazin' as he was closing his big overhead garage door, "Yo Blazin'? When's the break dance contest?"

"In 2 weeks! … Later," Blazin' said as he slammed the garage door down.

I walked home in the burning leaf air. It was the kind of night where you were almost listening for wolves or coyotes howling in the background. Not that they lived by our neck of the woods or anything; It was just that kind of fall night with the burnt orange moon, the strong smell of burning leaves, and the darkness of the night and all.

When I wasn't at school or at Brocks, I practiced my breakin' in my basement. My basement was a dark and dingy dungeon that I suppose is another way of saying it was an unfinished basement without furniture and dozens of spider webs adorning most of the corners. However, I liked it, it was my studio, it was the place where I had learned to be a bad to the bone breaker for the last five weeks or whatever it was. Before that, it was a spaghetti legs makeshift practice rink.

I started working on new moves in my dungeon the day after I learned about the break dance contest at the Big Burger. A couple of guys at school, Hazy and Dustin were showing me break moves in the hallway before school one morning. Well, it was mainly Hazy, he was showing me "crabwalks" and some other move that was called "flares," that reminded me of a gymnastic move.

As I was in my basement, I kept trying to walk on my hands in circles or "crabwalks" as Hazy called them. My boom box was jamming, "Jam on it" by Newcleus that sent echoes and tinny tingly vibration noises throughout the aluminum air ducts that were hanging above the entire basement ceiling. I laugh when I think about it because I used to hang out in a dark gray dungeon with creepy crawlies and strange noises that were emitting from the furnace but I loved it. There were creaking wood planks from above which kept cricking and cracking as the P's walked about upstairs. It used to spook me when I was younger, yet I now found that place to be a step away from heaven; what a difference a year can make.

Over the next few days I practiced my, "crabwalks" like madman. Or I suppose I should say I was practicing them like a mad crab. I worked on making my legs into a perfect, "V" shape, while attempting to walk in 360's on my two hands as fast as I could without any part of my body touching the floor - except my hands. I actually started to get the move down pretty good and darn quick too, as I said; I was practicing like a mad crab.With basement practice sessions, breakin' at Brocks, and hanging with the other breakers at school in the hip hop hallway, I was really starting to feel like I belonged. I was feeling like I belonged to this thing called breakin'. And life has never been the same ever since.

Chapter 4

Dorktown Mall

The weekend had arrived and I was stoked about heading up to the mall to check out the scene, check out the chicas, and get some new clothes for rockin' when I was breakin'. I picked up my phone and I gave Blazin' a call, "Hey Mrs. B. is Brock around?" I asked.

She told me, "No, he went to the mall already."

I was thinking, "You've gotta be bleepin' me!" but I said, "Alright cool, tell Brock I called Mrs. B." and then I hung up. You know what though? That was classic Blazin', I should have known. Check that, actually I did know, that's why I called him at 9am in the morning and the mall didn't even open until 10am. I'm telling you, that boy was always in a big hurry to get somewhere and he'll be in a big hurry to leave once he gets there too.

Instead of getting all frustrated. I grabbed a couple of winter hats and headed down to the basement to practice head spins. What sucked was that my P.s were working, so I had no ride to the mall. But the cool thing was that I didn't have to hide my head spinning for a change – that move really freaked out my P.s. And not the good kind of freaked out, like "Freak-a-zoid" kind of freaked out but the bad kind of freaked out where they would give me the third degree about how dangerous it was to spin on my head.

With the P.'s being at work, I had cranked up the jams, put on two knit hats and started practicing my head spins; taking my frustrations out on being unable to go to the mall. I'm not sure if you get this or not, so I'll tell you about it. I had to wear two winter knit hats as I spun around on my head because gravity and standing on my head put massive stress on the top of my head; the floor really dug into my scalp when I revolved around with head spins. In fact, it burned like fire sometimes, if I really have to complain about it to you. Truth be told I was a little worried that I was wearing down that spot on my head and eating my hair away from all of the head spins I had been practicing. I was always checking myself in the mirror for a bald spot or tapping that part of my head after I took the knit hats off to see if there was any blood. It always ended up just being sweat. If you think about it though, I was putting the weight of my entire body all focused on one little tiny spot on the tippy top of my head.

Try it with no hats on if you think I'm exaggerating. I bet you would lose a chunk of your hair after a while. Heck, hats off to someone who can HEAD spin with his or her hats off though. They are HEAD and shoulders above the rest. I'd even buy scalped tickets to watch someone HEADspin at a double HEADer without a hat on. Okay enough of that BALDerdash. I'll quit while I'm aHEAD.

While head spinning and listening to "Party train" by the Gap band it dawned on me – call Bruiser. I can call Dan the man Bruiser for a ride to the mall. Bruiser was a guy I knew from church. Every Wednesday night the P's would drop me off at church for Pastor Paul's youth group. It was for Jr. High and high school aged teens to learn about god and Jesus and the Bible and such. I kind of just went for the girls but I did like Pastor Paul, he was funny.

I had seen Bruiser at Wednesday night youth group for a few months but we didn't start talking until a few weeks ago when he saw me throwing down with breakin' moves on the tan carpeted upstairs floor at our church while we were waiting for group to start. I hadn't hung out with Dan Bruiser outside of youth group yet; he just gave me his number last week and told me to call him sometime. And the way I figured it, this was sometime.

When I first saw Bruiser camped out on the floor of youth group half lying down, half sitting up, just chillin' like a villain, and listening to Pastor Paul preach, I thought he might have been around thirty or forty years old or something. It turned out that he was just a senior in high school, only 17 years old. But he was rocking a big thick beard just as you'd expect to see on Jesus Christ himself. He had a stocky build and an adult look on his face. Even if Bruiser didn't have the beard rockin', you still would have thought he was in his 20's at least. He had that kind of face. Do you know what I mean, Jellybean?

I gave Bruiser a call and luckily he was home, "Yo Bruiser, Sup man, its Phil K Swift from church, I'm looking to get to the mall lickety split and see if there are any breakers up there causing a disturbance … I've got to check out some thread stores and that kind of stuff. Are you in?" I asked.

"Alright B – I'll meet you up there," it sounded like he was rushing me off the phone.

" -Wait dude … hang on …" I then got into it with Bruiser about how Blazin' was shakin' and fakin' and how he had scurried and hurried and how I was home alone and on the phone and I was just trying to find someone with a Cadillac brougham, so I could roam the mall, that's all." I was spewing out the old crambo to Bruiser like a champ as I was hoping to avoid being a tramp.

"What the heck in friggin' frack are you talking 'bout B?" he said while chuckling to himself over the phone.

"What I'm trying to say is – " I said

Bruiser laughed and cut me off, "You need a ride to the mall B?"

"Abso-positiv-alutely," I said.

Bruiser without delay said, "I know where you live B. See ya in a minute."

"You do?" I asked – I had forgotten I had told him.

"You said you lived by that house with the roof with that big thing on it, off Main St. … you called it your north star that guided you through the cornfields at night, when it was dark on your way home from old boys," Dan the man Bruiser said. (He knew about Brock, even though Dan hadn't met Brock yet, I had told him all about him.)

"I had forgotten I told you about that," I said.

Bruiser hung up the phone and started heading over.

Bruiser usually called me B or B-boy as in Breaker or Break boy. I was kinda new to this whole B-boy world, I admit it, but I was on my way to becoming a good breaker; B-boy.

At church on Wednesday nights Bruiser was usually sporting B-boy attire like most of the breakers I knew. You would usually catch Bruiser in a Black Kangol hat with the clear framed Cazal glasses, red suede gym shoes with white fat laces neatly woven to the top of his shoe. And that Jesus beard I was telling you about; Bruiser rocked it like the king of the Jews himself. (I hope lightning won't strike me for that.) But hey, how many people can say that Jesus Christ the B-Boy himself was on his way to their house? And at last, I was about to scoop up some freshy-fresh zipper pants.

Bruiser showed up at my house in less than the 20 minutes. I barely had enough time to finish my grub. He pulled up in his blue 'Stang with a boom box sitting in his backseat. I asked Bruiser, "Sup with the boom box brah?"

"I use it when I'm playing basketball at the park on the weekends," he said while running his fingers through his beard and hair.

"That's all fresh my man, we ought to bust out with that on Wednesday nights, right before group starts, I'll show you my copters I've got rockin' while you bump the box!"

"Alright B," he said and then he blasted his box.

I didn't live very far from the mall, by car at least, so we got there lickety split.

Bruiser pulled up by the food court of "Dorktown mall," stopped by the entrance, and said kind of mysteriously; "Alright B, I'll get back …" which in weeks past was his way of saying "bye" on Wednesday nights.

I was like, "What?"

Bruiser repeated with a curious look in his eyes; "Alright B, I'll get back wit ya," he said as his smile grew even bigger and more mysterious. It seemed so random.

"You'll get back? Wazup wit dat," I said out of surprise, since he made it sounded like he was leaving, and he was supposed to be my ride home.

And as usual, with all coolness, he said, "I had plans before you called," he paused and then smiled like someone who had just won a prize then said, "Dooooood – I'll get back, hurry up, I've got to go meet this girl."

Suddenly I got it. Bruiser's got himself a girlfriend and he was looking to get some smoochy-smoochy going. Guys always start acting funny when there is a girl on their mind.

"Cool my brother, when and where will I meet you?" I asked curiously.

"Don't worry about it," he said keeping his mysterious ways going.

"It's cool bro, whatever is clever. Do what you gotta do," I said.

As I exited his Mustang, in a deep voice, Bruiser said, "So you're staying here at the mall B?"

I nodded yes.

He reassured me, "I'll find ya B."

"Last time I had this much mystery I was watching a 'who done it' movie," I said.

I headed into the mall through the mirrored food court door, and I was digging me. I usually wore hip and happening clothes, so I really dug checking myself out. I was instantly greeted by two birds flying high inside the mall, right near the skylights which presumably made their way inside without an official invitation. I'm not sure why I even looked up as I walked in because there were three young kids giggling their heads off about the lollipops their mom had just given them and there was a baby crying inside the double doored section of the entryway that begged for everyone's attention.

The birds were flying right over my head. It made me think about a buddy of mine; Russ and what happened to him while we were at an outdoor festival called "Chicago fest" in downtown Chicago last summer. While we were standing in line to get some Chicago beef sandwiches at an outside vendors stand, a bird crapped runny brown and white goo all over his hair, shirt, and whatnot. And let me tell you, it was not pretty. So when I walked past the screaming baby and giggling kids I sort of crouched down and made my head as low as possible to avoid the birds. Then I laughed at myself; as if that would prevent bird crap from hitting my head or something because, you know, if they're going to get you, they're going to get you.

The mall is an instant sensory overload: I spotted three teen girls licking ice cream sundaes under a fake tree in the crowded foot court. An elderly couple was sharing one of those hot and huge fat pretzels with the large over sized salt sprinkles on them. And two cute moms that didn't know how to dress, but were still cute anyway, were pushing strollers and gabbing away while their babies were fast asleep.

I started looking at the three girls licking their ice creams again. They were right underneath the path of the flying birds. Their hot fudge and vanilla swirled ice cream had an eerily similar color scheme to my buddy Russ's hair that day right after the avian creature had dropped crap on him at Chicago Fest. If I was going to get ice cream at the mall that day, I was not now, or if I did, the colors would not be brown and white. One little incident in life can really ruin the way you look at things forever. Like the time I heard about rats crawling up the sewer pipes and into people's toilets. I have never sat on a toilet seat the same ever since. -and now, neither will you.

I'm not afraid of birds or anything but I didn't want to get crapped on, so I made haste inside. Two dudes who looked all artsy fartsy were sitting at the coffee shop sipping on their coffees like a bunch of know –it-alls; I could tell by their facial expressions that they thought their poo smelled like roses. Both of the dudes were wearing argyle shirts and one of them had a plaid knit hat as his lid. I mean, it was hot inside the mall, so obviously it was his fashion statement but you could tell that these were the same types of dudes that wore their knit hats outside in the middle of summer when it was 100 degrees outside, just for the sake of their fashion. But for whatever reason, his hat annoyed me.

They had their boat shoes shined sparkly clean and their polo shirts were buttoned up to the top. I mean, who buttons a polo shirt all the way up to the top? These freakazoids, that's who. I just knew they were having conversations about things that they really didn't even care about but they were just trying to look cool and sound cool for the people that might overhear their conversations. I could see it in their Richville know-it-all eyes.

I walked past the two rich kids and said, "Hey, I like your hats! Are you from Richville?"

"Thanks," The one dude said but he barely even looked at me.

"Yes, do I know you?" the other said in an: I'm better than you voice.

As I thought: I knew it, you spoiled brat.

"My grandpa has hats just like them," I said like a smart aleck, "Are you guys wearing those hats inside because you're chilly? Sup wit dat," I said as I changed my fake snobbish voice to a ghetto-fabulous swagger. I could tell that really bugged them, but they just looked at me like I was a kid and they were grownups; only they were teens like me.

They looked at me with their strained smiles, rolled their eyes at each other, and went back to talking about argyle socks, daddy's expensive car, and how rough their life was because they had to tell their maid repeatedly to tidy up their rooms for them. If I had any more guts I would have said it louder, but instead I sort of muttered as I walked away, "You guys should wear longer skirts if you're really that chilly." But either way, they weren't paying attention to me. Anyway, that was our mall; it was filled with a bunch of nut jobs, spoiled brats, hot chicks, kids, birds, and at least one cool breaker like me.

As I walked around the mall looking for Chess King I kept my eyes and ears open for my loud buddy Blazin'. He was certainly not the quietest cat around so, if he was at the mall, I'd find him. The mall was packed like a suitcase. Everybody was there to hang out, shop, or just flat out cause trouble but usually just innocent trouble like hide and go seek all throughout the mall kind of trouble. After walking around for a bit I was unable to find the clothing store or Brock - so I made my way to the Mall directory.

While I was peeping at the mall directory looking for the clothing store on the map, I saw out of the corners of my eyes a shadow of a dude down the hallway that was pacing around like a confident young punk. He captivated me in the same way my buddy Blazin' would captivate someone; just with his face and by the way he stood tough. Something in my gut said that this guy was a B-Boy. He was wearing a gray hooded sweatshirt – hood on, and had this certain swagger. What hat one wears can really tell a story.

The gray sweat shirted dude was not really doing anything in particular other than standing around the arcade looking tough and pacing once in a while. But it was the way he was standing and pacing that told me he was cool. He had this B-boy stance about him. Takes one to know one I guess. I started making my way over towards the dude but quietly, I didn't want to bug him.

His gray hooded sweatshirt was draped in sweat by his neck, his gray jogging pants were tight, but not too tight, and his white leather shoes were very white, bright angel white; if he ever got lost at night, he wouldn't need a flashlight kind of bright white. Upon closer inspection, I could see that the gray sweat shirted dude was not rockin' fat laces. Not that fat laces were a must, but most of the breakers I had met either had 'em or wanted 'em. It's not that fat laces automatically meant ones a B-boy. However, it means something. But even though he had regular laces, I still had an instinct that the cat was like me, a B-boy, a hip cat.

As I drew more near I could see that he was right around my age; 8th, 9th, maybe even 10th grade. I was wearing my red suede, fat laced b-boy shoes and my nylon windbreaker along with sweatpants. He caught a glimpse of me and started breakin'. The dude started top rocking all hip hop dance style while throwing me an occasional glance. He had more of a hop step to his rock than I had seen on most B-Boys. Old boy dove to the floor in a twist motion, his head and hands simultaneously hit the floor with the rest of his body perpendicular to the floor he began to revolve on his head in circles. He looked like a mini tornado. His gray hooded head was spinning around the floor while his hands rhythmically tapped the ground, keeping his head spins in action.

This B-Boy must have tapped around at least 20 revolutions on his head with his legs arranged in a V pattern. Then he closed his legs, which made him look like an upside down capital "T." His speed had doubled; he quit tapping the ground, put his arms out even with the ground, and continued spinning at least 20 more times no handed head spins until he finally succumbed to gravity.

He quickly stood to his feet, I yellled, "That's Chicago Bro that was straight up Chicago!"

He got this confused look on his face and said, "We are in Lombard?"

I told him, "No, I mean your breakin' is Chicago, Tall Chicago; Chicago is the windy city … a place with Large buildings, Large egos - Larger than life in fact. Saying that your breakin' is ALL CHICAGO is like saying that you are the coolest cat that has ever walked the planet is all I'm saying."

He looked at my shoes, then furrowed his brow while tightening his right jaw, and grunted, "You break kid?" He was a little out of breath still.

"You know it," I said.

"Show me what you've got kid," he said as he looked down to the section of ground that he had just rocked. He pointed his finger in an aggressive way and said, "Right here" in a gruff tone, and then stared me down.

I bounced around a little with a swaggerliscous top rock and then slid to the floor into footwork. After scatting around, which was more or less to loosen up and find my groove, I then plunged to the very hard, very slippery beige tiled mall floor and started rotating into fast helicopters; one after another, after another. While I was twirling around I felt compelled to keep on going. After watching that boy's head spins for days, it made me feel like I had to show him that I knew what was up. I finished off my copters with backspins and then I leapt to my feet. My counterpart was extending his hand out towards mine and said, "Sweet kid, sweet! You're rather Chicago too."

"Thanks dude," I replied while catching my breath.

I started to ask him his name, where ya from, how long you been breakin' and stuff like that but before I could even get any answers out of him he just point blank asked me, "You want to walk around the mall kid?"

"Sure dude, let's do the mall," I said. I instantly took a liking to him. He had a "tough guy" personality and he was a bona fide B-boy And I liked him.

He finally answered one of my questions as we were walking around but it came after about 2 minutes of silence, so it really seemed out of the blue, old boy said, "I'm Bob" and then he paused. I thought he was going to say more but he didn't. Then he paused for a million more seconds and then he blurted gruffly, "– and your name izzzz?" you should have seen the tough guy look he gave me. He was a smart aleck to the bone. But It didn't bother me. In fact, I think that made me like him more.

I told him my name of course and practically my whole life story. I really can talk my teeth off sometimes, especially if you get me going. Heck I was trying to talk to him just a few minutes before that and he had ignored all my questions. Maybe he had trouble hearing me I wondered, considering he was still wearing his gray hood and all. He never took it off.

Bob asked, "Where do you want to go kid?"

I told Bob about my quest to find zipper pants, and about how I might run into my flighty buddy Blazin', and I also told him to let me know if he saw Jesus Christ wearing B-boy clothing.

He laughed, gulped, and took a deep breath as he said, "I don't want to see Jesus just yet kid," then he crunched his eye brow and said, "Let's find that zipper pants store kid."

As we were walking around the mall I told Bob how I hadn't seen Blazin' yet and that if we didn't find him soon, he'd probably be leaving on account of his fiddle footedness. But Bob didn't seem to care whether we found him or not. He seemed content. However, Bob got a big old roar out of my use of the words "fiddle footed," which made me explain to him that I liked to read the dictionary for fun sometimes. Which made Bob roar even more – he roared through his nose, that's how he laughed.

I didn't want to sound like a "holder" or anything. You know someone who acts like everything someone says is great. Meaning: someone whose an overly complimentary person, but I told him anyway, "Yo dude those were some hella-straight head spins dude."

"You like to say the word dude a lot don't ya Dooood?!" Bob said with an odd smirk.

"Either way my man you've got head spins for days," I said with excitement.

Then I started telling Bob about how my buddy Blazin' and I were always practicing together in his garage and as if he didn't even hear what I had been saying to him, he interrupted and said randomly, "You can call me Boogie Bob or just Bob, Mr. Phil K Swift or you can even call me dude, kid. I was just busting your chops. I say dude all of the time, dude."

But something in the tone of his voice gave me the impression that he really did not like being called "dude." But I would also had bet that he called other people "dude" all of the time. He just didn't want to be another "dude." I've got no problem with that though. We are all hypocrites once in a while.

"Sup with the zipper pants that you're all high on kid?" Boogie Bob asked.

"They balloon out really big when the zippers are down and they will make my windmills look all bad to the bone when I'm sportin' 'em. And when you zip the sides all the way to the top, the pants tighten up all tough. And that my friend will make me look all cute for the girls," I said like a cool cat.

Bob made fun of me, smirked, and said, "Ok Mr. cutie-pie, let's go get you those pants."

I started heading to the Mall directory when Bob said, "Where you going kid?"

"The name of the store is Chess King," I said while scoping out the directory diagram.

"Yep, I know – follow me kid K Swift," he said while already in full stride towards the elevator.

Boogie Bob and I waited for the elevator for about five minutes. The elevator only held about four people at a time. But 4 moms, 4 strollers, and 2 old farts were already ahead of us waiting to get in. One of the old farts kept taking his credit card and rubbing it up and down his neck, getting his gray beard stubble all over the darn place; it was grosser than gross. When I whispered to Bob that I saw his whiskers falling off his neck, Bob told me, "Actually Phil, I think that is dead skin that is falling off his neck. Which forced both of us into dry heaves – practically make us puke all over the place, the rest of the while we waited for the lift.

When we got into the elevator, it had that elevator smell, like a machine, or sulfur, or something. It kind of reminded me of the smell of bumper cars at the amusement park. I couldn't quite put my finger on it but it just had that elevator smell. But thank god it didn't have that elevator smell like at the county general hospital. The maintenance man at the hospital once told me that skunks had made a home for themselves and their babies at the bottom of the elevator shaft and they can't seem to get rid of the skunks that had taken up residence there. I had been in and out of that hospital a few times over the past few years for asthma or boo boos or even just visiting grandparents and stuff like that, it always smelled like skunks, and it probably always will. I told Bob about that right when we got into the elevator and he said, "What's your point kid?"

"I guess I don't have one," I said, which made him laugh through his nose with this repetitious "hiss" sound that filled the otherwise quiet elevator. After that, to change the subject from uncomfortable silence, on a whim I said, "Take off your hood for a second."

I asked him that question because he was clearly a master of head spins and I wanted to see if he had a bruise on his scalp or a patch of hair missing on his head or something. I knew that I had put on two thick snowmobile hats while I was busting out with my head spins, yet the very top of my head would still hurt like heck, even though I had padded it like a madman. And Bob only wore his hood. I guess I was just wondering like heck if I was going to see a bald spot, a red spot, or a scab or something on Bobs head, I just had to see.

Bob began to take his hood off, which by the way, he had on ever since I had met him just 10 minutes ago. Then, as if it was in slow motion, he took off his hood while staring me square in my eyes. He was bald. I was shocked, and out of surprise I said to Boogie Bob, "You're bald."

He nodded and smugly said, "Thanks kid, I didn't know that." Then he smiled tough – like he usually looked.

At that point, I figured I'd ask him anyway, "Does it hurt the top of your head when you do head spins?"

Bob smiled, "Nahh, izz all good, kid," he said.

I continued asking him about his shaved head because I had been paranoid I was going to get a bald spot on my head one day from the head spins I had been practicing. Bob replied, "No, I didn't shave my head because of wearing out my scalp from head spins or anything like that kid," he paused for a moment then he continued, "I've been getting chemotherapy, I have blood cancer, they call it: A, L, L. or Acute Lymphocytic Leukemia, it's a bee otch but whatevvvs," Bob proclaimed.

I really wished I hadn't asked him to take off his hood anymore. Heck, I didn't even know he was bald under that gray hooded sweatshirt of his. I just wanted to know if the top of his head looked the same way mine felt. After that brief moment of awkwardness Bob still remained the same, he brushed it off as if I had only asked him for a piece of gum. The doors to the elevator opened up and Bob said, "Take a right kid, Chess King is this way" as he pointed down the malls hall.

"I hope this isn't un-cool of me Bob, but what is it like to have cancer? I mean, can you feel it?"

Boogie Bob responded, "Actually Boy Swift, now I know you are cool! Most people would avoid that question like the plague but here you are asking me what you want to ask me. You're not treating me different like I'm just some cancer dude; you're just asking me a question, the same way you'd ask anyone a question; just like I'm an ordinary guy – not some dude."

Bob was quiet for a few minutes, so it seemed. I mean, really he was probably just quiet for a couple of seconds, but this was the kind of conversation that made silence seem long.

Then Bob continued, "At first, I spent most of my time pretending that it wasn't really happening to me but that doesn't mean that I want other people to go on pretending. But at the same time, I don't want to be treated as, "cancer dude." Know what I mean kid?"

I nodded and said, "kind of?" I tried to understand, but I'm not sure I did.

Bob continued talking to me in this serious voice but at the same time, it seemed like he was smiling to hide his pain; mental pain, "I hate fake people Kid Swift, but I can tell you are for real Phil K Swift. You know what though?" Bob paused but then talked before I could even say anything, "Sancer Cucks! Cancer sucks say it ten times real fast! … but whatevvs," he yelled in the loudest voice I had heard him use since I had met him. In fact he was shouting so loud that everyone in the mall and everyone in the heavens could hear him; he really seemed angry. He had attracted dozens of eyeballs our way, that's for sure. But neither one of us cared.

"Word," I said, "How did you know you had it?" I asked.

Bob looked at me with a pale stone face and tiredness in his eyes and uttered with a slight gulp, "It started off as a cold or flu, well at least I thought that's what it was and I just couldn't shake it. I was sick for 4 or 5 weeks during the football playoffs; I kept waiting for it to go away but it wouldn't. As the days passed I kept getting more and more tired. Finally we went to the doctor's office but he just sent me home with some flu medicine. – Boy was that doctor wrong.

The next day my mom said, "Bobby, we are going to the emergency room so we can see what in Sam Hill is going on around here." Bob had used this mom sounding voice as he had said it to me - and if that was accurate, his moms' voice sure did crackle a lot. Then Bob continued, "The ER doctor ran some blood tests and within 24 hours I got the news that I had Acute Lymphocytic Leukemia; A L L."

I listened and nodded along as he told me about his cancer diagnoses and then we both said simultaneously, "There it is."

I smiled and Bob smiled back and then he snapped out of the glum look he had on his face and said, "Chess King, kid." He put his hood back on and we walked into the store.

Bob asked me again why I was so intent on getting the zipper pants. So I explained to him how every time I got some new hot happening threads and wore them to school, some random girl would come up to me and start asking me about my clothes.

This really got his attention. "So you mean, these zipper pants will get girls to start talking to you kid?" Bob asked.

"Well first of all my brother, I just think these pants are pretty damn cool but either way - killer threads get the girls talking to you … and you've gotta love that." Then I sheepishly said, "I never know what to say to girls in the first place, I mean, once they start talking to me I'm cool but I'm just not good at approaching them, so the clothes do my approaching for me," I said while I went through the clothes on the racks.

"Hey kid, I like that angle – whatever is clever," he said.

Bob and I were going through the clothing racks forever when Bob picked up a pair of pants and held them up high, "Yo Kid Swift, are these the zipper pants you're talking about?"

I rushed over to Bob and confirmed with a, "Heck yeah." I sifted through the hangers and sizes but to my dismay, they didn't have my size. I think I probably would have been pretty upset and disappointed about Chess King not having my size and all. But after meeting Boogie Bob, it really put things in perspective. Chess King didn't have my size pants and Boogie Bob had cancer. How the heck could I possibly be mad? Boogie Bob wasn't mad. In that moment I realized, there seemed to be two sides of Bob; when he wasn't being Mr. tough guy, he was all smiles; brow-less smiles.

Bob and I left Chess King and started circling around the mall, chatting it up, scoping out girls, and just enjoying each other's company. Bob was talking about chemotherapy and popsicles and I was talking about dark chocolate, the rink, and breakin'. Bob sure hated getting chemotherapy but he sure did love the unlimited supply of popsicles they gave him at the hospital when he was getting his chemo. Bob must have talked about popsicles for at least an hour. We revolved around the mall countless times; no sign of Blazin' and no sign of Bruiser but I really didn't care though.

Every once in a while we stopped off at one of the many arcades and messed around with breakin'. Boogie Bob without a doubt had his head spins down like a nonstop spinning top. I caught a glimpse of Boogie Bobs gray Swatch Watch and I noticed it was time to start looking for Bruiser. Even though Bruiser told me he would find me, sometimes that really means go find him.

I told Bob to follow me back to the food court where Bruiser had dropped me off. "You want to meet Jesus?" I asked him.

Bob half jokingly and half seriously said, "I'm in no hurry," then he told me, "I've got to bail kid, it's time for me to hop a bus. "

I grabbed Boogie Bob's phone number and as I was writing it down Bob asked me, "Are you in a break crew kid Swift?"

"Just me and my boy Blazin' so far," I said as Bob started walking away to head to the bus stop, so I yelled out, "Yo Bob, hey man you gotta join our crew!"

Bob smiled, walked in a confident circle, dove into head spins for a quick 5 revolutions, then popped back up to his feet and remarked, "Call me kid." And then he strode outside.

I started making my way back to the food court and who did I see? My man Bruiser, Chillin' like a villain. He was still hanging with his gal pal. I could tell that old boy was throwing down the mack! You can always tell when a guy is throwing down the mack; you know, trying to get some smoochy smoochy from some girl.

I wasn't sure if I should go up to him and say 'hey' or just keep on walking. I mean what if I go up to him and blow his deal. Say for example Mack Daddy Bruiser was in the middle of this big closing line, he's getting ready to lay some smoochy smooch on her, and I say something that puts the stop on this action. That would really suck. I mean, some chicks are like that you know? You get one chance to WOW the heck out of them and if you blow it, they bail. Girls are like that sometimes, you know. One wrong word and you're done. No kiss.

Bruiser spotted me and said, "Sup Brudduh? Who was that?"

"Oh, that was Boogie Bob," I said. He must have just caught a glimpse of him before he headed outside to catch his bus.

Then all slick like he asked, "Did you find your boy Blazin' Mr. Phil K Swizzle stick Swift?" he used one of those too cool for school type of voices that guys use when they are trying to sound all cool for the ladies. It almost made me laugh. I had to try hard not to.

I told him no and then I went into the story of how I met Boogie Bob, went to Chess King, and etcetera, etcetera. Then I noticed that Bruiser wasn't even listening to one word I had said. He was too busy with his gal pal. Which I understood. As I told you, one wrong word and you're done.

I ended up just hanging there like a third wheel for the next 10 minutes or so while I scoped out the eye candy and half listened to Bruiser lay down his miggety Mack.

Every once in a while Bruiser glanced at me randomly and if I noticed that his gal pal wasn't looking our way, I'd blow Bruiser a kiss just to taunt him about his sweet talking. You could tell he wanted to strangle me about it, yet laugh all at the same time.

Finally he was done rapping with his gal pal and she bailed. Bruiser and I started walking towards the direction of where he had parked his Stang. Bruiser bragged, "Were you taking notes B?" then he laughed like a hyena and said, "I was straight up showing you how it is done B."

"Yep, I was taking notes my man," I paused for a few seconds and added, "I was taking notes on what not to do when you're with a girl."

He scoffed, "Yeah right, you were taking notes from the master." We both laughed and then he asked, "So what's up with Blazin'?"

I told him how I never found him but it didn't really matter though because I was more excited about Boogie Bob's head spins for days and stuff. I didn't mind having to repeat myself, even though I had just told him all of that info a few minutes ago, but I got it. He had to pay attention to his girl at that time, not me. That's what you do when you are on a date, pay attention to your date.

We hopped into his Stang and started heading back to my crib, Bruiser asked, "So this boy Bob is joining up with you and Blazin'?"

I told him yes.

Then Bruiser said something unexpected, "If you guys get big enough, I'll help y'all find some Bboy battles or talent shows or paying jobs or something?"

"You mean like you'd be our break crew manager or something?" I asked.

"Or something B," he said.

Considering Bruiser was older than all of us; he did seem like someone that would be a manager of a store or something. Maybe it's the beard. People with beards are always managing something. Bruiser dropped me off at my crib and I told him that I would catch him later. I went into my house to chill like Phil the Pill for rill, that's the dill; there was time to do nill until tomorrow when I had to reinsert my will.

Chapter 5

Schlernious "SHLIRNEEUS"

The weekend passed quickly as they always did when there was school on Monday but at the same time, I couldn't wait to tell Blazin' about Boogie Bob. I had not talked to Blazin' about adding a new member to our break duo just yet. But after watching Boogie Bob throw down, I knew we had to have him on our side. Watching Bobs head spinning for days at the mall this past weekend got me to thinking about assembling an incredible break dance crew.

On the bus ride to school I thought about how Blazin' had blown me off and stuff but I wasn't really mad, that's just Blazin' for ya. I also thought that if I would have went to the mall with Brock, we might have left the mall too quickly or heck we may have not crossed Boogie Bobs path at all, because we would have taken on a whole new walking path at the mall. Any given path you take can really change your life in a big way. Some people say that everything happens for a reason, which I don't believe. Life is all about the choices we make.

I got off the school bus and headed straight to Blazin's locker. He saw me first, "Yo Swift, Sup Bro? Where were you all weekend?" If I didn't know him any better, I would have been mad.

"I was at the mall breakin' all day on Saturday ... ringing a bell?" I asked.

Blazin' looked at me all puzzled and said, "I didn't see you there? Nobody was there? So I left early." Then Brock beamed like he had a rocket in his pocket, he big mouth smiled, his eyes shined like flashlights, and he told me, "Lincoln center in downtown Downers Grove has an after school break dance club. Anybody can go there and dance." Blazin's eyes were wide and pure pump was coming out of his face when he asked, "Do you want to go?"

Of course I said, "Yes" and then I said, "I'll meet you here at your locker after school. Don't forget about me!"

Blazin' curiously surprised asked, "Why would you say it like that?"

I didn't even reply to that question. I ignored it. Since I wear my emotions on my sleeve, I probably gave him a "you've got to be kidding me look." But I truly didn't say anything. What would be the point in that, a leopard can't change its spots. I just told him, "I don't know how to get to Lincoln center so just make sure that you wait for me!"

Blazin' replied, "Word bro, word!" and then he hurriedly headed to his drama team that met every morning for fifteen minutes before school started. I didn't get a chance to tell Brock about Boogie Bob yet, so I figured, I'd tell him after school, on the way to Lincoln center.

After a gross day of dissecting a frog, labeling body parts, and getting kicked out of class for yelling, "Did the frog croak on his own? Or did they whack him?" – I was really ready for Lincoln Center. Only I hoped Blazin' hadn't forgotten about me.

I swiftly rushed down the stairs and headed to Blazin's locker, I didn't want to take the chance of heading to my locker first and missing the flighty Blazin'. I sped walked past the principal's office and then briskly walked past our vice principals office, Mr. Green suit and white sox himself was there making sure everyone was in line. I was only "speed walking" but he told me to "stop running" anyway. They called him, "Earl J white sox" because he always wore floods (pants that were a couple of inches too short) that showed off his white sox. Once I knew I was out of his view, I darted to Blazin's locker. I was happy to see that Blazin' was there. He was chillin' like Matt Dillon (from the Outsiders,) all tough like. I slowed down to a chill walk once I knew he was waiting for me.

"I'm thinking Lincoln," Blazin' said all pumped.

"Let's go to the center my brother," I replied eagerly.

Blazin' high fived me and we made our way out of the school building and started venturing north through the neighborhoods towards downtown DG. Every 5 minutes or so Brock and I would stop on a random sidewalk or temporarily empty road and bust out with break moves; swipes or scats or up rocks or freestyle - right on the hard and coarse pavement that we walked. Here we were breakin', right in the middle of the roads and sidewalks right in the middle of our neighborhoods when suddenly, in that instant, our crews' name was born. I said to Blazin', "Yo bro, we ought to call ourselves The Neighborhood Street Rockers!"

Blazin' replied in an instant, "Yeah Swift, I like it, let's do it – The Neighborhood Street Rockers."

Blazin' dove onto the ground with his now trademarked beach ball and immediately after bouncing back up to his feet he said, "Whoa dude that hurt" but he was smiling, so I wasn't too worried about him.

"I guess you better not do that move on rough concrete anymore," I said.

Blazin' shook if off though and went back into laughing and talking about our new fresh crew name. He said it out loud like 10 times, you could tell that he just really enjoyed the way it sounded coming out of his mouth. "The Neighborhood Street Rockers … The Neighborhood Street Rockers."

Blazin' wasn't the only person with a rocket in his pocket. "Yo Brock my man, in all of the excitement I forgot to tell you. When I was at the mall on Saturday I met this cat Boogie Bob. He can rock head spins for days! Days I tell ya. Anyway, I think we should ask him to join our crew, The Neighborhood Street Rockers," I said all cool.

Brock loved the idea. He was as pumped as bouncy house in an air factory. He was pretty friggin' pumped is what I'm screamin'. Crazy excited as all heck. "Now we've got three of us street rockers," he said beaming.

After a zig zagged route through the neighborhoods in Downers Grove, we finally made it to the red bricked 3 story building that was surrounded by a half dozen, old Victorian homes, you know the kind - with the turret shaped rooms; they look like spirals or rounded rooms that also makes them look like mini castles. A lot of the homes in downtown Downers Grove looked to be at least 100 years old – but the good kind of hundred years old, like historical society hundred years old.

Blazin' yelled, "Lincoln center, tharr she blows!"

We headed into the bricked building and started wandering the halls for signs of break dancers or music or whatever was supposed to be in the joint – nothing was really marked, there wasn't a receptionist or a desk clerk, so we had to just wing it.

We heard quiet sounds coming from the hallways, which I remembered were very echo-friendly hallways. There was an otherwise quiet feel to the building but down one hallway it sounded like a lady was talking rhythmically and playing classical music. I could tell that there must have been little kids in her class by her use of phrases like, "Do it like this sweetie and do it like that pumpkin." All of the other rooms were closed and dark that we passed, so when we hit the end of the hall, we looked in the open room and saw a lady teaching ballet to tots.

Blazin' and I turned around and started making our way towards this other hallway on the other side of the building that we had almost went down first.

"The road not taken," I said randomly as we walked to the other hall.

As we walked up the stairs to the "road not taken" we heard someone spouting unfamiliar words and spitting cackles coarsely. As we drew closer we heard, "I'm going to look cold man, COLD!" Then shrill laughter dominated the building drowning out the distant ballet teacher's voice. The unknown voice continued while Blazin' and I looked at each other with smiles of: what the heck is that?

"Schlernious! … Schlernious! … Shlur – nee- ouse Bro!" The tough voice spat.

Blazin' and I kept looking at each other like what in the heck is that all about. Then we heard an even louder and higher pitched cackle, as we got closer to the room.

It was the only other open room in that hallway. Blazin' and I slowly and warily entered closer to the room that had faint sounds of jazzy -hip hop coming from a small ghetto blaster radio that was sitting on the floor next to a water bottle and what appeared to be someone's belt buckle without a belt. We looked in from the hallway for a few seconds while we whispered with laughter about that "Schlernious" business and what in the heck it may have meant.

The room looked like that other ballet studio we had just seen the lady and the tots in, with its hardwood floors, a mirror covering an entire wall, and one of those bars that ballerinas hold onto while they point their legs to the ceiling and all of that. "I'm the baddest breaker," The dude inside of the room said. And in that instant we had both understood that it was the same voice that had said that "Schernious" word, which oddly enough drew us into the room inch by inch.

There was a tall lanky dude with a short black fro wearing maroon sweatpants and a maroon sweatshirt with gold letters across his back that read, "Rockefeller." This character, Rockefeller, caught a glimpse of us and continued talking all loud, "Man, when I show up in that place with my tabletops and with my CHaaayN! I'm going to be lookin' all tall. Straight up Tall …SHARP" Then confirming in Blazin's head and my head that we were in the right place, because neither of us was quite sure yet, the tall and skinny cat named, "Rockefeller," jumped into windmills. He had super long legs. The longest legged windmills I had ever seen. You'd have guessed he was ten feet tall or had stilts attached to his legs they were so long.

Rockefellers buddy who was half sitting and half standing on the wall was wearing jeans and a maroon sweatshirt that read, "Speedy G" on the front and "Wild Style" on the back. Speedy G (I'm assuming that was his name) reached down and flipped over the cassette on his boom box, another Jazzy hip hop tune began echoing throughout the relatively vacant room while Blazin and I inched closer inside.

And I think, but I'm not sure they may have requited our head nods and "Sups" as we walked in. Well, at least, Speedy G may have. I'm pretty sure he said, "Sup" even though you could tell he didn't really want to.

Rockefeller leapt back into his hypnotically slow motioned windmills; maybe it was just an optical illusion due to his 10 feet long legs but it really did seem like slow moe when he was breakin'. Watching that cat Rockefeller was very captivating because of his impressive size, grace, and smoothness of his slow motioned spins. You see, when I'm doing my windmills, I've got to spin around fast enough just to keep the momentum going – that's why his slow motion was a trick in and of itself

As I continued to be captivated by this cat Rockefellers' windmills and the slow mo of it all, it really started to feel surreal, like a dream, or a time warp, it's hard to explain but it was that mesmerizing. Then suddenly, Rockefeller in continuous motion rolled onto the top of his head and began revolving head spins without missing a beat. Then back into copters and then back into head spins again; all in a nonstop motion; slow motion.

The towering slender Rockefeller sprung back to his feet and then paced the floor in random figure 8 shapes with a serious, almost stern look on his face; he started to talk to himself in this tough tone, "Phony baloneys – don't know what's up! This cold cat breaker will take you out, Well – that's what's up!" Rockefeller laughed sharply and continued, "Nobody's goin' to want to battle me," he said confidently as he strutted around in long stomping strides. Then he laughed, "Aint nobody nuts enough to battle this cold dude," Rockefeller had said to nobody in particular. He then high fived his buddy Speedy G, who then turned up the volume on the cassette player while nodding in agreement.

Brock asked Speedy G what song was playing on his tape deck.

And he told us it was from a movie called, "Wild Style."

Rockefeller crouched to the floor and began circling around with hand walks or crabwalks; I mean, most people were calling them crabwalks but the way he was doing them – I'd have to call them "hand walks." He didn't look like a crab, the way he had done them. This cat Rockefeller was rotating around in 360 degree circles with absolute ease, save for the taxed expression on his face. His legs were stretched out stiff, held together; his body was spinning around smoothly in a straight line; straight as an arrow. In contrast to his seemingly slow motioned helicopter, his hand walks were steadily gaining speed; I swear I felt wind from his legs as if a fan was blowing on me as he hand-walked around in circles.

As a B-boy who was still learning how to do hand walks or crabwalks, I can tell you how impressive Rockefellers' breakin' was; his breakin' was bad to the bone, is what it was.

Blazin' and I were both so mesmerized by Rockefeller's display that we almost forgot that we were there to break too. Blazin' broke the ice for us as he beach balled a couple of times in between Rockefeller's routines.

Then I busted out into windmills of my own. I felt the need to show Rockefeller that I belonged too, so I kept spinning with sheer might. After I finished my routine with a backspin, I jumped to my feet and Blazin' cheered, "Yeah Swift, that was FRESH!"

Rockefeller interrupted us and bellowed, "Schlernious!"

Without hesitation, Speedy G chimed in and made fun of us, "Yeah, hey man that was real fresh man. Yeah Fresh."

Then Speedy G started talking with Blazin' and me about how Rockefeller and he found it funny how all of these new jack wanna-be B-Boys were all starting to talk like they were from the ghetto or from the city or they were trying to talk like they were hip hoppers and whatnot. When just a few short months ago they were all talking like suburbanite school kids with fancy pants vocabularies. Now all of a sudden everyone thought they were from the city.

Rockefeller laughed to himself while pacing around in zig zags.

Then Speedy G asked us, "So what's up with you guys? Are you all going to talk all of that slick talk?"

I plainly said, "We've got a couple of pals that are originally from the city, Miguel 2 tough and Gio- So some of that hip hop slick talk comes kind of naturally to us because it rubbed off on us."

That wasn't necessarily the whole truth, but it was kind of true. I had really said that just for the heck of it, because after all, I had just recently met

Miguel and Gio. But you know, I didn't want to be one of "those people" that he was talking about.

Blazin' interjected, "Sup guys I'm Brock and this is my buddy Phil."

Rockefeller muttered under his breath, "You guys seem all right," as he shook our hands.

"How long have you guys been break dancing for?" Blazin' asked them in the most "Vanilla" voice you have ever heard. This ended up opening a whole new can of worms.

Speedy G scrunched his entire face and mockingly said, "Ohhh hey that's real fresh breakkk! Dancinggg! Where did you learn to breakkk dance like that? ... breakkk dancing dude." Speedy G had said those words like a school teacher that was teaching the Queens English would have. It was quite obvious that he was making fun of us again.

Then Rockefeller jumped back into the conversation, "Yeah hey great, break dancing dancers can you break dance like a break-dancer?" Rockefeller used the most made-up Vanilla voice you had ever heard as he poked fun at us.

When suddenly, their making fun of us voices changed to serious and teacher-like voices, Rockefeller said, "I'm a B-Boy ... you might even call me a breaker. But don't call me a breakdancer – that's wazup. The word break dance is word from the media. That's what's up gents. I'm a straight up COLD B-Boy ... Cold B-BOY ..."

Blazin' chimed in, "I didn't know, I just heard lots of people calling it break dancing."

"Are any of these people cold ice B-Boys like us?" Speedy G asked.

Blazin' and I both shook our heads NO and Brock said, "Well hey guys you're right ... I first learned about breakin' from that TV show PM magazine ..."

Speedy G interrupted, "See what I'm saying ... the media taught you that word. If you want to sound like you know what's up ... we are B-boys ... Break boys ... NOT Break dancers."

I told Speedy G, "Well now I know that 'Breakdancer' sounds lame, that's cool"

"Now y'all been educated," Rockefeller boasted.

The next hour or so Rockefeller and Speedy G kept to themselves on one side of the room and Blazin' and I practiced our breakin' routines for the upcoming breakin' contest for the Big Burger on the other side of the room. It was a relatively friendly atmosphere in the room for the rest of the time. We were all there for basically the same reason; a place to break. However, Blazin' and I purposely kept our voices low as we plotted our moves for the battle. We didn't want Rockefeller finding out about the breakin' competition. He would have been a force to be reckoned with if he had showed up. So we kept our plans quiet. "Loose lips sink ships," I whispered to Brock when he asked me why I was so quiet about the battle.

Rockefeller however, was not very quiet and he really liked to boast about how great he was. Even though Blazin' and I were on the other side of the room and the boom box was blaring "Wild Style" music, I could still hear old boy saying, "I'm tall as all tallness boyeeee and I'm going to look all cold on that floor … straaaight upp sharp!" Rockefeller had spoken with such passion that you had no choice but to listen whether you were trying to or not.

Speedy G turned off his cassette tape and unplugged his boom box while Rockefeller picked up the water bottle and belt buckle that had a chain running through it. He placed it around his neck and began to saunter towards the door. The two of them strut past us with bouncing swagger and head nods as Blazin and I said, "See ya." Rockefellers face took on a whole new glow after he had placed his shiny metal charm around his neck; his necklace was a belt buckle nameplate made out of shiny metal letters that read, "G.T.R."

Rockefeller said, "See ya Gents Lay-trah … Got To Rock Crew is outta here!"

Rockefeller was a rather intimidating fellow when you first met him but it seemed like we were relatively cool with him and Speedy G. "Relatively," may be the key word. I was surprised he actually acknowledged us on his way out. But I was glad he did. He was an awesome breaker with much strut but I understood that. Sometimes, you've just got to strut. If you are going to pick a personality trait, would you pick "feather foot pansy" or "cool hip cat that struts?" I'm just asking.

After Speedy G and Rockefeller left, Blazin' and I began our breakin' routines for the big competition in earnest. Suddenly the room seemed so quiet and empty; it's amazing how just one person can really liven up a room.

After about an hour of creating b-boy routines, Blazin' and I began the hour long trek back to our cribs so we could be home in time for dinner.

On our walk back home, Blazin' and I guessed about what the word "Schlernious" may have really meant. We eventually came to the conclusion that we didn't know and we didn't even care. We just said the word over 100 times each in 100 different tones of voice in a 100 different sentences back and forth to each other, literally. We didn't talk about anything else the whole hour walk home.

"What's your schlernious cooking for dinner tonight," I asked.

Blazin' said, "Schlernious and noodles."

Then I'd say, "You've got to be schlernious. I am eating schlernious too."

It was schlernious this and schlernious that.

Blazin' belted out schlernious stuff like, "This walk home is wreaking schlernioius on my dogs (Brock always called his feet, "dogs." He meant his feet were starting to hurt.

And I would say junk like, "For schlernious my man, for schlernious!"

We figured that Rockefeller must have just made that word up and that he just liked to trip off of it once in a while. And now we were tripping off of it like big ol schlernious dogs too.

Brocks' crib came up first and we said our au revoirs and talked about how our schlernious crew was going to be better than anybody else's schlernious crew and then he told me to enjoy my schlernious when I got home and I told him I'd see him at his locker at schlernious tomorrow.

Chapter 6

Big Burger Break Dance Contest

I didn't see Blazin' that much the rest of the week other than in the hallways at school. Every time we ran into each other during school, all we wanted to talk about was the upcoming b-boy competition that was going to be taking place on Saturday afternoon at the Big Burger. Only we kept calling it the "schlernious burger jizz-oint," which drew giggles from the girls that were next to Brocks locker every afternoon after lunch period.

On Saturday morning I cut through the cornfields and made my way to Blazin's' garage so we could sharpen up the routines we had made up at the Lincoln center practice session earlier that week. When I got there we were both hitting all of the routines as if we had been doing them for years, only we just made them up last week.

Within a few minutes of practicing, I felt comfortable that we both knew our routines for the Big Burger competition so when Blazin' went to get his dad to give us a ride up to the Burger jizz-oint straight quick, I didn't think too much about it. I'd have rather busted out with more breakin' before we went, but I too wanted to, "see what in the schlernious was going on up there anyway," I told Brock. Which opened up that can of schlernious worms again; sparking Brock into saying the word, "Schlernious" about a million times over the next hour. That's the thing about Brock, once you get him going; he'll keep on going. Don't ever put a quarter in him or wind him up.

When we pulled into the parking lot of Big Burger, we couldn't even find a spot to park. We had to park on an adjacent side street that seemed like it was a mile away. The place was jumping like Jiminy crickets. Apparently the word had spread rather well throughout the surrounding towns that a break dance contest was happening that day because there were cars and people everywhere.

Throughout the week I was picturing a small crowd, maybe a couple of dozen people including the breakers at the joint. Now it was obvious that I was going to be breakin' in front of many dozens if not hundreds of people – which sort of put some extra palpitations in my heart to be honest with you. Breakin' in front of a large crowd was something I had never done before – at least not on that type of a stage. When I was at Suburbanite Roller rink or at Dorktown mall, people would randomly walk by and see me breakin', but nothing like the scene that was unfolding at the Big Burger. But I tried not to think about too much. If you think about that sort of thing too much you might pee your pants.

The sun was beaming brightly and it was a warm fall day for a change that made Blazin' say one of his favorite expressions, "It feels like Indian summer out here today," he said smiling brightly.

Teenage girls were wearing daisy dukes or hot pants and showing off their belly buttons.

Moms were dressed like Moms, shorts, tube tops, heels, and all. Dads were wearing tank tops or bowling shirts. Grandpas were wearing ugly colored shorts with even uglier colored socks with sandals; kind of like those nerds I told you about back when I was in grade school. By the way, don't be one of those guys; a guy that wears socks with sandals. And the kids were dressed like kids, snot noses and all.

Most of the boys and some girls that I presumed were going to be in the competition were wearing various styles of B-Boy clothing – mainly the trendy kind that was shown on TV in music videos and TV commercials. But we all sort of wore that; even Brock and I.

There was this one kid, probably about 5 years old that was wearing sweatpants, a hooded windbreaker, along with a bandana on his head that caught Brock and my attention. He was standing next to his parents, wiggling his arms around; poppin', wavin', and lockin' type of movements which would have looked phony, if an older kid was doing it, but since he was barely out of diapers, Brock said, "Not bad for a kid. "

The kid's parents overheard Brock and smiled at us and then said, "He taught himself."

Another boy about 10 was donning a black and gray track suit along with a gray Kangol, and gray suede gym shoes. I told Brock, "All that cat is missing is some Fatty Phat laces. Then he'd be straight up sharp - Schlernious, even." I instantly regretted saying, "Schlernious." It reopened that can of worms again. Brock said it over a thousand times in the minutes ahead. Even when I asked him a serious question, he kept laughing and saying, "Schlernious."

"Can you be serious for a quick second? I have a question about the break competition sign up?"

But Brock wouldn't let up, he responded with, "You want me to be serious or schlernious?"

So obviously, he kept on goofing around. But after a while, Brock went to sign us up for the contest and I kept sauntering around to scope out the competition and the talent.

As I swaggered around as if I owned the joint, I peeped another new jack wanna be hip cat wearing blue parachute pants and a blue and red windbreaker jacket; The kind of jacket that you have to pull over your head. This cat was eerily dressed just like me, I heard him say, "I'm going to be fresh today in the break dance contest."

The girl next to him replied, "You're great at breakdancinggg, Chucky," The way she put most of the enunciation on the G in "breakdancing" sounded all vanilla for rilla. This made me think back to last week when Rockefeller and Speedy G said that whole thing about people trying to talk as if they're from the city, yet they're not and about break dancing being a media term and such. The way she said "breakdancinggggg" really made me not want to use that word ever again. Even Miguel told me that he always called it, "breakin'" or used the term, "B-boy."

But honestly – even though I'm against it, I hear people say the term "break dancing" so much, I doubt I'll ever shake it. It's probably going to slip out once in a while. Now that I heard that girl say it all Vanilla, I finally understood what Speedy G and Rockefeller were griping about last week.

I thought for a moment about bustin' on them for their vanilla cracker talkin' and such; the same way that Rockefeller and Speedy G had busted on Blazin' and me the other week. But before I could even say something to his mom or heck maybe it was even his hot older sister, she said, "Hi" to me.

Once I noticed that, I suddenly didn't feel like bustin' on her anymore. Instead I smiled shyly and said, "Hey" in reply. It's funny how a cute girl makes you forget what you were going to say.

Then I heard her tell her brother or son or whoever he was, "You are wearing the same outfit as him." I really hated how the word "outfit" had sounded but I was really diggin' her outfit – if you know what I mean? - so I guess I didn't mind too much to be honest with you. After all of that, I just kept on walking though. I had no idea what to say to girls back then.

As I continued my way through the packed crowd, I could smell someone wearing coconut sunscreen but I was mostly whiffing the flame broiled cheeseburgers that were permeating the fall air and peddling themselves on peoples noses, subliminally making parents reach into their wallets to order a round of seared intoxicants for their spouse, their kids, and themselves. The bluish- white smoke was billowing out of the restaurants' chimney and into the crowd and reeling everybody inside to the cashiers who were cheerfully ringing their orders and taking their money. It all seemed like it was in slow motion. It was strange. I think it had something to do with my nerves but time had really slowed down that day.

Then I spotted this jack ass from school, Randal VanderNorth. He didn't used to get under my skin all that much before, I really didn't have much of an opinion about him at all to be honest with you. I knew he was some rich kid that always got his way and everything but I didn't care much about that.

What got me mad was when I was at this party a couple of months ago at the Chanecksons house and I overheard Randal talking some crap. By the way, this dude we went to high school with Brian Chaneckson had an older brother, he threw college aged parties, and half of our school would show up there. Some of the twenty-something's were drinking beer. We freshman didn't drink beer – I think it tastes gross; we all just drank sodas like mad. Brian liked to get all hopped up on coffee, suck on peppermints sticks, and he was also known for blowing off firecrackers when the mood struck him.

Anyway, while I was at that party I overheard Randal lying his lips off like a poop salesman. And the thing that got me angry was that he was lying to this really nice girl Gina; not lying to her face, but behind her back.

I overheard Randal VanderNorth telling Brian Chaneckson that he was getting close to getting a kiss from Gina. He was talking about this nice girl from our school, Gina D'agostio. She's totally hot, totally rich and she's a proud virgin. She has a rule that she won't kiss a guy until she has dated him for at least 6 months. She used to have a rule that she wasn't going to kiss a guy until she was sixteen and dated a guy for six monts, but now she's sixteen.

It's a good thing there are smart girls out there like her, because we guys are big idiots when it comes to thinking – when it comes to that kind of stuff, we just want to kiss – and we'll say anything we need to, to get one; lie even. I like a girl like Gina that could do the smart thinking for both people and tell guys NO.

You see, Gina was not running around being all fast and furious and willy nilly by sharing her lips with any dude that had hips. You've really got to admire a girl who didn't let any Tom, Dick, or Harry talk her into something she didn't want to do. Some guys and some girls don't even think about it. They let any old idiot or liar kiss them, but not Gina – she was smart and knew she was worth waiting for.

That was why it really started to get me mad. Old boy Randal was telling Brian, "Yep, it'll be any day now that Gina kisses me. My birthday is coming up and she said she is going to give me that thing I have been asking her for, for the past 6 months – you believe that Brian? This chick has made me wait 6 months to kiss her," Randal said like a jerk – which even irritated me more. It was obvious he didn't appreciate her.

Then Randal looked around and spoke quietly, he didn't see me takin' a leak behind the old oak tree, because it was thicker than me. I could easily hear him, I was that close, and there was no wind that night. All of the party people were inside Brian's house except for Brian, Randal, and me.

He whispered, "Little does she know that while I've been patiently 'waiting for her' (he even used air quotes, I saw him through the leaves) to kiss me and for her to gain my trust, I've been kissing Lucy Goosey from the bowling alley in secret. That girl kisses me whenever I want. So waiting for Gina has been a piece of cake."

I really wanted to say something at that point, but instead, I just zipped up my fly.

That's the thing about guys, well some of them, maybe even most of them; Girls can give guys all sorts of tests and questions and rules and waiting games and all of that kind of shiznit. And those guys can pass those tests with flying colors. But secretly many of those guys, and I'm not saying me - are scum bag liars. And I'm sure all of those girls that are with those, "scumbags" are saying, "Well not my boyfriend; my guy is good!" I'm sure Gina is thinking that her Randal is good. But anyway, that's why I don't like Randal.

There was no way that Randal was at the Big Burger for the break dance contest, he's not that kind of cool, in fact, he's not cool at all. I'd bet he was just coincidentally there to get food. And you know what? - If I was a bigger dude, I would have really liked to kick his butt for pulling the wool over Gina's eyes. You see, I try not to get into others peoples business, but at the same time, I hoped that someone would hook Gina up with the info about old Randal and his kissy face girl from the bowling alley - before I ended up having to be a tattle tale and blow his show.

I was right too, by the way, he wasn't there for the break contest. Randal grabbed his bag of grub, wiggled through the crowd, and made his way to his daddy's BMW that was filled with a bunch of older kids that looked like they were wearing golf shirts.

Before leaving, Randal sat on the hood of his car and smoked a square. I hate cigarettes. You should have seen this punk. He grabbed a cigarette from his gold cigarette case like it was a big deal; like he was operating on a brain; he had pulled it out so deliberately slow that you could tell he wanted everyone to see he had a gold cigarette case. He even made sure to hold it high and all of that jazz, just so everyone could see that his family had money. Seriously, you should have seen him; he made this big production out of lighting it too. Then he blew the smoke around as if he thought he was cool. These extra hard and long exhalations that he made while swaying his head from side to side made me dislike him even more.

His eyes watched the smoke until it disappeared into the sky and then he forcefully puffed down another drag. I was able to crack a smile though. He was giving himself cancer – at least that was the thought that had crossed my mind as I watched him smoke his cancer stick like some big shot. I mean, it says it right there on the darn box "smoking causes cancer."

As I waited for Blazin' to sign us up for the breakin' contest, I couldn't help wondering why one of the ladies in the crowd was wearing curlers in her hair. She was probably about 50 years old but the curlers in her hair made her look 70 – wouldn't you want to wear the curlers at home and then look good when you're out in public with your kids?

On the other hand there was a little old lady maybe 70 or 80 years old, heck she could have even been 90, wearing a babushka; one of those rain hats that wrap around your head and tie just under the chin. Little old ladies wearing babushkas are so cute, with their creaky walking and wrinkled smiles and such. She was probably at the Big Burger to cheer on her great-great grandson or GG-daughter. I sort of couldn't wait to see her cheering and shouting for some kid that was breakin' -saying stuff like, "Way to go sonny boy (or girly)!" That sort of thing really gets my rocks off to be honest with you. Little old ladies are so freakin' cute. I love how they call their purses "handbags" and steal packs of sugar from restaurants. Only old ladies can get away with that.

I was truly starting to feel nervous though as I took a look around the crowd and saw that there were probably 200 million people gathered inside and out of the big burger, just waiting for the contest to start. But at the same time, I couldn't wait to show everybody that the Neighborhood Street Rockers were a force to be reckoned with.

Blazin' had finally wiggled his way through the zillions of people and just in time too, because the competition was scheduled to start in 10 minutes. When I asked him what took so long, he told me that he was stopped by a few cats from school and he said he was talking his teeth off so much that he almost forgot to find me. - That's Brock for ya.

Blazin' and I quickly began slithering through the packed Big Burger crowd towards the stage where we saw official looking people trying to clear the linoleum roll that was laid out on the black top, which was going to serve as the stage for the competition.

There was a DJ manning the tape deck and turntable that was next to the large sheet of linoleum that was laid out on the asphalt with gray duct tape holding it down – just like in my basement. There were chairs right next to the linoleum with 3 guys wearing suits and ties and 2 ladies wearing dresses and heels – not the cute kind of dresses and heels but the professional kind. They looked like they were the judges of the competition or the owners and managers of the restaurant or something. They had an important look about them - that was for sure. Sometimes, you can just tell that sort of thing.

The thing about it was, Brock was in his loud, cackling, schlernious spouting mood when we walked by those "official looking people" and I just hoped that he wasn't irritating them with his loud ways and all. The last thing I wanted to do was irritate the judges. But maybe I worry too much about that kind of thing. But he was getting loud, that's for sure. I'm a loud person and he was too loud for me.

Finally battle time was upon us. The contest started with little kids doing centipedes on the ground and goofy wiggly worm movements with their arms that were sorry attempts at wavin', tickin' and poppin' – you could tell they were little kids. One kid did the James Brown – Michael Jackson Moonwalk but he didn't even do it right; he straight up sucked, I don't care how cute all the parents called it, he sucked anyway. One after another, little kids were attempting to look like breakers but in fact all they were doing was giving breakin' a bad name.

The flipside was that when Blazin' and I got our chance to get on the linoleum to do our thing, we were going to look like rock stars. And when I said that thing about "time had slowed down" because of my nerves or whatever. Well forget that. It wasn't standing still anymore. Time began to run like a shooting star, it was blowing right by super fast – and I think it was because of my nerves.

The MC of the contest announced, "Next up today are Phil K Swift and Brock Blazin' of the Neighborhood Street Rockers" the crowd cheered as we got ready and time had froze and sped up all at once, it was really quite queer.

"Freak A Zoid" started playing through the large ghetto blaster that Brock had brought with. We had the option of using the sound system that Big Burger had available but Blazin' was way too excited about using his own personal Boom Box – and so we did. We started the routine out with organized robotic and synchronized movements along with these King Tut routines we had made up. Then we educated the crowd with: up rockin', lockin' and floor glides; you know, moonwalk type stuff. But we rocked it right.

For the first time, the crowd was cheering their flame broiled burger breathes off. After our minute of theatrical routines, we finally got down to business. I busted out with crazy fast windmills then Blazin' busted out with his super fly beach balls. Then in the heat of the moment, I didn't even plan it, heck, to the contrary, I told myself I wasn't going to do any, but I busted out with head spins anyway. I had been working my scalp to the bone trying to get 'em down. Seriously, head spins had sort of put a bruise on the top of my head and I wasn't going to do them because of the pain, but my adrenaline had taken over and made me dive onto my head.

I was really trying to get lucky, I suppose, because I didn't really have head spins down just yet. I was only able to do a couple of them but the crowd still loved it anyway. By the look on all of the people's faces I could see that they were amazed. However, deep down, I knew that I didn't really do anything impressive. Impressive would have been head spins for days like Boogie Bob does.

On Blazin's next turn he busted out with copters then transitioned into backspins and then back into more windmills. Then he showed off swipes that made his body look like a flipping chair and his down rock made him look like a dancing spider. Brock was getting good is what I'm screamin'.

I got back out there one more time and rocked top rockin' like I meant it, and then I Brooklyn rocked against Blazin' just to show the crowd what wazup. Then I dropped into down rock that looked like dancing karate moves on the floor with all fours. I ended with backspins that made me look like a "tilt a whirl" into a kip up that had landed me back onto my fat laced suede shoes right as the song had ended.

Without a doubt we were the best contestants of the day up until that point, Hands down. The crowd got to watch real breakin'. I'm not even bragging though, the real deal was that the rest of the entrants up to that point were just wick whack wanna-be's. I'm not putting them down; I'm just telling you what they were, so you know.

Once we had finished our turn, Blazin' and I had to wait for the next entrants to do their thing. Some girl that was in the competition sign up line in front of Blazin', (he had told me,) was up next. And three other dudes were scheduled to go on last. The three guys had Blazin' and I concerned because they looked like they knew what wazup. They just had that look about them – a look that said they were going to be good. The same way that I knew that Boogie Bob was a breaker when I had first seen him - it was one of those feelings.

The MC got on the microphone, "Next up on the big stage we have our first and only girl of the competition – She goes by the name of Chee girl." The girl walked over to the MC, whispered something in his ear and then the MC got back on the microphone and said, "Sorry, let me correct that. Next up on the big stage is Chi-Girl (pronounced Shy girl – as in Chi-town, you know someone from Chicago) the crowd cheered their butts off, which I understood, finally there was a girl to enter the big show, you've gotta give her props.

Over the speakers, Cyndi Laupers, "Girls just wanna have fun" began to play at a low volume, but just as "Chi Girl" began her routine, the DJ turned it up. "She must be a gymnast or something," I said to Brock. She started way back off of the linoleum and then sprinted into flips, handsprings, and aerial cartwheels or some shiznit like that. I was not a gymnastics expert or anything, but I knew a gymnast when I saw one; she had rocked it out too.

She worked her way into a top rock with hip hop dancing and then sank to the ground into scatting and footwork hops. In other words, she was a little choppy but it looked good, it was her own style. She even did a coffee grinder; where one of your legs does a 360 circle completely around your body as you hop over the other foot that's holding your body off of the ground.

For her grand finale she kicked her leg up and around and twisted herself into backspins – super fast, she did a million of them, the crowd cheered loudly, which included Blazin' and me; we were both cheering just as loud as everybody else was. That's the thing about breakin', even when you're watching someone else, even if you're competing against him or her, you just can help but cheering for someone that's good.

Blazin' and I were actually impressed with her. She wasn't just good because she was a girl. She was actually just good no matter what. Chi girl had a complete package with the way she used her gymnastics into her routine and the hip hop dancing she did. The crowd cheered equally as loud for Chi-Girl as they did for Blazin' and me, so frankly, I wasn't sure what to expect anymore. "Chi-Girl was the only girl who had the balls to enter the competition. And you've gotta love that," Blazin' said.

"You've gotta love balls?" I asked Blazin' with a wise guy look on my face.

"You know what I mean," Brock said.

"Yeah, you love balls." I said.

"Dude, you know what I meant," Brock said. And I did, I did know what he meant, but I had a good old time messing with him anyway.

I whispered over to Blazin' after she was done, "We ought to get that girls phone number and see if she wants to be a part of the Neighborhood Street Rockers; the way I see it, adding a female breakin' gymnast to the mix would be smart."

Blazin' had instantly agreed with me, I didn't really have to sell him on the idea.

"Okay everybody," the crystal clear voice said through the speakers, "Last but not least, our final contestants of the day go by the name of the Suburban Break Crew; Slim Jim, Kid Mojo, and Jet Drinkwater you are up next."

I kind of laughed to myself about Slim Jim because, Slim Jim was not slim, in fact he was as big as a football player or a lumber jack, but for whatever reason big people get nicknames like "tiny" or "slim" sometimes.

The first guy up from their crew (Slim Jim) entered the linoleum stage gliding on his feet like an astronaut with moonwalk-esque movements that turned into wavin' and poppin' routines, first rate. Then the Big Red headed monster did these moves that reminded me of spaghetti legs and crazy legs that I used to do on skates but he was on the ground in shoes doing them, it was just an illusion that he was on roller skates, it was an optical illusion. You dig. It looked cool as heck though. And seriously, from far away, I bet you would have thought that he was on roller skates doing spaghetti legs.

The next Suburban Break Crew member made his grand entrance – I heard his break mates yelling, "Go Mojo, Go Mojo Go Mojo!" He began his routine with that move that Dustin and Hazy had tried to show me at school a few weeks ago in the hallway before first period – Atomic Flares. Only this cat Mojo had them down like a champ. His crew members called the move, "Thomas Flares" instead of "Atomic flares."

"Mojos got the Thomas Flares workin' … work it work it," Slim Jim said.

It was real cool to see the Flares in person, since I had only seen them on TV before during the Olympics – and that was on a gymnasts horse, Mojo was doing them on the ground. But at the same time, after that move, I was beginning to worry about our first place chances.

Next, this dude, Kid Mojo, transitioned into pennies, which were windmills where you grab your front pockets while you're spinning and revolving around and you just use your momentum to keep you going, instead of pushing off with your hands. Some people call them, "nutcrackers" but around our neck of the woods, people called them, "pennies" too. Kid Mojo boldly leapt to his feet and left the stage to numerous cheers.

Honestly the cheers were longer and louder than we had heard all day. And not those fake kind of cheers that were given when the 5 year olds were breakin'. Heck; if I've got to admit it to you then I will but I think I may have been cheering louder than anyone was after Kid Mojo had finished. Sometimes, you've just got to give credit, where credit was due – do you know what I mean Jellybean?

The last member of their crew was half the size of Kid Mojo and one quarter of the size of Slim Jim. His name was Jet Drinkwater. Some of the people in the crowd were cheering for him before he even did anything; it was mainly the chicks. They must had known him from school because a couple of them were yelling, "We love you small glass of drink water," The girls that were yelling it had really gotten a big old roar out of themselves. They must have said it a hundred times while they giggled their gooses off.

This "Jetty pooh" cat had busted out with helicopters, footwork and backspins. Which really made the crowd go crazy, you see, because of his height, it looked like a little kid was doing all of these impressive moves but in fact he was right around our age. He was good too though; I have to admit it to you.

Their grand finale was the three of them standing as one big helicopter. Slim Jim was standing upright in the middle of the pack. Kid Mojo wrapped his legs around the back of Slim Jim's head and the rest of Mojos body hung down Slim Jim's back. Jet Drinkwater wrapped his legs around the front of Slim Jim's head and his body hung down on the opposite side of Mojos, down Slims front. Slim Jim had four legs wrapped around his neck. The three of them had finished assembling their 3 man helicopter. Slim Jim began to spin around in circles; the force of motion made Kid Mojo and Jet Drinkwater extend outwards to horizontal. They both put their arms straight out to make their human blades that much longer. They were both even with the ground as Slim Jim turned around in circles as the crowd went bananas. They had formed a spinning capital "T."

"A three man helicopter blade," Brock said and then added, "That dude Slim Jim must be getting dizzy as all heck."

"Fo shizzle my nizzle," I said.

After the Suburban Break Crew was done, it was no surprise that the crowd was going straight up bonkers. They were going Izz-Off! They weren't just a good crew for this contest; they were a good bunch of breakers for anywhere. Blazin' and I had definitely hung tough with those guys but as far as that contest went, they had the upmanship on us and that was for sure.

The MC grabbed the mic and announced, "We will take a 15 minute break while the judges tally up the votes."

Blazin' and I both agreed that first place was out of question and we both agreed that we probably deserved 2nd place based on the breakin' alone. "If you factored in the crowd noise for Chi girl and if you factored in her gymnastics and such - Chi-Girl may get 2nd," I said as Blazin' just shrugged and smiled cautiously.

I spotted Chi-girl hanging with two girls who appeared to be her gymnastics buddies; based on the same warm up suits they had in common. I walked over to her by myself, while Blazin' headed over to talk to some of the guys from the Suburban Break Crew.

Chi-Girl saw me coming so she cut off her conversation with her buddies, "Hi – Phil … right?"

"Yep – Hey Chi Girl, you rocked it out girl," I said as cute as I could in a deeper voice. - It's funny how girls can make us guys act all cool and stuff like that. At least that's what I tried to do.

She smiled in an Awe Shucks sort of way and said, "Thanks Phil, you're not so bad yourself."

I was not very good at small talk to be honest with you, so I just got to it and asked her, "Yo Chi-Girl, I'm looking to assemble an incredible break dance crew and I think you should join up with us. We go by the name of the Neighborhood Street Rockers," I said while looking at her square in the eyes.

"That sounds awesome! Sounds like fun! I'm in," She said.

"Sweet, I'll tell my partner Blazin' that you're in, in like Flynn," I said like a hip cat.

But after that my mind had gone blank. Girls can do that to me sometimes.

Finally, she started talking and we just shot the crap around for a little bit: We talked about the competition. We talked about breakin'. I told her about Boogie Bob. But mostly I just smiled a lot and listened in as Chi girl and her buddies talked about an upcoming gymnastics meet.

I didn't hang out for too long though, I was too excited with the results that were coming, so I grabbed Chi girl's number and I told her I'd call her about breakin' practice sessions later on in the week. Then I wiggled my way through the crowded parking lot, past the spectators, who went out of their way to say, "Sup" and "nice job" and "cool break dancing" and other schlernious stuff like that as I shucked and jived my way back towards Blazin'. It was pretty cool to be treated like a celebrity by all of those strangers.

I found Brock who was smiling from ear to ear as he was chattin' up the guys from the Suburban Break Crew. We hung with them the rest of the way while we waited to hear the results.

"Wazup Blazin'?" I said

"Yohhh! This is my buddy Phil," he said loudly while patting me on the back with a wide smile that half assedly introduced me to them. "Check this out Phil – These dudes asked me if we want to hook up with them and become one big crew," Blazin' said while nodding and practically jumping up and down.

"We would dominate every crew out there," I said cocksure.

Slim Jim chimed in, "Yay man, you guys have some pretty sweet footwork and helicopters and routines and stuff."

Kid Mojo piped, "Hey hows it is goin'? I'm Kid Mojo –Your boy Blazin' said you're looking to build an incredible break dance crew," then Mojo cleared his throat, "… and by the way, Blazin' asked US if we wanted to join up with YOU guys and your crew, just to set the records straight, but I think that sounds cool."

"That's sounds tall Chicago," I said randomly.

And before I knew it, the MC had grabbed the mic. I had been keeping an eye on him ever since the battle had ended. It didn't seem like fifteen minutes had past, but that was probably due to my nerves again. I didn't even have a chance to tell Blazin' that Chi-Girl was going to join our crew because we were suddenly interrupted by, "Attention everyone ATTENTION! We have our winners – break dancers, please gather 'round."

The Big Burger was still packed to the hilt with customers, spectators, and breakers, so it took a while for everyone involved in the contest to make their way through the crowd.

"Coming in 3rd place … CHI GIRL," there was much applause, hooting, hollering, and all of that kind of schlernious jazz while she grabbed her prize. For a few quick seconds, I suddenly got an empty feeling in my stomach as I worried that one of those five year olds that had entered would get a cheap placement of second – just because they were five and "cute" - you know how that crap works, right? And just as I was worried that Blazin and I were going to get rooked and crooked -.

"Coming in 2nd place izzzz the NEIGHBORHOOD STREET ROCKERS", instead of happiness my first thought was relief. Then I was happy, and then I was mad. After all, second is losing, if I've got to tell you the truth. I know nowadays that everybody gets a trophy or ribbon for just entering any old friggin' contest - win or lose. But I've got news for you, if you don't get first place – YOU LOST! But I smiled anyway.

The crowd had hooted and hollered for us while we grabbed our trophy, 100 bucks cash, and gift certificates to Big Burger restaurant. I was glad they had a veggie burger on their menu too, since I've been trying to eat better. But mainly, I exhaled in relief and was just glad that we had won second. When it comes to judging, you never know how it can turn out, if you know what I mean.

"And coming in 1st place izzzzz the Suburban Break Crew." The crowd cheered extra loud like a bunch of silly little freaks for the first place crew. Brock and I looked at each other in agreement. We knew they had deserved it. They were a move or two up on us and everybody in the crowd knew it. After all, there were three of them.

Everyone that was in the contest shot the old crap around with each other for a little while but then good old Blazin' got in a big old hurry all of a sudden to leave. (Imagine that?)

Blazin' and I said our goodbyes to our new friends; Kid Mojo, Jet Drinkwater, and Slim Jim - formerly known as the Suburban Break Crew and soon to be known as the Neighborhood Street Rockers and we all planned on getting together ASAP to break together.

As we were getting ready to leave, I saw Chi-Girl waving across the parking lot. I waved back at Chi-Girl who then mouthed the words, "Call me," while placing her pinky to her mouth and thumb to her ear. I didn't try to go over to her; there were too many people to cut through but that's when I told Blazin' about our other newest addition to our crew.

After the Big Burger Break dance contest, Blazin' and I went back to our hood and just chilled in his garage for a bit and tripped off the day. We stared at his '67 that he talked about driving when he turned 16. Then we talked about girls - you know how we guys are when it comes to talking about girls.

Then we talked about breakin' in more contests with all of our new crew members and of course we talked about dominating the world and all. All the while Brocks ghetto blaster played mix jams and break beats for the whole neighborhood to hear. The whoosh and rush of cars driving by on Main Street was hypnotizing and relaxing for a great end of a busy day.

I know you haven't been there before, so I'll tell you, there was a stoplight by Blazin's crib so every once in a while we'd have an audience of people stopped in their cars by the red light that would watch us break in his open garage. Randomly a couple of people shouted from cars about how our breakin' looked cool and all. And a couple of times we even had girls whistle at us while we were just sitting there. That didn't suck to be honest with you. Now that I think about it that was the thing that had gotten us on the whole "girls" conversation in the first place. One little whistle from a girl and suddenly we were both Romeos and Don Juan's.

Anyway, after we had talked about taking over the breakin' world, we worked on some of the break moves that we had seen Kid Mojo, Slim Jim, and Jet Drinkwater displaying at the big burger competition that day. This snapped us back into reality real quick. We knew we had a lot of practicing to do before we could become the very best.

When I got home that night and then next morning I started calling our crewmates to figure out when we could all get together for our first assembly. As it turned out, it was too short of a notice to get everyone together right away. So after a whole bunch of back and forth with the guys (and girl) and after many call backs, we planned on getting together for our first assembly in three weeks.

Chapter 7

Lets battle right now

Do you know what rocks? My bus usually got to school 15 minutes early every morning. There were a few of us that scurried in a hurry to the hallways located by the woodshop classroom. A few of us cool cats would get our breakin' goin' there before school started on most mornings. On my way to the woodshop classroom hallway, (aka the hip hop hallway by us breakers) I passed by Big Ted's locker, (the gum salesman – and whatnot) I usually didn't see him until after I had been breakin' in the hip hop hallway and I was on my way to class.

This one morning he was bright and early for a change, but I'm sure it had nothing to do with a desire to learn at school. He wasn't that kind of a guy. His locker was opened wide that morning and I remember this morning because it was the first time I had noticed his locker speakers were gold. My locker was just a locker – boring. However, Ted's locker had speakers, a mirror that was taped onto the locker door with pink duct tape, and a selection of cologne bottles on his top shelf.

I sort of started to dance a little as I passed by him. Ted was fixing his hair and spraying on cologne from a black bottle, while throwing me a head nod and an eye brow raise, but when I said "Hey" he acted as if he didn't even hear me. Save for another eye brow raise that may or may not have been intended for me.

"Nasty girls," by Vanity was playing quietly from his battery operated speakers that sat on his top shelf of his locker right next to the cologne bottles. It was the shelf where most people would put their books - but I never saw Ted with any books. He was one of those kids that had managed to go to school the entire day and never crack open a book. Ted didn't appear to have any books in his locker either, not even on the bottom of the locker; save for a stack of Victoria Secret catalogues that he told me he had swiped from the mail.

After that day, I passed by his locker at least 10 times per week and he would always have something jamming from his locker speakers in between periods or before school or after school; Rick James, Prince, Michael Jackson, Madonna and stuff like that. They were jams I had always heard at the rink but he played the more soulful disco of the rink jams, which attracted some of the hotter girls from our school around his locker (that were also rink girls.)

It's not that Big Ted was a smooth talking Romeo or anything, but he did play the cool jams at his locker. Suzy and Betty were practically permanent fixtures at Ted's locker in the mornings and they always dressed like it was hot outside, even when it was cold outside. But the way they dressed had really given them a bad rep. if you dress "too old" or wear "too little" you can get a bad reputation. I'm not saying it's right, I'm just sayin'.

Anyway, after I passed by Big Teds locker, I could see down the hallway that Dustin, Isaac, and Hazy were already there getting on down in the hip hop hallway. One of them, I couldn't tell whom yet, was bouncing around off of the walls – Literally. Have you ever seen someone run up a wall and then do a back flip as his or her feet get to head high on the wall? As I drew more near, I saw that it was Dustin. Dustin had just nailed that maneuver. And he was setting up to do it again.

The ACA Collective, that's what they called themselves; The African, Caucasian, and Asian collective. They were a crew before Brock and I were technically a crew, so I never really thought about bringing them aboard to our crew to be honest with you. They seemed kind of clique-ee once in a while, so I really didn't want them on our crew anyway. It was obvious that I was some sort of an outsider to them, but we were still cool, just not best of buddies, that's all - you dig?

Isaac, screamed quietly, "Sup Boyeeeee Swifty?"

I high fived his outstretched hand and said, "Wazup?"

Dustin had just finished with his wall flip and said, "How goes it?"

Then Hazy jumped down onto his hands and did his signature move - the crabwalk, which were pretty tight and fast, if you asked me. "Impressive Hazy my man, Impressive," I said. He had really come a long way since that day he had first showed me them.

Hazy jumped up and smiled at me mysteriously then looked at Dustin and said, "Should I tell him?" He said it in an almost taunting sort of way too, which made me nervous. I even checked my zipper after his weird smile. He made me feel like my ding a ling was hanging out or something. I literally checked, but no, my fly was up.

"Sup dude? Wazza dilly o?" I asked.

Dustin and Hazy were now smirking like dogs with bones. Hazy told me, "You know that new guy, Devon at our school?"

I shook my head yes, "I eat lunch with him sometimes of course I know him."

Hazy continued, "Well your lunch buddy was just over here five minutes ago. He was looking for you. He said he wants to battle you!" Hazy bulged his eyes like a madman and grinned with taunt, probably just to freak me out, I figured. "He thinks you are getting too big for your britches."

"Battle me?" I said with surprise.

Hazy laughed at me like I was a dummy and said, "Yay, in a break dance battle, silly."

"Well I figured that, but that's cool, I'll battle anybody, I'm just surprised he's getting all like that – we're friends and such. Why didn't he just come up to me and try to battle," I said as I tried to act calm.

Dustin chimed in, "He heard you had won that break dance competition a couple of weeks ago."

"Of course he heard about it, I told him about it," I said with some sarcasm of my own.

" … Hey, over the weekend - Did you go to the mall?" Dustin asked.

"Yep, I went there Sunday with my P's, they hooked me up with these sweet new shoes," I said as I showed them my new gray suede-ed out break shoes with thick fat laces to boot.

Hazy jumped back into the conversation, "Well I guess when you were at the mall you were bragging to somebody about how you're some champion breaker and you think you can whip anybodies butt now, and through the grapevine, Devon had heard about it. So he said, he wants to put you in your place. You're getting too big for your britches, was the way he had said it," Hazy said as he grinned tightly with beady eyes just to send chills down my spine.

"I wasn't bragging to anybody at the mall," I said, and then I thought about it, "I did tell the shoe salesgirl and the cashier at the shoe store that I was just in a break-dance contest 2 weeks ago and that my boy Blazin' and I took second place. But the only reason I even brought it up was because they asked me if I was a breaker, on account I was buying fat laces for the shoes."

Hazy tauntingly jumped back in and said, "Either way Devon is looking for you." Then he smiled and smacked his fists in a way that shivered my timbers. It's not that I was afraid of battling anybody, but the way he had said it, made it sound like the biggest kid in the school wanted to kick my ass. At least that was the vibe that I was feeling at that time.

"Well, I'm right here, If Devon wants a battle he's got one. It izzz on … On like Donkey Kong," I said boldly, even though I was kind of nervous too.

The ACA Collective and I hung out for another 5 minutes or so, chatting, breakin', and this and that and there was no sign of Devon. Funny thing was - Devon knew where we hung out and what time we'd be there. He'd seen us there in the mornings breakin' many times and had even joined in on the fun; he knew where to find me.

The final warning bell had rung, giving me 2 minutes to walk briskly to my first period class. I passed by Big Ted's locker who wasn't there, which had made that hallway seem so empty. It's funny how boring that section of hallway was when he was not around playing his locker music.

It was 30 seconds on the clock when I was just about to walk into my class when I saw Devon walking up to me, all cocky with swag and an extra bounce to his ounce as he got all up in my face.

"Sup Devon!? … Hazy said you wanted to talk to me," I said while sort of playing dumb at the same time.

Devon looked at me with heavy weight boxers eyes and said, "You think you're all bad now, don't ya Swifty?"

I stopped playing dumb and said, "Word is that you want to battle me my brother?"

Devon grunted, "Darn Straight!"

I told Devon, just so I could beat him to the punch, "Okay my man – meet me over by the shop classroom tomorrow morning." He gave me a look of confusion, so I said, "The hip hop hallway - you know where I hang! We'll battle in the morning before school."

Devon scrunched his face and shivered his head as if he had just eaten a lemon and then in a deeper and louder voice said, "Lets battle right now."

"I've got to get to class," I said.

"Ohh, you're yellow? So now I get it, you're all yella!" Devon said.

"Yo dude, I just said I'd battle you tomorrow morning. I'm not a chicken my brother. I'm just trying to get to my class on time." I started walking away because the red second hand told me that I had 5 seconds left to walk 10 feet. I had already been late a couple of times last week because I had been getting all carried away and consumed with breakin' every morning with the ACA Collective guys and such. The teacher had even told me to start being on time or I'd get a detention.

I walked into my classroom as the bell had rung. I smiled at the teacher and the whole class and said, "Safe" as I put my arms out like an umpire calling someone safe at the plate in baseball. The teacher smiled and told me to take my seat. I could still hear Devon walking down the hallway muttering, "Yellow sissy boy," or some other schlernious shiznit like that, that I couldn't quite make out. But I could hear the anger in his voice; THAT, I could hear loud and clear.

In fact the whole class had seemed to overhear the whole conversation between Devon and I, because when I sat down at my desk, my buddy that I had known since elementary school, Fred, asked me, "What was that all about with Devon?"

"Devon is challenging me to a one on one break battle; he thinks I'm getting all cocky now that I came in second place in that Big Burger contest a couple of weeks ago. I told Devon that the bell was about to ring so I'd battle him tomorrow but that wasn't good enough for him," I said.

Fred crinkled his nose and said, "So battle him tomorrow."

"Oh yay fow show my man, for sure, I will battle him tomorrow … What is crazy though, is that I never even brag about second place. Second place means you lost, so I don't know what the heck he is talking about," I said.

Fred nodded and started getting his text book out and said, "You guys always sit together at lunch I don't know why he's trippin'?"

When first period was over Fred said, "Alright Phil, then I'll see you tomorrow, bright and early in the AM … Hey come to my locker first thing in the morning. I want to watch you and Devon battle."

"Absolutely, I'll come get you. I'll be at your locker at 8:20am," I said.

Fred nodded and told me okay and then we both walked together anyway, as we usually did after first period, since he wasn't with Reeny (his girlfriend), who usually didn't start walking the halls with Fred until after second period. From second period on: when you saw Fred, you would see Reeny, when you saw Reeny, you would see Fred. I bet you have those types of couples at your school too, don't ya? - The ones that always seem to be together in between every class period. Sometimes I wonder how they do it?

While we were walking to our next class and talking about our weekend, we spotted this dude Rory Ragz heading towards the drinking fountain with a purpose, as if his pants were on fire, at least, that's what Rorys eyes looked like. Isaac from the ACA Collective was already there slurping down the auga when he was suddenly interrupted by Rory.

This dude Rory had the exact same hair style that Michael Jackson had on the Album cover for, "Thriller." I knew Rory because his "thing" was poppin', just like Slim Jims "thing" was, and every once in a while Rory would show up at the hip hop hallway in the mornings to mess around with us. He was usually a pretty laid back brother but right then and there, Rory had this serious as a president talking about war look on his face as he got up in Isaacs space at the drinking fountain.

Rory poked his head over the drinking fountain and made his presence immediately known to Isaac, whose eyes widened as he picked his head up and stopped drinking. It was funny and serious all at once. Isaac had kept the handle pressed so the water kept flowing out and hitting his chin accidentally. I remembered thinking: why don't you lift your head up another couple of inches or stop pressing the water lever so the water would stop hitting your chin. But he didn't, he had the cleanest chin in school that day. I tried not to laugh because Rorys face was so serious but the water hitting his chin was hysterical.

Anyway Isaac looked up and said, "Would you like a drink?" Isaacs smile grew with panic as he started to read the facial expression on Rory's face. Water continued to hit him on the chin while his eyes and facial expression said: why are you all up in my face? Instead of getting angry or anything, Isaac just responded with a smile and said, "Can't a guy get a drink around here?"

Rory then without saying a word started Tickin', poppin', shakin', and wiggling his wavy arms like a man on a mission. A poppin' battle mission.

The fiercely powerful display of poppin' and tickin' along with the war-like eyes from Rory said -show me what you've got Isaac!

A boogaloo battle was on.

Meanwhile Rory's buddy Rodd Get down was laughing in the background and saying, "Oooooh, aint nobody going to match that." Rodd was practically jumping up and down being Rory's cheerleader and yelling the word, "dayg" repeatedly; I knew he was sayin', "dang" but it sounded like dayg. Rodd kept talking trash by saying stuff like, "That's my dawg throwin' down." Or "You can't touch that –cant even touch it."

Rory still had not said a word just yet; he only spoke with his eyes and with his poppin'. But his pal Rodd was making up for his silence with his taunting snickers and taunts of, "OOhhh boy, he's got you stuck. Isaac, he's got you all stuck."

Isaac finally jumped into the ring and busted out with some king tut poppin' and some MJ and James Brown moon walking and such, but Isaac more or less admitted to Rory in his actions and in his comments that he thought he was better than he, "Yeah man, Rory you're good, that was cool man." The poppin' battle ended just as quickly as it had started. It was obvious that Isaac wasn't really into it.

That was the thing about Isaac though; he was just a cool cat, just trying to have some fun with breakin' and poppin'. He just wanted to entertain or have fun; he was not really a battle breaker like me. And really, at that point, he was just trying to get a drink of water.

The bell was going to ring in a minute or so, so everyone started to scamper. I heard Rodd laughing as we all sped walked away, "My boy Rory schooled Isaac, boy!"

As I walked on to my next class, I wondered if Rory and Devon had planned the day together? Did they both plan to battle their counterparts that day as a pact. On the other hand, was it just something in the air that day, or was there a full moon that made them want to battle? I bet you Isaac would say it was something in the water.

I didn't run into Devon the rest of the school day, which was odd since I usually saw him at lunch, even on the days that we didn't sit at the same table, I still usually saw him in the cafeteria sitting at the black table. For whatever reason, the various ethnicities in our school, usually sat amongst themselves. But I took turns sitting wherever and with whomever on any given day; whatever their color, race, or preference, I didn't care, I was friends with a variety of people.

When Devon or Fred weren't around at lunch time, I sat with Gary and Gloria, who were a "couple" that were "dating" but everyone called them gay behind their backs. This gave our melting pot of a table the label as the "gay table" but actually I'm straight and I sat with them because they liked to listen to the DJ "mixes" just like I did, so really, we were the "mix music table" if you ask me.

Anyway, that's whom I sat with that day while I looked around for Devon. I kept waiting for him to show up at my lunch table and talk some more trash to me but he was nowhere to be found. But good ol Logan Gelderring made sure I wasn't lonely. He was one of those dudes that made fun of Gary and Gloria to their faces about their orientation. And he made fun of me because of where I sat sometimes. But he really didn't have any room to talk.

Logan was one of the grossest dudes I had ever met. Every day, after he got done eating, he would take out his keys from his pocket and start picking his teeth. He would even walk around the cafeteria and pick his teeth with his keys while he talked to you.

"How's life at the queer table?" Logan asked me while picking his teeth.

"Quit picking your teeth you gross jack ass …. How's life at the chick table … Chick?" I asked him, since he sat with all girls that included his sister and her friends.

"Devon is going to take you out dude … it's all over school that you're yella," Logan said.

"I told him I'd battle him tomorrow … aint nobody yella-fella, I said.

"Alright queer, we'll see. - Devon's from Chicago and you're just a suburbanite, you don't stand a chance," he said.

"Buzz off Chick table Chick," I said to get rid of him.

"Maybe I shouldn't say anything about you and where you sit. I mean, Jesus sat with the leopards, so I guess you're just being Christ-like for chrissake," Logan said trying to be funny.

"Its leppers Mr. wisenheimer," Gloria said.

"What? … It's Gelderring," Logan said.

"Jesus sat with the leppers … people with leprosy … not zoo animals," she said, "and you are a wisenheimer; a first class wiseacre, Mr. Gelderring," She added.

"Whatever," Logan said, blowing it off as he walked away.

"I can't stand him," Gary said in a quiet sneer as he walked away.

"Have you ever noticed how none of his sisters' friends talk to him? No one likes him at his table. You can't say mean things to people and expect to have real friends," I said to Gary and Gloria to try and quell that punks comments. Then we talked about me battling Devon the next day throughout the rest of lunch and ignored all of Logan's teeth picking comments.

The school day came to an end. I headed straight home. I wolfed down dark chocolate, slammed a glass of water, while watching Tom and Jerry cartoons on the TV, and thought about the break battle against Devon for the next day. I don't know what it is, but I swear, even when I become an adult, I will still watch the "Tom and Jerry" cartoon. And you can take that to the bank. They really floor me.

Later, I rearranged some of the furniture in my family room so I could practice my pennies, flares and crabwalks. I put, "Candy girl" by New Edition on the P's stereo and kept Tom and Jerry playing in the background while I thought what a punk Devon was for calling me chicken, when the fact of the matter was, the bell was seconds away from ringing. The thought of Devon calling me a chicken made me practice even harder though. When I felt like my arms were going to fall off, I kept going anyway. Finally the day had come and gone; another turn of the globe; another sunset and all that mattered was tomorrow morning.

The globe had spun enough for the bright celestial sphere to shine through my bedroom window, right into my eyes, begging my bones to arise for the pending break battle at school. The battle with Devon was the last thing I thought about when I went to sleep that night and it was the first thing I thought of when I woke up that morning.

On the bus ride to school a couple of people called out my name from the backseats. I was sitting in the middle of the bus and thinking about the break battle against Devon, when I looked back and saw, Jenny Quade and Jocy Rezza staring at me. Jocy said, "I heard you're breakin' against Devon Hornsby today."

I asked her how she knew that and she told me, "It's all over the whole school Mr. Phil K Swift the best breaker in the world," and by the way she had said that, I knew that the grapevine was alive and well at our school. Boy did she sound snotty – even though we were friends.

Then Jenny said, "I heard Rory schooled Isaac yesterday." And even though Jenny had said it to Jocy, I jumped in and more or less stuck up for Isaac and said, "Isaac wasn't really trying his best, he was just trying to have some fun. Rory was the one getting all serious."

Then Jocy said," Yay, I heard Rory totally took him out yesterday. Isaac just stood there all frozen … he was stuck." Then they went back to talking amongst themselves before I could even reply. I mean, they never even gave me eye contact again. That's really kind of annoying, if you really must hear me griping about it.

When I got off the bus I hurriedly headed to Fred's locker which was right next to the girl's gym locker room door where Ms. Demimonde, who was the girls P.E. teacher, was always standing and waiting for her students to enter the locker room for gym class. Ms. Demimonde had butchy short dark black hair with gray swirls; a very, "Alice from the Brady Bunch" hairdo. She was a stout boyish looking woman that stared at students in this creepy sort of way.

On two separate occasions, from two different girls that had Ms. Demimonde as a gym teacher, we heard that Ms. Demimonde made all of her students take showers after class. Then after all the girls were done with their showers, she would make them to go over by her, where she would then rub or feel every girls' back individually, to make sure that their backs were wet, to make sure that they had actually taken a shower. She said she wanted to make sure that they didn't just walk through the shower line and not get wet. Or whatever her excuse was. Rather creepy, dontchya think? I guess she had never crossed the line enough for anyone to complain. However, you could tell that all of the girls who had her as a gym teacher were all thinking: What the heck? But nobody had ever complained against her. But if you ask me, she had figured out a pretty sneaky way to cop a feel. Someone should have told their parents at least.

Most guys in our gym class didn't even take showers. We just rubbed on the pit stick or sprayed on cologne, and were done with it. Taking showers at school was the kind of thing that could really mess a guy's life up; because some guys were furry as all heck, like a monkey. And some boys didn't have fur just yet – not everybody hits puberty at the same time.

Some of those students that were as furry as gorillas really liked to rub that crap in too. It really was pretty damn nuts that whether or not you had hairy ones or bald ones could spread your name around the school like the common cold. Speaking of "cold" let me tell you, you don't want to see anybodies thing-a-majiggers when their cold – they shrink you know. It's scientific in fact. When it's cold out, they shrink in an effort to get closer to the body for warmth from one's own body. Can you imagine telling the whole school why your what-u-muh-call-its were so small and then answering everybody with that scientific answer? Even though its science, it still would get you razzed a whole bunch. But that's why most guys in my gym class would get a little testy when it came to disrobing, showering, and showing off the testes.

It's just as bad for girls though. One girl I know, I won't say her name, got caught stuffing her bra. And it was because of the whole required shower thing; when she got into the shower - her pears had became grapes; it was all over the school by the next day. But I didn't care what people said about her. I still thought the girl was cute. She had a pretty face, really knew how to dress, and she was nice too. If a girl is nice and can dress nice, sometimes that's enough.

Anyway, Fred's locker was right by the girls gym locker doors and that's what threw me on that whole story, but now I'll tell you what happened next. I saw Fred bouncing down the hallway; he had this bounce to his walk that was very obvious, you could pick him out in a pack of jumping kangaroos. "Sappenin Phil – I take it you're still battling Devon?" Fred said assumingly.

I boldly said, "You got that right, Fred; I'm going to show him Wazup!"

Fred opened up his locker, grabbed his books while he laughed under his breath, and started shaking his head in disbelief. He quietly whispered, as he was trying not to be overheard yet he was still loud enough that I'm sure she could hear, "Mz overly-friendly is hanging out bright and early this morning, I see." He was talking about Ms. Demimonde. He too thought this teacher was way too close to crossing the line with teenagers, so he always made wiseass comments around her.

Before I could respond, I could see in the shadows of the narrow hallway that led to our small gym, near where Fred and I were standing, that Devon was there. Practically at the same time we both said, "Is that Devon?" and then we both were certain of it just as soon as we had asked it. We both started walking down towards Devon in the narrow Hallway.

Devon boldly yelled, "Oh I see you showed up Mr. Swift." He didn't waste any time starting the break battle either. He twisted and turned into some move that looked like maybe it was supposed to be a windmill or maybe it was a failed attempt at tracks or head glides (a move I had only heard about). I wasn't sure because seconds into his break routine his legs or maybe it was even his head had hit the lockers due to the very narrow section of hallway that he was breakin' in.

I looked at the hallway and I tried to picture myself doing crabwalks or backspins or windmills, heck even head spins, which would take up the least amount of space, but the hallway was definitely too narrow to attempt anything. I looked at Devon's expectant eyes and said, "Let's take this over to the hip hop hallway where we will have more room."

Devon arrogantly said, "We'll do it right here Swift boy!" He circled around the hallway with his arms spread apart to attempt to make room in the hallway that was now packed with students. The students were gathering around because some of them had gym class in the small gym for first period and some of them seemed to be gathering around because Devon was becoming loud. You know how students love a good fight? Devon's voice sounded rather fight-like which really helped reel in the crowd - but he wasn't trying to fight me, that was just how it probably sounded to the students.

"Come on Swift, you said you weren't afraid to battle me and we have 5 minutes before the first period bell rings, show me what you've got Bo-aye," he said trying to egg me on.

"Devon my man, you just hit your whole body against those lockers because this hallway is too narrow. Let's take the 1 minute walk down the hall to the shop class and I'll show you what is going on. I'm not afraid of you. We said yesterday that we would meet in the hip hop hallway, so let's do what we said we were going to do," I said.

"Ohhh okay! Okay! You are a chicken! That's what's up!" Devon said.

I whispered In Fred's ear, "This hallway really is too narrow, I wouldn't be able to do any of my moves."

I then said to Devon, "Dude why can't we just go over by the shop class, I'll battle you right now."

Devon laughed and said, "That's what I'm trying to do PhILLLL-uhhPPP (he said my name so darn sarcastically) – battle you right now!"

I started walking away and said, "If you follow me to the shop class hallway we can battle there right friggin' now."

Devon yelled, "Right here is fine Swift, we can battle right here – all of your boys are by that shop class – that's unfair."

I stopped dead in my tracks, turned around, and said, "Hazy, Isaac, and Dustin aren't my boys. They are the ACA Collective. I am a Neighborhood

Street Rocker … How about this dude, you want neutral?" I asked sincerely and then I paused to see if Devon was listening, "We can battle each other at the upcoming Thanksgiving school dance on Wednesday night. I'll be there for sure, no matter what. There will be plenty of room there … Are you in?" I asked.

Devon turned around, looked at his boys, then he looked back at me and said, "Alright bet!"

The warning bell for first period rang to alert us that we had 2 minutes to get to class. All of the students that did not have gym class started running quickly as if someone had just blown a massive fart.

Throughout the day I had a few cats here and there call me "chicken" or "yellow" because that was what Devon had called me. But what most people talked about was that Devon and I were going to be battling at the Thanksgiving school dance on Wednesday night to see who was the best breaker in our school.

It's amazing how rumors or truths can spread around a school by the end of the day. The other rumor that was flying around the school was that Devon was going to bring some of his boys with him from his break crew, to teach me a lesson. However, the other rumor floating around the school was that I was bringing all of my crew with me too; the Neighborhood Street Rockers. But that was not true. I planned to go to the dance alone. So I also figured that Devon was probably going to be flying solo too.

Chapter 8

Fart bully

Even though it took forever, Wednesday had finally arrived, the night of the Thanksgiving school Dance was waiting for me and I couldn't wait. I still had to go to my classes for the day but I won't bore you with those kinds of details. I'm sure you don't really care to hear about my math class or about how I had learned in home economics class to sew hot pads that were supposed to be oven mitts but I made them wrong so they became just hot pads.

However, I will tell you about how I literally ran into Diana Woodgrow for the third time, during passing period, on the day of the Thanksgiving school dance. And when I say literally, I mean, literally, she ran into me in the hallway with a bang right into me. I think she did it on purpose too. I think she timed it by waiting until I had been looking down at my books to reorganize them or she had waited for me to look at the hallway clock and then BOOM it would happen right out of nowhere – I never saw it coming.

I've never bumped into anyone else at school in that way, just Diana. It must have been her way of saying hi, I figured. I really wasn't sure if she did that to everybody or just me. It was all cool though, I actually found it rather cute. Every time she did it –she had knocked my books down, she gave me a big warm smile and said, "HI Phil" as she opened her arms really wide and gave me this – I want a hug look.

I gave her a hug as usual and for whatever reason, I had to hold my books over my pants the whole walk to science class, and that's all I'm going to say about that, it's a guy thing. It's hard to explain; pun intended.

The bell rang, I strolled to my chair, and sat down sort of hunched over to hide myself a little bit – and I tried not to look too much at this girl who sat next to me, Julie, who was wearing a short skirt and bobby sox. I wasn't trying to re-aggravate the situation to be honest with you. All I wanted to do was stop sitting so hunched over.

When our science teacher, Mr. Goenaddes walked into the classroom, my problem was solved, it just fizzled out. Now that I wasn't hunched over, I noticed the teacher had the windows open. It was one of those warm fall days that Blazin' loved to call, "Indian summer."

Class was just about to start but I still couldn't straighten out my seating posture just yet because of MS Bobby sox but when we were asked by the teacher, "Please put your belongings under your chair and take out something with which and on which to write for your test today." I finally was able to sit straight. His stuffy voice could kill any mood.

Mr. Goenaddes had been rumored to throw a desk from across the science lab room because one of his students had mouthed off to him. He was a big guy; a serious, stuffy, and dry looking man that looked like he could have been a judge or something. He had a tightly groomed beard and mustache that made me think he was strict. And for whatever reason, his particular style of beard and wrinkled forehead made me believe the rumor.

Anyhow, I used to be a big time class clown in grade school, although I swear this time, it was accidental but midway through the science test I sort of disturbed the class. A couple of students were done early with their test and as they were dropping their test off with the teacher, I overheard the mumblings of Mr. Goenadds "- Yes … you can smell the geranium flowers …"

I then, without thinking, from across the room, said, "Ohh, no kidding – I thought it was my breath?" which made the whole class crack up. Truthfully I wasn't even trying to be funny. I kept having this weird taste in my mouth; as if I had dry morning breath and I had just got done taking gross medicine. But I hadn't. I had been trying to figure out what the gross taste was for the last 5 minutes. The smell was so strong that I could taste it in my mouth. So when he said "it's the geraniums" it was an instant understanding.

Instantly Mr. Goenadds sternly yelled, "Phil - go stand in the hall!"

My sudden understanding had earned me a trip to the hall.

"But I …" I tried to say.

But before I could get a word in edgewise the teacher interrupted me and said, "Phil – hallway."

In disbelief, I started to head to the hall. But not before I said, "Yo man this is schlernious … straight up schlernious!"

Mr Goenadds didn't even know what to say at first, so he just stood there with a crinkled forehead and blank stare. He was probably wondering what the heck schlernious meant. – Not that I could tell him.

Moments later, he replied, "What's this schlernious business? … You walk around my class with this certain swagger … who do you think you are?"

"Many people have asked me that very question Mr. G. - They ask me … Phil, what's this swagger and bop to your hop? … and you know what I tell them?" I asked Mr. G (and the whole class for that matter, whom were now listening in) "I tell them: Yo I'm from Chicago, Tall Chicago, and I am a Neighborhood Street Rocker; a bad to the bone breaker, and even though you call it SWAG-GER, I call it my nature." – everyone started laughing their butts off, which definitely didn't make Mr. G happy.

"You can walk your way into the hallway young man," he said in a serious voice like I had never heard him use before.

I wasn't even trying to be a smart aleck or anything. I was just telling him the dilly o. I mean, he did ask about my swag, so I told him. But either way, he didn't like it. So he grabbed my arm and took me into the hallway with a firm gorilla grip on my shoulder that confirmed in my mind that he had most definitely thrown that desk across the lab room, just like the rumor had it. Sometimes the grapevine was true, you know.

While I was standing in the hallway I thought about how I hadn't been kicked out of class since the 6th grade, where I got kicked out of music class by Mr. Gaylord because I had farted in class. Yes farted; really loud too. The thing about that is and I'm still mad to this day- How the heck did Mr. Gaylord even know it was I that farted. I was sitting way in the back. My classmate Jim Zeke was the one laughing his butt off after I had farted, so why didn't he get blamed? In fact he was even the one telling jokes. Telling jokes so crazy, that I laughed so hard, I farted.

If Jim Zeke hadn't been telling jokes that day I probably wouldn't have slipped it out so forcefully. I would have done it secretly and probably had made it a silent but deadly affair. Well, that happened about 3 years ago or so and that was what I thought about while I stood in the hallway when people walked by and stared at me. I thought about how at least I didn't have to tell them I got kicked out of class for farting. I was kicked out of class because "I thought it was my breath."

Have you ever smelled something so strong before that you could taste it? I wasn't even trying to be funny or disruptive. The longer I stood in the hall; I started thinking about how my science teacher really blew an excellent chance to teach us about science. For instance the teacher could have told the class: Hey that's interesting Phil, so you mean you are in-taking the smell of geraniums via the sense of smell, yet you are genuinely tasting the geraniums with your taste buds. I was then picturing him running to one of his bookshelves and grabbing a science book and saying something like: what you are experiencing Phil is the thing they call, "olfactory taste osmosis." Then he could have talked about the famous scientist Pavlov and his salivating dogs and such. But no! Nothing like that happened. I was sent to the hall just like the old days.

When the bell rang, the students rushed out and after every last one of them was gone, the teacher poked his watermelon shaped head out of the classroom and told me that I could finish taking my test after school if I would like. Before I could even reply Mr. Goenadds removed his oval head from the doorway and then I heard the door close. It reminded me of an expression my grandma used to always use, "Children should be seen and not heard."

At the end of the school day I walked back into Mr. Goenadds class and I finished my test. When I was done, the next thought on my brain was: it's Wednesday and school is over; Devon is going to get served! I handed Mr. G. the test and darted out of the door. Neither one of us said anything to each other - no bye, no see ya, or have a nice Thanksgiving, - only silence, except for my footsteps as I walked down the hall.

Just before the stair case, I looked at the clock quickly, and then I ran faster, hoping that my footsteps were out of Mr. G's range. I realized that I still had a minute to catch my bus if I ran. But of course Mr. Bearded Watermelon head yelled from his desk, "No running in the halls." He probably didn't know it was I for sure, but he heard someone's feet at near gallop and of course he had to bark.

Once I hit the stairwell, I made double time, Mr. G. didn't stop me, I still made it to the bus. "I am still Chicago, all Chicago … Tall Chicago." I said to the bus driver as I got in, but he just looked at me as if I was nuts, gave me a smirk, and told me to take my seat. The second I sat down Cedric the bus driver took off. Anyway, that was how my school day went, the day of my Thanksgiving school dance. And I told you about it because I really felt like blabbing about it to someone and I knew you'd be listening.

I was nearly out of breath from the dart to the bus, so I took my seat and sat next to Witty Dee who was calling somebody names in the mean jack-ass way he always did. He was calling this big dude a, "Girly boy and girly man" or some shiznit like that. Witty Dee really did have a mean streak. I mean, he would pick on someone way bigger than he was. Witty liked to taunt people, just for the sake of bullying. He didn't even need a reason. I actually liked when he was teasing somebody because that usually meant that I was safe from his teasing of me, at least in that moment in time. And if I jumped in to stop him from teasing someone else, like I had done before – then he'd start teasing me. So I had learned to keep my trap shut around Witty Dee, when he was in one of his taunting moods, which was almost always. I'm not saying it's right; it's just the way that it was.

I hadn't seen much of Witty Dee lately, other than on the afternoon bus. I had been off doing my breakin' thing all of the time and Witty Dee had been hangin' tough with Muffy – his new girlfriend. I asked Witty Dee if he was going to the Thanksgiving Dance but he said, "Maybe" and usually when people say "maybe" they really mean "no." Besides he started talking about some movie that Muffy wanted to go see. And I know Witty doesn't like to dance, so the last thing he was going to do was tell her about our school dance. (She went to a different school)

Witty Dee asked, "Are you ready for that break dance battle tonight with Devon?"

"Foe show my man, I am going to rock that joint," I said in a confident nod. He wished me luck and all that kind of schlernious shiznit and then we just shot the shee-ott the rest of the bus ride home. I told him about how I almost missed the bus because of Mr Goenadds and Witty told me that he had Mr. Goenadds for second period and he is on his bad side too, "BIG TIME" he even said. He told me that he was always standing in the hallway outside of his class for no good reason. He once got kicked out of class for smiling.

"Smiling?" I asked.

"Yep, the jerk kicked me out of class for smiling …. I mean, I smiled when he accidentally bumped his knee on the lab table, but WHAT EVER?" Witty said.

I told Witty that I got kicked out of class for "thinking I had geranium breath," which was kind of true, if you think about it.

Then Witty told me that In Mr. G.'s class, he sits next to this kid named Chris Smith who was always letting out loud, squeaky, juicy farts, "I've never heard someone fart so long and so loud before in my life; you would think he had a microphone and speakers attached to his butt. I'm not kidding ya man," Witty said as he waved his hand in front of his nose as if the story had stirred up some smelly memories. Then Witty added, "Chris just doesn't care, I think he eats beans and broccoli right before class just for the fun of it." He said with a scrunched face. The kind of scrunched face people make after they had just whiffed a big smelly fart.

Witty started cackling even louder and told me," Dude, check this out, last week, we made a pact and we both ate beans, sauerkraut, and broccoli in our omlettes for breakfast just so we could fart our butts off and then blame poor Sabinta who sits in between us, it was hilarious," he said.

Witty went on to tell me that Chris and he farted like mad all over the classroom on that bean, sauerkraut and broccoli day and then passed off the blame of this gas attack on the unsuspecting quiet and shy girl named, "Sabinta." Witty said that Chris and he always shouted out loud for everyone in the class to hear, "Ohh Sabinta how could you," and "Ahhh Sabinta your farts smell." I could tell that Witty really enjoyed his misplaced blame fart game.

"You're a FART BULLY," I said with a smile.

Witty laughed and said, "I know." Then he said that Sabinta just sinks to her desk and doesn't even try to stand up for herself. That's Witty Dee for you; he loves to taunt! I think he even gets a kick out of making people shrink in embarrassment.

He finished his story with a half hearted attempt at acting like he was sorry, by saying, "Poor Sabinta – too shy and too nervous to say anything." His big choppers, crinkled nose, and devil may care in his eyes told me, he wasn't too sorry though. I read pure joy in his fart bullying eyes, if you really must know.

We had made it to my bus stop and just in time too, all of that joking around had put a devilish twinkle in Witty Dee's eyes. If I had stayed on that bus any longer, he would have certainly aimed his taunts at me. As I was exiting my seat to walk off the bus Witty Dee yelled, "Good luck tonight Phil."

"I don't need any luck Witty – Its all skill me boy, it's all skill! I am the master of the art of luck. The more I practice, the luckier I get," I said cocksure.

I was excited for Wednesday night but the following Saturday was going to be the first time that all of us NSR's were going to get together at McCollum Park. So I started making some phone calls before I went to the dance that night just to make sure everyone was ready for the weekend.

First I called Miguel 2 tough. He told me, "I'll be there without a care Swifty … does that sound nifty?"

"Right on Miguel, it's all well, I'll see you on Saturday," I said.

"My brother is coming too," 2 tough told me.

Then I asked him how he was going to get up to the park since I knew he lived too far away to walk and I knew he didn't drive yet. He told me that his Mom was going to be dropping him off.

"Is your sister coming? The one who picked you up last month at Suburbanite? …Your sister is cute," I said.

Miguel laughed and said, "I don't have a sister …. You think MY MOM IS CUTE?" he yelled loudly, "Hey Gio, Phil thinks Mom is hot!"

"Well don't keep yelling it or anything; I don't want your mom to hear that. I'm going to feel like a goof around her if she hears it," I said.

Miguel told me, "My mom is standing right next to me, she just smiled and said, naughty boys … boys will be boys," which made my face feel warm the rest of the time I talked to him on the phone.

I first saw Miguel and Gio's mom at the roller skating rink that first night I had met them. She walked into the rink and I remembered asking Miguel if that was his sister. Miguel did his usual closed mouth smile and didn't even answer my question - not a word, so I wasn't sure, until that phone call I had just told you about.

I got off the phone with Miguel 2 tough before I said anything else crazy but he told me that he couldn't wait to get together with us guys again. He was referring to Blazin' and I. He was totally cool and excited about meeting some new cats and making one big crew. We said our goodbyes and that was that.

Next on my list was Blazin'. I wanted to see if he was coming to the school dance tonight even though I knew he wouldn't be but I figured I'd remind him about Saturday anyway. I guess I was hoping that he had a change of plans for tonight. Instead, He was going to a turnabout dance at some catholic school across town with some girl he met a while ago. I guess you could call her his girlfriend but they hardly ever saw each other so I'm not really sure what to call her? Heck Blazin' doesn't even know what to call her? He just said, "This chick-a-dee wants me to take her to some dance at her school." He was kind of complaining about having to go to this dance on account he wasn't going to know anybody there and he really wished he could have been going to the Fall Dance with me so we could have gotten down and did some serious breakin' in front of the whole school.

However, I knew that he was only complaining about not going to our dance just to make me feel better. Really he wanted to hang with that "chick-a-dee" … and I can't blame a guy for that! But that's how good of a friend Brock Blazin was, he even pretended to not want to go out with some chick, just to make me feel better.

I hadn't really hung out with Blazin' at his crib over the past couple of weeks all that much, on account that he had been busy with Drama club and choir practice and that kind of stuff. But yay, really I just called Blazin' to shoot the ol shiznit around a little bit. But after a minute of chatter, it became clear that he needed to get going so he could get ready for his turnabout dance with that "chick-a-dee." However, not before I hit him up with the main thing that I really wanted to know about, "So I'll see you up at McCollum Saturday at noon right?"

Blazin' said, "Heck yeah my brother, I can't wait for the jam session in the cypher!" (A cypher is a circle of breakers – break dancing.)

Then Blazin' told me that he had already talked to Kid Mojo, Slim Jim, and Jet Drinkwater and he told me that they would all be there on Saturday. Then Blazin' quickly said he had to go; you'd have thought his pants just caught on fire by the way he rushed me off the phone.

I rang up our one and only B-Girl, Chi Girl and asked her if she was in?

She was all excited about meeting up at McCollum Park on Saturday and said she would be there, right after her gymnastics meet. But then I sort of got confused for a minute when she asked me," What should I wear?" For a split second I was thinking … what? Then I realized this was a girl; Girls are always asking questions about what they should wear?

I just told her, "Dress like a B-Boy … I mean, dress like a B-Girl … be there or be square! I'll be there like sab wah faire, it's all Chicago baby … Its all Chicago," I said as I hung up the phone. I was pretty sure that I didn't answer her question or anything but I tried.

Lastly I called Boogie Bob. I've talked to him on the phone numerous times since that day that I had met him at Dorktown mall. He already told me that he would be there if he could, but with his cancer chemotherapy medicine and being in the hospital and all, he wasn't exactly sure if he would make it or not. Turns out, the day I had met Boogie Bob at Dorktown mall he actually wasn't even supposed to be at the mall that day. He told me the whole story about how his Leukemia had went away, it was cured, but then a few months later he found out that his Leukemia had came back; he had a relapse.

The day that he was at mall, he was actually scheduled to begin another round of chemotherapy medicine -that morning even, but he left his house early without his parents even knowing. He snuck up to the mall to have some fun before he became a "prisoner at the hospital again." He told me that he wanted to "do some normal kid things, like walk the malls for girls and breakers and stuff," which I'm sure was the reason that we had been getting along famously ever since. B-boys of a feather flock together.

That's what the mall was: girls and breakers, and … oh yeah … stores.

I guess he had his parents worried sick, they called the cops and everything. So when he got back home from the mall that day he immediately went to the hospital and began his 2nd round of chemotherapy. And he's been there ever since. I've called him nearly every day.

Boogie Bob answered the phone; I had the direct line to his room, "Cancer sucks hotline how may we not help you?"

"Boogie Bob, it's your fellow Neighborhood Street Rocker, Sup my man?"

Bob sounded happy to hear from me, "Hey Swift, what's going on kid?"

"We are having the big NSR get together at the park on Saturday that I've been telling you about; I hope you can make it."

Bob replied cheerfully but I knew he was hiding his sadness, "I've got to get some more of this chemo shee-ott, so it doesn't look good kid – but I'm seriously thinking about skipping out on this chemo crap and meeting up with you guys anyway," he said while thinking out loud.

That kind of got me nervous because I knew he had already delayed his cancer medicine in the first place, which is why I had even met him that day, so I told Boogie Bob, "Why don't you finish up that chemo shiznit and then meet up with us on some other day when the chemo is done?" I paused and Bob said nothing so I continued, "Don't they have any chemo to go crap like asthma patients use an inhaler or something?" I asked.

Bob replied, "I wish they did, believe me kid. I already asked the doc that same question but it's all messed up – I've gotta stay here kid. But you're right, when it's done – we will all meet up and get on down with some crazy, goin' izz-off berserk breakin'.

I can't go skipping out on this chemo thing again. Momz was pretty mad at me that day I went to the mall and ended up being late for our appointment. In fact, I think it was the first time that I had seen her mad at me in months; she hadn't been mad at me ever since I got cancer. It was kind of nice. You know, my mom getting mad at me. I know it sounds crazy but in a weird way it was actually really nice having my mom get mad at me. It made me feel normal again … for a few minutes at least," Bob said. I could tell his wheels were turning when he added, "I don't know what to do?"

I told Bob, "Look, I don't want you to miss your chemo treatment. How about this bro – I'll stop by the hospital first thing in the morning before I go up to McCollum Park and we'll hang out! Is there anywhere for us to break in that joint?"

Bobs voice picked up ten notches of pump and he replied, "Yeah man, I'll find us a place to break."

I rambled on for a minute or two and Bob had stopped talking more or less. Then there were a few seconds of silence, it almost felt like a few minutes. Even though I couldn't see his face and I didn't know what he was thinking I could tell something heavy was on his mind. Sometimes silence weighs a ton and is louder than bombs.

Bob started talking again, "You don't have to come meet me at the hospital. This place is very depressing; it's a sad place. Every once in a while there will be a friend that I've met, hung out with, had popsicles with, laughed with … by the way these friends are also cancer patients … but anyway out of nowhere, these friends of mine will disappear without saying goodbye, you just don't see them again, suddenly their bed is empty.

What makes it worse is that all of the nurses will have wet eyes and sniffly noses and stuff but oddly enough none of the doctors ever seem to get the wet eye thing, they are just people with white coats and stone faces who write scripts for medicine. But yay, the nurses, they are a whole different story. They sniffle all over the place. I don't know if you want to hang out with a bunch of cry babies?

Like this one time, I asked one of my nurse's, Nurse Mary, Hey where's Jimmy? Who was a buddy of mine here in the cancer unit last time around, just before I got better, but she didn't answer my question right away, she just got all sniffly and said something like, He's in a better place. Then another time I asked, Hey where's Sandy? Whom I had met from my very first day of cancer treatment. She was such a happy girl. She had this great smile, pretty face, and everything; if she weren't bald you would never even know she had cancer. But Mary answered my questions in such weird ways: She's having dinner with

Jesus right now or she's playing the piano with the angels. She could never just come out and say it. Eventually, when she had to, she'd say something like: Oh Jimmy or Oh Sandy - …their beds are empty now. And that's the closest she could come to actually saying it. Then she'd start crying with rainstorms coming out of her orbits. Orbits – that's a doctor's word, I learned that here kid … you told me that you liked words, so that's one for ya kid, ORBITS.

Anywho, what the heck man, I mean - what the heck man? It's just an empty bed. Lord knows someone will fill that darn thing up again … So if you're sure you want to come here to the cancer unit and deal with people that get wet orbits over empty beds for no reason, then come on through. But if that sort of thing bothers you, I understand. Heck I don't even want to be here kid," Bob said plainly.

I cut Bob off from his rant and said, "That's all cool Boogie Bob – Saturday is the day where all of us Neighborhood Street Rockers get together and practice for a bit. And you are a Neighborhood Street Rocker, so of course I will come on through and practice with you," I said.

Boogie Bob said, "That'll work kid. Umm,huh, ohh, yay that Chi girl chick you were telling me about last time we talked – is she going up to the park too? Is she cute?" he asked.

"She's confirmed and yep she's pretty cute, but I'm trying not to think about her too much, I don't want to mix business with pleasure," I said like a grown up. Then somehow the mood struck me to say, "And listen dude, you're not dying, you're not one of those cancer patients, you're a breaker, you're a B-Boy and you just happen to be getting treated for cancer. But it does not define you. Breakin' defines you! "

Obviously I couldn't see him through the phone but I knew that Bob was now smiling his bald brow-less head off; I could hear it in his voice. I don't know why I even used the "D" word or anything but something made me to say it.

"Alright Swift kid, I've got to go, but hey, I think they are switching rooms on me tonight or tomorrow, so when you come here; you might have to ask for Robert Charles room – they don't have me listed under Boogie Bob, Okay kid," he said.

"Gotchya brudda … I'll see you in the morning on Saturday, meanwhile I've gotta get ready for this battle against Devon tonight," I said.

"You'll school 'em kid," Bob said.

I hung up the phone with Boogie Bob and I could tell that he was happy that he was unable to talk me out of coming to see him. I never really thought about the fact that some of the people that Bob was hanging out with on a regular basis at the hospital ended up just leaving without saying goodbye. That's the thing about meeting people, you'd like to be able to say goodbye to them when they leave – that's all, that's the only thing. I was happy to have talked to Boogie Bob but I was also confused about his warning of the sadness that is around his hospital.

Suddenly I had this weird feeling floating around in my head. I was totally looking forward to the school dance that was just a couple of hours away but I was also a little sad to hear the way Bob was talking about the hospital and such. This was some grown up shiznit to have to deal with and I was just a teen.

On a brighter note, my "NSR" belt buckle nameplate had arrived in the mail that day in a big manila envelope but I didn't see it till later. Do you remember what I'm talking about? Rockefeller at the Lincoln center was sportin' one that day I first had met him. His read, "GTR" and of course mine read, "NSR" for Neighborhood Street Rockers. "Now I am going to look All Chicago when I hit that dance tonight," I said aloud to my P.s as I put it around my neck for the first time, which made them shake their heads about my crazy ice slang.

I was kind of talking to myself and sort of talking to my P.s when I said, "Rockin' this NSR nameplate 'round my neck tonight is going to get everybody talkin' for shizzo; talkin' bout this cat right here, Phil K. The Funky Groove King Swift and his bling thing, know what I mean … I can already hear everybody at the dance saying:" then I used this girly voice, "That NSR plate you're sportin' is ALL Chicago Swifty …" I said to myself.

You should have seen the look my P.s gave me. They thought I was nuts.

"Nobody will be saying anything to you unless you get those dishes done son," Mom said plainly.

After doing the dishes, I grabbed my winter hats and got ready to head to the school dance. It was about that time; time to rock, time to jack, time to break, and time to face off with that cat Devon.

Since Blazin' was going to turnabout with his semi-girlfriend and since Witold Dee was going to a movie with Muffy. It looked like I was flying solo that night. I yelled down to the old man about my ride to the dance while I fixed my hair, "I'm about ready to rock, when we doing this Pops?" I asked.

He yelled back, "I'm waiting for you," even though a few minutes ago I was waiting for him, which was the only reason I figured I'd re-do the spikes in my hair.

I took one last look in the mirror, I checked out the NSR nameplate, and my new fresh fat laced kicks and I made my way to the old man. I couldn't stop looking at myself in the mirror to be honest with you. I was looking all fly, straight up fly; Chicago fly. I was looking way too fly not to admire myself in my Bboy attire. "The mirror is loving me," I said.

"I just hope the mirror doesn't crack," My dad wisecracked.

Chapter 9

The High School Dance

On the way to the school dance, dad was pumping Chic "Le Freak" over the car audio system; he was snapping his fingers and boppin' his head like one cool dude. My old man grew up on the Southside of Chicago where he learned about Harold Melvin and the Blue Notes, Al Green, The Temptations, The Four Tops, and stuff like that back in his day at his school. In fact I don't think my dad had ever missed an episode of "Soul Train" on TV – so he knew what wazup with this disco funk thing.

I arrived at the school right on time for the dance, which kind of sucks when you're flying solo; it really makes you stick out. I exited the ride and I walked towards the front doors of the school as I heard the trees rustling in the wind, while dads' car stereo was getting quieter by the second as he drove away, and suddenly I started to feel alone. The most alone I had felt in a long time. I mean I had spent plenty of time alone in the basement of my crib practicing my breakin' but this was a different kind of alone. This was a -Boogie Bobs conversation about empty beds -kind of alone.

I patted my right pocket just before I walked inside the school and indeed my knit hats were still there. I'm crazy like that. I can know that I just put something in a pocket. I can even know it for sure yet I will check my pockets again to see if the darn thing is still in there. I then checked my left pocket and what do you know, my other knit hat was there too. I was no longer feeling alone anymore; I was there with my thing -that thing is Breakin'.

I was good like that, you know. I mean, I could really get upset about something but I could usually snap out of it pretty quickly. Heck sometimes I could even avoid the whole thought of something bad all together, that way I could avoid getting too depressed about something. For example, sometimes I would break out in a thousand zits all over my darn face, which would make me hideous and gross; which could depress me for a quick second like a little kid who had just accidentally lost his helium balloon into the sky. Then out of nowhere, I would snap out of it pretty fast and be re-inflated.

And don't even get me started on Zits. Zits sucked because they would freak me out and make me not want to talk to any girls. When you're all blotched up, no girl is going to want to look at you – I thought. But when I got older I learned that I could have just dated the other girls that were zitted up too, and we would have gotten along famously; zits and all, but I didn't figure that out until later. And there it is in a nutshell. Whatever you think you have wrong with you; there is someone else that has something wrong with them too. So if you are an ugly freak. Don't worry there's an ugly freak out there for you too. Now doesn't that make you feel better?

However, my big zits didn't matter anyway. Instead of thinking about my gross zitted up face back then, I blocked it all out and I just focused on the fact that I was a bad to the bone breaker. In fact, I did that all of the time, like an obsession even. I thought about breakin' only. I was all good. I was no longer a zitted up kid; I was a breaker.

I guess my point is that I had shaken off that whole empty bed thing by the time I had walked up to the school doors, just like I could shake off the zits thing. And when I started to remember the battle against Devon, I got my hop back to my step too.

As I approached the 6 door entrance to our school I could see that other students were already inside the lit up hallways. The school looked so different at night. It was weird. The hallways were the same but different. Heck the students were even the same, but they looked different too, it even made me feel different, it's hard to explain.

Just before I entered, a girl was looking at herself in her compact mirror, checking out her makeup, checking out her hair, checking out her cheek, "What?" she said to herself as I walked into the schools corridor. Then I got a closer look – zits. That explained why she started putting tan make-up all over her face. It got me to thinking. I wish guys could wear some cover up over our zits the way girls could. But we can't, unless we wanted to look like a pansy or something, we have no choice but to walk around all over the place with a spotlight directly on our zits.

I got lucky as all heck at the dance that night though, I wasn't zitted up like a madman for a change. I was feeling pretty good even, good enough to say, "Hi" to Cassandra and Anna who were chit chatting right as I walked inside the school.

Cassandra and Anna didn't used to talk to me, that is, until I had become a breaker. I didn't really know those girls all that well but I saw them every day at lunch. They sat at the "Latin table" that was next to the black table, which was just a table away from my usual table.

Now, I kind of know Cassandra a little bit because her boyfriend Tito is a breaker who I had met a couple of times after school. He was usually parked out in front waiting for Cassandra in his blue rusted out Cadillac. He was always bumping the bass and Bboy jams from his car; loud and proud.

One time I was throwing down with Top Rock on the sidewalk because our bus was running late. This dude who I now know is Tito, yelled from his car window, "Nice Top Rock player!" So we started chatting a bit. Cassandra saw us talking that day and ever since then she has said hi to me at school.

Tito and Cassandra both had this very thick Chicago-Ghetto accents working for them. Expressions like, "I'm going to go ghetto on you" and they both called everybody "players" or "playettes." She said it at least a thousand times a day. I'm pretty sure that every conversation I have had with her had consisted of the words: player, fer real, nasty, and tight. Everything was either tight or nasty.

Not everybody at Cassandra's lunch table talked like that though. One of the girls had more of an accent that made me think she had just moved here from South America or somewhere like that. And another one of the Latin girls at the "Latin table" was very well spoken, bilingual too. She was always reading books during lunch which sort of made me want to "go out with her." I once heard her use the term, "Avant-garde" to a teacher in the hallway and I always thought she was pretty hot after that, even though, I had no idea what that word had meant until I had looked it up.

After I passed those two "Latin table" girls, I kept walking slowly towards the large gym where we were having our school dance that night, when I heard Cassandra saying, "No ah ahh, ohh no he didn't, that's nasty!" It was so odd hearing these kinds of words coming from her mouth too, because if you looked at her you'd think she was this cute, petite fragile girl; but her personality was opposite to what she looked like.

I happened upon a couple of "burnout" buddies of mine, which some people called them that because they were known for being down with "420" and not just occasionally. I had known those cats since elementary school, we were casual friends, but we didn't hang out all that much, but every once in a while we'd walk home together. So I kind of new them. It's just that 420 is not my thing.

They were hanging out in front of the principal's office, laughing and licking their lips. One of them, his name was Donnie Blacklung, was happily talking about cotton mouth, baked-ness, munchies, and stuff like that. He really seemed to be enjoying his own words that were coming out of his mouth.

Both of them had been caught smoking during study hall last year. They really blew it too (pun intended) because this teacher was really cool and they had the perfect study hall going – but not anymore. This teacher was cool enough to let Don Blacklung and Seth Coughman play their electric guitar during study hall in this small room just across from study hall class. – But now that was over.

It was just the two of them in this small room that was more or less, unsupervised for a bit as they played their guitars. When they thought the coast was clear in their private room they'd sneak a smoke, they would keep on jamming their guitars and smoke the gross stuff like madmen. They used to take these empty paper towel rolls and stuff fresh scented dryer sheets into the tube. They would then exhale their smoke into the paper towel roll; the dozens of dryer sheets that were clogging the tube would turn their smoke into the fresh smell of a spring flowers all throughout the study hall air.

What they did not know was that the red burning cherry on the end of their cigarette made smoke too, that would fill the private study room. Nor did they realize that someone would walk in the room in the middle of their smoking. So as the story goes, they were very familiar with the principal's office. So maybe that was why they were hanging out in front of the office, it was like their home away from home. I laughed to myself. They were down to earth dudes and I was friendly with them, but I hated smoke, you dig?

"Sup Don … Sup Seth? Is this your home away from home," I said jokingly.

They both look at me with a blank face and said nothing, so I explained my joke, "The principal's office – Is your home away from home – you practically live there," I said. But their expressions only became more murky, "Never mind," I laughed.

They must have mulled over my joke as they both started laughing in this phlegm filled smokers cough and said, "Right on!"

And "Sup Phil."

Even Blacklung and Coughman were dressed up for the school dance that night. "Looking Dapper tonight Seth," I told him.

He nodded thanks and said, "You breakin' tonight dude?"

"Of course," I replied. This made him laugh, but everything made him laugh.

Donnie had on what looked like a brand new dark blue jean jacket and black dress shoes. I looked at him and said, "I feel under dressed with y'all dressing up and all. Even you burnouts are dressed up sharp," I said with a genuine smile while walking away and giving them the rocker wave, which was a pinky finger up, index finger up and thumb out; the three fingered "rock on" wave.

There's something I didn't tell you about that had happened with Donnie Blacklung, Seth Coughman, and me - so I'll tell you now, I'd rather you hear it from me than someone else. I'm not the only blabber mouth out there, you know. I was walking home from school with them one day, I usually took the bus, but on this day I stayed after school because there was a big fight between these two known tough guys from our school Mike Fitzgerald and Paul Woodson. Paul won blah, blah, blah. Anyway, after the fight Don, Seth, Blazin', and I walked half way home together. Only Blazin' and I were taking the long way home, since Coughman and Blacklung lived north of the school, and Blazin' and I lived south; it was the very long way home. I guess we just got carried away with talking about the fight and such that we ended up following them towards their home.

After a few minutes of walking, we all stopped off at this place they called, "the wreck" by Barth pond. Blacklung pulled out a pipe, which he called a "bowl" that he told us he had made from parts he bought at the hardware store. He packed it up with Mary Jane, lit it up, and began passing it around in a circle. I put the bowl to my mouth, lit the flame, kind of sort of inhaled, but I didn't put the smoke into my lungs. First of all, I didn't know how, I had never done that before. I even tried, just from the pressure of it all, but inhaling while a hot flame was rushing down my throat sort of hurt – maybe I did it wrong, or I don't know. In addition, I didn't really want to try it anyway. However, I didn't want to be rude. - Okay, well honestly - I almost screwed up.

Peer pressure can really be a punk ice bee-otch sometimes. But I was glad I said NO. In the middle of trying, I realized it was something I didn't want to do, so I said, "Never mind, I don't want any."

Seth said," Dude, it's cool, it won't hurt you, just try it."

"No thanks man, I'll just skip it," I said.

"Come on, go ahead, it's awesome," Donnie said.

"No bro, I don't want any, but hey … do you want one of THEEZ?" I asked.

"One of what?" Seth asked.

"One of THEEZ farts?" I said while pointing my ass at him and laughing like a freak-a-zoid.

They both laughed like madmen and then I stepped back a few feet from them and they stopped bugging me about smoking. Smoking sucks I thought.

I was offered "smokes" again by those dudes on a different day but the next time I was prepared and I just told them, "I have asthma and that Shiznit will Eff me up." They busted my chops for a minute or two but they eventually gave up and we just hung out. They smoked while I just hung out and watched them. I no longer felt the need to try and fit in anymore, they bought my asthma excuse, which was actually true. I did have asthma and I'm sure my doctor wouldn't recommend my smoking. It didn't really matter anymore, they were cool with me whether I smoked or not. I didn't go out of my way to hang out with them outside of school that much anymore though; because birds of a feather really do – flock together. And -second hand smoke really did mess up my breathing and eyes, and not to mention it would stuff up my nose. But I guess some people like that sort of thing. OKAY – I'll stop sniveling.

I had smelled 420 a few times at the roller rink too, even back when I first started going to the rink in 5th grade and I didn't know what the smell was just yet. I later learned from Witty Dee's older brother, Robbie, what the smell was. I said something like: I just smelled a sweet "burning leaves" type of smell."

And Robbie said, "That's pot you idiot."

And that was my first official class on drugs education.

I could still hear Coughman and Blacklung cackling in the quiet hallways as I walked away, along with Cassandra and Anna's ghetto fabulous conversation. And that was when I had realized what made the school seem so different that night. Usually the hallways were teeming with hundreds of students and hundreds of voices, but since I had arrived early, it felt like a ghost town. I could hear everyone's conversations. Voices really travel and echo down the hallways when their empty.

As I slowly approached the large gym I could hear muffled music issuing through the doors. "Boom boom boom boom," was faintly coming through the gym doors. It would have been a cool moment until I saw Randal VanderNorth and a few of his pals standing by the gym doors. They were considered "Preppie yuppie punks" by most people that I knew and most people generally didn't find them all that friendly. Most classmates usually called them "snobs," "stuck up," or "silver spooners." But I just called them rich punks. To be completely honest with you, I'd rather be a rich punk than a broke ass but that didn't stop me from calling them "Rich punks" behind their backs.

I suppose if you were one of them and your family was rolling in the dough as their families were, then they were probably friendly but otherwise they were high brow, stick up their butts, rich punk-know-it-alls. I knew a little bit about them because of their hand me down expensive cars and their big houses and stuff. And they always seemed to have anything that was expensive before anybody else. They all had big screen TV's in their houses before anybody else even knew what a big screen TV was. And they bought all of their clothes at Oak Brook Mall – very rich, very expensive.

As I drew more near to them, I heard one of them whispering, "They'll let anybody into this dance."

And another silver spooner said, "Rock on dude" in a mocking tone that was obvious he was making fun of them. Basically those rich punks were ripping on Don and Seth who I was just talking to. At first I thought they were talking about me, but the "rock on dude" made me realize it was about them.

Randal VanderNorth looked my way but didn't so much as throw me a "sup." Then he joined his rich punk buddies and sarcastically whispered, "Oh hey, yeah let's crawl around on the floor and call it dancing." I wondered if he thought I couldn't hear him or did he purposely say it loud enough because he wanted me to hear him? Either way, it was bunk.

I wasn't afraid of those Rich punks though, so I said, "Good one dude, crawling around on the floor and all that jazz. - Because hitting a small ball with a club into a hole and listening to people whisper with their golf claps is cool as ice," I said because I knew he was on the golf team. Which I like golf to be honest with you, but it was the only thing that I could think of off the cuff.

Then I looked at Randal's two buddies, who I couldn't remember their names but I knew them from around school and said, "I'm not sure if Don and Seth could hear you guys talking about them? But I heard you! … Why don't you speak up so they can hear you better … tough guys."

All of them looked at me with this "what?" silver spooner, high brow, expression on their faces, and then went back to talking amongst themselves and ignored me of course. I'm sure they weren't expecting me to be so confrontational – I was usually not, with them at least. I've got to really be in the mood to be confrontational but sometimes my balls are bigger than their britches; which can really get me into hot water without even trying. But I've learned, sometimes you've really got to stand up for yourself; otherwise you will get walked all over. It's better to put yourself in that occasional situation where you might have to defend yourself than to be a permanent whipping boy.

As it has turned out, most people who talk a lot of smack, just do that; talk a lot smack. When you confront trash talkers, they usually shut the heck up. I know it's usually better to say nothing, but like I said, sometimes, I just get in the mood to be confrontational.

I've told you about Randal VanderNorth before. He is the dude that had been pulling the wool over his girlfriend Gina D'Agostino's eyes this whole time. And Gina was the knockout that bragged about her virginity to everybody, which is totally cool!

Gina still didn't know that Randal had been sneaking around with back alley Sally and Lucy Goosey from the bowling alley, and god only knows whom else. Which really sucked too, because Gina was one of those girls at school that everybody liked; she was nice to everybody whether you were rich or not, cool or not, "in" or not; or were zitted up that day or not – even though she was rich, Gina would talk to you - I hated seeing a girl like that get rooked. All she wanted to do was save that "first kiss" for a guy that was willing to date her exclusively for six months. And she was getting lied to.

Moments later Gina came walking out of the girl's bathroom smiling as she usually did. The thing was, nobody really knew about that bowling alley chick that Randal was smooching on the side, except for Brian Chaneckson, Randals buddies, and me, but they weren't going to rat him out. And I only knew because I happened to be outside of Chanecksons house that night when Randal shot his mouth off about how he was grabbing some lips on the side while he was supposedly waiting for Gina to kiss him. The whole reason he was given this waiting period by Gina was because she wanted to know if he would wait or not. And she really believed that he was waiting, but he wasn't, that's what really made me mad.

I turned around and came back so I could say "HI" to Gina before I headed into the gym for the school dance. But I mainly did it then and there because I wanted Randal to know that I wasn't going to back down from him, especially since he had made that rolling around on the floor comment. But she beat me to the punch.

Gina said, "Phil ... Hey, how are you ... Where's your buddy Brock?" Gina had choir class with Brock Blazin'. Sometimes when I would run into them in the hallways, just after class had let out, they would be laughing their teeth off about some inside joke that nobody else ever got, because it was a choir class joke. Even if they explained it to you, it still didn't make any sense. But old Randal VanderNorth and his "golf clap laugh" would always laugh along and act as if he got the inside joke but we all knew darn well that he didn't. What a flippin' phony. The thing was, only the people who could have possibly understood their inside jokes would be the people that were on the "inside" of choir class, which Randal was not, just as I was not. As if I needed another reason not to like him, but we can add "being fake" to the list anyway, that works for me. It was really obvious that Randal got all jealous of Brock and Gina's inside jokes and such. And I loved it. I loved every golf clapping laughing minute of it.

I responded to Gina, "Yeah, Brock's at some other school dance right now taking out a girl who got dumped at the last minute, just to be nice, he didn't want the poor girl to have to go to the dance all by her lonesome," I told her. Actually I had made that "dumped" part up, just to get that whole "Awww thing goin'" and it worked. I was being a wingman for Brock without even trying.

Gina said, "Awwww …. How sweet … what a sweetie."

I continued to lay it on, "Brock talks about you all of the time Gina - telling me how funny and nice you are too," I said as I gave a look or two over at Randal, just to make him mad. Maybe I was hoping he'd insult me and force me into ratting him out or something. But mainly I was just trying to get him angry on account he had just ripped on us breakers.

She talked about what a sweetie Brock was while smiling – as she always did, for the next couple of minutes or so while Randal and his boys sneered, snarled, and got hotter by the minute. I was diggin' it, to be honest with you. I don't know why but their anger made me happy.

Seth and Don were still hanging out within shouting distance of us all, so they probably had made me feel stronger, if I've got to give you my best guess of this all. Because what I said next was out of character for me.

"I've got to get going Gina … I've got some serious business to take care of" (I was referring to Devon) then cocky as all heck I said, "… Hey Randal! How's Lucy?" you should have heard me, I said it smug as all heck. Then I just strode away, it's not as if I was trying to take on all of them anyway, and I wasn't sure just how much help Don and Seth would have given me anyway, so I just left before it got ugly.

"Good luck tonight – I heard you're breakin' against Devon," she said as I was sort of walking away.

"Thanks – you should come and watch, however I'm sure your swell friends won't want to, they were just making fun of breakin'," I told her.

I kept walking and waved goodbye. I could hear Gina say to Randal, "I like break dancing; I think it's cool," then a big pause, "…Whose Lucy?"

He whisperingly brushed it off with an, "I don't know" and I'd bet you that he had shrugged his shoulders too, he had used that kind of confused tone of voice. I didn't turn around to look but I would bet you that the big fake phony had kept that confused look on his face for hours.

As I made my way towards the large gym doors to enter the dance, I heard Randal say, "Come out with me for a smoke Gina. You ought to try one. I rolled my own with tobacco from Europe, it's an aristocratic blend of leaves my love … it will calm your nerves," he said in one of those snobby rich voices that really bugged me. If I didn't already dislike that dude, I now had a reason. Mainly because I happened to know that Gina was a non smoker.

One day last year, Gina and I were both standing outside after school when someone lit a square. Both Gina and I walked about 20 feet in another direction to avoid the second hand cigarette smoke. We were both laughing about how we had both purposely walked out of our way to avoid the smoke. We both even admitted that we always dodged and ran away from people with lit squares anywhere and everywhere we went. I told her, "I dodge second hand smoke as passionately as I dodge bees and hornets at a picnic."

And she said, "I dodge second hand smoke as if someone had just farted." She once got out of line at a concession stand at a baseball game because someone was smoking in front of her, even though she had already waited in that line for twenty minutes. And I once took a different route home from the store when I was walking behind someone that was smoking because I didn't want to inhale someone's second hand cancer smoke. That's why Randal and her dating each other didn't add up to me. But he was a good looking dude whose parents had money and that didn't hurt anything.

But I still didn't get it, the more I thought about it. I knew she was un-cool with second hand cigarette smoke the same way that I was, yet she was going out with Randal VanderNorth who was a smoker. That's one thing I'll never figure out though … Girls.

Anyhow, Gina responded to Randal by saying, "No thanks, you know I don't smoke."

Then Randal repeated the same crap, "The tobaccos from Europe, its top quality tobacco … It's even healthy for your lungs, it's pure tobacco without any chemicals … don't be a goody-goody Gina … at least come out with me while I smoke for Christ's sake," he began to demand.

Gina being the nice girl that she was, said, "I'll go outside with you but I don't want one."

Randal the chump said, "It won't kill you if you try a drag."

They started heading outside and I had half of a mind to blow his cover but I didn't.

Laser lights, strobe lights, and police lights were bouncing off of the small glass windows on the large gym doors. I opened up the door to the gym and the muffled boom boom boom turned into crisp boomk koosh zeek zoit boomk koosh zeek zoit; an electronic dance track that I had never heard before. The DJ was in the middle of his mix and by the time I had made my way all of the way inside of the gym, I knew what song it was. It was, "Planet rock" by Afrika Bambaataa. To my delight, the DJ was straight up playing B-boy music.

When it comes to DJ's, it's like a white elephant gift; you never know what you are going to get. I was only in the gym but a second but it was so far so good. I sauntered with swag to Planet Rock throughout the large gym which was still kinda empty. There may have been about 30 people in there so far which included the chaperones, teachers, the DJ, and me of course. I guess I didn't get the memo about being fashionably late. I know how some people like to be fashionably late to make a grand entrance - to seem cool – as if they had something more important to do beforehand. But I didn't need to be fashionably late, just to seem cool. I was already cool: early, late, or on time. I'm all Chicago baby; totally cool.

It was weird; it was like nobody was there, but after I looked up from having grabbed a punch from the punch bowl, people had really started to filter inside of the big school gym dressed in their "hip" and "sexy" clothes. I started taking a reconnaissance of the Thanksgiving Dance crowd and none of my friends had shown up yet. Only people I knew more casually were "in effect."

It looked like I had shown up at the dance at a good time too, because one by one the place was quickly starting to fill; the crowd had tripled since I had walked in.

I spotted Hazy and Dustin walking in together right as, "Watch the closing doors" came over the speakers. They were with their girlfriends Brandy and Wanda. They were both cheerleaders and were good dancers too, I had caught a glimpse of them and the whole cheer squad for that matter at a school pep rally one time and they really knew how to dance pretty hip.

They were all boppin' to the groove as they entered the gym, save for Dustin who walked in looking stiff, yet he tried to look cool – which I thought was his way of not having to dance. Even though he was a breaker, it didn't mean that he could shake his money maker. It sort of ruined their grand entrance, if you asked me. He was a distraction to the eye, if your friends walk into a party dancing – you've got to dance too. That's all I'm saying.

I started sauntering towards Hazy, who spotted me and started up rockin' as he stared me down and moved towards me. We began up rock battling against each other from across the room. We were at least 100 feet away from each other when we had started. The closer we got, the more animated we both had become with our combo top rock-up rock. We eventually crisscrossed and crossed paths and up rocked against each other for real while Brandy and Wanda kept dancing and Dustin stood around looking stiff.

It was time, I swiftly walked around in a circle and I started throwing down with crabwalks, which was Hazy's specialty but I wanted to show him, heck everybody; that nobody had anything on me.

That was the first time that Hazy had ever seen me do crabwalks and I could tell he didn't like it. It removed his upmanship that he thought he had and it had probably given me the advantage. I had been practicing them like a madman and had them pretty friggin' fast too. I knew this dance was the time to unleash 'em. I even straightened out my legs; Rockefeller from GTR style, just to show off. I exited the break circle cocksure as all heck and Hazy gave me this weird smile. A smile that said: you're a biter, but you rocked 'em, so I can't say a darn thing – that's the kind of smile he gave me.

Hazy jumped in next and did his usual tricks; Scats, crabwalks, backspins, and swipes. While I was watching him, I thought about how I wanted to save my pennies and head spins until Devon got to the dance. I didn't want to show all of my stuff just yet. You see, I knew what moves everyone in my school had, unless some of them had been holding out and not showing me their moves like I had been doing. I had been holding out in the hip hop hallway the past couple of weeks and not showing off all of my newest moves. But either way I wanted to wait for loud mouthed Devon to get to the dance before I showed everything off. I didn't want him to see me through the gym doors and get scared off. I was that sure; cocksure.

I kept my eyes peeled for Devon from the moment I had got there, but there was still no sign of him even an hour into the dance. I chalked him up as one of those "fashionably late" cats.

Dustin had finally shaken off his rust and got into the break circle when Rick James had come on the spinning platters. He started poppin' and floor gliding, which didn't interest me much. It was the power moves and down rock that usually had kept my attention. I mainly kept scanning around the room for my battle mate. I couldn't wait to prove that I was the best.

Frankly I had a really weird vibe going on inside my head that night; I had been trying to block it out all day or maybe I had been trying to shake it off even. It was odd; I was happy, sad, and excited all at once. I was happy that I was breakin' and excited to watch my fellow breakers, yet I was sad because I thought about Bob once in a while - how he couldn't enjoy something so simple, like going to a high school dance. I didn't usually feel that way. I usually was not such a rollercoaster ride. And it all started right after I had hung up the phone with Boogie Bob, and it had been sticking around ever since.

The DJ threw on my jam, "Boogie down Bronx" by Man Parrish. That song had totally changed my mood from cancer to dancer. Music can do that to me you know, zap me out of a bad mood that is. I entered the break circle. I started top rockin' around and boppin' my head while staring everyone down that was in my path, in an effort to grow the cypher. All eyes were on me and I wished Bob could have been there.

After Top Rockin' like a swaggerlicous B boy, I did a round of windmills and backspins and then I had sprung to my feet and back into a mad pace around the circle. It was obvious that I had impressed the heck out of Hazy, Brandy, and Wanda; however, Dustin played it off as if I had done nothing. He was playing all cool and bored all at once. I knew what it was though. He didn't want his chick to be too excited over my skillz, is what it was. – And she was, I could see it in her eyes. And he didn't like that, I could see it in his eyes.

All Dustin really had was those walk up the wall flip things that I had told you about, and other than that he was kind of lame. I'm not hatin', I'm just telling you like it was.

I had abruptly ended my routine when I thought I had seen Devon coming in through the gym doors. I was just about to jump into head spins for my routines finale, but I stopped myself, when I saw Devon and his swagger walking around the crowd. It ended up being a false alarm though, it was really Isaac. But by the time I saw it was Isaac, someone else had taken over the cypher.

The cypher had started to grow with other dudes from our school that I didn't even know were into breakin' but they were giving it a try anyway. Most of them were just hacks though, you could tell they never really practiced and some of them were trying it for the first time even, which made my mind wander. They weren't even as interesting to watch as those five year old breakers were at the Big Burger contest.

I started to think about the opposites; party people at the dance were drinking down the punch while Boogie Bob was at the hospital drinking down the chemo. Everyone at the dance was dressed to impress and Bob was probably wearing a dowdy hospital gown; the gowns that make your butt cheeks hang out all over the place. But I was more mad than sad when I had thought about that.

Isaac had made his way to the cypher in no time flat and jumped right in with a casual smile. He was one of the few cats that I had ever seen break, that could look casual while he was breakin'. Most of us breakers had serious and stressed looks on our faces when we were breakin', but not Isaac; he was as cool as a cucumber. Suddenly, I sort of got irritated.

A couple of girls that were standing by our break circle were complaining as they walked by me; one girl said, "What is this DJ playing?" as she made a stink face.

And the other girl said, "Not my cup of tea." I didn't know these girls names but I had seen them in the halls before. They were very hall monitor, goody goody, and teachers pet looking types of girls.

I leaned her way, tapped her on the shoulder and said, "My boy Boogie Bob is sitting in a hospital room right now wishing he had your problems."

"What are you talking about?" she asked me.

"Did you just say this music is not your cup of tea?" I asked her.

"Umm, yeah," she said in a whine.

"My boy Bob wishes he could complain about lousy music at some school dance but he was unable to leave the hospital this weekend. He just wishes he could listen to some lousy music right now, but he can't, he's too busy getting chemotherapy right now. He's just a teen like us. But he can't enjoy good or bad music right now. He wishes he had your problems," I said and then I turned my body back into the cypher. By the way, the music wasn't lousy, but in her opinion it was, that's all I was saying.

After Isaac finished his poppin', king tuttin', and down rockin', I decided to rock the joint again. Heck, I didn't need a personal invitation to get into the cypher anyway, so with no further ado I slipped into the break circle.

I felt my heart start to pump; clang, clang, bang. I began my confident circle around the ever so packed crowd with both of my arms opened wide in an effort to increase my breakin' room. Our breakers circle had seemed to shrink like a shrinky dink because the school dance crowd had reached near capacity. I started a wild up rock. I was kicking my legs buck wild and herky-jerky in an effort to make the breakers and spectators back up that much more – sometimes you've gotta do, what you've gotta do. I finally hopped to it, I couldn't help myself. I knew that a lot of eyes were on me. Everybody was watching me top rock like a b boy on a mission and I felt it. Even though I had originally meant to save my best stuff for Devon and our battle, I just couldn't wait anymore.

I pounced into windmills right from standing, as soon as I gained top speed, I then grabbed my crotch while continuing to windmill into even faster pennies. I could hear the "Whoas," "ooohs," and "aahhs" from the crowd as I revolved around in fast motion, yet my mind felt like it was in slow motion – it was like a dream, making my adrenaline pump that much more, which forced me to keep going.

I did at least 10 or 20 pennies in that round and it may have been even more to be honest with you, it felt like I had spun for days if you really must know. But truthfully I lost track after the 3rd or 4th"no hander. I'll tell you this though; my pennies were more elevated than usual that night, which was surely due to the adrenaline that was pumping through my body with force that had produced the side effect of me banging my forehead down to the ground that much harder with each revolution of my no handed windmills.

I used my forehead to push off the ground while doing pennies (or nutcrackers) instead of my hands. Some people used momentum to keep their "nutcrackers" going, but I pushed off with my head. In all my haste, and with all of that power, my hats had flung off my head while I was spinning. It was giving me a floor burn on my head from scraping the ground and such, but it was too late to stop, I was in too deep. Having awesome pennies was more important than a little floor burn on my forehead at that point in time.

Towards the end of my routine I reached around my back and did a couple of " businessman windmills," which is where you put your hands behind your back while your windmilling; some breakers called them, "handcuffs" but I suppose that depended on what side of the tracks you were from. I was all business.

I bolted up to my feet and boldly exited the circle and slipped away from center stage. I stood next to the wall of people that were surrounding the break circle. I was a little dizzy from the revolutions I had just spun and I was trying to gain my balance when I felt a couple of pats on my back. When I looked in each direction I was dropped a couple of compliments from classmates that I knew by face but not by name. I didn't know most of my classmate's names to be honest with you. But I smiled and said, "Right on."

Once the gym had stopped spinning and I regained my balance, I decided to walk around the dance and say, "Hi" to everyone that I knew, which was only a few. Since I didn't know most people's names like I just told you, I ended up doing a lot of smiling and head nods instead.

After a minute or two of boppin' around the dance, I spotted a couple of my friends - Fred and Reeny. They were in the middle of the gym looking all lovey-dovey into each other's eyes, sharing a sweet romantic couple's moment. And me being the cat that throws manners out of the window sometimes and also being the cat that just can't mind his own business; I interrupted their "private moment" and said, "Sup guys …. Your lips are going to get sucked off with all of that face sucking you all are doing!" I sort of said it all loud and annoying, so in that moment, I had realized that I had probably shouted right in their friggin' ears on accident. Which made them offer me a bulgy eyed: thanks for screaming in my ear – look. But they smiled it off, Reeny sort of rolled her eyes and Fred just gave me a smirk. Then he mouthed, "Is Devon here?"

"I haven't seen him? " I said quietly (this time) while shrugging my shoulders. I doubt he heard me over the loud music. However, he did read my lips.

They looked away from each other's gaze only briefly, just long enough to smile and wave and then they immediately went back into their face suckin' as if they were all alone, yet we were in a packed gymnasium. They were boyfriend and girlfriend - and I was alone. But I hung out by them anyway, trying to not feel so alone – flashes of Boogie Bob being in the hospital had blipped through my mind once in a while, which made me feel alone, but I tried not to think about it too much.

While I was chilling by Reeny and Fred I was sort of talking to them but sort of not; mainly because they were too busy smooching each other's lips off and also because I had one eye out searching for Devon. I started to slip away from them but not too far – I didn't see anybody else that I really knew, not well at least. So I kind of stood by them, but sort of not, if you know what I mean?

By chance, Gina and Randal began hanging out right by us. I had moved over close enough so I could eaves drop on old Randal. I wanted to know what kind of schlernious Bull-shee-ott he was going to tell her. I kept my back to him as to play it off as if I wasn't paying attention to him though. I was sort of pretending to talk to Reeny and Fred who randomly came up for air once in a while and looked in my direction with vacant eyes. I mean maybe they weren't even really looking at me?

If anybody had paid close enough attention to Fred, Reeny, and me, they would have thought that I was just plain old off my rocker or something because I was really just talking to myself and pretending to talk to them. I didn't want Randal to know I was listening to him. I can really be a weirdo sometimes, you'd better watch me.

And here's where I sound weird again. I really wanted to smell Gina's fingers like a madman. I wanted to know if her fingers smelled like cigarettes. I knew she might have smelled like cigs, just because she had gone outside with him. But if she had smoked, her fingers would have smelled. Like I said, you had better watch out for me – I can be a real freak.

Something in Randal's voice, reminded me of that night at Chanecksons keg party, so I really focused my ear on his voice. He was talking about "smoking," "money," and crap like that but something in Randal's tone drew me in and made me listen harder. I kept my back to them, but secretly I was all ears.

… But what I heard next had really set me off.

I heard Randal say, "With it being my birthday tomorrow I think you should go outside with me and have a smoke." That comment made me turn around.

Gina shook her head no

But Randal continued to try and talk her into it, "Really Gina, get with it; after you give me my birthday present tomorrow … and we both know what that is," he said with a liars grin, as he grabbed her hips, drew her in closer, then kissed her on the cheek. Then he continued, "After we French kiss baby, you're supposed to smoke … haven't you seen any movies in your life before," he said in a belittling tone, "… after you French you're supposed to smoke a cigarette … any girl of mine needs to know how to smoke a cigarette after we kiss. It's the thing to do," he said as if he thought he was cool.

"I have been waiting forever for you girl – I have been as celibate as a nun … I've been getting none … nada," he said drolly. " … I have been saving myself for you, you know that girl?" He even said it in this most sincere voice that almost made me believe it, even though I knew it was a lie. It made me want to Ralph big piles all over the darn floor.

Then he said, "You've made me wait 7 long months for this. -I've done that for you," then he raised his voice, "now you can do this for me." Then he practically demanded, "Let's go Gina, let's go outside I will show you how to smoke a cigarette, so you will know how to do it, after we have our official first kiss on the lips," he said with a punky laugh as he grabbed her hand. Then the freakin' scumbag Randal smiled like a used car salesman as Gina began to shake her head in a reluctant yes.

I had been looking at them ever since I had heard him trying to convince her to smoke. I walked over towards Gina and looked her square in the eyes and said, "Hang on, don't go anywhere with that two timing punk ice bee-otch. Ask him about Lucy Goosey from the bowling alley. He hasn't been waiting for you or saving himself for you, that's Bull shee-ott.

And as far as that smoking shiznit - Don't even do it. Yo check this out Gina, I'm about to grab that mic from the DJ and tell y'all wazup. Watch this," I said confidently as I strode towards the DJ rig while looking back occasionally to make sure she had waited. It was weird though, dream-like even. As I walked quickly towards the DJ stage I was in this dreamy haze that I can't even explain. And what I did next wasn't even me. I became someone else.

I stormed the DJ booth and I told the DJ, "Yo give me the microphone bro, I've got something to say."

The DJ obliged and handed me the mike.

I grabbed the mike swiftly and talked into the DJ's ear without any fear.

He then fingered through his crate while I swaggered my gate.

He picked out a 12 inch. I said this will be a cinch.

I began to walk around the dance with a certain kind of prance.
I had my B-boy, top rock, saunter and then I rocked it like this and I became Randal's taunter:

"The ploys by Randal
Has me flyin' off the handle
It's time to take his joy
And blow out his candle

He's been pulling the wool over your eyes
With his celibate cries
The truth is, he's dealin' in lies
Don't fall for his disguise

Randal is just a love vandal
And you're his next scandal
Gina hit him in the butt
With your shoe or your sandal

I'm goin' to tell you wazup
He can kiss my rump
Randal's really just a chump
Take him to the dump

He's trying to make you smoke,
Sayin' he's a celibate bloke
Claims he's waiting for you,
Really -he's just another Jamoke

Smoking cigs is a joke
Don't take a toke
Mess with them long enough
They will make you croak

It tastes like butt crack
You ought to just pass
It's for the low class,
They make you look crass
Toke 'em long enough
You'll be six feet under grass

Yo girl:
Don't put ciggy butts in your mouth
Don't put butts in your mouth
Don't do it
Don't put ice in your mouth
Don't put ice in your mouth
Don't do it −He's a smokin' jack-ass

Your boy Randal blows rings,
 Second hand devil wings
Streams and zings,
Makin' my eyes stings

Watch out for his lips
With all of those two timin' flings
I betchya his lip stings
Stay away from his lings –
He's a ding a lings lings

He's been kissing the whole hood,
 Not doing what he said he would
Giving away his smooch
He's just a low down pooch.

He told you he was waiting
Really he was fabricating
 Nothing 'bout him is real
He's just a pig, make him squeal

He's got girls from the alley on the side
He's not the one for you, don't let it slide
He's trying to make you smoke
But he's a lying joke
Don't go with him to do that tokety toke toke

Don't put those dastardly sticks in your mouth
Its disastrously, your health will go south
Read my lips, my mouthety mouth mouth
Those cigarettes make me wanna Ralph Ralph

It makes your lungs all black
 Your clothes will smell whack
The gross phlegm in your mouth, hackety hack hack hack
That's the fact jack.

Hey Randal:
You're putting ciggy butts in your mouth
You're putting butts in your mouth
You're putting jack-ass in your mouth
You're putting ice in your mouth
You're putting ice in your mouth
You two tym-inn Jack-ass"

In the midst of my rappin' I saw Gina giving him dirty looks as she tugged
away at his grip, which gave me added inspiration to rap a few more digs,

"Well, I'm done with you son
I had to tell you hun
Putting squares in your mouth is a loaded gun
Now one more thing son -she knows about your fun
And now -yous will be getting' NONE

I'm about to hit the floor with breakin' for sure
Not shakin or fakin' spinning for her
What's that you called it punk? "I said as I put my hand cupped around my ear and stared Randal straight in the eyes while I continued to rock the cordless microphone,

"Yeah, that's right,

You called it crawlin' on the floor
You made fun of my folklore
Now you're shakin' galore
While I'm rockin' this floor – you bore

Gina's got you groveling for more
But your jack-ass can head out the door
You're now a part of something Gina will call the days of yore
Beat it dude you're a smokin' cheater to the core

But go ahead Randal on your way out:

Put that ciggy butt in your mouth

You're puttin' butts in your mouth
You're putting jack-ass in your mouth
You're putting butts in your mouth
You're putting ice in your mouth
You two timin' Jack-ass."

By the second time around of my chorus everyone in the whole school gym was singing along:
"You're putting butts in your mouth
You're putting jack-ass in your mouth
"You're putting butts in your mouth
"You're putting jack-ass in your mouth
YOU Jack Ass."
I put the mike back on the stand by the DJ who then high fived me like I was Air Jordan. I watched from across the room as Gina slapped Randal VanderNorth across the face. Moments later, Reeny and Gina went briskly walking out of the large gym doors with Gina crying in Reeny's shoulder.
Fred gave me thumbs up, nodded and smiled, and then I lost him in the crowd or should I say swarm. I was then swarmed by all of the dateless girls at the dance as if I was Michael Jackson or Simon LeBon. Half of them were telling me that they didn't know I could rap and such. But I just smiled like a

rock star and said, "I didn't know I could do that either. I'm not really a rapper or anything – I'm a breaker but Randal got me mad," I said to some of my new 'fans.'

As I walked around the school dance as a new "mini celebrity," a few people who hadn't seen me break yet, asked me to "do some breakin'" So I did at random. Well I mainly engaged the girls. How do you say no to a cute girl who says: "Swifty Can you show me some of your breakin'?" you can't. Whether I was tired or not, I just had to do what I had to do. I'm such a sucker for a pretty face.

I didn't want to be out of energy when Devon showed up, so I tried to chill when I could, but I was also starting to wonder where the dude was. I had made my way around the entire dance party a million times and I had asked everybody I knew if they had seen him. But nobody had.

Another hour went by and still no Devon, then to my surprise, the DJ said, "This will be the last slow song of the night." and somehow that made me feel like breakin'. My feelings and emotions had been fast and slow, happy and sad, overwhelmed by crowds, yet feeling alone all night. Therefore, it only seemed right to break during a slow jam. I busted out with all of my routines and all the while I was breakin' I couldn't believe that Devon hadn't shown up. He did all of that loud mouth taunting and ranting all week about battling me. And I had spent the whole week planning, practicing, acting, and expecting to face Devon in a wide opened free for all so we could settle it, once and for all; who was the baddest breaker in our school - and he didn't even show up. It was a big nothing, a big let-down to be straight up honest with you.

I had fun breakin' and rappin' that night, which I didn't even know where that whole rap thing had come from because I wasn't a rapper. But I guess the moral to the story was: don't get me mad; you might get rap attacked.

The DJ played another slow jam, "This will really be the last song of the night," he said. As I made my way towards the exit where I was grabbed by everyone; some of the students I could tell had partied a little too hardy that night. Everyone wanted to talk to me: The jocks, the preps, the nerds, - everyone had said, "HI" or "Bye" or "that was cool" and crap like that. I didn't realize that grabbing the mike like that was going to make me into a big deal or anything. I just did it to stop Gina from making two bad decisions.

As I talked with a couple of classmates that looked totally "blown" I thought about how I was just glad that I hadn't gotten into any of those things (drugs, cigarettes, or alcohol.) Other than the "almost inhaling" incident I told you about before. But you see, I was already cool, I didn't need to add any smokes or drinks to become cool; I was cool, I was straight up Chicago YO! I had a blast breakin' and everything but I was mainly glad that I had stopped Gina from doing anything with that punk ice bee-otch.

After I finished my goodbyes with my friendly "burn-out" friends, Blacklung and Coughman, I started making my way out of the gym. I didn't really feel like saying bye to anybody once I hit the halls, if I've got to tell you the truth about it. Saying goodbye can really be kind of sad sometimes if you think about it.

In the Native American language spoken by the Seneca Nation of Indians they actually do not have the word "goodbye" in their vocabulary. Instead they say, "I will see you again" – (ENHS GONH GENH AH-AYH)

Either way I was not in the mood to say goodbye to anybody as I made my way through the more or less empty hallways –as I was among the first to leave. Everyone else was either clogging the exit doorways with chatting, or checking their hair in the bathrooms mirrors, or taking leaks in the can and stuff like that. I wouldn't have minded seeing Gina again, but she was nowhere to be found. I guessed she was off crying in Reeny's shoulder somewhere.

I quickly exited the school and I stared at the cars one by one. I didn't see my old man's car just yet, so I paced around. There were about a million cars parked in the school lot filled with parents that were waiting for us teens to come on out. Engines were running on most and exhaust was everywhere, which was highlighted because of the cold. It almost looked foggy.

Suddenly I felt anger as a cars bright red dot drew my eye. It was a bright red cherry that had just been lit from a lighter by some parent that was nice enough to have his window down, so I could inhale his second hand devil wings. And when I say "nice enough" I am being sarcastic – in case you couldn't tell.

After that whole rap attack thing, I looked at cigarettes differently than I had ever looked at them before. I looked out into the dark sky, half cloudy, half moon lit night. Then I looked back at the car with the glowing red cherry and the smoke coming from the half drawn windows and I thought about the rap I had just done that night.

I had half of a mind to start telling this parent about the smoke fumes that he was second handedly making me inhale but I only had half of my energy left at that point, from breakin' half of the night. The adrenaline rush from breakin' and my rap attack had worn off by that point. And you've really got to have your swag going if you're going to tell someone's parent off.

So I let the half wit keep smoking his half finished cancer stick through his half opened window under the half moon while I half cared and I thought for a moment on one half of my brain that it was half of his life that he was cutting in half; not mine.

My old man's car slowly strutted down the street and I began to bounce towards him. The dance must have been completely over by then because the students were starting to come out in droves. I walked fast towards my ride and hopped in the car as fast as someone would, who had bees chasing him. I really wanted to get out of that smoke filled outside air is what it was.

The old man had on the mix jams playing loudly as all heck, as if he was a teen or something too. I started telling the old man about how, "That kid Devon didn't even show up and stuff," and dad started making a scrunched face. You see, I had told my dad the whole scoop on how I was going to battle him in breakin' before he had dropped me off at the dance, so he knew what wazup.

Then my dad said in true dad fashion, "That sounds typical to me, lots of people talk a lot of crap - but then when it's time to put your money where your mouth is…. Aaaahh, there's just a lot of chumps out there! Screw 'em," he said. Dad couldn't have given any better advice. The rest of the car ride home we listened to the mix jams on WMIX 103FM Chicago's mix station and I thought about how I had foiled Randal's plan. I didn't tell dad about that though. I didn't feel like talking about kissing and cigarettes with the old man, if you really want to know the deal. I wasn't doing either of them anyway, and I really didn't want to hear anything about it.

When I got home I just went straight to my bedroom, I said my prayers for Bob and I went to bed with the same mixed emotions that I had been experiencing all day but I had the satisfaction of knowing that I had showed up ready to battle. I wasn't backing down to anybody. I would sleep well knowing that I had showed up. My last thoughts before drifting to sleep were: what if I would have waited all night for Devon to show up to unleash my best break moves. I would have never shined; I would have saved my best and most impressive moves for the big moment … and that moment would have never came.

I was glad I didn't wait all night for that moment. Devon's not showing up made me realize that it was always time to shine! I learned that night to not let your life revolve around other people; other people will let you down. Do what you want to do; when you want to do it!

Chapter 10

You're playing with your butt - but I'm the idiot?

I arrived at the hospital bright and early on Saturday morning. My mom gave me a ride since she had to be at work at 8am anyway and it was more or less on the way. I would usually get out of bed at 9am on Saturday, watch cartoons, and slowly wake up -at least that's what I was thinking about while half asleep, as I sat shotgun next to my mom, while she drove, and put her makeup on at every stop light we hit.

If you met my mom, you would think that she was like the first lady of the white house, or the queen of England, or a model or something; she was always dressed in nice and expensive looking clothes; Mom accessorized like no other. She was very aware of her appearance, which was good though, it had rubbed off on me – I too, dressed to impress.

My mom was a counselor or therapist, whatever you want to call it, so I thought about telling her how crazy my emotions had been about Boogie Bob; about how I was happy one minute and sad the next, and how I couldn't stop thinking about Bob's reality and such, however, I did not. I knew that would be like opening up a big old can of worms at 730 in the morning and I didn't feel like opening up that can. I could barely put one solid thought in my mind that early in the morning and I didn't want mom trying to put a million more thoughts in my brain while I was still trying to clear the cobwebs out of my morning head.

I knew I would be alright though, I was just a little curious about things like: Should I walk into Bob's room with a big old smile on my face that said: it's all good in the hood, life is great. Which maybe that would be considered fake because really I had been concerned about Bob's bed becoming empty one day. And what if he didn't even say goodbye? And did I want him to say goodbye? Or did I want him to say, "I'll see you again." You see my problem? I did not know what to say to him.

When we had finally arrived at the hospital, Mom said, "Have fun visiting your friend sweetie." Which made me think: If mom only knew I was going to the cancer unit and hanging out at deaths door she probably would have said something different. But I was glad she didn't say something different.

Since I had arrived at the hospital early that morning, I took my time walking. I was thinking about how cancer patients were faced with thoughts that people usually didn't have to think about until they were at least 100 years old. Cancer patients must face Mr. Reaper square in the freakin' eyes; he's an unavoidable fellow that forces you to think about it all. Then I thought about Moms comment and I thought: yes, I will have fun visiting my friend Boogie Bob.

Before I could even ask the lady at the hospitals information table any questions she said, "I like your necklace!" I had worn my "NSR" belt buckle nameplate around my neck on the outside of my jacket.

I told her, "Thanks Doll face." I never had used the expression "doll face" before, it kind of just slipped out. I think it was the way she had complimented me that made me flirt. This girl had to be at least 30 years old and she had no rings on her fingers, I happened to notice, so that's probably why I flirted with her. If she had been my age I probably would have been a stone cold chicken. Then I told her, "I'm here to see my buddy Boogie Bob, he told me to ask for Robert Charles' room, kid's cancer unit, not that I'm a kid, I practically have my driver's license," I said with more flirtation.

She told me, "Give me a minute cutie, while I look up his room number – no one's answering on the unit."

"Sounds good darling," I said. – Boy, I can really be a flirt when I know it won't go anywhere.

The information desk girl, Phoebe, told me while she was waiting on hold, that she knew Robert Charles. She said she had to work the night shift last week and, "There was a boy that was break dancing right there," Phoebe had said as she pointed at a section of smooth tile. "He was spinning on his head, quite a few times and his mom kept saying that's enough Bobby … and what did you call him Break dancing Bob?"

"His name is Boogie Bob, but yep, I'm sure we are talking about the same Bob," I said.

Phoebe whispered to me, "Hang on sweetie," while taking the phone away from under her chin and replacing it to her ear.

Then she told the person on the other end of the phone, "Okay, thank you Darlin'."

Then she smiled at me and said, "Robert Charles room number is 2410. Just follow the brown tape on the floor all the way to the 2nd set of elevators. Then go up to the 2nd floor. Then follow the blue tape until you see the sign that says Pediatric and Adolescent cancer unit, okay cutie," she said while twisting her hair in circles. This made me wonder if she was flirting back at me, or if she just wanted to fix her hair. I had no idea about that kind of stuff. But that didn't stop me from crushing about it. I can get a crush on any girl; I'm a real love sick puppy.

I told her thanks, smiled, and started walking down the brown taped hallway. Then she yelled out, "I really do like your necklace."

So I yelled back but in a shy way, "I really do think you're hot too!"

"Thanks sweetie," she said.

I could be really bold when I was walking away from a girl.

As I was walking towards Bob's unit, I thought about how brown tape was really a sad color of tape to have on the floor, it reminded me of brown dead leaves that fall off the trees in the autumn. As I got on the elevator, which smelled like skunks and lemon cleaning products, I remembered how I had first asked Bob to take off his hood while we were on an elevator at the mall.

I exited the elevator and started following the blue tape, which made me wonder: who the heck picked out these depressing tape colors that were on the floor of the hospital. I wasn't trying to feel blue or maudlin (which means sad like Mary Magdeline from the Bible that cried at Jesus Christ's feet) but having sad colored tape on the floor really didn't lift my spirits very well.

I nervously hoped that I wouldn't hear the term, "code blue" yelled out loud while I was at the hospital that day. – and I was not even exactly sure what "code blue" meant, but I knew that it was nothing good. The blue tape on the floor, for some reason, had me thinking about blue faces though.

I had to get buzzed into the kids cancer unit where I was greeted by a male nurse who started giving me the rundown on all of the things that I needed to do before I went in to see my buddy Bob (or Robert as he kept impersonally calling him. Which I didn't like, it really started to sound like he was just another name or just another number or just another "dude" when he called him "Robert.")

"First, you have to wash your arms and hands very thoroughly. Then grab this bag. Inside the bag you will find clothing that looks like hospital scrubs. There are coverings in the bag that you will need to put over your shoes. Plus there is garb for you to put over your pants and shirt as well; along with sterile gloves, a mask and a item that looks like a shower cap. Please put all of these items on before entering the unit," he said in an annoying voice. He wasn't trying to sound annoying – he just did.

As I was putting on all of those items, it was really starting to make me feel the seriousness of the situation. It felt much heavier to me, like a ton of bricks heavy –as I was putting on the surgeon looking clothes.

When I was done putting on my cancer unit "visitor's clothes" I left the dressing room and entered The Kids Cancer Unit with extra weight on my shoulders. I started looking on the walls as I walked in the direction of Bob's room; there were pictures of kids and teens on the walls that had "beat cancer." There were also pictures on the walls of people climbing mountains, swimming, playing tennis, baseball, and junk like that. I had noticed how everyone in the pictures were smiling too, they were all happy, and all of the people in the pictures had hair. I found that rather funny. I suppose they didn't want to put pictures on the wall of the people who didn't make it. I suppose they didn't want pictures of people on the wall that were bald, skinny, and wasting away either. I mean, they didn't have any of those types of pictures. I got a little mad to myself about it, to be honest with you; I mean, don't the people who didn't make it matter? The pictures on the walls seemed to send the message that only the people who mattered were the ones who had made it. Yet, at the same time, I got it; they were trying to inspire hope. But what about the people who didn't make it. Don't they matter? Well, that's what I thought about silently in my head as I neared Bob's room.

Room 2410: I entered Bob's room and he quickly jumped up from laying down to sitting. "Sup Boogie Bob," I excitedly said.

"Phil K Swift, sup kid," Bob said as he looked up at the clock on the wall and grinned, "You're early! …. Cool, I'll skip my treadmill run this morning."

I started to apologize but Bob cut me off, "No I'm glad you're here kid, come on in, sit down. I'm usually up early, the nurses are always coming in here checking my blood pressure or pumping my veins with some of this friggin' bull shee-ott chemo medicine, and waking me up anyways." I leaned over to Bob and we exchanged one of those half hugs that guys give each other; like were Bro's. We are Bro's and it was a Hug, so sometimes we call it a "BRUG."

"What have you been up to?" Bob asked. Even though, he already knew. We had been talking everyday on the phone since we had met.

I told Bob mostly about all of the Breakin' that I did and how I "rap attacked" that dude Randal last Wednesday, which Bob really got a big old bang out of. Then I told him that Devon didn't even show up and stuff, and he was just as irritated as I was. He even called him a chump, just like my old man did. Bob already knew all of this, since I had told him about it over the phone on Thursday and Friday, but talking to someone in person is way more fun. I had fun talking about it again.

Boogie Bob got this playful look in his eyes and said, "You know Swift kid, with all of this talk about breakin' that you did this week, you've really got me into the mood to throw on down with some breakin'." Bob started to get this tough smile and trouble-maker look in his eye that I had become very familiar with that day I had met him at Dorktown mall. It was the exact look that I had remembered most about Boogie Bob.

He pressed the "nurse help button" and told me, "I usually just yell for her, but my voice is rough, seeing how I hadn't had my morning popsicles just yet. Anyway kid, they have this room down at the end of the hall; it's like a family visitors section or something. There is just a couch and a few chairs in there. We can move them around and do some breakin' in there! … but sshhh," he said as he put his index finger to his lips.

A voice came over the intercom, "Yes Bob?"

"Can you come in here Mary?"

"OK," she said.

"Are you going to be able to break with all of those needles and tubes sticking in your arms and such?" I asked quietly.

"I'll figure it out," he said with a sneaky smile, "I haven't really been in the mood to break ever since I got here …but I am now kid."

"The receptionist Phoebe at the information desk told me that you were throwing down with head spins the night you checked in," I said as I high fived him.

Bob smiled and said, "No kidding, she told you that? YEP, that was the last time I had rocked out."

The nurse came into Bob's room and Bob asked her to unhook him from all of his machines for a few minutes because he wanted to go down the hall to the family room and hang out for a bit. The nurse, whom Bob called, "Nurse Mary" unhooked the lines and tubes and re-hooked them to this portable "IV stand" that made it possible for Bob to leave his room. He moved the "IV stand" around his bed with what I thought to be bags of chemo-medicine, saline, and god only knew what else were in those "intravenous bags." Then we strode out of his room with a B-boy, top rock, bop about ourselves as Bob pulled his I.V. stand.

I followed Bob down the hallway as the squeaky wheels from the "I.V. Stand" that carried his bags of medicine led the way. I asked him, "How are you going to break with that medicine stand alongside of you and all of those tubes coming out of you?"

Bob whispered, "Sshhhh!" as he scrunched his face, "I've got a secret," he said as he looked at the pictures on the walls that I had looked at when I had first walked into the cancer unit. Moments later he grunted, "Where are the pictures of the breakers?" but I didn't say anything. Then he started laughing through his nose; you know the noise it makes when you're blowing air out of your nose? That's how Bob sounded when he laughed, quick bursts of air rushing out of his nostrils. It started making me laugh. And for the first time, I had forgotten that we were in the cancer unit.

We walked into the family room where cartoons were playing. Bob told me to move the chairs and sofa out of the way. The room was at least 15 feet by 15 feet and was rather boring to be honest with you, save for the Woody Woodpecker cartoon that was playing in the background.

Bob started unhooking his lines from the medicine bags and told me, "I've watched the nurses unhook and re-hook them enough times that I know how to do it. I've just never had a reason to do it before."

Bob finished unhooking all of his lines from the I.V. Stand, which were three different bags. Bob then rolled up the I.V. chords nicely and tied them together around his waist.

"They let you break with all of those chords and needles in you and stuff?" I asked stupidly.

Bob replied, "Cuck Fancer, Chuck Femotherapy. I'm a breaker! I'm not one of those cancer patients. I'm just a Neighborhood Street Rocker who happens to be getting some medicine for cancer," he said as I high fived him.

"Right on," I said, as I couldn't argue with that logic.

Bob got this devilish look in his eye and asked, "Do you have one of those winter hats on you kid?"

I reached my hand inside of my hospital scrub pants to get to my street clothes which were underneath. Bob jokingly stopped me and sarcastically said, "I don't want a jimmy hat you sicko, I want a winter hat."

It was nice to see Bob still joking around. I laughed and then continued to pull out the winter hat that I had in my front pocket of my pants, and handed it to Bob, "Very funny," I said as I thought about what he had said.

We both started laughing our butts off and Bob was still doing that air blow laugh through his nose thing like a madman. It made me wonder if he always laughed like that.

Then in true Boogie Bob form he dove and spiraled to his head like a tornado and started tapping around in head spins. You'd have thought that Bob had been practicing all day and all week; he didn't miss a beat. Bob revolved around about 10 times, with his hospital gown covering his body from his waist to his head with his underwear showing and everything. All I could see was two spinning legs, underwear, and a hospital gown that covered his head, but it was Bboying at its finest.

"I'm sure the hospital didn't think about people doing head stands or head spins while wearing those hospital gowns and getting chemo and such. But in the future maybe they can redesign those hospital gowns for breakin' patients, so I don't have to look at your underwear," I told Bob jokingly.

When Bob was done head spinning; he smiled with tired eyes and said, "This chemo Shiznit Sucks, let me sit down for a minute."

I sat down right next to Bob and I started digging into my hospital scrub shirt. Bob started looking at me as if I was strange. I finally grabbed a hold of it and pulled it out. "Check this Shee-ott out my brother!" I showed him my "NSR" nameplate which was now on the outside of my hospital scrub shirt.

Bob thought it was awesome, with his mouth opened wide he said, "Dude I want one, you've got to get me one, I'll have my mom bring money next time she comes. You've got to hook me up!" It was like Christmas morning in Bob's eyes as we sat in the family room of the cancer unit. Bob then added, "That is the baddest to the bone-est bling-est thing that I have ever seen."

"Now it's my turn," I said as I dove to the ground into windmills, which turned into pennies that evolved into a couple of businessman copters. I went for as long as I could until I lost my steam and fell to the ground.

Bob clapped, "You've figured out the no handers, huh kid?" I then joined Bob on the couch. Bob quickly stood back up and pounced into tornadic head spins again. He tapped around a few times at a fast rate, then he purposely slowed it down for effect, and did a few slow-mo - no hander's, and then he began tapping ferociously fast again.

In the midst of Bob doing his head spins, the strict looking nurse with a serious face walked into our "break-room," and gave us a stink face. It was the nurse that had told me the rules of the cancer unit and handed me my scrubs when I had first got to the unit. "Nurse Marvin, I aint starving," Bob said to him after he had stopped head spinning, "I thought I saw white shoes while I was revolving," Bob added.

Marvin's hair was combed to the side like a comb-over but it wasn't a comb-over and I could tell by the way he had looked at us that we were about to get a lecture. He sighed and gave us a parental look. Then the straight laced white shoed nurse said, "You can't do that Bob."

Bob stood up.

Then I said, "But he is, and he can, and he was rocking it strong!"

This made Bob smile.

Nurse Mr. Goody two shoes said, "Bob you are a cancer patient receiving chemotherapy and we must be responsible to treat you effectively."

I yelled, "Yo man Boogie Bobs not a cancer patient! He's a breaker, who happens to be getting chemo. He's a Neighborhood Street Rocker!"

"It's all good Marvin, I know you're just doing your job," Bob said as he sat down to catch his breath again.

I continued yelling at the nurse, "Can you rock out head spins like that?"

The party pooping nurse quietly said, "No."

I sarcastically replied, "Then maybe you're the cancer chemo patient around here? Maybe you're the one who needs medication. My boy Bob can do head spins for days; he's as healthy as a stallion. We will ring for you if we need you. You can go now," I said tight lipped, with my chin flexed out, while sporting bug eyes to boot.

The nurse left without saying a word. Bob high fived me and I dove to the floor like a quarter had been flicked. Bob cheered, "You've really got those pennies going kid, your pennies are up and running!" I bent my knee, transitioned into a half of a knee spin, and then posed in a freeze.

Over the next hour Bob and I just sat back on the couch and shot the Shiznit around while trippin' off the Woody Woodpecker cartoons. Half of the time we took turns making fun of Nurse Marvin who tried to rain on our parade. We both tried to come up with the nerdiest, mocking, and goody two shoed voices that we could. In a lisp voice I said, "Umm hey there fella, you can't do that break dance stuffy things."

Then Bob one upped me and used this real stupid sounding voice, "You can't do those spinner ma bob thingy's, you might get cancer or something – oh wait a minute, I already have cancer," Bob jokingly said as he pretended to be Nurse Marvin scolding him. We made sure to speak loud enough so anybody around could hear us. We didn't care, we were having too good of a time.

Moments later Bob's doctor entered our "break room" with a stone face and said, "Bob we need you to get back to your room, we are adding another medication and we need to draw some blood. Thank you."

Bob replied, "Yes sir."

Bob looked at me and said, "He's an okay doctor, lets head back. I was thinking about heading back anyway, I have a surprise for you," he said while grinning with full moon eyes, he would have been raising his eyebrows too, if the chemo hadn't taken 'em.

We entered Bob's room when moments later the angelic looking Nurse Mary, who was wearing a cross around her neck, and all white clothes, started hanging up the new Devilish red I.V. bag for Bob's chemotherapy treatment. Out of nowhere Bob said, "They are shooting me up with poison." I gave him a look of no-way and then he said, "They are trying to kill all of the cells in my body; good cells and bad cells alike. Then they are hoping that when the cells in my body are all dead, the good ones can win and the bad ones will stay dead, and make me cancer free."

"Hey Mary quite contrary," Bob said to the nurse.

"Yes Bob," she said with a warm smile.

"Can you hook up Phil the Funky Groove King Swift and me with some popsicles," Bob said with his brow-less brow raised.

"Sure thing Bob," Nurse Mary said.

Nurse Mary walked out after she finished taking his vital signs and listening to his heart, then Bob looked at me and said, "I told you I had a surprise for you my brother, these popsicles are the Shiznit my man, they are absolutely the best. Truth is, I can't really hold down much food these days, so the popsicles are really all I've got," Bob said quietly. "Until you came today

Phil, popsicles were the only thing that I really got excited about around here, other than my parents coming to visit me," he told me sincerely.

"Yo dude, when you get out of here we are going to get into some break battles or contests or talent shows or something … When are you getting out of here anyway?" I asked.

"I heard that I may get out of here as soon as three weeks," he said and then paused for a moment. I could tell he wanted to say something, so I kept quiet. "You reminded me that I was a breaker, not just some cancer dude in a hospital getting chemo. I don't want people treating me as if I'm dying or dead guy walking. I mean, we are all dying at some point or another. It happens to everybody, not just cancer patients. But you know what kid? … I want people to treat me like I'm a breaker, that's all. I am a B-boy and that's that."

"Okay boys, dessert is served," Nurse Mary said as she brought in the popsicles.

As she handed me my Popsicle I said, "I guess I will have to take my mask off to eat this thing, right?"

"Technically you don't really need the mask on, just everything else, unless you're worried that you have a cold that you could pass onto Bob and the other patients" Nurse Mary told me.

Then Bob jumped in, "Yep, I have no immunity, don't give me any colds or anything, especially cancer, don't give me any cancer," Bob said smart assedly. (its not really contagious.)

Mary walked out and Bob said, "Yo Phil raise that popsicle up high!"

I looked at him with a weird look on my face but I did it anyway. "Wazup?" I asked.

"Cheers my brother, Cheers," Bob said as he touched my Popsicle with his Popsicle.

As we clanged Popsicles together I told Bob, "Awesome, right on, cheers back at ya, I have never toasted with popsicles before," I said out of surprise.

"Now you have kid, now you have. It's the most exciting time around this joint, Popsicles; I love 'em," Bob said as he slurped it down.

Other than talking about breakin' and popsicles, Bob's eyes really lit up when he started telling me about his girlfriend. "There's this girl here in our unit that I run treadmills with, I call her purple bandana girl, she loves that, purples her favorite color. Anyway, kid, she is the hottest bald chick you have ever seen in your life. No bull shee-otting. Bald is beautiful," Bob said.

"I'll have to meet her sometime," I said.

Grubby mitts off bro, she's bald, she's beautiful and she's mine," he said.

While Bob and I were eating popsicles he told me, "This is my second round of chemotherapy, once they get me cancer free again, I will do some radiation treatments, and then they will give me my second bone marrow transplant or BMT, the doctors call it 'BMT' with their stuffy beards and their serious faces and such." Then Bob took a deep breath and continued, "I was in remission for a few months but then this crap came back; the leukemia came back, so they're trying to get rid of it again. I'm hoping to be out of here within 3 weeks," he said with a tired looking face.

Bob stopped talking for a few minutes but his heavy eye lids and his tensed lips told me the rest of the story before he even told it. He said, "I'm getting tired of them frying my body with poisons. I mean, check this out Phil, they are putting poisons in my body to make me better. Sup with that?"

I couldn't think of anything to say, but Bob filled in the gaps for me, "I'm getting worn and tired of all the pain and sadness that I'm putting my family and friends through, especially my girl Bella. I wish Bella didn't have to deal with a situation like this.

But you know this time is it! When I am done with all of this chemo and radiation and bone marrow transplanting and stuff; we are hitting the mall, the rink, and wherever the breakers are … I am there," Bob said with a half hearted brow-less smile. I almost got the feeling that he didn't truly believe his own pep talk but he wanted me to believe it. He didn't want me to worry.

"Well my brother, I've got to make like Geeta," I said.

"What's Geeta," Bob asked.

"Geeta frig Outta Here," I said with an added Chicago style accent. (I grew up in the suburbs, so I didn't necessarily talk like a Southsider as my old man did.)

Bob smiled big and rapidly laughed through his nose, almost snorting.

"But for real, I've got to get going. I have to start making my way up to McCollum Park. I wish you could come with bro, but it sounds like you will be joining us in about 3 weeks, right?" I questioned Bob with hope.

"Yes Swift kid, I will be done with this place in about 3 weeks. Thanks for stopping by Phil," Bob said.

"It was awesome Bob! By the end of the day I will have danced with all of us Neighborhood Street Rockers. But hey - you know what? - I can stop by again next weekend. My mom works across the street in the medical building as a therapist, so I'll hitch a ride with her again. So I'll catch up with you next week. I'm Audi 5000," I said all slick-like.

I pitched my empty Popsicle stick into the garbage can and then I put my surgical mask back on.

"You don't have to wear the mask on the way out," Bob said with a snicker through his nose.

"It's cool bro, I kind of feel like wearing it for some reason," I said. I was too nervous to take it off until I got out of the cancer unit. I mean, what if I was on the verge of a cold and I didn't even know it.

Bob grabbed my "NSR" nameplate and groped it like it was pure gold. He practically pet it like you'd pet a dog, and then he told me, "You've got to get me one of those kid!"

"Of course my man, of course, I'll hook it up," I said.

As I walked out of his room he said, "See ya kid Swifty."

"I will see you again," I said.

As I was exiting the cancer unit I sort of got into this robotic or zombie type state of mind. I mean, I knew that I was supposed to take off the scrubs, the hat, the mask, the footie's, the gloves, and stuff, but I didn't; I couldn't. I just made my way down the hallways wearing my cancer visiting garb, while following the blue and then brown lines on the floor.

It wasn't as sad on the way out. I think that visiting Bob was kind of like therapy in and of itself, because I really felt better afterwards. Now that I had seen him break again and now that I had heard him say that he would be outta there in 3 weeks, I felt much better. But something had me puzzled. Something I had heard his doctor say over the phone as I was walking out didn't make me feel all that great. But I hoped it was nothing. I mean, I didn't know all that much about medical words, so I tried not to worry too much.

By the time I had made my way outside of the hospital I decided that I wanted to wear the scrubs getup on the way to the park. I think it was my way of paying respect to my friend Boogie Bob who couldn't make it to McCollum Park that day.

Before I could even make it off the hospital campus I spotted 2 nurses smoking cigarettes just a few feet outside of the hospital doors. Even though they were standing far enough away from the hospital entrance and exit doors, their second hand smoke and the cool fall wind had its own idea of who should get this smoky crap into their noses.

I wondered if either of those nurses worked in the cancer unit or in the heart unit? Then I wondered: would I want those nurses working on me if I was a patient here? I mean, here I was walking out of a cancer unit, which was a place that was trying to cure my buddy Bob from his cancer of the blood or A, L, L as Bob called it. Yet, some of the hospitals very own nurses were smoking cigarettes which were known to cause cancer. And to top it off - they were blowing their death smoke in my direction. Life is filled with opposites like, "Smoking nurses" or using, "Poison to cure cancer" and I didn't like the thought of either one of those.

I love what I did next, check this out: I made this deep bass voice and said, "Hello girls!" I knew my young looks were hidden since I was still covered from head to toe in surgical clothing, so I figured I would have some fun. I started feeling a little devilish and their second hand devil wings (smoke) were my reason.

The nurses both replied, "Hello" and "Hi" and then went back to their conversation with each other.

I made my voice deeper still and as adult-like as I could and said, "Do cigarettes cause cancer? ..."

There was about a 5 second delay until the short blonde said, "They cannnn? … My grandma always said everything in moderation" and then she went back to smoking and gabbing away with her nurse buddy.

I kept on walking to get away from the bad direction of the wind when I heard one of the two nurses giggle and say, "Some people should really mind their own business."

"Do you like putting that butt in your mouth?" I asked sarcastically which made both of them look at me more closely and then I continued, "you've heard people call them ciggy butts before, right? When you get to the end of your cigarette they call them butts, right?" and at that point, I was using the most smart aleck voice I could think of. You should have heard me. I knew I had really irritated them by that point. I was close enough to see their faces, the taller brunette scrunched her nose, moved her eyes to the upper corner of her orbits, tilted her head down, and said, "Umh yeaaah, I've heard of that – what's your point?"

In a fake deep grown up voice I said, "I just wanted to be clear and make sure that we both understood that you are putting butts in your mouth."

Then the punky teen in me started having a little more fun, I started shouting in this taunting (na na na na boo boo voice) as I was walking toward the parking lot, "You guys are putting butts in your mouth, you guys are putting butts in your mouth." I even put my thumbs on the sides of my head and wiggled all of my fingers; I knew I was being childish, but sometimes that sort of thing is fun to do. You can never be too old to act like a child.

I kept going on and on for another minute or so while I strode towards the lot, "How's the butt taste in your mouth?", "You like butts in your mouth," and other schlernious stuff like that. At the end of my rant I said once and for all, "My buddy Bob is in your cancer unit trying to get rid of cancer and you're out here trying to give yourself cancer. Sup wit dat?"

I must have finally gotten under their skin because they yelled back, "Mind your own business!"

I turned around and took a few steps towards them to make sure they could completely hear me because I was now a good football field away from them, and I spouted back, "You made it my business when I had to inhale your second hand smoke from your butt – and your butt smells!"

They shouted something back that I couldn't hear but I was done with them at that point. The Blondie was pretty hot and everything, but in light of the fact that she was a smoker, I had to knock her down a few notches on the hot list, if you know what I mean.

While walking down the sidewalk on Main Street in Downers Grove on the way to McCollum, I must have had a car honk at me every 5 minutes. I wasn't surprised though, I'm sure the people in the passing cars were wondering why someone was walking down the street wearing surgical scrubs with a mask, cap, and the scrub footie's to boot. But I had my reasons; I suppose I was taking Bob with me to the park that day by wearing those hospital scrubs or maybe I was just shocked by what I had overheard his doctor say just as I had left the cancer unit floor.

Halfway through my trek, a group of high schoolers in a car purposely slowed down; a teen in the back seat of the car had his butt hanging out of the window with his pants pulled down. I was straight up getting mooned with ghost white cheeks by some young punk. The dude was spanking his own butt and spreading his butt cheeks apart while someone else from the car yelled, "It's not Halloween you idiot!"

They kept driving and I kept walking and I started thinking, well actually I said it aloud to myself: I'm the idiot? … You're the one who just pulled down your own pants, showed your butt, spanked your own darn butt and then spread your butt cheeks apart … but I'm the idiot?"

I had a few more honks along the way, but I was almost there. I was probably about three quarters of the way there, practically in my own neck of the woods, so I stopped in the 24 hour pantry to scoop up a bottle of juice.

Some redneck looking dude that was bearded up, tattoo-ed up, and smelling of cigarette smoke said, "What's up Doc," he had used this voice that sounded like Bugs bunny which sounded pretty funny coming from a big dude like that. Then he added, "Did you forget to take off your Halloween costume last month?"

"Hey that's pretty funny guy, but a car load of teenagers already beat you to that joke. … You're not going to pull down your pants and start playing with your butt, are ya?" I asked sarcastically.

This big tattooed dude that looked as if he could have and would have kicked my butt if I had kept on smarting off to him said, "What the heck are you talking about boy?"

"A car load of teenagers just mooned me and did all that stuff I just told you about while I was walking down the street; they mooned me and yelled something about Halloween.

All I'm doing is paying respect to my friend Bob who wishes he could be hanging outside in the fresh air but instead he is cooped up in a hospital room getting poisons pumped into his body … he's got cancer, I just got done visiting him," I said.

The tough-redneck looking dude told the clerk, "I've got this dudes drink" he said as he pointed to me.

I told the dude, "Thanks" and then we both walked out of the store basically at the same time since he had sort of struck up a conversation with me. He was talking so random. He talked about cancer, Agent Orange, fishing with his dad, life is too short, and something about bubble gum – all within 15 seconds. Then as he was getting into his car he told me that his dad had cancer a few years ago. He slammed his door, waved, and drove away and it was pretty clear at that point that he was thinking about his dad. Either that or he suddenly got a big case of the sniffles.

Chapter 11

McCollum Park

I started speed walking the rest of the way to McCollum Park; it was 5 minutes till noon and I was still about 15 minutes away, which, "aint no thing but a chicken wing on a string wearing some bling bling, ting ting ting. I am almost there Cha Chinggg," I said out loud to myself.

As I drew near to the park I could see off in the distance by the tennis courts and the cemented sidewalk areas that there were some cats already there: spinning, grooving, gliding, popping, and straight up rocking that place. I couldn't make out any faces yet. I was still too far away but I could tell by their colors that it was my posse. I wanted us to have uniforms so I asked them all to wear Black and gray.

Once I was close enough I saw Kid Mojo bangin' windmills and Blazin' was twisting spinning top backspins right next to him; they were tornadoes of gray and black on the shuffleboard courts, rotating shades of gray were taking over the pavement. My blood started pumping, my face felt adrenalized and I couldn't wait a second more. I started sprinting towards my fellow NSR's yelling, "B-boys in the house."

Behind me in the parking lot I heard, "YO Phil!"

I looked back behind me, stopped dead in my tracks, and accidentally squealed like a pig, "Bruiser!" I swear my voice had never reached that high of an octave before and of course he busted my chops about it.

Bruiser and I walked the rest of the way together. He was strolling coolly with a roll of linoleum under one arm and a ghetto blaster playing, "The Message" in his other hand.

"How did you know it was me?" I asked Dan.

Bruiser told me, "I saw you scampering past me while I was waiting at the stoplight a couple of minutes ago. I thought that was you in that hospital getup. I could tell by the way you walk," he said with a smirk.

"By the way I walk?" I asked.

"Yay dude," he laughed, "you've got this certain hop to your step, and I know your walk anywhere," he told me with a wink. "But anyway dude, I blew it off and didn't think anything when I saw you leaving the 24 hour pantry because you made such a big deal about wearing black and gray, so I said to myself: Self, that can't be Phil he's in green scrubs and not black and gray Bboy regalia, like he said he would be.

Then I remembered as I was eating my lunch in the car, just a few minutes ago, that you said you were going to visit Bob in the hospital this morning. Then when I saw you run with that hop step in your bounce, it confirmed it for me 'that's my boy Swift!' I said to myself." Bruiser smiled with a big laugh coming from his lungs, and then he motioned to me with his eyes as if he wanted me to carry something.

Bruiser asked me, "You want to grab one?"

Which one do you want me to grab?" I asked.

Bruiser shrieked, "Grab One of THEEZ FART CHEEKS!" he said as he squeaked one out.

"Ha ha, you got me," I said.

Then Bruiser said, "For real though dude, grab this linoleum for me." I grabbed the linoleum and then Bruiser asked while grunting and wheezing, "Can you grab the other one?" he seemed so stressed out.

"The ghetto blaster?" I asked quietly.

Then Bruiser got this irritated look on his face, distressed tone in his voice, and said, "No grab the other one!"

"Grab the other one of what?" I asked frantically with equal distress. He really seemed to be buggin'.

Bruiser laughed, "The other one of THEEZ FART Cheeks! ... You're too easy," he said as he let one rip again.

"Ohh Shee-ott bee-otch! You looked so stressed dude, I was trying to help a brother out and here you are messing with me," I said.

"You're stressing on THEEZ farts cheeks yo," he said drolly.

We both laughed and started heading towards our fellow NSR's that were breakin' on the shuffle board courts. As they say, boys will be boys.

We were both bopping along to Melle Mel as it played through his ghetto blaster, while we both scanned through the crowd in delight. Other than us NSR's, it was cool to see that my boy, Witty Dee had actually showed up with Muffy. He never got into breakin' or anything; he just came to hang out. I was glad to see him there since I hadn't seen him all that much (except on the bus), ever since he had met Muffy and I started breakin'. It was almost weird to see him in his "Romeo" mood when he was with Muffy because he was usually in a taunting mood when he was on the bus.

While walking, I did a quick head count and saw that almost everyone from our new crew had already shown up. Even Chi Girl was there. She had told me that she was going to be late because of her gymnastics event but in fact she had beaten Dan and me there. "That's Brock Blazin' getting on down on the shuffle board court," I said to Dan as we walked.

"Yep, that is old boy," Dan said.

When Brock had finished his breakin' routine, Chi Girl had jumped into the cypher next with flips and aerial cartwheels with some twists, turns, and other shiznit that was a combo of breakin' and gymnastics moves that drew cheers from our crew members that were checking her out for the first time.

Not on purpose but because of the scrubs and surgeons mask, I snuck up on my fellow NSR's. Blazin' noticed my eyes first and asked with laughter,

"What's up with the hospital scrubs bro? I thought you said to wear Black and gray?"

The rest of the breakers that were near Blazin' had moved towards us, and I answered, "I just came from the hospital. I was visiting Boogie Bob our head spin specialist. He's in the cancer unit getting chemotherapy to battle blood cancer – they call it A.L.L. or Leukemia or some bull shee-ott like that, acute something or other, but these scrubs are a reminder that our fellow B-boy Bob is with us, since he can't make it in person," I said in a serious voice.

"Word," Blazin said.

"Heck yeah," Bruiser agreed.

"But look, I've got the black and gray rocking underneath," I said as I lifted my scrub shirt up and I showed everyone that I was in fact wearing black and gray. "If it's okay with y'all I'm going to wear my scrubs for the day, it makes me feel like Boogie Bob is with us … I know it sounds nuts, but cancer sucks! And somehow this helps."

"Heck yay boy, rock it," Kid Mojo said.

"Word," Dan Bruiser agreed.

"Yay man, cancer sucks," Slim Jim sympathized.

"To Bob," Chi Girl shouted.

"Hey nice nameplate Phil," Brock said about my "NSR" belt buckle that I had around my neck.

"Oh yeah bro, I'm sportin' this nameplate big time bro. This NSR belt buckle is a big deal for real," I said cocksure.

"Word," Blazin' said.

All of us breakers started high fiving each other, clapping, and whistling and some random breakin' broke out on the pavement at McCollumn Park. We were chatting and getting along famously with one another while checking out each other's break moves. After all, most of us had just met each other over the last month or so and many of us had never even met in person just yet. This was our first official assembly together as a crew.

Slim Jim approached me and said, "Nice necklace Phil" as he touched my NSR nameplate, putting it into his hand, while it was still around my neck. He looked at it with amusement as if it was made out diamonds.

"Heavy, sort of," Slim Jim said.

"Heaviest necklace I ever had," I agreed.

Chi Girl approached next and said, "Were you just walking down Main Street in Downers Grove about 30 minutes ago?" and before I could answer she swooped in for a hug.

The way she was smiling made me smile even bigger than she was, only she couldn't see it because I was still wearing the surgical mask, "Yep, that was me; I wore this getup all the way from the hospital to here. It made me feel like I brought Bob with me or something," I said sort of sadly, yet I was still smiling underneath the mask.

Chi Girl smiled, "That's cute; I can't wait to meet him!"

"Yeah for real, Bob was just telling me that he should be done with all of his chemo and radiation and bone marrow transplant crap within 3 weeks. He can't wait to meet all of you too," I said.

Miguel and Gio had finally bopped their way towards the rest of us, they were the last two to show up, but they were only seconds behind Dan and me.

They walked right by me at first, since they probably didn't know that it was I underneath the surgical mask. Gio set his boom box down next to Bruisers' and they both started chatting about their ghetto blasters. Bruisers' was a double tape deck with crazy large knobs and 4 super large speakers; his blaster box was the size of a television set.

Miguel and Gio's boom box had a single cassette deck with a microphone input, a dozen or more tiny speakers and multiple flashing lights; along with digital sound meters that had flashed to the beat; red, orange, and green danced to the kick drum. In addition, it had additional VU meters right above the cassette deck, which I'm sure was just for the sake of making the boom box look flashier.

Blazin' took it upon himself to unroll Bruisers' linoleum that I had set down. He told me that it was cool as heck that I had brought linoleum with, but then I told him it was Brusiers' which sparked Brock into this loud display of thanks and excitement as he unrolled the linoleum, "Dan the man Bruiser - sweet dude, sweet, awesome, you brought linoleum. Now we can break like rock stars." You'd have thought that Bruiser had just handed him a thousand bucks or something by the way he carried on to Dan about the linoleum.

"Yo Poppin' G, Wazup, I saw you guys bopping and grooving from across the park, sup my brother. What Izzz going on?" I said with swag.

"Oh? Phil, that's you, huh? I didn't recognize you with that stuff on," Miguel said.

"Is there a doctor in the house?" Gio (Poppin' G.) asked.

I told Gio (and Miguel, who was listening in) my story about why I was dressed in hospital garb and such and 2 tough said, "Right on" as he gave me the biggest smile you could ever imagine someone giving, but he showed no teeth as usual. He had cornered the market on closed mouth smiling.

Poppin' G. or Gio, whichever you prefer to call him, walked closer to me and quietly asked, "Who's the old man with the ghetto blaster?"

''That's no old man, that's Bruiser, he's only 17, don't let the beard fool ya. He's going to be our break crew manager," I said to both of them.

Poppin' G. got this look of disbelief in his eyes as he raised one eyebrow up and furrowed the other one down and then said, "Really? I was wondering if maybe he was your dad or something."

"Speaking of parents … Is your mom coming up here today?" I jokingly asked with a boys will be boys grin.

Poppin' G. playfully pushed me back and said, "Hey man, don't go hitting on my mom."

I smirked like the cat that had ate the canary and walked away. I started going around to all of the guys (and girl) and introduced everybody to everybody. First, I called over Chi Girl, "Hey Chi Girl, this is Gio a.k.a. Poppin G."

Gio then smirked as if he had eaten a canary of his own and said, "Hey nice to meet you sexy."

"Easy there pal, she's one of us guys; she's a Neighborhood Street Rocker," I said.

Giovanni just played it off and said, "I'm not doing anything, I was just saying, "hi!"

"You never call me sexy," I said sarcastically with a girly voice. Chi girl got a big old roar out of it and was smirking and enjoying our conversation.

Gio shrugged his shoulders some more so I just told Chi Girl, "Just watch out for this one Chi Girl, he's a player."

Gio responded, "Nah man, I'm a good boy."

Chi Girl stiffened her neck and said, "I have an older brother who has already given me the run down: he told me that guys will lie to girls so they can get what they want from them. They will tell you that they love you so they can get you to kiss them. They will even try to pressure you or make you feel stupid if you don't give them what they want. However, it's all good. I have already decided that I am going to remain celibate while I am in high school. I want to make something out of myself before I get all involved with some girl crazed, hormone ragin', teenaged boy that changes the course of my life forever." Then she looked at me and gave me a wink.

"Word Girl … Word! You are one smart chick, Chi Girl," I told her.

"It's okay Gio, I have seen the likes of you and I aint mad at ya," she said with another wink.

"Can't blame a guy for trying," Giovanni conceded.

"Can't blame a girl for being smart, knowing better, and waiting till she makes something out of herself either," she said while pointing her index finger at Poppin' G, while pressing her thumb onto her finger as if she just shot him. She even made a, "P-cheww" sound as she shot him. It was really cute.

"Where are your friends?" I asked her.

"They couldn't make it at the last minute," she said.

"I'm glad you're here though, come meet my boy Bruiser," I said.

Chi Girl and I walked over to Bruiser while Miguel, Gio, and Slim Jim followed along, "Sup Bruiser, I want you to meet Miguel, Gio and Chi Girl … you already met Slim Jim," I said.

Bruiser smoothly said, "Nice to meet you guys, now don't listen to this crazy cat Phil, he's trying to tell everyone that I'm your guys manager or something … If I can get you guys some battles, I will. If I can get you guys some talent show gigs, I will. If I can get you guys … and oh sorry, girl too … some sort of paying performance gigs, then I will. But I'm just here to hang out and have a good time watching you all break."

I cut Dan off, "Ohh okay, so you're going to do managerial duties but just don't call you a manager," I said sort of smart-ass-edly.

Bruiser replied with an equally as smart aleck tone, "Yay something like that Dr. Swift boy!"

After I had introduced everybody to Dan, everyone more or less knew each other's names by then. Over the next two or three hours, everybody mingled, busted out with his or her break moves, and had a rip roaring good time, to say the least.

I busted out with behind the back businessman or (handcuff windmills), just to show the crew how I had improved. Brock Blazin' was impressed too; he hadn't seen me break all that much since the Big Burger contest since he was always busy with choir practice, drama club, and whatnot, and I had come a long way since then.

"You're getting good bro," Brock said.

"Phil K Swift is getting swift," Kid Mojo said.

After Kid Mojo handed out his compliment to me, he then whirl winded down to the ground and busted out with atomic flares. Dan Bruiser who was a few feet away from me raised his eyebrows in amazement and said, "Now dude! That is straight up strilla for rilla ... sah-weet!"

Slim Jim took center stage next. He started with his signature foot gliding; walking on air movements that seemed to defy gravity. It almost looked like he was being held up in the air like a marionette as he "walked on air." His B-boy movements were basically moonwalks and waving that had been taken to the next level. He also busted out with boogaloo style of poppin', tickin', and lockin' flows that had ended with crazy ice contorting theatrics –something you'd expect to see from a circus performer; he even made his belly wave but just to joke around. Slim Jim was our pop lockin', foot gliding, and waving moonwalker specialist.

After he finished his routine, I started to get this chill down my spine. I felt moved to jump into the action again. I started walking around in a viscous circle while nodding my head all cockily with a playful smile. I began to skip, rock, and bop around a bit while staring at whoever's eyes were available. Then I spun on one foot as if I was a ballet dancer, into a freeze position as if I was a statue for a second or two, then I busted out into top rock, to down rock then footwork swipes.

I remembered Bob while I was rockin' it. I'm not saying that anything paranormal was going on, but without thought, I felt compelled to dive to the ground into tap head spins; almost as if someone was whispering it to me, but no one was.

I tapped around into 8 or 9 revolutions with my legs spread in a "V" shape that sort of slowed me down but it helped keep my balance. All of the other times I had practiced my head spins at home in my basement I was only able to pull off about 3 head spins at the most. And I am telling you, my mind could really wander when I was breakin', because in that moment, I thought about Bob, the scrubs, my new crewmates, and how that had been my best head spin routine ever. It was amazing what sorts of things I would think about while I was actually breakin'.

I walked off the linoleum like a cocksure cat, over towards the boom boxes, which were now blaring Miguel and Gios cassette of some mix they had recorded from the famous, "WMIX FM." I was greeted by Bruiser who said, "I didn't know you could do that B!"

I quietly told him, "Neither did I my man." He was talking about my head spins.

Dan randomly said, "It's cool that we've got a chick in our crew."

"Yep, she's one of us ... a Neighborhood Street Rocker, I said. I was glad to see that all of the boys were treating her like one of us too; you know how boys can be (except for Gio, who was still giving her the eyes and all.)

Next, Miguel 2 tough pounced into the ring, "Now that's the Shee-ott, Bee-otch," I yelled to Miguel as he twisted around.

I was very glad to have met Miguel, to be honest with you; he had really sped up my breakin' skills a whole bunch by showing me windmills that first night I had met him at Suburbanite Rink.

Miguel exited the limelight after he did reverse windmills and started top rockin' by himself over by the drinking fountain, where a couple of cute chicks were standing nearby giving him the googly eyes. He had the kind of looks that made girls give him the googly eyes all of the time. When he was born and God was passing out good looks, he must have gotten in line ten times. Lucky son of gun.

Poppin G. then took his turn on the linoleum with a 1990 routine, which is a one handed handstand where you are spinning around in 360 circles on one hand while the rest of your body is reaching towards the sky. Gio must have spun around 6 revolutions in a row before gravity took over. He abruptly exited the linoleum and said to me, "I'd have done more, but out of the corner of my eye I saw mi hermano talking to some chicas at the fountain, so I'm going to go over there and help him out," he said like the ladies man that he thought he was while adjusting his pants.

"I don't think your brother really needs any help my brudda," I said playfully. But Giovanni just smiled and walked towards them anyway.

As he walked over, I fixed my eyes in their direction, I could see the girls were in fact, "looking pretty fine from afar," I had said to Dan as Gio walked away. But I also told Dan, "But what do I know? Almost all girls look good to me from far away, I swear. One time I saw a girl sitting on a bus stop bench and I was thinking about how cute her legs were looking. So I started making my way over to her to get a closer look and when I got there, I realized that her hot tan legs were really just brown paper shopping bags from a grocery store that she had sitting on the ground in front of her. – and hot? She was not! ... But those chicks Miguel is talking to, really do look fine from here," I repeated to Dan, which made him practically pee his pants from laughter.

When he finally calmed down he said, "Yo dude, those are actually elderly ladies with walking canes and shopping bags, maybe its Miguels grandma?" Dans tone and facial expressions were so sincere; I bought every word of it.

"Really," I said in a high pitched, red embarrassment of a screech, that started him laughing again – and I knew I had been busted; my chops had been busted by the master.

"No, dude – I'm just messing with you, they actually do look like some pretty fine chicks," he said.

"Right on brizzo. I'm going to go hit that break circle again," I said while walking away.

Anyway, by the end of the afternoon I could tell that everybody had gotten along famously and incredibly. In fact, we all had made plans to get together again at Suburbanite roller rink on Friday. The word was that the rink was having a skate session from 8 to 1030pm and then they were going to stop the skating and have a dance party out on the rink floor from 1030pm till midnight.

Kid Mojo put it this way, "Breakin' is becoming so big that they want to make room for us breakers to show up at the rink."

"House music is starting to spread like wild fire too," Dan Bruiser added.

Everybody agreed and planned to meet at the rink on the following weekend.

Chi girl left first because she saw her moms' car in the parking lot waiting for her. She told everybody good bye and vowed to see us next week at the rink. When she said bye to Gio she playfully yelled, "Watch it buddy or I'll kick your butt."

Oh yeah, by the way, Gio and 2 tough more or less struck out with those two girls by the drinking fountain. Gio explained, "One of them turned out to be 25 years old and the other one was her mom who was probably around 45 ..."

2 tough chimed in, "The mom wouldn't reveal her age and the daughter didn't want to date a younger guy," Miguel told us with his usual coy smile.

"You were sure over there for a long time, considering you all gots nada," Bruiser said.

"The milfy was kind of into it … if milfy would have been by herself, I'd have closed the deal," Gio said cocksure.

All of us NSR's barked out some, "Yeah rights" and "you wish" and crap like that. But Gio just kept bragging about his "Don Jaun" abilities or how he's a "real Romeo" or some crap like that for a little while. After a stretch of Gio telling us about all of his past "girlfriends," in his attempt to prove he was a real life "Romeo," we all started to wind down a bit as the sun sank into the land.

Blazin' helped Bruiser roll up the linoleum and he told him again how his linoleum was the shiznit. And I was thinking: it's just friggin' linoleum. Then Brock was all kissing his ice about how great his boom box was and about how fresh his music was and on and on he went. We were all saying our "peace outs" and "au revoirs" and "catch you on the flip flops" and such as the bright had turned towards twilight. I made sure to tell everybody to bring 20 bucks with them on Friday, so I could order NSR nameplate belt buckles for everyone. By the way, everybody wanted one like mad, mad I tell ya.

As I looked through the swings by the tennis courts I saw Witty Dee and Muffy making out like a bunch of horn dogs. For a split second, I almost forgot he was even at the park. I did sort of remember that he was sitting there because I looked over there a couple of times while we were all breakin' and chatting, and stuff. However, he was always mashing and rapping with his chick when I saw him, so I never bothered going over by them. It would be like walking into someone's bathroom when you knew they were dumping. I know it was outside in a public place and everything but they were really smooching like monkeys. So I left them alone.

I yelled in their direction as we were leaving, "P.D.A. in the freakin' hizouse." But they only ignored me. Like I said, they were really going at it.

The funny thing about it all was that I had invited Witty to the park because we hadn't hung out in a while on account that I had been so consumed with breakin' and he had been so consumed with his gal pal and I figured that we'd be able to spend some time together. But we both ended up doing the same things that we had both been doing for the last couple of months; hanging out with our loves: Witty with Muffy and me with breakin'.

Blazin' and I helped Bruiser bring his ghetto blaster and linoleum back to his car. The three of us were all trippin' off the incredible breakin' that we had seen and were a part of that day. I mean, it was quite obvious by everyone's smiles and cheering that we were all very excited about our newly assembled break crew.

When we made it to Bruisers' car I started to take off my hospital scrubs when Bruiser whispered, "Is Bob doing okay for real or what?"

I told Bruiser and Blazin' who were listening closely, "He seems to be doing okay but I'm not sure; he definitely seems to be in high spirits and Bob said that he would be breakin' with us within 3 weeks - once he was done with all of his chemo treatments and such – so I guess so," I said.

After we got done loading the linoleum, Bruiser slammed the trunk down and urgently asked Blazin', "Hurry quick – Can you hold these?"

Blazin' quickly scampered over by Bruiser with an equally as urgent look on his face and asked, "Hold what?"

Bruiser blinked his eyes quickly and licked his lips, and as he was about to say it, I saw it coming, so I joined in; and we both simultaneously said, "THEEZ fart cheeks!" with a little extra oomph and taunt in our tones.

Blazin' got this stink face for a quick second but then he smiled and said, "Okay you got me, you got me, I'm holding your farts, I get it, I get it – you burned me – ha ha ha."

Bruiser wasn't about to let him off that easy, so he taunted a little more, "Oh yeah dude, you're holding 'em. You're holding 'em like they're going out of style."

We all high fived each other and then Blazin' started his trek across the parking lot to his house which was not even a hop skip and a jump from

McCollum; if you spit into the wind at McCollum Park, Blazin' would have had to wash the windows on his house.

"Later Brock," I yelled.

"See ya Mr. Blazin'," Dan said.

"Later guys," he yelled back.

"Hop in B," Bruiser spouted to me as he pushed the cassette into the deck; the music came on, and then he revved his engine. I was walking distance from McCollum but I hopped in and threw my hospital garb into the back seat of his car anyway. "Al Naa Fyisch" by Hashim was jamming his deck and we both listened as the DJ was busting out with a scratch on his mix tape, "Chit, chit, chit, chit, chit, chit chewwwww."

Then Bruiser turned down the cassette deck a bit, just enough so I could hear him better, yet he still had to shout over the music. He asked me, "Are you feeling alright about your friend Bob?"

"I'm really glad I went to go visit with him today, it made me feel better, you know? Some of the things he had told me over the phone the past week or so, really made me a little nervous for him. But seeing him alive, and well, and breakin', really put my mind at ease – if you know what I mean bro," I said sort of choked up on the verge of crying, but choked up and crying in a happy way.

"You saw him breakin' at the hospital?" Bruiser said with eye brows raised in surprise. This made me think about Bob's brow-less brows.

I told Bruiser about how we were both breakin' in the hospitals "family room" and how we got scolded by Nurse Marvin, which really surprised Bruiser. He was mainly tripping off the idea that he had unhooked his tubes, lines, and all, and then was able to bust out with head spins. I was shocked too, to be honest with you. I mean, the more I thought about it; Boogie Bob was a breaker to the bone! I already knew that, but now there was even less doubt in my mind, and there was never any doubt.

As I sat in Bruiser's car I realized what had made me think strange and scared thoughts about Bob and what had made me feel almost paralyzed into not wanting to take off my scrubs today. I must have blocked it out of my memory until now. In fact, I hadn't told you or anybody yet. But I decided to tell Dan about it on the quick ride home to my crib. "Well, Dan the man, the one thing that really freaked me out about my visit at the hospital today was when I accidentally overheard a phone conversation that Boogie Bob's doctor was having with another person over the phone while I was about to exit the cancer unit.

As I was slowly walking past the doc's office I heard him say in a serious doctor's voice, "Considering Robert Charles didn't even make it a year without a relapse, I must be honest with you - that isn't a good sign. We can try another bone marrow transplant, Mrs. Charles, but Bob's A.L.,L is extra tough this time around. We may want to consider hospice."

Then I walked away and I exited the cancer unit. Now I didn't know exactly what all of that meant but I knew he didn't say: Hey Mrs. Charles, Bob is doing great – I hope you are sacking away the dough for his college tuition." That last comment had inspired a half hearted, sort of queasy chuckle from the both of us.

Bruiser responded, "I'll say a prayer for Bob." And that was about it. He was sort of quiet after that. But I got it. It's hard to say something after that.

We arrived at my crib and I asked Bruiser, "Yo brother, my parents ordered a pizza for dinner, we have plenty extra; do you want some pizza?"

Bruiser replied, "Ahh straight up, yay I'll take some pizza."

"A Pizza THEEZ fart cheeks," I said with a boyish smile.

Bruiser chuckled and said, "Alright there B, you got me back, it took you forever, but you finally got me back."

As I was exiting the 'Stang I asked Bruiser, "How'd they taste man, how'd they taste? Thanks for the ride Bro, I'll catch ya when I catch ya."

"Alright B-Boy, I'll get back atchya, peace out," he said as he was slowly reversing out of my driveway while sticking his head through his open window, smashing his black Kangol hat in the window frame of his door, and laughing loudly to himself and muttering, "One minute you're talking about cancer and the next minute you're talking about THEEZ fart cheeks."

Chapter 12

Opposites Attract

It seemed like Monday mornings were the hardest of all of the mornings to wake up, if you know what I mean. I'm telling you this because I remembered having wet hair on the bus on the following Monday morning, the weekend after I had seen Bob at the hospital and the rest of us NSR's at McCollum.

I overheard a couple of football players on the back of the bus talking about some weirdo that was walking down Main Street on Saturday wearing a Halloween costume. I suppose I could have walked to the back of the bus and tried to explain to those guys that a guy our age was sitting in a hospital room, pumping his body full of poisons and hoping to kill his cancerous leukemia cells. Then hoping that the good cells could take over once the process was done - which was how Bob had explained it to me. But I really didn't think that those dudes would have seen things my way, no matter what I would have said. So I kept my mouth shut. I really didn't need to hear myself talk; at least not about that kind of thing.

I got off the bus and headed straight to the hip hop hallway but nobody was there that day. That sort of sucked to be honest with you. I couldn't wait to trip off my weekend to all of the break boys at my school. But that's Monday mornings for ya. In addition, I was really hoping to run into Devon that morning or find someone who knew what had happened to him that night of the school dance. Maybe I was just hoping to gloat, but I really did wonder what had happened to him.

Finally by lunch time I saw Devon sitting at the "black table," where I sometimes sat on occasion, when Fred was sitting with his soccer buddies or Gloria and Gary were in one of their moods to talk about their "real significant others." They got all private when they talked about their love life.

I grabbed my Fried Chicken, mashed potatoes, and green beans through the lunch line and headed over towards Devon. This dude Darnell had flagged me down to come over and sit with Devon and him - even though that was already my plan, anyway. I really wanted to talk to Devon.

Darnell said, "Sit right here in between Devon and me and make us into an Oreo!"

I wasted no time and asked Devon, "What happened to you on Wednesday night? I thought we were going to have a break battle my man?"

Devon went into this big story, "My mom works 2 jobs and by the time she got home from work it was too late for her to take me to the dance and all." Devon shook his head in a sort of sadness and added, "I heard you were busting out with some nutcrackers at the dance?"

I nodded like a tough guy.

Devon continued, "Dog gone it, man, I heard you threw 'em down pretty good too, I've gotta get me some of those goin' for real."

It was like freakin' night and day, from the last time I had talked to him. There was no more battle talk or chicken this or that coming from Devon's mouth whatsoever about how he could out break me. I suppose I could have gotten all tough guy with him, but I kept quiet, just the same. I already knew that I could out break him. Plus, we were friends too.

However, I did keep smiling smugly and nodding like a cocksure punk and I think he knew it too. I could tell by the sideways glances that he had given me once in a while that he knew I was quietly gloating. But I kept on doing it anyway. It almost felt as good as shooting my mouth off to be honest with you. Sometimes silence is the best thing you can say.

The rest of the table went back in line once the smell of fresh baked chocolate chip cookies had yelled at them. You could smell them all throughout the cafeteria while they baked in the oven, practically every day at that time. Devon and I remained at the table, as we always did. We were both slow eaters. I told him, "My crew, the Neighborhood Street Rockers and I are going up to Suburbanite Rink on Friday.

Then on Saturday, there's this other rink that some of the cats in my crew (Miguel and Giovanni) just told me about last night on the phone, it's called, Chicagoland Rink but really it's in the suburbs, but I guess a lot of people from the burbs and Chicago hang out there. It is supposed to be swarming with B-Boys, B-Girls, and people that listen to the mixes; you know, hip cats like us," I told him, "Our crew is trying to drum up a battle and supposedly it's 'the place to be' for that sort of thing. Either way we are going up there to get down with some breakin'. If you want to come up there, you can," I said without gloating, as to make a truce.

Devon told me that he already had plans and such. So I left it alone. But I really felt like calling him a chicken, just for the fun of it, not even in the tough guy way that he had called me one, but I left it alone. I wasn't sure if he would have found it funny or not.

After lunch period I passed by Donnie Blacklung and Seth Coughman's locker, when they spotted me, Coughman said in a wacky voice, "Hey Phil are you going to do some break dancing?"

He was always asking me that whenever he saw me and then he'd laugh, but come to think of it, he was always laughing about something. I think it had something to do with that wacky tobacky that he messed with. (You won't catch me doing that crap.)

Then, while Coughman was practically inside of his opened locker, I watched him secretly but not so secretly pull a clear plastic bag out of the inside pocket of his jean jacket; inside the bag was a small bottle with gold-ish liquid, some of the liquid had leaked out of the bottle and into the bag. Seth put the bag to his mouth and sucked the excess liquid off of the bag. I naively asked him, "What is that?"

Seth spelled, "B – O – Z."

"What's Boz?" I asked, sort of loudly.

Then in a yelling whisper voice Seth said, "Booze dude!"

"Ohh Booze," I said while whispering back to him. Then I thought about how fitting it was that someone bringing booze to school in the middle of the day would misspell the word. I hate mispelt words.

Donnie Blacklung leaned over to me and asked with a big smile, "Hey Phil did you bring your asthma inhaler with you to school today?" I could tell by his tone that he was more or less busting my chops, but I didn't care. You see, he asked me that almost every day, ever since I had told those guys that I wouldn't smoke with them. He was forever busting my chops about it. I knew he was mocking me and he had probably figured that it was some sort of a phony excuse that I had given him to not smoke, but I didn't mind. He was still my friend. Sometimes you've got to take a little razzing and smile about it.

"Yep, I've got my asthma inhaler with me," I said with a smile.

"Cool man, then we can walk over to the wreck today after school and Seth and I can smoke you out, your inhaler will save you," he said to mess with me.

I stiffened my neck and said, "No way dude that crap tastes like ice; butt ice! I don't want to put ice in my mouth Duuude!"

Seth jumped in and said, "Nah man, izzz all gooood, and it tastes sweet."

I raised my voice, muscled my eyebrows, and said, "Dude do you like the taste of butt farts? You want to put butt in your mouth DUDE?" I smirked and continued my good natured taunting, which was making them laugh too, "You two are going to share the taste of butt together – how sweet." The more I zinged 'em the more they just kept laughing like the wacky smokers that they were.

That's what I liked about those guys too. They could dish it out, but they could also take it. I patted them both on their backs, smiled, and said, "Enjoy smoking that butt - later," while I walked away. They usually had some sort of come-back for me, but this time, all they could muster was wacky laughter.

As I was walking away though, Donnie yelled out, "Go do some break dancing dude!" I could hear them both laughing at me in those high pitched smokers cough cackles that they had always had.

Even though, they had just said it to mock me, I did it anyway. The hallway was clear; I had room, we were in one of the wider hallways, so I obliged them. I dove into 7 or 8 windmills into a backspin and then I sprung to my feet and walked away like one bad brother. I heard Blacklung laugh and say, "Whoa dude that was cool!"

I yelled back, "That's how I get my high!"

The rest of the school week Donnie and Seth kept calling me, "Break dancing Phil" and I would remind them, every time, that I was Phil K Swift the Funky Groove King." It had become our thing.

Friday after school I was sitting on the bus by myself because Witty Dee had skipped the bus and walked over to his girlfriend Muffy's house. I usually sat with him on the way home, so for a change, my bus ride home was quiet.

On the way home while looking out of the bus window, I spotted this very nerdy looking guy on the corner, just about to enter the crosswalk. He was holding hands with this hot chick that was without a doubt, way out of his league. The dude had no fashion sense, heck he was even sort of ugly – if you asked me, and he had this weird angle to his face. He had his arm around the girl, and she really seemed to be interested in him too, she even leaned in and kissed him a couple of times while they waited for the "walk" signal. Talk about opposites attracting.

This made me start to look around the bus to see if there were any other "ugly and cute" or just straight up "opposite couples" on our bus. Check this shiznit out, I noticed 2 other couples that sort of fit into that "opposites attract" category. They were the couples that had been together for most of the school year and everybody knew about them. You know the type - It's a guy and a girl; you see them together in between every class period in the hallways at school, holding hands, giving each other googly eyes and kissy faces – and they were always together; being all lovey-dovey – enough to make you puke puddles all over the place.

As I took a closer look at these "items" that were on my bus that day, I realized something. What started to stand out to me was that the girls in those couples were pretty, cute, nice looking, and all of that shiznit, BUT THE GUYS in those couples were straight up goofy looking freaks; freaks of nature – I'm not kidding you. You could tell that when the girls in those "opposite couples" got older that they would get prettier. However, the guys in those "opposite couples" were going to remain nerdy and ugly looking dudes.

Then it occurred to me that I have seen some older "opposites attract couples" about town or wherever – and they were married. For example, I know there is one of these hot chick -ugly guy couples at my church. And another that lived across the way from us when I was a kid. And another ugly dude-hot chick couple that owned a coffee shop together, but the point is: they are out there.

While I sat on the bus alone, I wondered: why is that hot older girl with that ugly, dumpy, geeky looking guy? – And I'm not talking about the geeky looking dudes that are loaded with cash! That's a no brainer, I'm talking about the hot chick with the ugly dude and the dude is driving in a beater car. Then it hit me, I think I had figured it out. They had probably met in high school before "the hottie" was old enough to realize that she was going to be a hottie and before said hottie was old enough to realize that her high school boyfriend was going to grow up to be a gross looking dork.

Well anyway, that's what I thought about on the bus ride home to my crib while checking out these hot chicks with their dorky boyfriends. Get the hottie when you're young, before she gets old enough to realize you're really an ugly geek is the moral to that story. So if you're pretty sure you're going to look gross as heck when you're older, then hurry up and get one now.

If you don't get your girlfriend while you're young, it's okay. The good news is that for every gross looking guy out there, there is an equally as gross looking girl out there too. So in the worst case you will get yourself an equally as gross looking boyfriend or girlfriend - you have that to look forward to if you look gross. Yep, that's what I'm here to do; make you feel better – You're welcome!

Chapter 13

Breakin' at Suburbanite Rink

I was excited to return to my old haunt: Suburbanite Roller Rink. I hadn't been there since I had first met Miguel 2 tough and Poppin' Giovanni and had caught my first glimpse of breakin' in real life. It felt like so many moons ago upon my return to the rink, but really it had only been a couple of months.

All of us NSR's were going up there that night and it was going to be a stone gas! I got to the rink early as usual – of course, but this time, I didn't even bring my skates, which felt strange; I even felt a little naked not having roller skates in my hands. I must have gone to Suburbanite roller rink 1000 times and every time I had skated from open to close. Now I was entering the rink as a breaker. I was there to break, dance, and just straight up rock it. And gawk chicks of course.

Even though breakin' had taken away my interest from skating, I still liked watching everyone skate. I sat down on the bench for a bit and watched some of the skaters whizz by for old time sake. Some of them were speed skating, some of them were spaghetti leggin', and some of the dudes were trying to sweet talk the girls, because that's what the rink was; it was a gossip pool and place to meet somebody first and a roller skating center second. It made me feel good for some reason to see that skating was still alive and well, even though I didn't really care about it anymore.

I was chill-axin' and waxin' nostalgic and just waiting for my crew to arrive when it occurred to me, now that I was a straight up B-Boy I no longer cared about fitting into the skate rinks "in crowd." I was feeling tough in my own right. And not the tough guy kind of tough, but Tall B-Boy, all Chicago tough. I was feeling like I was 20 feet tall while I was sitting down in the shadowy rink benches watching these skaters whizz by. I knew they couldn't rock the breakin' floor like me and that made me feel cool. My NSR crew and I were our own, "In crowd." Not intentionally or anything either, we were just cool, without even trying and that's just the way it was.

As I was sitting on the bench maxxin' out and scoping out the scene, a slow song changed the mood of the grooving rink floor. In a deep low and slow cool voice, the rink DJ said, "Couples skate only, that's right couples skate only," to my surprise Witty Dee and Muffy took the floor. I didn't even know Witty was going to be up there that night – that's how out of touch we had become, yet we were still "buds."

Witty Dee was skating backwards and Muffy was holding his hips as they skated around lovey-dovey and smiling at each other to, "Faithfully" by Journey. I yelled out, "Witty Dee" at the top of my lungs but he didn't see me. He kind of looked around a bit, but gave up looking after a while.

After they were out of my line of sight, a weirdo was skating by with his couples skating partner. He was probably about 19 years old, sporting a fro; he was a white boy sporting the fro. It was 1984 and somebody forgot to tell him that froes for white boys had died out in the 70's, the day they were born they had died out; froes for white boys were in and of themselves: stillborns. Some white boys could rock the froes fow show like, "Greg from the Brady Bunch" and such, but most white dudes, just couldn't rock it.

Anyway, this weird looking dude with raggedy facial hair somehow managed to have a girlfriend. (One of those "opposite attracting couples" I had told you about earlier.) So this 6 foot something, jean overall wearing, perverted smiling guy was skating backwards with his "girl" who appeared to be about my age; 14 or 15.While they were couples skating, this dude was holding her shirt by the neckline. She was wearing a regular kind of t-shirt, nothing too low cut or anything, but the weirdo was grasping her shirt at the collar and neckline with his fingertips and pulling it a few inches away from her body to give him a bird's eye view right down her shirt. Really creepy, really perverted. – she looked shy. He made me want to vomit Olympic sized swimming pools filled with puke; he was that creepy. He was so creepy, I felt molested and I was only the innocent bystander.

The girl was "girl next door" cute and she seemed so passive about it all. It really felt funny - watching this freak frolic his female's fabrics. It felt funny as heck to be honest with you. Hey, I can be a rubberneck like the next guy but this dude really made the whole thing look cheap.

I yelled out randomly, "Lose the zero and find a hero," but I'm not sure either one of them heard me. I just hope that if she didn't want him doing all that staring at her boobs thing, that she would find a way to get away from him and then tell someone, like her friend or her mom or something. I hated to see this girl get taken advantage of.

Witty Dee and Muffy finally spotted me and waved as they did another couples skate lap around. I stood up immediately after they had passed me because I had simultaneously noticed a couple of dudes walking with a bop-hop to their step that told me: they owned the floor that they were walking on.

I shouted out as I exited the shadows of gawking, "NSR in the hiz-ouse" but none of them really heard me. A bunch of them had walked in at the same time: Blazin', Kid Mojo, Jet Drinkwater, and then came Slim Jim, who was actually the first one I had noticed, even though he walked in 4th. He was just that Big and tall, that's all.

"Sup y'all?" I said to the bunch.

Blazin' came running up to me, "Sappenin' Swift my man? Suppp???" Blazin' said in his usual pumped up way. He said everything in an excited way in case you haven't figured that out yet.

I energetically shook his hand and said, "What took you guys so long?"

"We were all waiting outside for everyone to show up. I kept trying to get everyone inside but nobody wanted to come in, everyone wanted to hang outside," he said. He had said it in a way that I could tell that he had probably bugged everyone to death about going inside the whole time they were outside.

I told Blazin', "Witty Dee's here with his chick … and Chi girl will probably be up here later."

"Witty's here, awww, cool man, I haven't seen that mug in a minute," then Blazin' made a "W" shape with his lips and said, "Cool is the rule – We are all Chicago Bro … Tall Chicago, NSR is here." He had said it like a millionaire, so I had to high five him.

Then he sort of complained, "…They all wanted to walk in at the same time and make some 'big appearance'," he said mockingly, "so we hung out outside like a bunch of idiots. It took me forever to get them to come in," he said with this distressed look on his face.

Kid Mojo broke into Brocks and my conversation with a tough Chicago, crossed arms pose while nodding with a playful smug smile, "We'll mess anybody up," Mojo said playfully for no particular reason.

Then Slim Jim shook my hand and started Poppin' as the slow jams had ended. Couples skate ended and, "Give it to me baby" was thumping through the system.

I reached into my backpack and started approaching each Neighborhood Street Rocker one by one to pass out their NSR nameplates, which had just come in the mail that day. I had used my own dough to buy them in advance and I hoped they had all brought money with them to pay me back but you know how that will go. People hardly ever pay you back but I wasn't too worried about it.

I went to Jet Drinkwater first and put the "NSR" belt buckle necklace around his neck and said, "NSR is in da house … you're sportin' it now."

"Right on Swift, now I am sportin' it!" Jet said.

Once everyone had seen that I was passing them out, everyone in our crew started waving me over but Jim just couldn't wait.

Slim Jim came up to me and randomly said, "Sup Brizzo for shizzow my nizzo, where's my bling? I want to be king! Do you want to hear me sing?"

"I would rather go to Sing Sing," I said drolly. (That's a prison in New York)

"Fretty Punny; pretty funny, Sonny, now give me the honey," he said.

"Not until you give me the money Mr. Funny," I said with a smile. I wasn't really worried about the dough. I just felt like keeping the rhyme goin' – you know? Joe Blow, go suck your toe, all the way to mexico. Anyway – So -

He then leaned down and I donned him with his big ice gaudy NSR necklace that had made us all one. Slim Jim's face lit up like a bonfire, he couldn't stop staring and grabbing his new "NSR" belt buckle that was now draped around his neck. "I am all Chicago now boyeee," Slim Jim said cheerfully.

In fact, as I scanned all of my crew mates I could see that everyone was touching, looking at, or talking about their new necklace. We were now ONE as the NSR crew.

"AEIOU" by John Rocca started jamming through the speakers, Chi Girl had told me last week that it was her favorite song, so it made me think of her. I began asking some of the boys if they had seen her outside of the rink before they had come in. But no one had seen her yet. But somehow that got Brock back into his big spiel about how long they had to wait outside before they came in. And how it took him forever to convince everyone to go inside and blah blah blase.

"You're always in a big hurry to go somewhere," I told him, which made him laugh and walk away.

There was still another 10 minutes left on the skate session, and after that, they were going to open up the hardwood rink floor to us breakers and dancers and whoever. Meanwhile, Kid Mojo was foot workin and swipin' on the carpeted outskirts of the rink in the very spot where I had first met Miguel and Gio a few months before.

Every time I looked at Slim Jim, he was poppin', moonwalking, and staring at his new nameplate.

Blazin' was chattin' with Witty Dee while Muffy had skated off with her "in crowd" friends.

Jet Drinkwater and Too tough were up rockin' against each other in a ferocious dance battle. 2 tough must have just walked in too, since I didn't even realize he had shown up yet, so I made my way over to him. "Sup my brotha, Mr. Too tough? ... Here is your bling," I said.

"Thanks Mr. Swift, now I'm looking straight up sweet mi hermano," Miguel Too tough said just before he dove into windmills. It wasn't until about his fifth windmill that his necklace had flown off him, but I picked it up and handed it to him after he was done.

I saw a girl with very blonde hair that almost made her look brow-less; she was that blonde. But that only made me think about Bob. I thought for a moment and wished in a happy way that it would have been cool if Boogie Bob could have been with us that night. He would have dug all of the excitement in the air for shizzow. But before I could get too sentimental about it, in came Chi Girl. She came with a couple of her girlfriends; one on each arm; they had strolled in like best buddies. They were casually struttin' their stuff, looking from side to side, yet they seemed to only be interested in each other's company, not in a stuck up way, they were just chillin' was all. I don't think they had spotted any of us, since we had moved away from the entrance a bit in anticipation of the rink floor opening up to we breakers and dancers.

Chi Girl was walking in the middle of the threesome and it was obvious that every single guy in the rink was checking those three out. I'm not even kidding you; half of the guys in the joint had dropped their jaws. Even the girls were throwing jealous glaring scowls at them; perhaps it was no exaggeration to say that every eye in the rink had been on them at one point or another. What I remembered liking the most about it was that they were a part of our crowd; the NSR crew. I was no longer on the outside looking in. I was in; in like Flynn.

They looked as if they had all just came from their gymnastics class because they were all wearing blue and white tight body suits under their just unzipped and opened winter coats. I had never seen Chi Girl look that way before, with her hair done all cute and her smiley face and all. She usually had this serious looking face when I had seen her those two other times.

The threesome walked up to me first, Chi Girl hugged me and said, "Hey."

"What izzz doing girl?" I said as I hugged her. Our bodies made an upside down "V" shape. It was a hug that was opposite to Diana Woodgrows hug, (you know, the girl that had knocked my books out of my hand.) Anyway Chi Girls and Diana's hugs were completely opposite and that's all I'm going to say about that.

One of Chi Girls friends was sporting pig tails and a sweaty face that I guessed was due to their gymnastic practice. She just stood by Chi Girls side and smiled with shyness, practically looking at nobody, while Chi Girls other friend that was sporting a pony tail, looked around as if she knew how hot she was. She had made it a point to catch everyone's eyes that night, just to let them know, that she knew, she was hot. That's the kind of eyes she had working that night.

I caught this one dudes eyes from the rinks "in crowd," looking at "our crowd" – well mainly Chi Girl and her buddies but I remembered thinking: how does it feel to be on the outside?

Let's just say, it felt good to have the hot chicks hanging out with us for a change.

Chi Girls' sweet smelling perfume drew me in and for whatever reason; I started to speak like an idiot. I reached into my backpack, pulled out her NSR nameplate, and then I motioned as if I was going to put it around her neck, which made her bow, towards me.

Then, here's where I sounded all crazy and such, I said, "Are you ready?" Which made her hunch over even more and then I placed the NSR necklace around her neck and said, "With this bling, I thee wed" and right when I said it, I wished I hadn't. I knew it sounded corny as all heck, but it was too late. I had already said it.

Chi Girl and her coy pig tailed buddy, whom was still standing next to her, laughed this corny ol oink snort of a laugh right through her nose. One of those laughs that made me wonder if she needed a tissue to clean her nose. But to be honest with you, this worked out perfectly. This made me feel better about the corny line that I had just used. When some hot girl starts snot snorting through her nose with laughter, it makes you feel better, if you know what I mean.

"Nice laugh Tabitha," Chi Girl said making fun of her, which made her turn red and look even shyer than before.

"I'm glad you and your friends could make it up here tonight. We are all here except Bob, of course."

Chi Girl smiled, "Yeah, I can't wait to meet him."

Chi's other friend with the "I know I'm hot eyes" was wrestling her tight coat off when she looked at me and said, "Hi, I'm Sabrina," and then she stared at me squarely which kind of made me nervous; the kind of nervous where I almost forgot to say hi back to her.

I thought to myself: don't say anything stupid, so I went with, "I'm Phil," which earned me a hug from Sabrina.

"I'm sorry, by the way, these are my friends Tabitha and Sabrina, we are on the same gymnastics team, and in fact we just came from class tonight," Chi Girl said.

"Yeah, I think I remember seeing your buddies that day of the Big Burger contest," I said.

"Yep they were there," she said as both of her friends nodded in agreement and smiled.

"You wear your hair like that to gymnastics class?" I asked curiously, since Chi Girls hair was all dolled up.

The three of them shyly laughed until Tabitha jumped in and said, "You should have seen us girls, combing our hair, spraying our hair, lip glossing like mad, and primping and everything in our compact mirrors in the dark back seat of her mom's car on the way here."

"You're all looking hot!" I said which I wished I hadn't said it like that, but I suppose I could have said worse. Since they all smiled and said thanks, I figured I must not have screwed up too much.

"Tabitha and Sabrina really wanted to come up here and watch us break, is that cool?" Chi Girl asked.

"Absolutely that's cool," I said in this Sauvé, cool cat, Rocky Balboa voice, and then I spoke without my filter again, "We Neighborhood Street Rockers could use some groupies, so I'm glad you came to watch us."

The three of them giggled like the school girls that they were when Blazin' finally swept into our conversation with his usual huge and cheesy grin. I was glad to see him. He joined us just in time too. I was one of those guys that definitely needed a wing man. I was running out of things to say to be honest with you. Cute Girls can really make me forget what to say, you know.

Blazin' started chatting to Chi Girl about her new NSR nameplate like it was a million dollar piece of jewelry, when she joked that she had just received a marriage proposal. But she winked at me, so I figured we were all good. Then just as I was going to flirt with Tabitha, which means I was probably going to say HI and then walk away. Slim Jim muscled his way into a conversation with her about how he liked her laugh, which he had heard over the rinks music, even though he had been ten feet away at the time. It turns out, she always snorted loudly as she laughed. Every time she laughed she sounded like an elephant was yelling out of her nose. She laughed about everything, even if it was just KIND of funny. I heard Jim tell her that he "liked her laugh" but I could tell that he was really busting on her, but I don't think she caught that. But they got along famously anyway.

Sabrina started a staring contest with me, which made me tell her out of nervousness that I felt like busting out with some breakin', "Watch this girl," I said with swag. I started top rockin' in a flirty sort of way as I looked at Sabrina's deep staring eyes. Now you see, If I was top Rockin' - I could stare any girl down, but if I was standing around doing nothing, I would get sort of nervous.

Once she broke eye contact; I began dancing, up rock battling, and top rockin' around, until I had her full attention again. Then, I kicked my legs into the air and landed into fast rotating windmills. I could hear random girls screaming, in girly-girl shrieks that had given me even more desire to keep on rotating my windmills around, which turned into nutcracker-windmills.

I heard in the background one of the guys from my crew yell, "Yeah boyee, wind 'em up, wind 'em up!"

Then another yelled, I think it was Slim Jim, "Uh oh, Swifty's getting it goin'!"

I sprung to my feet and as I gained my balance again, I heard murmurs of either Tabitha or Sabrina saying, "He was good."

And," That was cool."

And that really grew my swag, if I've really got to brag.

Just as my dizziness had worn off, Bruiser had entered the building. I saw him go through the rinks turnstiles as he handed the rink guard his ticket to get in. I spotted him from a mile away, which wasn't really like me; I was as blind as a bat sometimes. I didn't always trust my vision from that far away. But how many guys do you know that are a dead ringer for Jesus Christ himself, that also wear B-Boy regalia? I knew of one, so I Yelled out, "Yo Bruiser, sup my brother from a different mother?" he was still kind of far away, but I had yelled it pretty loud.

Bruiser had waited a few seconds to get closer to me, and then he said, "I'm just chill like my main man Phil who fits the bill for real …. Sup dude," he said while laughing loudly. Then he shook my hand and said, "Looks like everybody made it."

Then at the same time, we both said, "Except for Bob." It was as if Dan had read my mind.

I was out of breath from the breakin' I had just rocked, so I told Dan, "Give me a minute." I went over towards the bench where my backpack was, so I could get Dans' nameplate. Sabrina was busy talking to Tabitha but she stared me down the whole walk over, which was something I wasn't really all that used to, to be honest with you. I really sucked at picking up girls if I've got to tell you the truth, but I was starting to find out that being a b-boy and good at breakin' had its perks.

I handed Bruiser his NSR nameplate and he remarked, "Dude this is strilla sweet my nilla, thanks B!"

"Now you've got some straight up bling … now go do your thing," I said.

"How long did it take you to come up with that rhyme?" he asked.

"At least I didn't say to you, with this bling I thee wed," I said as I was still feeling strange about it.

"Who the heck did you say that to?" he asked as he scanned around the room until he blurted out in a roar, "You mean you straight up said that to Chi Girl? For strilla my nilla, straaaaight up?"

He couldn't stop laughing the more he had thought about it. You see, Dan was used to me saying crazy ice shee-ott and putting my foot in my mouth and stuff, so he really got a big old bang out of it. Once he stopped laughing he said, "Dude, don't go using your own pick up lines … just stick to the Tom and Jerry pick up lines that you're always messing around with, like that, 'Is you is or is you aint my baby,' stuff. At least maybe that way, you'll sound half way decent." Dan said just to mess with me.

Then he laughed some more and added, "Don't go off on your own, that doesn't do anybody any good … No, I mean it, the only way you are going to pick up any girls is if you stick to cartoon character pick up lines," he said with a stone face. Then he busted out with harder laughter just to throw salt into my wounds. He must have laughed for an hour but I really didn't care all that much.

I can totally laugh at myself most of the time. After all; I know I say corny ice shiznit.

Out of the blue, Bruiser remarked, "But dude, whatever you did say, you must have done something right because all 3 of those schmoe diddly okin' gals are scoping you out big time. They are scoping you like a dog scoping a bone," he said. (He was talking about Chi and her buddies.)

"Did you say I am bad to the bone?" I asked in jest.

"Easy there Romeo," he said.

Then Bruiser lowered his tone and got this serious look on his face, "I've got some news for you guys. Are you ready?"

"Yes," I said curiously with a hint of reluctance.

"No dude for real, are you ready?" he asked again with a brighter face.

I wiped the playful look off my face and said, "Wazup dude?"

"Two of my buddies happened to be chillin' in the lot outside this joint, they are both breakers, and I know them from school. I talked to them, just before I had come in here, and I told them that I might have some boys inside the rink that are looking to get into a break battle. And when they heard me say 'battle' they got all gruff and tough and excited. I know them from school, they're cool and everything but they get a little cocky and loud sometimes. Anyway B., they'll be in, in a few minutes to battle you all," he said.

"Do I know them? What are their names?" I asked half paying attention.

"The B-Boys I just told you about?" he asked, "Their names are Rockefeller and Speedy G. They'll be in soon to throw on down. So go tell all of the boys … and girl; there is going to be a battle tonight fow show!"

My jaw dropped to the floor, I think I may have even had an out of body experience to tell you the truth. My face felt flush and even though I was still standing upright, it felt like my body had collapsed to the ground. I asked Bruiser out of shock, even though I knew I had already heard him, "Did you say Rockefeller and Speedy G?"

"Yay dude," he said with a smug smile. Then he grinned bigger as he understood that I had practically just crapped my pants. "Sup B?" he asked with curiosity. (At that point, I had never told him about Lincoln Center.)

So, I told Bruiser the quick version about Blazin's and my experience at the Lincoln center that fall day after school when we had first met Rockefeller and Speedy G.

"His bark is louder than his bite, he's just here to break my man, he's cool," Dan reassured me.

"I guess I better start telling all of the NSR's that we've got a battle brewing," I said as I took a deep breath.

I walked over to Miguel Too tough and told him, "We are going to be battling some real bad to the bone B-Boys tonight named Rockefeller and Speedy G – so get ready – Bruiser hooked it up," I said like a coach. Then I asked Miguel where his bro was, since I usually saw them together.

He told me he was in the parking lot having a square and chatting up some chicks. I thought about telling him that smoking sucks, but I didn't. Miguel didn't smoke and Gio wasn't the sort to preach to, so I didn't plan on saying anything to him when he got in. Some people you just can't say that sort of thing to, unless you enjoy talking to yourself.

Miguel almost looked a little nervous though; "I thought Gio would have been in already," he said while he looked at the rinks turnstiles.

"Well, you said he's talking to girls … you know how that player rolls," I said to reassure him.

We both knew that at any given moment trouble could be brewing outside in the rinks parking lot; I must have seen a fight in the parking lot every other weekend.

As I was telling Miguel that we had a battle tonight, the rink DJ turned on the lights and announced that the skating session was over. All of us B-Boys knew what that meant; that meant that as soon as all of the skaters could get off the floor, we breakers and dancers could take over the rinks hard wood floor for the rest of the night. It was on: on like Donkey Kong; that was the plan like Pac Man.

Miguel flashed his magnetic smile as Poppin Gio came walking in, wearing a tough gray turtle-neck sweatshirt that had black cursive letters that read, "FANDANGO."

"Sup with this Fandango business?" I asked him.

Gio looked at me all serious and said, "Sup man, I go by the name of Fandango now."

I looked over at Miguel who shook his head in agreement yet smiling. I looked back to Gio and said, "Your name is Fandango? Where'd that come from? Poppin' Gio, I mean, Fandango."

"That's just my name now Mr. Phil K The funky groove king Swift …You got a problem with that?" he asked in an exaggerated Chicago accent that he didn't usually have.

"Can Fandango do the fandango?" I asked playfully with a smile as I started to up rock around him a bit, attempting to interest him into an up rock battle.

Fandango replied, "No but I can do the Tango while eating a mango," he said while widening his eyes because he finally noticed the threesome of chicks that were hanging with Blazin' and Kid Mojo. "What is going on with that? - Funky Groove king Swift," he said with hormone filled eyes as he peered at the girls.

Like a big older protective brother or an old man guarding his lawn, I said, "That's Chi Girl and her buddies … grubby mitts off!"

"I didn't even recognize her," he said.

Fandango did a double take of the girls, and then leapt into the air in flip-like fashion, ultimately landing onto the ground into 1990's. A few cheers from our crew and random rink regulars filled our ears as the artist formerly known as Poppin' Gio ended his routine.

He had landed on his feet with his legs spread wide. As he was closing his legs at the same time; like a pair of scissors, I said, "Nice bro, Nice 1990's … on carpet, without anything in your hands to make 'em slippery. NICE!" I was truly amazed, since I had tried it before on that very same rink carpet where I had torn my palm up with red hot rug burn when I had tried it bare handed and all.

"I got a lil rug burn too, but it's all good in the hood. You've gotta do what you've gotta do sometimes," Fandango said. Then he marched away and joined Kid Mojo and Blazin'. At least, that was his way of getting over there. Really I knew he had just implanted himself there so he could gawk, hawk, and lay down the mack to Chi Girl and our new "groupies."

I kind of kept my eyes on Fandango or maybe I was keeping my eyes on Chi girl, like a big brother guarding his little sister. Fandango could tell to, he kept looking over at me with innocent eyes; fake innocent eyes; and shrugging his shoulders as if he wasn't doing anything. Heck, I didn't even say anything to him; he just had a guilty conscience. Either way, he saw my eyes keeping guard, so he stayed away from Chi Girl.

Even though the other two were "fair game," I was glad to see that Tabitha had her gawk fixed on me though, because Gio or should I say, "Fandango" really did know how to impress the heck out of the girls with his sharp tongue and everything. He was a genuine Mack daddy. If you looked up "Mack Daddy" in the dictionary there would be a picture of Fandango right next to the word.

I rejoined Fandango and everybody and I coolly without saying a word put his NSR necklace around his neck but I didn't give him a speech like I had with everybody else. He was too busy trying to sink his hooks into Sabrina, Chi Girls NOT SO shy friend. They both seemed to be smiling their lips off at each other so I didn't want to mess up his game. If you want to have a wing man you have got to be a wing man, if you know what I'm screamin'?

Plus, I had other things on my mind at that moment; I was on a mission. I approached every last Neighborhood Street Rocker and put them on alert that we had a battle brewing. I probably got a little coach-like too, but I was really taking it serious, that's all. I told most of them in this serious voice to "Get your stretches going and be ready for battle." I even told a couple of them "Get your game face on," and I don't even know what that means?

Chi Girl was the only one who had acknowledged me though. She began stretching out on the floor, probably the way she had always stretched out during her gymnastics class with her legs spread all wide and everything. However, we weren't at a gymnastics meet, we were surrounded by a bunch of peeping Toms. Love 'em or hate 'em; boys will be boys. I suppose my name was "Tom" for a second or so too, but what can you do?

The rink DJ got on the mic and said, "Aahhh yeah! We are opening up this floor to all of the dancers, breakers, guys and girls. Everybody dance, hang, or mingle, if you're single please make your way to the DJ booth, I'm giving out free hugs to the ladies."

DJ Steve started the session off with, "Dominatrix sleeps tonight" which prompted us "NSR's" to begin taking charge of the hardwood oval rink floor.

Everyone in our crew was rocking the nameplates. Everyone in our crew knew there was a battle lurking. And everybody was wearing the gray and black B-Boy clothing that night just as I had asked. Everything felt right. We looked like one big crew, The Neighborhood Street Rockers.

Even Chi Girl was sportin' dark gray suede gym shoes with light gray fat laces that she had made her mom buy last night. It made me realize that she took our crew seriously, just as Blazin' and I did. I mean, she told me, she made her mom go out late last night to buy her gray fat laces for her shoes, instead of the white laces it had come with. That's how serious she was.

Kid Mojo started us off on the rinks hardwood. He broke out into his lip wave, then his eyebrow wave, and then he pulled up his shirt to show his belly wave. However, he was only goofing around. Because he then got this goofy look on his face as if to make fun of himself and said, "I was doing all of this stuff last year – and to think that I thought this was a big deal back then." Then without haste Kid Mojo dove to the hardwood rink floor and began revolving into hydraulic pennies (where your body lifts completely off the ground, about a good 2 or 3 inches, while you're nutcracker-wind milling around. Then he transitioned into a set of Atomic Flares and sprang up to his feet and said, "That's just how I get loose gents, that's just how I get loose," then Kid Mojo smirked and walked away.

Realizing I had pounded down a couple of big glasses of water at dinner and another in the car while mom drove me up to the rink, I quickly snuck away and strolled towards the restrooms.

While I was making my way to the John, I heard, "Yo Phil" coming from the skate benches, which was roughly in the direction of where I was heading. I was right under a large speaker, so I wasn't exactly sure if I indeed heard my name or not, but as I walked towards the John I saw that it was Witty Dee. He was laughing like a banshee as I approached, "Are you deaf? I was calling your name like 20 times," he said.

"Sup Witty? Where's your skeezer?" I asked.

Witty threw this dumbfounded look on his face and asked, "Who?"

And I realized that he didn't understand any of our "b-boy vernacular" or maybe he did, but he played dumb just to rip on our style of talking. I say that because every once in a while, he would say crap like, "Speak English dude" or "take the marbles out of your mouth," crap like that.

"Where is your girlfriend?" I said slowly.

He smiled and then gruffly said, "She had to go take a crapper." That was Witty Dee for ya, a crude rube. He could make any girl sound ugly.

"Nice! ..." I said in shock about his description he used to explain where his girl was. I mean most girls will say: I've got to go powder my nose, so they could make the whole ordeal sound cuter. But ol Witty just made his girl sound gross as heck. "I've got to use the John too, I'm getting some pizza. You want a pizza?" I asked Witty sincerely.

Witty said, "Sure!"

"A Pizza THEEZ fart cheeks," I said in a horselaugh.

As Witty smiled with his typical mischievous look that only Witty Dee flashed from time to time, I knew I had set myself up for him to get me back; Witty always had to get you back.

A couple of seconds of smiles and silence were followed with Witty eventually nodding and acting as if he was agreeing that I had burned him. He bowed his head and without giving eye contact he continued to smile while saying, "You got me dude, you got me ... good one, good one." Then he extended to shake my hand and I remembered thinking that it was odd for him to be such a good sport about that kind of a thing. But I shook his hand anyway. He wasn't the kind that took razzings all that well. But maybe having a girlfriend had made him change or something – I briefly thought.

Then his true colors began to show -As I started shaking his hand, he firmed up his grip, squeezed harder, and then pulled my hand right to his butt and then farted. He kept a firm grip on my hand and started yelling louder than a baby who dropped its pacifier, "Dude stop trying to grab my butt you pervert, I like girls, I like Girls, stop grabbing my butt PHIL … Hey everybody, Phil's grabbing my BUTT! … Get your hand away from my BUTT, I've got a girlfriend," he kept saying it while using all of his might to keep my hand on his dairy air that had just rumbled a massive fart.

I finally was able to strip my hand away from Witty's firm gorilla grip, which left red marks on my wrist and hand. And I don't know why but I smelled my own hand, I had felt the rumble and vibration, but I guess curiosity had taken over. "Dude you farted on my hand," I yelled, "You freak."

"Who had a pizza THEEZ fart cheeks NOW my brother?" he devilishly cackled through his mouth while squinting his eyes in laughter. We were both laughing at that point but Witty was certainly laughing 10 times louder and 10 times harder than I was. Witty Dee had conceded nothing. A steady girlfriend had done nothing. That's Witty though, if you burn him; he will make sure to get you back 100 times harder and tougher than you got him. That was just how he rolled. But if you don't burn him every once in a while, he'll look at you as an easy mark, and he'll get you anyway, more often even, so you had to get him once in a while and just suffer the punishment.

Witty Dee ended up following me to the snack shop where the Johns were also located. He had seen that his gal Muffy was already in line to order grub. "She must have finished taking her crap," Witty said as we walked towards her. Like I said, he could make a princess sound disgusting.

He really got a big old bang out of saying, "how'd it smell man, how'd it smell?" every time he looked at my hand.

She turned around when Witty and I were by her, I threw her a, "Wazup girl," and then I quickly walked towards the bathroom. As I heard Witty cackling under his breath to Muffy about how I had just had a pizza fart.

I turned around one last time before I hit the "John" and saw Muffy was shaking her head in this: Silly boys will be boys sort of way.

Witty saw me look back and yelled, "How do you like your fart hands?"

I walked into the rink John where Big Ted from school and Curt Columbus were seemingly just hanging out in the bathroom shooting the crap around – pun intended. Neither one of them were washing their hands or draining their lizards, or anything relevant that I could see, they were just hanging out.

Ted raised his brows and whispered to me, "You got some papers on ya braugh?"

I was by chance staring through the bathroom mirror and it became rather obvious that Curt was holding a bag of wacky tobacky in his hands. Curt hurriedly hid the bag, when he saw me looking through the mirror but Ted reassured Curt, "Phil's cool, he hangs out with Blacklung and Coughman once in a while."

Curt pulled the bag back out of his pocket again and Ted repeated, "Do you have any rolling papers dude?"

I told them both, "NO" and then I said, "I have asthma, my lungs stopped working right, so I don't smoke, plus I think it sucks." I said.

Remember? I sort of tried it, but sort of not – which I regret even kind of trying it that one day at "the wreck."

Ted raised his eyebrows and said, "Right, your lungs stopped working … right." Ted concluded, "Sucks to be you."

Curt looked at Ted and said, "Hey let's try using that paper towel you were just talking about?"

I unzipped and unleashed the beast and said, "Besides, it kind of tastes like jack-ass doesn't it?" However, they both ignored me; they were too busy trying to see if they could use a paper towel as their "rolling paper."

While using the pisser, out of the corners of my eyes, I watched Curt pinch some tobacco out of his sack and start sprinkling it into a smaller section of paper towel that Ted was holding. And just to be the peanut gallery I said, "How many idiots does it take to roll a cigarette?" Ted raised his eyebrows and smirked while Curt kept sprinkling Mary Jane over the paper towel.

After Curt was done sprinkling that junk onto the paper towel, he told Ted, "Hey we can use this liquid soap to seal it shut."

I pulled up my fly, and figured I'd exit the John quickly. I skipped washing my hands because I didn't want to be in the wrong place at the wrong time. I heard Ted counter the soap idea with, "Dude I'll just lick it."

I walked out of the bathroom but not before I turned around and said loudly, "Dude you're going to lick it?"

Ted spouted back, "Good one dude."

Then he said to Curt, "You got the lighter?" and then I heard the flicking sound of a lighter as I exited the John and entered into the busy crowd of people grubbing down. Most of them were the skaters who had just left the skate rink floor, to make room for we dancers and breakers.

I walked over to Witty Dee and Muffy's table that was accompanied with two other girls. The more I looked at those girls, I realized they were the same girls that I had almost said "hi" to, but Bruno had cut me off at the pass. Remember that?

I sat down with them and Witty started talking about me in a mean and mocking way, as if I wasn't even there, which was typical Witty D. He tried to bust on me and my breakin' and such. He was saying crap like, "Phil's a fart cheek grabber" and "he likes to talk all that ghetto slang," and junk like that. But his plan sort of backfired because the more Witty talked about breakin' and me, the more Muffys friends became interested.

"Oh cool, I like break dancing," Muffy said.

"Awesome, can you show us some of your breakin'?" Muffys friend asked.

I was never formally introduced to those girls, so I didn't know their names just yet and it wasn't like I was expecting my friend Witty to introduce me. Instead, I knew he was too busy trying to figure out some more ways to burn me, because I was sure in his eyes; we were still not even because of my "do you want some pizza" wise-crack I had made. Until Witty gets you back ten times harder, he will be busy minding his plot for revenge. And that's just the way that it was.

Moments later two smiley faced and squinty red eyed smokers exited the bathroom with a cloud of smoke looming around the florescent lights affixed to the ceilings of the snack shop. The way the disco lights from the rink and the snack shop lights played off of each other had made the plume of smoke very noticeable, especially since I knew what was going down just seconds ago in that John. Most of us in the snack shop could now smell the smoky smell of leafy burnt skunk drifting around the room.

There were lots of people with curious looks on their faces. It was obvious that they were trying to figure out where the smell was coming from. I heard someone at the table in the far corner by the Pac Man 'sit down' arcade game yell, "Whose smoking around here?"

The manager of the snack shop was intently sniffing his nose and looking around feverishly; I could actually see his nose flexing; it looked just as a dog's nose would look when it was offered a treat.

I heard someone yell in a good natured, yet scolding tone, "Ted and Curt what have you fellows been up to?"

Muffy's friends said, "It smells like a grateful dead concert around here."

"It's a 421 on someone's watch right now, because the 420 is over," Muffy said.

I told everybody at the table about the bathroom shenanigans and then I heard the DJ play Shannon, "Let the music play," and for whatever reason, that song made me remember that I needed to get back to my crew. I didn't want to miss a thing.

I stood up and said, "I'll catch you all on the other side I've got some breakin' afoot with my good foot." That was a James Brown reference, that whole "Good Foot" thing, but I don't think any of them caught it.

"Have fun rolling on the floor - you fart cheek grabber," Witty said.

All of the girls at the table smiled at me as I was leaving and one of Muffys friends said, "We'll be on the floor a little later to watch you."

As I was shuffling my way out of the snack shop I spotted the manager speed walking to the men's bathroom. Which I happened to know was currently empty; Ted and Curt had made their willy-nilly exits minutes ago. Although, something told me that Ted and Curt would be back in line at the snack shop in a few minutes to cure their newfound munchies.

My zig zagged path back to my crew through the sea of dancers, rink regulars, and wallflowers was a long one. The rink was really getting packed. I stared at the Donkey Kong machine in passing, and out of habit and out of reflex, I sort of considered dropping a quarter, but I really had no intention of playing whatsoever. Really, I couldn't wait to get back to the cypher because the break circle that I couldn't see but I knew was there was the real thing that was on … "On like Donkey Kong."

As I got closer to the cypher, I started to see the spinning and twirling through the legs of dancing rink goers, which made me pick up my stride. I went over and stood by Bruiser, who was chatting with Chi Girl and company, while I watched my fellow breakers rock the floor.

Blazin' was sitting in the background with a deep thinking look on his face - he was getting battle ready.   When Brock saw me, he came over," Where did you go?" he asked.

"I had to unleash the beast," I said.

"Drain some rain from the main vein until it wanes," he said.

Blazin' then suddenly swooped in on Bruiser and with a sparkle in his eyes and a tickle in his throat he said, "Yo Dan the Man Bruiser, the snack shop over there has some pizza. Do you want some pizza?"

Bruiser laughed, "Dude, don't even try it!"

Blazin' kept trying anyway, "Dude, do you want some Pizza?"

Bruiser kept brushing him off.

Then, Dan Bruiser looked at me and said, "I know this cheap skate isn't about to really buy me some pizza."

Brock admitted with laughter, "Yep, you're probably right on that one."

"Go eat a pizza your own fart cheeks … you wacko," Dan said playfully.

During the joking around, I noticed the cypher had become empty, it was begging me to enter. I strutted to the middle of the break circle and cockily hop danced to, "Electric kingdom" that was blasting through the tweeters and woofers while my crew was eagerly watching me strut. I top rocked and danced around in a circle and then dove into pennies and then attempted to bounce into a head spin but I didn't quite make it; I luckily wound up spinning around on my shoulders a couple of times at an upright position.

I stood up after my spinning routine and saw that my entire crew was wide eyed and impressed. Kid Mojo yelled, "Shoulder spins! Blammo!"

I exited the circle and rejoined Bruiser who asked me, "When did you learn that move? - that was strilla for Rilla!"

"I just learned it right now," I told Bruiser.

Blazin' bounced into the middle of the action next. And of course, he started doing his thing, beach balling and coptering when suddenly, as if thunder was booming while we were watching Brock throw down with his routine, a deep and loud chant had filled our ears.

A ranting raucous had grabbed everyone's attention like a tornado siren during a storm. Even though the gap band was grooving through the system loudly and groovily, I could still hear the chant of "GTR … GTR … Tall GTR." It was an unmistakable obtrusiveness and confident swagger that could have been none other than Rockefeller … Rockefeller had entered the building!

   I had only met the cat once before, but his voice was memorable and unmistakable. His confident swag was like no other. And just like last time, he was rockin' his GTR nameplate across his neck. I had first learned about the belt buckle nameplates that day at the Lincoln center when I had seen Rockefeller sporting his like the tall Bboy that he was. And now my whole crew and I were donning one. - I was a biter (copy cat), aint no doubt about it. Guilty as charged.

   Rockefeller continued to walk onto the rinks hardwood like the brave, confident soldier that he was, "I hear there are some school girls up in here that want to get schooled … Tall GTR is here," Rockefeller cackled with sheer irreverence, "Where are these breakers at?" he demanded as he looked around at all of us.

   Then Rockefeller hopped to it, he wasted no time as he entered right into the break circle which had just been abandoned by Blazin' upon Rockefellers grand entrance. He floated right to the ground into his straight legged hand walks which looked even faster than I had remembered from a couple of months ago – and his hand walks were fast then. He then switched into a straight legged floor exercise that was similar to the atomic flare but with his legs closed together instead of spread apart. There was no doubt about it; the tall skinny cat named Rockefeller was the most graceful breaker I had ever seen - even more graceful that Kid Mojo.

ATOMIC FLARES

One by one all of us breakers took our turns showing off our moves in the cypher and to my surprise, Rockefeller was a good sport. He cheered when someone from our crew, "Got off!" or was a, "Cold Cat" as he had put it. Heck, I even got a head nod after my routine. One on one, Rockefeller could have certainly taken each of our guys out, but collectively as a crew, we had him beat.

The NSR vs. GTR battle of the crews really ended up being more of a breakers showcase than a battle; a jam session in the cypher. I think Rockefeller realized that we had numbers and a variety of break moves, and it was just him for his side. His friend Speedy G was there with him but he never even got out on the floor. I don't think he was a breaker – at least not like his boy Rockefeller was; he just liked hanging out. Rockefeller was the force to be reckoned with.

The rest of the night I socialized, rocked a move from time to time, and just chilled with all of my crew mates and our groupies (as I liked to call them) Tabitha and Sabrina. Hanging out with girls, seemed to have its perks too, other than the obvious. It made me look even cooler or something because while I was gabbing away with Chi Girl and her girls, other rink girls who I had seen around at the rink over the years, but had never talked to, were suddenly approaching me.

One girl said, "Hey I like your break dancing you've got to teach me how to dance dude!"

Another girl, (Muffy's friend) slid her way into our group and told me, "Cool breakin' Phil." And she even sort of brushed her hand on my hand and everything. I wasn't sure if she had done it on accident or on purpose, but either way, I didn't care; flirting was flirting. She probably would have stuck around a little longer too, but Tabitha monopolized the conversation by butting into everything Muffys friend tried to say. Tabitha had even grabbed my hand at one point as if she was going to hold it, but then she let go when I had looked at her. This was something that I wasn't really used to. I mean, girls trying to flirt with me and all. I was probably supposed to grab her hand back, but like I said, I wasn't really used to that whole thing.

Heck, it was just a couple of years before that, that I was wearing thick pop bottle glasses, momma picked out clothes, with a bowl hair cut, and nobody was paying attention to me —at least not in the cool and good looking sort of way. I was really kinda new to this whole "chicks diggin' me thing" but I'll tell you this, it didn't suck. Breakin' had made me.

The night had flown by like a sonic boom; it was a blast, I was still in Mack Daddy mode when it was time to leave and Bruiser knew it. He was my ride home but he told me, "I'll give you a few more minutes to lay down your mack, big daddy Swift; Blazin' and I will be waiting outside for you. Bruiser had to get up early for work the next day, so he was in no mood to chill like a rill. So as soon as I hit some awkward silence with Tabitha, I gave her a hug and then made my rounds and said my, "See ya's" to everyone.

I whispered sweet nothings to the girls I had talked to that night; Denine, Tabitha, Sabrina, and even Chi-Girl who I had to remind myself was just one of the "guys." I briefly wondered if I had become a "mini Fandango." But the difference was, I had no idea what I was doing. They had all approached me.

When I said, "See ya doll face" to Muffys' friend Roxanne, she was very touchy-feely, so the more I thought about it, she most definitely had intentionally grabbed my hand. She had whispered her phone number in my ear as I was telling Witty Dee goodbye. I had three numbers in my pocket and one number in my head that I was repeating over and over again like a madman until I got to the cashier's booth.

After borrowing a pen from the peppermint gum smelling, pigtailed chick that ran the cash register room at the end of the night, I hung out in the lobby long enough to see if I could make it 5 numbers. I mean, I had NOT gotten any girls numbers EVER before, and suddenly I was looking for five. I can really be a crazy ice madman sometimes, I really can. But after hanging out in the lobby for a couple of minutes, I made my way to the parking lot. Four numbers would have to do.

The rink parking lot must have had a million cars in it which made me wish I had asked Dan where he had parked before he had walked out.

However, I was too busy being a "Romeo" so I didn't think to ask, but at least his car had a distinctive sound. Really I think he needed a new muffler, but I was glad that he hadn't bought one yet. Otherwise I may have never found his car. I walked towards the blue exhaust and loud not so muffled sound of what I hoped would be Dan's car.

I walked past this one car that had semi fogged up windows and two smoochy teens with octopus arms moving all about. I couldn't make out what they were doing, but I'll tell you this, they were kissing so much that I could hear a smacking sound. I continued to walk towards Bruiser's Stang. Then ...

As I was continuing my trek towards the blue Stang, which I could finally see, I caught a glimpse of a scuffle through a small opening in the rink fence that led to a taco stand on the other side. Bruno Capone had Curt Columbus pinned up against the fence. He was holding him by the neck of his shirt collar. I couldn't hear what was being said but a war-like look sketched on Bruno's face and an intimidated and scared look drawn on Curt's face painted the picture that something was awry in the rink's" in crowd" circle.

It took a few seconds for them to be out of my line of sight because I had purposely walked all zig-zaggedly to keep my rubber neck at the best vantage point for as long as I possibly could. However, still to this day, I have no idea what that scuffle was all about and how it all ended.

I opened up the door to the Blue Stang and I told Blazin', "Hey I forgot to give you my CD; you're going to love it!"

Blazin' replied excitedly, "Ohh cool, What CD?"

"CD's fart cheeks," I said freakin' loud as I climbed in through Bruiser's half lifted front seat. He closed the door hard, put the car in drive and started driving slowly past the opening in the fence, but I could no longer see anybody on the other side from our vantage point.

Then Bruiser said, "Yo Phil, don't give Brock such a hard time, he's just trippin' off the fact that he didn't get to break with Howard Yu tonight."

"Thanks Bruiser," Blazin' said, "... Who's Howard Yu?" Blazin' asked.

Bruiser mischievously smiled, "Howard Yu like to smell THEEZ farts?!"

A battered Blazin' bellowed begrudgingly, "Oh shiznit you punks!"

We must have razzed Brock for a good while but after we were done busting on him, Bruiser asked Blazin' and me, "Who wants to grab some burgers from the Big Burger drive thru?"

It's funny though, Blazin' and I were silent at first, neither of us wanted to say a word. Blazin' and I were both trying to figure out where he was going with that burn or question or what the punch line was?

Then Bruiser yelled, "No for real! Does anyone want food from the burger joint?"

We both slowly said, " ummm Yes" as we all start laughing at our cautiousness.

"It's like the boy who cried wolf around here," Bruiser said.

We had arrived at the drive thru lickety-split, mainly because we had luckily hit every green light on the way there. Bruiser even stomped the gas at a couple of ambers because he kept telling us how he was, "Starvin' like Marvin."

And like the smart ass that I was I said, "I'm hungry as all heck after lugging all of these phone numbers around in my pocket all night."

"Easy there Romeo, " Dan said.

"Oh shiznit … you don't even know if the numbers are real dude," Brock said tauntingly.

The voice over the drive thru intercom greeted us instantly, " Schhhh. 'an I 'elp u?"

Bruiser replied, "Give us a minute please."

The voice over the speaker gated, "'ake er 'ime"

Bruiser finally ordered after a little thought, "Okay were ready: we'll take 3 burgers, 3 fries, and 3 colas … and HEY can you give me extra sauce on the burgers?" But before the drive thru attendant could answer Dan's request, Blazin' leaned over me, and popped his head from out of the back seat and partially stuck his head out of the driver's side window.

Brock then, with a huge smile – practically foaming at the mouth, and glee in his eyes, blurted out into the Big Burger drive thru intercom, "Hey, hey, hey - you guys know Phil? Do you guys know Phil?" he asked the drive through clerk.

At the time, I remembered thinking - why is Blazin' asking the drive thru attendant if they know my name? Is it because he was wondering if people still remembered us from the break dance contest from a couple of months ago? I even thought: Why not ask if they know your name? Why are you asking them if they know me? I was confused as all heck … but only for a few seconds.

Then the voice over the drive thru speaker replied, "NOhhh?"

Then Blazin' started giggling as if someone was tickling his pits and said, "You know Phil … Phil THEEZ fart cheeks!"

Bruiser sharply yelled at Blazin', "Dude, don't mess with people who are about to make our food!"

I shrugged and shaked squeamishly as I pictured the burger makers spitting in our food. And to make matters worse Brock kept yelling, Phil THEEZ cheeks Phil THEEZ farts" as I pushed him back to his side of the back seat.

When we pulled up to the drive thru window; Bruiser pulled out his cash and said, "My treat guys" and suddenly I thought about how I really wasn't that hungry after all.

Bruiser offered an apology to the drive thru attendant, "Don't pay any attention to old boy about that "THEEZ farts" business – he's a nut job. "

"No problem – I took care of it," The drive thru worker said as he sniffed his nose like a lunatic. Bruiser grabbed the bag of grub and the sodas while putting his car back into drive while simultaneously asking the cashier, "Hey bro, did you all put the extra sauce on the burgers?"

The Big Burger cashier answered in a creepier and deeper voice than he had used before. I'll never forget it. He scrunched his face and said, "Ohh yeah man … we gave you the extra sauce alright, it was my pleasure," and then he sniffed his nostrils again like a madman and then wiped his nose with his index finger as Bruiser drove away. It was the creepiest voice I had ever heard. It gave me an instant eerie feeling in my gut. We were all immediately weirded out. It was rather apparent that we were all thinking the exact same thing.

"That sounded a little creepy didn't it?" I said. "And what did he mean by: I took care of it?"

Brock's eyes bugged out, "Yeah, did you see the sinister look on his face?" Blazin' said.

"He probably spat some hockers in the sauce on account of the Phil THEEZ butt cheeks jokes and everything," Bruiser had said as he stared at Blazin' through his rear view mirror.

Blazin' jumped in and defended himself though, "Dude, never order extra sauce from a drive thru, duuude … you're just asking for it!" I ended up eating my fries and drinking my cola but I was no longer in the mood for a burger. In fact I almost tossed my cookies having to watch Brock and Dan throw the hockered burgers down. (By the way -Do you call big loogies and spit phlegm balls: "HOCKERS" where you come from?)

Chapter 14

I need a Popsicle STAT

Saturday morning I woke up to the dripping sound of melting icicles hitting the metal wheel barrel that I had accidentally left outside for the winter. I suppose there was nothing accidental about it, but It sounds better to say it was an "accidental" thing rather than saying I had just been lazy last autumn, doesn't it? What a difference a week or two makes though, when you're from Chicago. One week it's warm and the next week there's snow.

I grubbed down breakfast straight quick and had an early start of it. Mom wanted to leave earlier for work that day on account of the icy and snowy roads. I was anxious to go see Bob that morning. Like last time, I got dropped off early at the place that gives sick people toxic poisons in their body which makes them puke like madmen but ultimately and hopefully makes them better. That place is also called the cancer unit in a hospital in case you weren't pickin' up what I was puttin' down.

I didn't see Phoebe that morning. Remember? - The older hottie at the "information desk" that I had sort of flirted with last time. Instead, it was some old lady that rocked gray hair, polyester clothing, and smelled like liniment and cough drops. She was just as friendly and smiley though. And she kept calling me "dear" which if you think about it, it's kind of the same thing. When a girl calls you "honey" or "darling" and an old lady calls you "dear"; it's all the same thing.

After being called "dear" and a "nice boy" like a million times, I made my way towards Bob. I remembered how to get to the cancer unit and I tried not to think too much about dead leaves and code blues. I was buzzed into the unit and then I went through the routine of making myself as germ free as possible; I washed my hands, put on the scrub pants, scrub shirt, hair net and footie slippers. I skipped the grim reaper mask this time or surgical mask, whatever you call them. The nurse said they weren't necessary and I'd rather not wear it anyway. This time I felt as if I could visit the cancer unit without the mask as my hiding place yet still act normal.

I walked into Bobs' room and he blurted out, "Phil K Swift … Neighborhood Street Rocker in the hizzy! Me brizzy."

He shook my hand and then yelled, "Nurse Mary … will you be so merry as to bring your merry self in here to marry me, Mary?!" Bob could have pressed the "nurse button" on his TV remote control but he liked yelling better.

"Right on, it's not crazy to ask someone to marry you if you're just joking around?" I said randomly.

"Who's joking around?" Bob smirked.

Moments later, Nurse Mary walked in with swollen red eyes and sniffles but she had flashed a smile at us to hide what she may have been thinking. She cleared her throat and kept smiling to hide her tears, "Hi Bob" she said.

Then she looked at me and said, "Hey I remember you from last week, Bob talks about you and his break crew every day." Her face had finally changed to happy (well, sort of), and with a bright look in her eyes she said, "I'd ask you what you want Bob, but I can tell by that tone in your voice … I know what you want."

Bob replied, "Yep, you know!"

"Red or orange this time?" Mary asked as she was half way out of the room.

"Red for both of us," Bob said, "STAT," he yelled. "That's another hospital word kid, Stat. It means right away."

I suddenly realized, "Ohh popsicles?"

"It's never too early or never too late for popsicles; popsicles for breakfast, popsicles for lunch, and popsicles for dinner. Can you guess what I eat at snack time?" Bob asked while raising his brow-less brows.

"Popsicles?" I smirked.

"You know it kid," Bob said while smiling with his whole face. Then he whispered to me, "Mary has been crying today, one of the rooms next to mine now has an empty bed. She's crying over a flippin' empty bed again. Doesn't she know that someone will be filling up that darn thing again in just a few short days? … Women … Always crying over empty beds or broken heels or something," he said.

Mary walked in swiftly and passed out the popsicles while laughing half heartedly, "Here is your icy cold popsicles to combat the fire-ee hot chemo - as Bob likes to say," she said while looking at me.

We both took off the Popsicle wrappers like a kid opening a birthday present and then Bob clanged our ice cold popsicles together and said "Cheers kid!"

"Nostrovia," I said.

"Ohh, you're a Polak?" Bob asked, " … Me too! Mowamy po polsku?"

"No," I said, I never learned how to speak it. Even though I didn't speak Polish, I had heard my grandma speak it enough to know what he had asked me.

While sucking down the popsicles I reached into my pants pocket and pulled out Bob's NSR nameplate. I draped it around his neck and said, "And now … NSR is officially in the hizzy!"

Bob smirked and then told me something with a smile, which seemed to hide his true thoughts. He seemed to be hiding something but NOT necessarily to be mean, "I have some good news and some not so good news, but I don't like not so good news, so I'm only going to tell you the good news. In fact, it is great news," he said as he paused, looked at his NSR nameplate, smiled and then continued, "They are stopping all of my chemotherapy. I am going to receive blood transfusions about every week or so ... Hey, check this out kid - once my immunity level goes back up; meaning my body can fight off colds and flu's and stuff, I am going to be free and clear to get out of this crazy joint!"

"That is awesome news," I said.

I looked at Bobs I.V. bag stand and I noticed that he only had one bag of saline pumping through his veins. Bob took his nameplate off and was staring at it happily and said, "So anyway, I should be out of this dump by next weekend ... We can all go breakin' together at those rinks you've been telling me about. The doctor told me: Bob, you're a young man; you should go out and enjoy the things that young men are enjoying. Go live your life, life is short, so enjoy every minute of it... So Swift kid, be ready, Boogie Bob is going to be rockin' out somewhere next Friday or Saturday night," he said with his eyes looking upwards.

I told Bob, "The whole crew can't wait to meet you! I've been telling them all about you and it'll be cool, it will be a stone gas!"

"It will kid, I can't wait to meet everyone too," he said.

Bob and I talked back and forth for about an hour or so; but he was not as awake the last half hour that I was there. Bob would say something that kind of made sense for a few minutes, then he would drift into sleep or a state of mind and conversation that didn't necessarily make sense. In his state of confusion he said, "Did you know Phil - when you die and you go to heaven they give you chocolate and feathers? ... chocolate because it tastes good and feathers so everyone can get tickled all of the time, it's a nonstop place of laughter ..."

I just laughed and said, "Oh yeah?" You see, when Bob said that I wasn't sure if he was quoting a line from a movie. Or just trying to be funny? Or what. On the other hand maybe he was just having a weird reaction from his medicine? Either way he was not making a whole lot of sense anymore.

After that Bob asked, "Hey Phil, Can you go get me some water? ... And HEY (he said gruffly as I started towards the nurses' station), don't get me any of that foo foo flavored water shee-ott ... NO FOO FOO water! Just get me some plain water ... H2O."

I walked out of the room, grabbed water from the nurses' station water cooler, and Mary commented, "Non foo foo water for Bob?"

I smiled and said, Yep."

Upon my return, I gave Bob his water, he took a sip, and then Bob turned on his side to see me, with wider eyes than he had shown in a little while and said "Hey man, I'm going to give you a ticket."

"A ticket for what?" I asked confused.

Bob chuckled, "I'm going to give you a ticket for not drinking."

His seemingly strange remark begged me to ask again, "Wazup my brother?"

"You don't have a drink in your hand; I'm going to give you a ticket," he said.

I finally understood and said, "Oh, you want to have a drink with me, you don't want to drink alone, you're joking around … ok, I get it."

Bob shook his head yes into his pillow and painfully smiled. I darted back to the nurses' station and told the nurses that Bob wanted to have a drink with me. But when I got back, Bob was kind of drifting in and out of sleepiness more than he had before.

I wasn't sure what to make of Bobs random comments; was it the chemo withdrawal, was it the leukemia, or maybe he was just tired. I wasn't sure. However as I sat there I thought about how Bob was going to be joining us NSR's outside of these hospital walls in just one short week, so that made me feel better, as I watched Bob fight to keep himself awake.

Bob eventually drifted off to sleep in the middle of my story about the previous nights adventures at Suburbanite. He liked hearing me talk about the breakin' that had been rocked out by us NSR's and Rockefeller. And he laughed like a freak show about the nitwits that had used paper towels to smoke their wacky tobacky. We both agreed that smoking sucked and breakin' gave us our only "high" we really needed or wanted. I also told him about the smooching in the parking lot, and all of that junk, but he fell asleep during the best part of my story, about how I had finally scored some girls phone numbers. I guess it's not always a good idea to save the best for last.

I hung out for a few more minutes, just in case he woke up again but it became obvious that Bob was going to continue napping, so I bailed. The only thing that bugged me was that I didn't get a chance to tell him that we were all going up to Chicagoland Rink that same night. I wanted him to feel like he was a part of every moment but I didn't want to wake him. Bob was holding his NSR nameplate in his hand while sleeping as I walked out into the cancer unit hallway. I took off the hospital scrubs this time and headed home.

Chapter 15

The infamous Chicagoland Rink

I don't think I told you yet, I think I forgot, so I'll tell you now. On Friday (yesterday), all throughout the school day I was getting warnings about "Chicagoland Rink." - You know - the place we are going to hang out at tonight?

When I was in my typing class, I was talking to this smart girl Savannah just before the bell was about to ring. I told her I was going up to this rink called, "Chicagoland Roller Rink," to hang out and do some breakin', when she cut me off and gasped.

"There are a lot of gangbangers that hang out there all of the time. My brother told me all about that place; my bro won't let me go there … and he won't hang out there anymore either because of all of the riff raff." Savannah had told me just as the bell rang, so that's all I knew … UNTIL….

On that same day, in gym class, this dude Riley said: one day his Uncle Mike was there (at Chicagoland Rink) and someone got shot inside of the place, right in the leg, with a pistol.

Then this other dude in my gym class, Anthony, chimed in and corrected Riley, "In fact someone did get shot at Chicagoland Rink but it was in the parking lot, not inside the rink. It was all over the TV news and in the newspapers and everything. And he got shot in the butt, not in the leg," Anthony had said. The way Anthony explained it made me believe him but I tried not to think about it too much.

The more people I told I was going to Chicagoland Rink; the more people that had stories for me about how I'd better be careful if I went there. It made me feel like I must have been living under a rock or something because I had never heard any of those stories before.

Also on Friday, during my lunch period, when I was waiting in line to order my food, these two girls; SummerWind and Mariah told me, "We know of Chicagoland Rink because our neighbor from down the street told us how we better be careful if we ever went up to Chicagoland Rink. Something about, if you get caught wearing the wrong colors up there you'd find yourself in a heap of trouble or whatever," Mariah said as she rolled her eyes and then added, "as if," in a tone that meant she wouldn't be going there anyway. She was a preppy bookish type that obviously didn't "wear colors."

"As if we would go up there," SummerWind agreed, who was also a very straight laced girl.

Anyway, everyone I had talked to about "Chicagoland Roller Rink" last Friday had something shady to tell me about that place- and that was the only thing that sort of had me buggin' after I had visited Bob. I had meant to ask Bob if he knew anything about that place, but he had fallen asleep by the time I had remembered to ask him.

It's weird, I didn't think of Bob as a cancer patient the whole walk home on Saturday. I just kept thinking about how he didn't like Foo Foo water. Which I guessed was anything that wasn't just pure H2O. When I wasn't thinking about foo foo water, I was picturing Bob's bald head eating chocolate and getting tickled with feathers. I can really think about the weirdest things. Anyway, I thought about all of this junk while I walked home from the hospital that day: Chicagoland Rink, feathers, "real H2O," and chocolate - I'm such a scatter brain sometimes but that was what was on my mind and I wanted you to know – I hope you don't mind?

Chapter 16

What you be about?

It seemed like it was only a few minutes that I had been home from visiting Boogie Bob, but in fact it had been a few hours. Time flies when you're breakin' in the basement, I guess but it was that time on the Tic Toc to start making my way towards the infamous Chicagoland Rink. - Especially since Blazin's Dad was driving, I knew I'd better be ready early. I could guarantee you that Brock was going to bug his dad like mad until he got into the car to start picking everybody up. Brock was so early for everything that he would show up for a morning "early bird" breakfast, the night before.

And I was right of course, Blazin' and his old man showed up early to pick me up, just as I suspected. For whatever reason, Blazin' and I started talking about that TV show, "PM Magazine" again, that we both saw a couple of months ago. The show aired clips of teenagers break dancing - it was love at first sight, It was the first time that I had ever even heard of or had ever seen this thing called – BREAKIN'. At least, that's what I had told Brock that night as we drove to Chicagoland. I knew I had sounded like a romantic fool when I had said that Love at First sight thing, but I didn't care.

Then, I was laughing sarcastically when I told Blazin', "The reporter on the show said that New York gangbangers had set aside their differences and weapons and decided to duke it out with break dancing instead of fighting. Even though I can be pretty naïve sometimes, I know that gangbangers weren't going to stop fighting just because they were dancing. However, it probably did keep some kids busy dancing instead of fighting, so maybe there was a little truth to it.

But Blazin' was practically getting mad at me, he said, "Dude … Phil … that's what the show said … why would they make it up? All of the bangers break dance instead of fighting now, that's awesome!"

"Ohhh … you're a sweet boy Mr. Brock Blazin' … it's just some kind of crazy journalism spin or slant, but whatever you want to believe is okay with me … even though it's wrong," I said to get his goat. Even though I was young, I had learned that even TV news stories can be lies. "I'm sure it's keeping some kids out of trouble, just not all of them," I added.

Moments later, Fandango and 2 tough got into the ride and we continued onto Chicagoland Rink.

Blazin' asked Fandango and Miguel about their opinions of the whole gangs giving up their guns for break dancing thing when Fandango chimed in with his own spin – ignoring Blazin's question, as if he thought Blazin' was just kidding, at least that's the kind of smirk Fandango gave.

Fandango said, "Breakin' got its name from guys like: DJ Kool Herc and Africa Bambaattaa who I heard were the most influential DJ's in the foundation of breakin'. Have you guys ever heard of them?" Fandango asked us.

Blazin' said, "I've heard of Afrika Bambaataa, but not the other one."

"I know Afrika Bambaataa too ... because of his song, "Renegades of Funk," I added.

Then Fandango continued, "Yeah, everybody knows Afrika Bambaataa but Dj Kool Herc was just as important too. I heard he played a lot of extended breaks when he mixed his jams at his club in New York and that's when all of the "break boys" would bust out with breakin' – during the breaks of songs. You see, DJ Kool Herc would take two copies of the exact same record and keep repeating the breaks live, right there on the spot – and that's when the boys would bust out with their spinning on the floor, hence the name "break boys" or Bboys.

But yeah, someone from the media called it 'break dancing' and the term break dancers grew from there. But B-boys and B-girls were clubbers that were rockin' to break beat music in these New York clubs." Fandango told us.

As if a light bulb just flicked on, Blazin said, "No shee-ott Bee-otch?"

Then Fandango added, "By the way, for those of you who don't know, breaks are the part of the song where a DJ either mixes in or mixes out of the song. Usually just drums and percussion make up the breaks. "

"I know ... Bruiser was telling us about some of this stuff a couple of months ago," I said.

"Word," Blazin agreed.

Then Blazin' while still in his uproarious and debating mood said, "Some people say that breakin' started because of James Browns song called the, 'Good Foot.' The legend has it that James Brown himself, and his fans, would butt spin, back spin, or do some down rock type stuff or moon walking during his concerts, and this carried over into the clubs of New York. ... And this was back in the 1970's man! When we were just babies," Blazin' said with passion.

Miguel 2 tough finally broke his silence and entered the conversation, "I have seen Karate movies with martial artists kicking their enemies while doing windmills or helicopters on the ground which is where some breakin' moves had come from. I thought they called it break dancing because people like Bruce Lee would break someone's bones as they were wind milling around, kicking them and stuff. But it's pretty obvious that gymnastics and acrobatics play a big role in breakin' too," he said. Miguel wasn't shy, but he was soft spoken – and we were all listening.

Fandango looked at his brother and said, "I told you about DJ Kool Herc and what Crazy legs had said ... Remember? ... originally Bboy meant Brooklyn boy, remember?"

"I know but even after you told me that, I still thought that Karate movies with fighters getting their bones "breaked" or broken -and stuff was where the name had come from," Miguel said.

I had my own take on all of this, so I told my fellow B-boys in the now steamed up car from all of the hot air blowing around, "I might have to argue that Thomas Edison was among the first fans of break dancing. In 1898 Thomas Edison recorded on video, an Arabic street dancer doing head spins on a sidewalk. (Look it up at the library of congress for yourself) … no Shiznit, no Bull Shee-ottin! 1898! How ironic is it that Thomas Edison who invented the turntable ,which DJ's use to play the music that we breakers listen to while spinning around on the floor, also made the very first video recording of someone doing head spins over 100 years ago." Everyone was eagerly listening to me with serious looks in their eyes when I started joking.

"Maybe we should really be called Edison dancers or E-Boys … but hey, whatever you want to believe about break dancing or b-boying or breakin' and how it got its name and who invented it, is all cool with me. Maybe it's a combination of all of that stuff, but I don't care who invented it or where it came from. All I know is that it was hip then and it's even more hip now," I said.

We all ended up agreeing that we didn't care what anyone called it as long as we were all talking about the same kick ass style of dance with head spins, windmills, up rock, down rock, freezes, power moves, and all of that shee-ott.

We arrived in the parking lot of the infamous Chicagoland Rink just as we had finished our talk about where breakin' had come from. I was glad that none of us said anything negative about the rink on the way up there because one nervous parent equals all of our parents getting nervous, if you know what I mean?

When we got out of the car my eyes were drawn to two fly girls that had just been dropped off, just as we had. One of them had worn bright neon green socks and a matching neon green mesh woven shirt. The two girls had disappeared into the entrance doors of the rink before I could get a real good look at their faces. But I knew I'd find them again; that neon would shine in a blackout. My boys were too busy sorting out who had really started breakin', so they didn't see them. I didn't say anything to the guys though. The way I saw it, I didn't need a million guys looking at the girls I had found anyway.

Both of those fly girls were rockin' black high heeled shoes, the kind that had the straps that wrapped around the ankles, which were wrapped, strapped, and walking through my mind as all of us NSR's started our journey inside the rink. I wasn't used to seeing girls our age wearing high heeled shoes, except at church on Sundays. It was usually the 21 and uppers that wore that kind of thing when they went out on the weekends. But my first impression of Chicagoland Rink was different than whatever I had heard at school on Friday. It's funny how girls can make a place seem different.

By the time my friends and I had entered through the doors of the rink, the two fly girls were already inside and out of sight. We were instantly bassed in our face with grooving Chicago house music. House music was starting to take over the Chicago airwaves, the speakers at the rinks, the dance parties … everywhere. Even Big Teds' locker at school had been thumping Chicago mix jams from his cassette deck, in between class periods the last couple of weeks. DJs had become torn between pop, hip hop, and house music as the crowd requests played tug o war with each other. At least that's what DJ Steve was telling me at Suburbanite Rink last night.

The cinder blocked walls of the lobby at Chicagoland Rink were covered in graffiti. It looked like it had been professionally done, very thought out and good use of colors; it looked like a scene out of a comic book. I thought it looked cool; it wasn't that gang bangin' graffiti tagged crap you'd see on the side of buildings, done all quick like. It was real artwork that looked like it had taken a while to paint.

Miguel 2 tough offered to pay my freight to get in and I couldn't find a reason to tell him no.

You're a gentleman and a breaker," I told him.

"No problem amigo," Miguel said as he handed the cashier our admission fee.

I continued my search of the rink for riff raffs, girls, and breakers while I went through my first ever "Frisk line" to get patted down. I guess they were looking for guns, knives, and stuff like that hidden on my body. This made me think about all of the warnings that my friends at school had given me about this place. The pat down, in and of itself spoke volumes about what Chicagoland Rink may have had in store for me, but I tried not to think about it too much.

As we walked into the main room where the large skating rink was located, I saw three young kids skating around the rinks oval hardwood floor and a few moms and dads sitting on the benches along the sides. I know I had just been frisked and everything but seeing those girls as I had arrived in the parking lot and seeing the kids skating around the rink, made me feel like the place must be safe. I even told that to Brock, but then he started singing Whodinis song, "The Freaks come out at night."

I quickly noticed some breakers off to the far right side in a smaller section of the building – not on the actual rink itself, that were not a part of our crew. They weren't breakin' just yet, but I could tell by the way they had dance-top rocked for a quick second and by the way they were dressed, that they were one of us.

I started walking over towards them to get a closer look while the rest of my crew hung back. They were wearing knit hats inside a rink that was plenty warm, so that told me something. Plus they were donning tight tracks suits that screamed breakers. And when I say "tight" I mean the opposite of nasty. As I drew closer, the two dudes started to up rock more seriously and ferociously against each other. They were pretending a straight up street fight and pretending to use weapons against each other and shiznit like that but it was all a part of their up rock. One of them was busting out with bow and arrow charades within his up rock, which I found quite queer but, art is art I guess, it doesn't always have to make sense. The other knit hat wearing Bboy had acted like he had numchucks for his up rock battle against his friend. This made me think about what Miguel had said about breakin' coming from Karate moves and everything. It looked very "different" to watch those two up rock like that, but to each his own, I guess.

My friends sort of hung out by the popcorn machine that was by the entrance, so I walked back over towards them after checking out those two Bboys, when I saw all of my homies checking out this group of twenty something's that were housing it up and jack dancing to the rink DJ's house jams. They were all groovily engaged in disco dancing to this track called, "Disco Circus," which is a song I had heard in the mixes on the radio a few times and I had always wondered what the names was, until that night, when Fandango had told me.

"Sweet … the DJ's playing Disco Circus," he said.

"How do you know?" I asked.

"I know," he said smugly.

Fandango and Miguel always seemed to know the names of the records that were getting mixed at the rink.

That group of twenty somethings or "house people" - we called them, all looked very wild-eyed and in their own worlds while they danced around to their vibe. I wasn't used to hanging out at places that were all ages, but that's what Chicagoland Rink appeared to be - teens and twenty something's and whatever.

Eventually the kids that had been skating with their parents had left the building as the night had grown older, which ended up putting the song virus (or ear worm) in my head: "The Freaks come out at night."

After a couple of my guys had bought popcorn, we NSR's moved and set up camp near the other B-boys that I had told you about a minute ago. We had our own dance floor that had these white Christmas type lights constructed into the framework of the partially plexi-glassed and wooden dance floor. And let me tell you, that really got Blazin excited –as if he needed something to get excited about. He yelled out, "AAhh man dudes! … Breakin' on a lit up dance floor is totally choice, it's kind of like the dance floor in the "Billie Jean" video, you know guys, you know?"

Slim Jim had just arrived at the rink and overheard Brock – he was that loud, so he joined in our conversation about the dance floor. He had heard Blazins' enthusiasm a mile away, "Hellz yeah my brizzo, skizzo fow shizzo. The floor is all Saturday night fevered out. Dance around Brock - maybe the beavers will shout," Jim laughed to himself.

Blazin' shouted, "Yeah dude, Saturday night fever, that's what this floor reminds me of … the Saturday night fever movie!"

Slim Jim belly laughed, "Or Billie Jean, whatever? It's caz-zool, fool."

"Yay dude, that's what I just said, Billie Jean," Brock said as he shook Slim Jims hand.

The DJ played Herbie Hancocks, "Rockit" next, which seemed to inspire the two breakers that I had first seen when we had got to Chicagoland Rink, to start breakin' again. They started top rockin' around and stuff, which led to one of them swiping and back spinning while the other one started head spinning. Not as many as Boogie Bobs head spins, but he did all right.

Miguel, Blazin', Fandango, and Slim Jim were chatting each other up and admiring each other's B-Boy clothing like it was a fashion show. "It's not just girls who admire each other's shoes or skirts or blouses or hairstyles," I said to them in a lispy soft voice, just to mess with them.

"We guys like to rock the pimpin' clothes too," Miguel said.

"Sweet outfit," Brock added, "I really like your outfit man."

I sort of faked a girl's voice and said, "Outfit or should you have said ensemble sweetie?" Then I looked at him with a crazy smile just to egg him on, "Dude, it's not an outfit. My mom wears outfits. Its B-boy regalia or B-boy attire, but don't go calling it an outfit my brother," I said.

Brock just brushed me off with a scrunched face so I left it alone. I mean, I was really in the mood to mess with them and everything but I was really more curious about the whereabouts of those two fly girls I had seen when we had first got to the rink. If good ol Witty Dee had been with us that night – he would have messed with them.

Since I was left out of the conversation for the moment I began scanning the room for neon sock chick with the mesh shirt, while I listened to "Jam on it" in the background. I hadn't seen either one of them since we had gotten inside. We were on one end of the building and most of the other people were on the other end of the rink.

The DJ finally got the lights going! The disco ball rotated specs of light everywhere, the laser lights flashed randomly throughout the joint, and after having been blinded about a million times by the laser lights, suddenly my eyes had been drawn towards the rink entrance. The outside street lamps were sneaking inside and creating a shadowy entrance for all of the new comers that were coming from the outside. When someone new had walked in, all I could see was a shadow entering inside.

Some people you can see from a mile away, even if it's just a shadow of them. As I looked towards the entrance I saw this new cat entering inside of Chicagoland Rink as if he owned the place; he looked tough. The way he walked from the center of his body and marched his legs forward before he placed his feet down flat footed, made me know that it had to be none other than Kid Mojo in the hizzy. By nature, he walked almost zig zagged, it's hard to explain; it was queer. But he slammed his feet down and walked zig-zag.

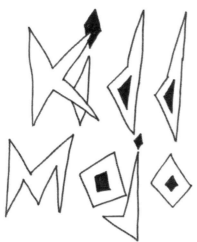

I couldn't be totally certain it was he because of the way his Kangol Bermuda hat played hide and seek with his face. It made him look like the character on the, "neighborhood watch sign," like the kinds of signs you've seen posted on your own neighborhood street that warn the community to look out for riff raff. Well, that's what Mojo had looked like – hat tilted to hide his face, trench coat, and all.

The shadowy neighborhood watch figure was slowly moving towards us with his head swaying from left to right as he marched on beat to the Boogie Boys jam, "Fly Girl." Since I was pretty sure it was he, I sort of walked slowly towards the entrance. He seemed to have looked our way right after he had paid and he was heading in our direction right from the get go; like he meant to.

Then confirming my suspicions, he busted out into floor gliding, moon walking, poppin', and tickin' and such as he drew more near – that was just how he walked, which inspired Slim Jim to walk towards us and yell, "Kid Mojo – in the hiz-ouse!"

Kid Mojo reached out his hand, "Sup Mojo, I thought I saw you walking in. You're dressed like the neighborhood watch sign with your black Kangol and all," I said as I shook his hand.

"Sup Mr. Phil K Swift," Mojo the kid said with a smirk.

"We are going to be breakin' like madmen tonight, " I said.

"Yep, we'll mess anybody up," Kid Mojo said, then he mysteriously disappeared from Slim Jim and me and made his way around the rink by the rest of our crew to let them know he was in the hizzy.

"Sup Swift, my Brudda, there are some straight up skeezers and fly girls up in this joint, right!" Then he bit his lower lip, flared his nostrils and laughed, "Fow shizzo my nizzo, they are strilla for rilla magillla … word up!" he had said as he started to pop, wave, and tick. He really liked to rhyme his mumbo jumbo while boogalooin'. Half of the time I didn't even know what he was saying but he laughed, so I laughed.

"Say there Slim Jim, tell me dude, when are you going to make me one of those jackets my man?" I asked. Jim was wearing a dark blue jean jacket with a 15 inch by 15 inch patch that was sewn onto the back that had graffiti painted on it.

"Where did you get that pimped out jacket from? You were telling me about it last night until those chicks came by … sorry for blowing you off."

"Don't worry about it bro, that one chick was smooth … smooth as ice," he said with a devilish grin.

"And nice eyes too," I added. She really did. (He meant Muffys friend Roxanne from Suburbanite last night.)

"Anyway Swift, I made it myself brizzo, I'm the pimp – you know."

"Big Pimpin',' I said.

Slim Jim then took off his jacket and handed it to me so I could take a closer look. He started pointing out all of the details on the jacket and then explained about the sizes of brushes he used, the color names of the paint he used: like midnight blue, flesh tone peach, burnt orange and shee-ott like that. But my undiagnosed ADD kicked in and I had trouble following him – too many details. But that happened to me sometimes when I was talking to Slim Jim; his mouth could move at a mile a minute and once you got him going he could talk your ear off. He could give you Vincent Van Gogh syndrome if you let him; that's how much he could talk your ear off. (Van Gogh is the famous artist that had cut his own ear off, in case you didn't know.)

Slim said that he even sewed the patch on himself; so I called him, "LIL Suzy homemaker" but I really was impressed. I wasn't trying to rip on him; not really, I just sort of said it. He scowled for a second then laughed and put his jacket back on, pulled out a stick of gum and then gave me a serious look.

"Did you see that thick book of graffiti art that I brought with to McCollum Park a couple of weeks ago?" he asked.

"I checked it out for a minute but I didn't really get to scope it out all that much, someone swiped it out of my hands. –Why?" I asked.

"Well that's the book that I use to draw my burners and sketches … all of my graffiti art and doodles or whatever is clever is in there. So if you saw anything you liked in there, I can make it for you as a patch to put on a jacket or whatnot.

I'm not some Punk ice Bee-otch that spray paints on someone else's property. That's whacked, jacked, heart attacked. I'm like Einstein with my melon, not a felon," he said as serious as a heart attack as he fixed his sleeves. "I only paint graffiti in legit places where I have permission."

"You've got to make me one of those jackets Brudda," I said.

"Fer strilla Swifty, it'll be nifty," he said. Then, Slim Jim started throwing down with poppin', wavin', tickin, and lockin'. He was more of a boogaloo cat rather than a breaker.

"Slim Jim, do it to it and like a witch: brew it," I said with a wink.

"I'm like a warlock and I'll put y'all in shock; -doc tickety tock see you in outer space Mr. Spock," he said slyly.

"Nice bruh," I said.

Slim Jim had this style of pulsating poppin' that was as exciting as lightning. I mean, he didn't do those been there done that, type of moves that everybody else did. He really struck the on lookers with lightning when he boogalooed. He really did.

Slim Jim started quickly vibrating his fingers, joint by joint. Inch by inch he transferred his flow to his palm, then wrist, to the fore arm, then elbow, and so on; it looked like he had just stuck his fingers into a light socket, which in turn sent a shock wave through his entire body. By the time his vibrating poppin' reached his chest it got me to thinking; I bet you Slim Jim didn't even have to use towels or one of those hot air hand dryers after he was done washing his hands. Slim Jim just had to bust out with some of his pulsating poppin' and then BAMM! His hands would be dry.

"Alright Slim Jim, I've got to run to the other side of this Jiz-oint, some female has been eyeballing me TALL. I'll catch up with you in a few, after I get her phone number," I said cocksure.

I boldly walked toward the direction of where I figured Ms. Neon green socked girl would be, as I dodged through the now busy rink crowd. Truth be told, neon green sock girl wasn't really eyeballing me, it was the other way around, I was scoping her out, but it just sounded better to say it the other way, that way if she turned me down, nobody had to know. Guys can really razz another guy about that sort of thing. You know?

As I walked around and started to look for her, I sort of wondered if she looked any good or not. - that paper bags for legs incident will haunt me forever. I even started freakin' myself out too, to be honest with you. I wondered if she was going to be the epitome of femininity or the essence of a calamity. Hot or Not? that was the question – not that I was either.

I didn't finish telling you about Slim Jim's jacket though and as I walked around looking for Ms. Neon Green, I sort of thought about it. The patch on the back of his jacket that he had designed, drew and then painted himself had: a red bricked wall in the background, with the mortar finely painted with fine grey brush strokes in between each red brick. There were 2 breakers as the focus of the jacket; one B-Girl was down-rockin' and the other B-boy was executing Atomic flares, you could even see "NSR" spray painted on the bricked wall - that's how detailed he had made it.

The setting was a street corner sidewalk in Anytown USA. The ghetto blaster was positioned next to the red bricked wall, right where the two bricked walls had merged and formed an outside street corner. The ghetto blaster was sized as big as one of the breakers, but it looked cool. I mean, even though the ghetto blaster was drawn crazy large, it still looked cool as heck. Slim Jim even drew squiggly lines pointing outwards from the boom box speakers to show that the stereo was playing music. He had thought of everything.

I really did want one of those jackets too; I wasn't just saying that to pump his ego or anything. I had meant it. It would have really helped finish off the look that I was sporting that night too. I was rockin' dark gray suede gym shoes with light gray fat laces, gray slippery parachute pants with a gray and black pullover tracksuit top and of course I had my NSR nameplate as the focus. I also had on a black sweatshirt underneath because sometimes when I was wind milling, especially nut cracking, the slippery jacket made me lose traction, so I usually took the slippery pullover off, especially on slippery floors. When I was breakin' on carpet, like the outskirts at Suburbanite were, I'd keep the pullover on, you dig?

I kept heading towards the DJ booth, vending machines, and restroom area where I thought I had last seen the short skirted, neon green socked, cutie. I watched the DJ grab a twelve inch record from his crate, he put it on the spinning platter and then we all heard, "The roof is on fire" by Rockmaster Scott and the Dynamic Three. I paused next to a large subwoofer and listened to the cut as it moved through the sound system; a definite B-Boy jam. He kept flipping the record over and remixing, "Request line" and "The roof is on fire" back and forth and back again – the crowd was going crazy.

After a while, I went over to the vending machines out of nerves and got a couple of chocolate bars. I guess my plan was to offer her one, to sort of break the ice or something. What better way to say "hi" than with sweets. At least, that was my plan at that point.

I had looked around everywhere and there were no signs of her bright green colors, so I figured she and her friend must have been in the bathroom ever since I had made my way over there. The girls "John" was the only place I hadn't checked, so I started hanging out with the chocolate bars in my hand and thought about what I should say, while also trying to look calm, yet standing all tough, cute, and cool; all at once. It's really hard to pull all of that off, with just a certain kind of look on your face and stance, but I tried. I just hoped that my tough-cool-cute face didn't look like my "I'm takin' a dump face" both faces can really use a lot of facial muscles if you know what I'm screamin'?

Then over towards the boys' bathroom, I spotted 2 unknown BBoy looking cats strolling my way. BBoys can really stick out of the crowd and not just by the way they dress but by the way they walk too. You see, we BBoys really own the floors that we walk on – not just when were ready to rock, but always.

Both of the Bboy looking cats were wearing black jogging suits, which was my first clue that they were breakers, but it was more about their swagger that told me they could floor rock. The taller dude of the two was sportin' a dark green scarf draped around his neck untied, a Black Kangol as his lid, with Black

Cazals to hide his face. And the other cat donned a dark green knit winter hat that sat on his head off to the side – like he didn't finish putting it on all of the way and he also had a dark green scarf, just like his pal, only his was tied around his neck tight. And this time when I say, "tight" I mean snug and firm.

They were both walking with purpose and swagger; sheer cockiness and toughness was written on their faces and they appeared to be heading straight towards me. As they drew more near, I was sure that I didn't recognize them but I was also sure that they were coming towards me. Their nonstop eye contact seemed to pierce right through me. I even looked behind me, but it was just a wall. Maybe they could tell I was a breaker? Maybe they wanted to hang out or something?

They engaged me with firm eye contact that felt like it was going to bite my head off. The dude wearing the black Cazals and black Kangol got uncomfortably close to me, squared up and said, "Yo Boyyee, what you be about?!" He had said it with this very threatening tone and mean face as he poked his index finger hard into my NSR nameplate which had thumped my chest. Then he flicked my necklace with might; I could feel the belt buckle nameplate shifting from side to side from one chest to the other like a pendulum. It all happened so fast, he was bulging his eyes like a psycho and blinking like a madman. In that instant I remembered the warnings from the students at my school about how "gang bangers" had hung out here.

Before I could respond his buddy chimed in by echoing him in this tough yet mousy voice, "Yay, what you be about? – Who you ridin' with people or folks?"

Meanwhile, out walked the pretty dark haired, nice smiled, neon greened, short skirted, high heeled Chica. She had just put her dark hair into pig tails while she was in the girls' room. She had matching neon green hair ties and green hoop earrings to go with the rest of her ensemble. My heart was racing like mad – for more than one reason.

The thought blipped through my mind that I had probably looked as Curt Columbus had looked when he was pinned up against the fence by the taco stand last night at Suburbanite rink. Admittedly these cats really did catch me off guard with the flicking of my nameplate and that 'what you be about' business. But when I caught a glimpse of "that girl" I quickly bowed my neck and snapped out of it.

"Sup guys, I'm just a breaker; no people or folks or any of that. I'm just a B-Boy … I'm here with my break crew; the Neighborhood Street Rockers."

And I bull shee-ott you not, right as I had said the word "breaker" the two fine mini skirted girls with the meshy shirts looked my way with a smile. They casually started walking their way over towards me, but slowly – trying to not look obvious.

The two not so friendly bangers were still giving me this hard ice gangbanger look. My being a breaker didn't make them instantly want to be my new best buddy old pals or chums or anything. My face stayed focused. Their face remained mean. Yet they stopped talking for a moment while they figured out their next move.

Neon greens buddy that was wearing a black bra that was peeking through her white mesh shirt like the Madonna "like a virgin" look - asked me, "Hey are you a breaker? I love to watch breakin'."

I forgot for the moment that my safety was at risk, my girl craze took over, and I said, "Yep I am a b-boy extraordinaire, I can rock out with breakin'!"

It's funny how a girl can really snap a guy back into his swagger. I didn't even mean to get tough in front of those hard punks but my mojo took over. (And I'm not talking about Kid Mojo; I am talking about my swag mojo)

"You're a breakdancer, huh?" she said with a cute smile.

"Yep, breaker, b-boy, that's what we call it. I mean sometimes I'll call it break dancing out of habit but that is really a term the media came up with for B-boying or breakin' but it doesn't really matter to me as long as someone can rock the floor," I said as I started to ramble out of nerves.

Now that I had a closer look at the two girls, I saw that they were both wearing thigh high stockings, not socks. It was hotter than hot and I was glad that it wasn't paper bags this time.

Then the mousy looking gang banger chimed back in, "Breaker, b boy … pshhht, you aint nothing!"

The girl with the pig tails and neon green thigh highs said, "I like your spiked hair – when are you going to break? I want to watch you."

It was a cause and effect; the more the girls talked to me, the angrier those dudes facial expressions became. I couldn't even answer her question because, the finger flickin', Kangol and Cazal wearing banger piped, "I bet you he breaks like a pansy … you girls want to see some real breakin'? … I'll show you some real breakin'," the gangbanger said.

Both girls rolled their eyes as the macho mousy banger with the dark green scarf and the dark green winter hat chimed in, "Yay, this boy aint be about nothing … he's with the Neighborhood Street Rock a bye babies," he said trying to get me mad.

Out of the corner of my eye, I saw Slim Jim driving through the crowd like a Mack truck, along with Blazin' who had his horse teeth showing as usual because he was usually trippin' and laughing about something. But the crowd had been getting packed by the minute because it was prime time, so they were still kind of far away, due to the zillions of party people they had to weave through, if you know what I mean?

My mojo started to kick up a notch when I realized they were heading my way. (You know, I had some back up.) I turned to the girls and said, "My crew and I, The Neighborhood Street Rockers are going to be breakin' all night over there," as I pointed over towards the far section of the rink. (The Billie Jean-Saturday Night Fever Dance floor.) Then out of sheer mojo, I said to the girls first but then threw a look towards the gangbangers that were still throwing me hard looks, "My crew the Neighborhood Street Rockers can beat any crew in a break battle, NOT a gang bangin' battle. We are breakers. I am here to break." Then I smiled, looked at the girls, and said, "And I'm also here to talk to the pretty girls," which seemed to paint more anger onto the green scarved gangbangers faces. (I refuse to call them B-boys because a B boy in my opinion shouldn't be a gangbanger ... because it's all about the breakin'. Breakin' is our way of life.)

The black and dark green clad bangers moved inches closer to me. When mousy dude whined, "Your crew can't beat shee-ott, bee-otch ... Our crew the Hip Hop Breakers versus your crew the Neighborhood skirt rockers, next week, right here, at Chicagoland Rink, show up if you dare!"

I confirmed with toughness, "We will be here! It is on ... On like Donkey Kong."

"We will battle 50 bucks each man and shoes. The losing crew will give the winning crew their shoes. Unless you're scared and you know you aint shee-ott bee-otch, In that case we could battle for flowers, pansy," finger jabbing banger had said in a mean yet funny way.

But I didn't let it phase me, it may have scared me a little, if I've got to be honest with you, but I knew my boys were on their way over. So I confidently said to both of the cats from the Hip Hop Breakers crew, "We will be here, next week."

"Alright bet," Macho mousy guy added in his chip-monkey weasel voice.

"Bet, 11pm sharp," the finger jabbin' banger said in a gruff sounding voice. Then they walked away with hopping swagger but they made sure to eyeball me from time to time with every other stride.

I talked with the two girls for a bit while Blazin' and Slim Jim tried to squeeze through the packed crowd of skaters, breakers, housers, and bangers – I guess some of the rumors I had heard from my classmates at school yesterday had some truth.

Blazin' must have seen the past few seconds of my exchange with the Hip Hop Breakers so he held up his hand using "the okay symbol" while he raised his eyebrows in wonder.

I held up my hand and nodded to confirm that I was okay which sent Slim Jim and Blazin' into the can to download the brown load – at least that's what Slim Jims face looked like; he looked like he had to take a crapper –sometimes you can just tell that about someone.

Now that the gangbangers had left, I was finally able to ask her name and shoot out some small talk all the while I got back into my tough-cute-cool face, that I hoped didn't look like my "I'm growing a tail at a sit down" face. – You know – taking a crapper face.

Kelly was the one in neon green and Marie, her friend, wore mostly black and white, but I was more focused on Kelly. Kelly never took her eyes off me and I did the same.

Kelly told me, "Sylvester and Angelo are loud mouth gang bangin' punks. They go to my school, don't let them scare you. I've got big friends here at the rink that can squash those punks. I won't let them mess with you," she reassured me with a nice smile.

"Thanks doll face, that's sweet but I've got my boys up here too," I said while trying to stand tall.

"I'm glad you stood up to those punks, no one at my school likes them because they are always acting all tough but when the football players mess with them… they aint nothing, they shut up." Kelly said.

"So, you'll be up here next week then?" I asked her.

"I'm up here every week," she said, "I'm usually skating but Marie and I just went shopping at the mall and we wanted to show off our new clothes and shoes," she said.

I smiled like a kid in a candy store and said, "I'm glad you did, you're looking bee you tiff full! Foxy even, Fow show!" Then I told her how I used to rock out with roller skates too; I talked about trick skating, spaghetti legs, and crazy legs but I could tell I was losing her, she wasn't really into all of the trick skating talk. So I told her how she had great fashion sense and she started to smile again. Like I said, I have no idea what to say to girls.

Then I made her eyes light back up, "But ever since breakin' came into the fold … well I've just been smitten ever since," I had said the word "smitten" about breakin' but I sort of tried to hint that I was smitten with her by the way I had smiled and looked deep into her eyes. You should have seen me, for the first time in my life I think I may have actually pulled off that thing they call flirting.

I think she had picked up on my hint too because she smiled and said, "I think I am a little smitten myself Phil K Swift."

I took that as my cue to make my exit. I knew I was liable to say something stupid, so I decided to bail. It's always best to leave on a high note and there was nothing higher that could have happened at that point. So I told Kelly and Marie, "I'll catch you girls in a little while, I'll be right over there hanging with my break crew on the Saturday night fever dance floor," I said as I pointed towards our section of the room again.

Kelly smiled, "Yeah, I like how there are lights in the floor over there. By the way, I hope you and your crew can beat those Hip Hop Breakers next week."

"We will, you'll see," I said with swag.

Then I went in for a hug and she said, "Mmmm" in my ear.

As I walked away I spouted back, "I really like your style girl, you really know how to dress!"

"You're not so bad yourself Swifty," she said as she waved good bye.

Moments later, Slim Jim and Brock Blazin' showed up. "What was that all about? What were those dudes talking to you about … were they breakers?" Brock asked.

Slim Jim jumped in, "Yay Phil we thought you were in some trouble or something? Were those guys messing with you?"

Blazin' eagerly jumped back in, "Yay dude, we got here as fast as we could but by the time we got here, they walked away so we just hit the can man."

I filled in Slim Jim and Blazin' on the whole story, well not the whole story; I figured I'd wait for the right time to tell them that I had wagered and anted our shoes and 50 bucks a man and all of that jazz. That's the kind of thing that I'd rather tell them when the moment seemed right. After all, coming up with 50 bucks a man wasn't going to be a piece of cake for some of us. – including me.

I knew when I got back to the other side of the rink where all of us NSR's were hanging out, I would have to break it to them. That's what happens when you're trying to impress a girl; you start talking out of the side of your neck.

The three of us walked back through the grid locked rink and towards our boys. Bruiser had finally made it. He was getting frisked for entry.

The second dance floor (where we breakers were hanging) was getting shared by the breakers and the house head jack dancers. When we got back, the DJ had switched vibes to jackin' house music, which little by little had been taking over Chicago.

Two tall guys were dance stomping to the beat like Clydesdale horses on the Saturday night fever dance floor; side by side with the breakers I had told you about when we had first walked in, the two that had pretended fighting with their up rocks and such. And our boy Jet Drinkwater was hanging with them too. They were mostly working on their head spins. – and I say working on, because none of them could rock more than one or two of them in a row.

Anyway the stomp dancer dudes were stomping so hard to the beat that it appeared, at least from where I was, that they were stomping on one of the breakers hands as he had switched to a down rock, foot work, scat. I couldn't tell if it was on purpose or if the jack dancer was just so pumped that he didn't pay attention to the breakers around him as he stomp danced.

Next, I saw Jet Drinkwater enter into a routine of his own that included swiping and down rocking - but he too had to shuck and jive to avoid getting his hands stomped on, and I was sure of it now. I could tell by the nasty looks that Jet had given the stompers that he had almost been stomped on.

And I didn't get it either. There was plenty of room for everybody to dance, yet the stompers stayed close to the breakers. But when I got closer I realized what was going on. Everyone was vying for the "Billie Jean" and

"Saturday night fever" floor space that was right underneath the speakers. It was all about vying for the bass in the face and the lights on the floor. Everyone wanted to dance on the same spot.

I joined in with these unknown breakers and Jet and we formed a cypher, which managed to make those jack stompers move their action down a bit as our break circle grew by the minute as my fellow NSR's began to show up.

Eventually all of the NSR's had joined the breakin' cypher. We were all getting down with our top rocks, up rock battles, down rocks, and power moves. But the stomp dancers didn't go away, they just moved on down the floor a bit. But it seemed as if everyone was happy now. None of us breakers had to dodge stomping feet for the moment.

The DJ took notice of the stompers that were now in front of him. (By the way, there was a second set of turntables and a second DJ, in our "Saturday night fever" section of Chicagoland Rink.) The jack dancers and the disco house steppers were showing up everywhere on the dance floor like disco ducks on steroids, so the DJ threw on another Chicago house music track to keep 'em movin; "Its House" and "Time to Jack" were playing through the system which made everyone pick up their dance pace a notch. Even we Bboys were diggin' the house music. The track was that slammin'! We breakers had grown to love and break to House music however, we still dug our "hip hop, don't stop the rock rock"

But when you are from Chicago, sometimes, you've just gotta have house.

The DJ was taking doubles of the records and remixing on the spot. The more jack trackin' the DJ played, the more jack be nimble I had to be about where I had walked and breaked and placed my hands because those stompin' dancin' cats were getting their freaks on even more crazy than before.

After walking through the gauntlet of stomping, I had struck up a conversation with our manager Bruiser. I thought he would be the perfect person to deliver the news that I had just got us into a battle with some hardcore breaker bangers.

I told him the details about their attitudes and that "what you be about" business, and I sort of shouted in his ear on accident – I saw Dan moving his head away from mine; I had shouted that loud. I had to compete with the music the DJ was thumping. Then I loudly whispered, "Oh yay by the way, I wagered our shoes and 50 smackers each. The losing crew gives their shoes to the winning crew."

Bruiser shouted back with wide eyes, "You wagered the whole crews shoes and 50 bucks each?!" A couple of NSR's looked our way but I don't think they could hear what was being said over the loud music, but they knew that Bruiser shouted something which made them curious.

After hippin' Bruiser up to the details of our break battle along with all of the seedy details. He pretended wiping his brow and said, "Whew, I think you got a little too big for your britches Swift." Bruiser laughed and added, "But that's a good problem to have, isn't it?" Then he thought about what I had just told him, he shook his head, and repeated in this, holy crap sort of way, "Shoes and 50 bucks, this one's on you B, but I'll let everybody know the details."

Bruiser slowly had made his way around the rink, hippin' up the crew about the battle next week, but I decided to jump in and start telling some of them too. The waiting was killing me.

I talked to Blazin' first, my right hand man. I gave Blazin' all of the details in one big sentence and one big breath and when I paused for air he told me, "I already told you … We will serve those punks! We will show 'em wazup! … I thought something was going down when I saw you over there by the bathrooms."

Out of the corner of my eye, I watched Bruiser talk to Slim Jim when moments later Slim stormed over in a panic, "Yo Phil, My mom will kick my butt if I lose these shoes. It's the only pair I have. She just bought me these shoes, they were 70 bucks and she told me: I'm not buying you anymore shoes until next year. In fact, I had to talk her into buying me these shoes for 6 months. She made me put duct tape on my old ones for three months – just to make 'em last longer."

Blazin' jumped in, "Dude, we are the Neighborhood Street Rockers bro! We are going to win. We are the baddest crew around bro," he had said in the loudest voice ever, aimed right at Slim Jim.

Meanwhile Bruiser was making his way around the rink like a hot potato. He'd tell a new NSR what wazup and then move on to the next one.

After Dan had delivered the news, one by one the NSR's were coming up to me and giving me their thoughts. Miguel 2 tough approached me and said, "I'm all about it Swift, let's show that crew what's up! …Bruiser told me the story. They were messing with you, huh? … Calling us names and shee ott? … Babies or something? We'll show 'em wazup for realz!" Miguels wink and smile made me feel better.

"Did anyone tell your bro yet? What's Fandango going to think?" I asked Miguel as we both scoped Fandango in the corner laying down the tall mack on a Chica Latina.

Miguel reassured me, "He'll be cool; he'll be in – in like Flynn, no worries."

Next, I walked up to Kid Mojo and he told me in his usual cocksure way, "We'll mess anybody up!" That was how Kid Mojo usually was; arrogant, yet playful all at once - and he meant it. In fact the rest of the night, Kid Mojo must have come up to me at least 20 times; like every 5 minutes, at random - saying "Yo! We'll mess anybody up … Yoppp, we'll mess anybody up." I wish you could have heard the voice he used when he had said it; he used this made up, playful, tough guy voice while he powerfully slammed his hands together and making his mouth huge, "Anybody … we'll mess anybody up."

The news about our first big battle with money and shoes on the line went off better than I had expected, except for Slim Jim who was still worrying about his mom kicking his butt and such. "But at least she won't be kicking your butt with your own shoes if we lose," I said to him, just to mess with him.

"You're not even funny, sonny," Jim said nervously. It was sort of strange to see such a big dude get so nervous. I never really picture big people getting nervous, so it looked kind of weird.

The rest of the night I walked around the rink trying to gather as much information as I could about the Hip Hop Breakers. 4 of them were there that night. Three of them had green scarves. One of them was wearing different colors, so I wasn't sure if he was a part of their crew or not but he was hanging and breakin' with those cats Angelo and Sylvester all night, so I assumed that he was a part of their crew. After I had watched the four of them break from the shadows. I suddenly didn't want to watch them anymore. They were good – too good.

My wanderlust led me back to Kelly and Marie who introduced me to some of their friends who had more info about those Sylvester and Angelo dudes. I learned that the Hip Hop Breakers were a real deal break crew that had battled before – and they hung out at Chicagoland rink every weekend. One of Kellys' friends Jackie said that half of their crew was from Chicago and the other half was from the burbs. "They are the real deal; they can do head spins, flips, and spinny twisty thingys," she had called it.

But just like that, the end of the night drew to a close when they flipped on the bright white fluorescent lighting. I didn't quite notice that there was more detailed graffiti on the walls on the way in because the bright lights were off and the disco lights were on. Or maybe I didn't notice because I kept trying to look for neon green socks the whole night. But there was a lot more graffiti art on the rink walls than I had told you about. And not gang bangin' kids vandalized graffiti - but artwork graffiti; it was purposely and professionally painted graffiti ART. Cooler than Pluto.

There was a graffiti mural of an afro headed guy holding a boom box right next to his ear in one hand while the other hand had big rings that read: "HIP HOP RAP." It was stretched across 4 of his fingers in gold, his hand was drawn as big as his head, but it looked cool, comic book, and cartoon cool. And of course he was drawn with skates on his feet, since this place was mainly a skate rink – until us B-boys and house people had started taking over. I didn't know much about graffiti art, but it looked fantastic - bad to the bone.

"Very fresh, very cool," I said to the rink cashier as I pointed at the mural while walking towards the exit. The cashier nodded and was about to say something to me when Kelly who had been coincidentally behind me came walking out of the rink with her friends and said, "See ya next week Phil. I can't wait to watch you take out the Hip Hop Breakers, you're going to crush them," she said all crazy loud.

I started talking tough and pumping my fist, when I noticed that one of the Hip Hop Breakers was behind us a bit and was within ear shot of us, which sparked him into our conversation. I did not know his name, but he was this cat that had rocked Atomic flares. I had seen him when I was checking out the HHB's from the shadows, "Easy, easy, aint nobody takin' us out!" he said.

In the midst of it all, the cashier had looked at me with this concerned look that said: "You're not going to gang bang at my rink – are you?"

Since I thought I was reading the cashiers mind, I said, "Kelly is talking about my break crew taking out this other break crew in a break dance battle - just two dance crews, dancing against each other."

The cashier (who seemed like she may have been the owner; she had that look about her) replied, "Oh, Break dancing? Well, okay, that's fine then."

When I looked back to see what that "atomic flare" cat and the other HHB's (Hip Hop Breakers) were doing, I saw this taunting and smug smile coming from Angelo as he mouthed the words, "What's up?" the way he had said it to me, made him look like a dog that had just barked at me. I knew he was trying to start something but I just turned around and ignored him.

Our exit of Chicagoland Rink was herd-like, so I had made it outside of the rink before those cats could even catch up to me. Blazin's old man was already waiting for us too. We hopped in our ride and left before anything else had happened.

The car ride home was silent all things considered, mainly because we were all beat from hours of breakin', heck 2 nights in a row. I told the guys that I had heard through the grapevine (some of Kelly's friends) that those Hip Hop Breakers had been trying to drum up some break battles for the past couple of weeks but everyone had been afraid of their "thuggery" as Marie had put it. I guess rumor had it that the rest of their crew was scoping out some other rinks and nightclubs that night, in hopes of drumming up a break battle. "So I guess I walked right into their trap," I told Blazin'

"You can't trap the hunter," Brock Blazin' said boldly. Then Blazin', who felt a little playful, tried to mess with Miguel."Yo 2 tough, well, you know Phil? – Right?" he asked Miguel.

In this: 'duhhh' tone of voice Too tough said, "Yaayyy?"

Which made Blazin' start laughing like a freakin' hyena; he could barely talk he was laughing so hard, "Phil Mckracken – you want to Phil McKracken?"

In the most droll and sarcastic tone I said, "Ohhh wow Brock finally burned someone."

"Aren't you supposed to say: Do you know Phil McKracken? Then if the person says "yes", you say. You know Philly my crack in? What do you know about filling my crack in?" Miguel said as he rolled his eyes and explained to Brock that he had told the joke wrong. But that didn't stop Brock from laughing his crack off anyway.

However, this did make Blazin's dad look into the rear view mirror with this strange look that said: don't they teach these kids anything better to talk about in school? And to confirm that I had read his look accurately, when we had all finally shut up, he said, "You kids and your corny ass jokes."

But with Brock already in a playful mood, he started asking everyone if they had ever eaten corn and then looked at their crap the next time they had dumped. Which drew a few dry heaves from the bunch, and coincidentally or maybe it wasn't coincidentally, this made Brocks old man crank up the radio but not before he said, "I didn't say corn, I said corny," as he shook his head at our corniness.

Anyway, after we had dropped off Miguel and Fandango, Blazin' asked me, "So Phil, do you really think that we can school those punks for real? – I saw you checking them out." He meant the HHB's of course.

"As long as we can get our entire crew to show up next Saturday I think we will be golden. Boogie Bob said that he will be out of the Cuckin' Fancer unit by next weekend and Chi Girl and her flips will be icing on the cake, "I told Blazin' sort of loudly, which drew Brocks dads eyes on me for a quick second; mainly when I had said that whole, "Cuckin' Fancer" thing. No one wants to hear the "C" word and no adult wants to hear an 'almost swear' or a swear from a kid.

Then I continued, "… And Bob told me that the first thing he wanted to do once he was out of the cancer unit was to hook up with all of us NSR's at one of the rinks I had been telling him about. Dude, last week when I was at the hospital, he was spinning around on his head like a madman with needles sticking in his arms and everything. - As long as everyone shows up next week, we are in; in like Flynn," I said cocksure. – Even though, deep down inside, I was really worried about the HHB's – they looked tough.

Blazin' suddenly realized that Chi Girl wasn't at the rink tonight, so he asked, "Where was old girl at bro?"

"Chi Girl?" I asked.

He nodded yes.

"It's all good in the hood my brother from a different mother. When I talked to her on Friday at Suburbanite she was already telling me not to expect her to be there on Saturday because her mom only lets her go out once on the weekend nights because she's an "A" student and she spends one of her Fridays or Saturdays reading. She told me that she likes to read anyway so she doesn't really put up much of a fuss or anything. She wants to get into a good college so she can make lots of dough when she's older, she was telling me – but I will call her up tomorrow and I will make sure that she keeps her Saturday night open as her night out. - So izzz all good mi hermano," I told Brock as I shook his hand since we had just pulled onto my block.

Blazin's old man pulled into the driveway to drop me off, and as I was getting out, Brock could see that I had this seriously worried look on my mug; almost as if I was in pain, I urgently asked, "Whew, I almost forgot, thank god I remembered. Don't forget to grab those and bring them inside or they'll get ruined."

Blazin' looked at me all puzzled and concerned and said, "Oh okay, grab what?"

Cackling my butt off I said, "Grab THEEZ FART CHEEKS!" I shut the car door and headed to my crib door. I looked back as I was pulling my keys out of my pocket and I saw the shadows of Blazin' and Blazins' dads' heads shaking back and forth as they pulled away. This made me laugh so hard I practically peed my drawers. It must have taken me an hour to open up my door I was laughing so hard.

I don't know what it is about THEEZ FARTS jokes that never gets old, it's a guy thing, I guess. It makes me wonder if girls ever say: hey do you want to grab one?; ONE OF THEEZ FARTS?

I'm sure it's just a guy thing.

CHAPTER 17

Its Rock N Roll

My Uncle Wes's Rock band was playing at "Meadowbrook Malls" indoor atrium at their annual winter festival, the day after our first trip to Chicagoland Rink. I had made plans with Dan the man Bruiser to pick me up so we could check it out.

My Uncle Wes was quite the rebel. Well first off, he is an awesome guitarist and he's been in a band ever since I can remember. When I was little, like 5 or 6 years old, my cousin and I used to stay at my grandparents' house (Uncle Wes's and my Dads parents) and watch him and his band mates practice.

What was cooler than Pluto was that his rock band had its band practices in the basement every weekend, so my cousin and I usually checked it out. When it came time for his band to take a break or something or maybe it was just because they needed to add some fun to their day – my uncle and his band mates would start messing with us. Uncle Wes would start whispering in between songs to my cousin and me, "Hey Phil, hey Mike, pssst come here." Then he would say in a secretive and sneaky voice, "Do you want some Whiskey?"

I didn't know what whiskey was back then and of course I know what it is now but I knew it was something we weren't supposed to be doing. Uncle Wes would grab a couple of shot glasses and a very green bottle of "something" and then he'd continue his game and quietly say, "Okay nephews, do you want to have a shot of whiskey?" He could barely even keep a straight face he would be laughing so hard, "Here boys, drink a shot of whiskey."

My cousin and I would go, "bottoms up" and drink down the lemon juice. It was only lemon juice but I didn't know it at the time, he and his band mates would get a rip roaring real good bang out of this whole thing. Looking back, I swear that my cousin Mike who was also my age, must have known what the word "whiskey" had meant because he would start acting all weird and wobbly and such after we had gulped down the "Whiskey." And that would even get a bigger roar out of my Uncle Wes and his band mates, because they all knew that is was really just a placebo; a pretend adult drink. I can still remember watching my cousin stumble and fall all over the place like a drunkard; a lemon juice drunkard.

Anyway, that's my crazy rocker Uncle Wes. There's actually way more, I could go on for hours but I don't have time to tell you everything, but let's just say this; my cousins and I had to endure our fair share of fart machines, which I'm sure you can figure out what that was. And we had been given plenty of "hot treatments." The hot treatment consisted of my Uncle taking us for a car ride, and then he'd crank the heat up in the car on a summer 100 degree day for 100 hours in a row and keep the windows SHUT! Well, actually it probably only lasted about one minute, but when you're five or six years old, it seemed like hours. But you know what? An Uncle is supposed to corrupt their nephew in some way shape or form otherwise they might get their Uncle card revoked. It's true.

Everyone gets hazed once in a while, nowadays any kind of hazing and you make nationwide news, but anyway you ought to see my Uncle Wes thrash some licks on the guitar. He doesn't just play rock n roll and blues. He plays other very complicated cool stuff; like Beethoven, Bach, and other classical pieces that he has reworked into guitar solos. It's pretty darn cool to watch, that's for show YO! Heck Uncle Wes can even light the guitar on fire and play with his teeth, it nearly burns his eyebrows off but he's that good. Well, maybe I'm exaggerating a little bit, but it's hard to describe just how good he is unless I tell it to you in that way.

I had a couple of minutes before Bruiser was going to be at my crib to pick me up for Uncle Wes' show, so I started making the phone calls. Boogie Bob sounded the same as yesterday morning. He was wide awake one minute and then drifting in and out of sleep the next, which I guessed was because his chemotherapy medicine still needed to wear off. And his nurses said something about a lack of red blood cells but blah, blah, yada, yada; I'm not a doctor.

I told Bob about the break battle, the shoes ante, and the 50 bucks and he was all cool with it, he sounded excited as all heck for a minute or two. I guess I'd be excited about anything that meant I was no longer in a stinkin' hospital anymore too. Then he must have drifted off to sleep again because the phone went quiet. So I shouted in the phone to wake him up, he answered, "Phil … Kid … I will be there in high spirits … for the battle – you said 50 bucks right? … but come by this joint in the middle of the week … I've got to tell you something. Okay kid?"

"Fow show my man, I'll be there like sab wah faire," I told him.

Bob still tired, repeated, "Just come by in the middle of the week."

He hung up the phone or fell asleep before I could even say, "I will see you again."

Next I rang up Chi girl. When I filled her in on all of the details about the wager and such, she was hardly thrilled, but took the news like one of the boys and said, "Well Phil, we better win this thing; I don't want to explain to my mom why I am coming home in socks. So we better win. That's all."

Moments after I got off the phone, I heard the rough sound of Bruiser's muffler or lack thereof in the driveway. "Sup Bruiser? What izz doing?" I said as I got into his ride.

Bruiser replied, "I'm just chill for rill! So do you think that there will be any breakers up at this mall today?" he asked as I got into his ride.

"A couple of breakin' cats from school told me that they would be up there," I told him.

On Friday at school, I had told Hazy and Isaac to meet me at the Laundromat in Meadowbrook Mall just after lunch time on Sunday. The Laundromat was only a five minute walk to the music festival. I picked the Laundromat as the meeting place because they had a yellow cabinet, stand up Pac Man arcade game in there and I was somewhat of a Pac Man addict to be honest with you. I have even been diagnosed with "Pac Man Fever" before, there's a whole song about it. Well, that's why I picked that Laundromat as our meeting place.

I had never hung out with those cats outside of school before but when we were in the hip hop hallway last Friday and I told them that I was going up to "Meadowbrook's Winter Music Festival" and droppin' some breakin' to rock and roll, they were all over it. Hazy told me, "Dude I've never gotten down with breakin' to rock and roll before - that sounds all crazy."

And Isaac added, "Dude, the punkers have a mosh pit but now we can give your Uncles rock band a breakers pit." Anyway that's what my friends from the hip hop hallway at school had said about breakin' to rock and roll, which really seemed to interest Dan too.

Bruiser pulled up to the Laundromat and I tried to see if they were there yet, but I could barely see inside the fogged up glass windows, except for the yellow cabinet of the Pac Man machine, a neon sign that was in the shape of a hanger, along with another neon sign that was flickering, "OPEN."

Someone was standing by the yellow Pac Man machine, wiping away some of the steamed up glass, and looking outside as Bruiser and I got ready to get out of his ride.

Hazy, Isaac, and Dustin were all huddled around the Arcade game, "The ACA Collective is in full effect," I said to Dan more or less at random once I realized it was them. As I hopped out of Bruiser's ride, Dustin and Isaac came out to greet us with poppin', lockin' and wavin', while Dan's car stereo was still jamming.

Bruiser's car sound system was playing: "Din Daa Daa" by George Kranz, sparking Dustin into top rockin' and Issac into chanting along with Bruisers' cassette player, "Bim Baa Baa Bim Boe Boe – Bim Baa Baa Bim Boe." While Isaac sang it, he was looking at this girl, just down the mall.

We all caught on pretty quickly that he was singing a parody of the melody because there was this totally hot, skimpy clothed girl, dressed like a "Bimbo" standing just down the mall from us. She was dressed in clothes that were 2 sizes too tight and too small. – Not that any of us minded or anything. But if a girl dresses like that; she's going to get talked about, I'm not saying it's right, I'm just saying. Young boys will be boys. If a girl shows off too much of herself, guys will say mean things. I know it's not right; it just is what it is. Wear more clothes if you don't like all of the "boys will be boys" talk. We'll like you just the same, we really will.

Bruiser turned off his car and cassette deck and then Dustin started to chime in with Issac. Even though the song was no longer playing from his car, the chant had kept going anyway, "Skee bop ba Skee bop ba Skeezer, Skee bop ba Skee bop ba Skeezer"

Then I joined in the fray, "Rump rump rump rump rump rump hey yo rump rump rump rump rump rump hey yo."

Bruiser had no choice but to join in on the fun too. The four of us were singing "Tromenenz" in parody as loud and hip as we could while passersby watched with smiles; even the hot Bimbo-ed out chick had smiled at us – she probably didn't know we were busting on her. Everyone just thought we were singing; fire barrel singing without the fire barrel.

We had even been loud enough that we could see Hazy, who was still inside of the Laundromat playing Pac Man, was grooving his shoulders, boppin' his head along, and mouthing the words to, "Din Daa Daa" as he rocked his game.

Hazy had finally been eaten by a monster and came out of the foggy windowed Laundromat to join us outside, "Sup Phil K Swift," he said while shaking my hand with his usual smug smile. He was a real smug punk, but we were still friends.

Isaac and Dustin were still vibin' as Hazy said, "You guys were grooving it for real, I was dancing along while I was playing. I was diggin' it."

I cut off Hazy out of excitement, "This is my buddy Bruiser, he is my manager.

"Manager of what?" Hazy said with a sideways glare.

Bruiser jumped in, "I'm a manager of a bunch of knuckleheads is what. "

Bruiser locked the doors on his car and the 5 of us started walking towards the indoor atrium where the winter music festival was supposed to be taking place. While walking, Hazy commented on my nameplate, "I haven't had a chance to tell you yet but your sharper than sharp NSR plate is totally fresh!"

Dustin chimed in, "Yeah fresh!"

I briefly thought about Rockefellers mocking comments about suburbanites that use the words "fresh" or "straight up" and other shiznit like that to sound like they're from the "city" and all. But I didn't say anything; I was one of those suburbanites that talked like that once in a while too. Sometimes I used that vernacular when I was really in the mood. And sometimes I used words like "vernacular" when I was in that kind of mood. I was not trying to pose, I just liked the way all the different words sounded – that's all. I like words, whether they're from the dictionary or from the streets; it's all good in the hood.

So anyway, I told Hazy, "Yep, having one of these nameplates around your neck is just like sporting a swagger … SPORTIN' DA SWAGGER!" which sent out a cascade of all five of us saying that phrase like a million times each. Brock and I always said it, but the other three had never heard our expression before. They couldn't stop saying it. After a few minutes Dustin, who didn't get it, asked, "sportin da swagger... around your neck? What are you freakin' talkin' bout?"

"This NSR nameplate lets everyone know that I am for real. That's what it means. When I say I am 'sportin' da swagger— I am saying that I have swag, confidence, I'm cool, and I'm lookin' good," I said loudly. "This NSR nameplate around my neck lets everyone know that I am the shiznit gents."

"We are all the shee-ott," Dan Bruiser said.

"I can hear some banjo twangin' coming from yonder," I told the guys as we got closer to the "winter music fest."

"Sup with that? You said it was a rock concert," Bruiser said.

"I guess my uncle wasn't kidding when he said the music was going to have variety."

Hazy and Dustin started singing, "Din Daa Daa" again, but this time they added a little yodel twang to their pitch as they sung along to the banjo, only this time they had used the actual lyrics.

I shrugged my shoulders, "I guess that's the band that goes on before my Uncle Wes because I know he goes on in about fifteen minutes or so."

By the time we had made it inside the atrium where the winter music fest was being held, "Mr. Banjo man" had finished. I saw my Uncle, "Wes Lee K" tuning up his guitars, chatting with his band mates, and whatnot.

Uncle Wes had rock star messy hair that was the Beatles meets Bon Jovi. He was sporting leather pants, a leather vest, and he had no shirt underneath. Wes spotted me, waved, and then got back to getting ready for his show with volume checks and all of that shee-ott.

Practically at the same time, we all noticed some cats rockin' the B-Boy regalia from across the packed atrium: Some of them were rockin' track suits, Kangol hats, Cazal glasses, tight fitting body suits and one of the cats was carrying a boom box radio. B-boys had been sprouting everywhere lately, so it was of no surprise that we had ran into some other breakers that day.

Bruiser started fooling around with the ACA cats and me, "Alright guys, get ready ... I'm going to go over to those B-Boys over there," he said while pointing to the guy that was holding the black boom box, "I'm going to tell them that you guys want to battle for pants. Loser has to go home in their underwear," Bruiser said as he stared at me with this mocking look in his eyes and winked.

Then Hazy jumped in with a smart assed look on his mug and said, "Who would be stupid enough to battle total unknowns for something crazy like clothes or shoes or something."

I looked at Bruiser and said, "I take it you told Hazy about our battle next Saturday with the Hip Hop Breakers?" I knew it had to have been Dan, since I hadn't gotten around to telling Hazy yet.

Bruiser shook his head "no" but said, "Yes" then he shook his head "yes" and said "no" with a smart aleck wink and smile.

Hazy continued, "Dude are you going to wear your new 70 dollar suede gym shoes with the fatty fat laces when you battle those guys next week?"

"You got that right, I'm wearing them on battle night, we are going to win, out of sight … aint that right," I said.

Hazy laughed and said, "Heck no, don't be low, cuz I said so, but if you lose your gonna be po."

Then Hazy slipped away from me and started top rockin' by this group of girls that looked like "rocker girls." They were wearing suede jackets with the fringe around the waist, they had long hair with bangs, and one of the girls had an "AC DC" purse. All the while I watched in excitement as my Uncle was taking the stage.

I watched my Uncle "Wes Lee K" and his band mates dart to the stage in a hurry. They grabbed their guitars, bass, and drum sticks and jumped into their set. The way they had all ran and then jumped onto the stage had made them look like paratroopers would have, if they had landed on the ground with instruments in their hands and then just started jamming. Their entrance was that grand is what I'm saying. The crowd of probably 300 or more started going nuts as they stomped on the gas and got into their set.

Uncle Wes was strumming a danceable rock melody with his lead guitar; the drummer kicked it in extra hard while banging his head to the rhythm, and the bassist followed the excitement by plucking some hard ice bass swing.

Wes began to captivate the crowd with a monster guitar thrashing while the look on Uncles face told me that he was giving it everything he had – his guitar solo was very Eddie Van Halen-esque in my opinion. The screaming crowd of hundreds started to get me amped. I started to stretch out a bit without trying to make it obvious. But Hazy who was only a few feet away from me, started reading my mind and began up rocking in my face.

We started up rock battling against each other right there on the spot to Uncles mad guitar solo. Bruiser circled around us a bit, sensing that we were about to get on down with some breakin', as to make room for us. I started to feel some of the crowd's eyes on me as Hazy and I went at it. It felt kind of different, yet cool, to up rock battle against Hazy to rock n roll instead of hip hop or house for a change. It felt like a mosh pit. It really did.

Uncle Wes spouted into the microphone, "Yeeeah! How's everybody feeling out there?"

The crowd cheered.

"Phil K Swift is rockin' the floor right now … show us what's up with that B-Bop Break dancing Phil, " Uncle Wes said like a rocker and then put the microphone back on the stand and jammed his guitar like a madman.

Without further ado, I leapt down to the ground into super fast pennies but I was abruptly stopped by some random spectator who wasn't paying attention to the break circle. He had walked right into my windmills in mid spin, which totally stalled my routine. I'm sure it hurt him more than it had hurt me but neither one of us was all that happy about it. I had to stop and shake off my wounds for a minute, but it was all good, Hazy started top rockin' again and I just watched my Uncle Wes rock it for a few.

Then Hazy jumped into the circle and started crab walking. Wes Lee K got back on the mike and said, "Alright rockers, breakers and rollers Wes Lee K band is going to shake things up, turn things out, and show you all what it's all about!"

It seemed like out of nowhere, our cypher had thickened up with breakers. I didn't even see them coming, it was as if everyone had just appeared. As they got closer, I recognized a few of them too.

"Braun, AJ Fresh, Pauly G … Sup Y'all … if I'd have known that was y'all standing by the snack stand I'd have come over to y'all sooner," I said to the three cats that had just joined our cypher.

"Sup y'all," Braun said with a funny smirk that mocked my "y'all" while the others gave me handshakes.

I had rocked breakin' with these guys a few other times around town and such. AJ Fresh was the dude that was holding the black boom box that I told you about when we had first walked into the winter music fest, only he was far away at that point and for all I knew his boom box was really just black paper bags. - And oh yeah, that "y'all" thing I had just spit out. I can really throw the "y'alls" out da side of my neck sometimes. I vacationed in Georgia a few years back and it sort of grew on me, so it slips out once in a while. Y'all know what I mean?

I also knew Braun Drix and AJ Fresh from hanging out at McCollum Park on random weekends or after school. When no one was around my hood to hang out with; meaning if Blazin' wasn't around, I would go up to the park and they would be there. It seemed like every time I went there, they'd be there. I'd go up there by myself and they would be there rockin' with AJ's boom box on the shuffle board ground, next to the cardboard they had brought with. The third B-boy of their bunch was, Pauly G., whom I had met at McCollum Park originally but had also run into at Suburbanite rink the other night. Everything Pauly said was in a rhyme. At Suburbanite, he said something like, "Do you know where the can is man, I've got to go pee before it flees down my knees and everyone says jeez Louise."

I forgot I had told him about the winter music fest, otherwise I might have recognized him from far away. It looked like he had worn his Bermuda Kangol hat a zillion times, it was the most flat, and tattered hat you have ever seen. Gilligan from the island had nothing on him. Pauly must have touched his hat every five seconds when he talked – and he was always talking, rhymin', and rappin'.

The music was crazy loud but that didn't stop ol Pauly from spouting his rap lyrics at me like a madman. Pauly had come up to me and started spitting his rappin', beat boxing, and some shiznit like that, right in my face; he wasn't good at giving people their own space.

In fact, the first time I had met him, he came up to me and acted as if he had known me for years – only I barely knew him. He got "all up in my grill" is what I'm saying. But he was cool, he didn't mean anything by it, he just didn't understand "personal space." He was just a "close talker" with a tattered hat who rhymed every darn word out of his mouth. Even his coughs and sneezes had patterns.

My Uncles band was rockin' freakin' loud, so other than the first words Pauly had said to me that day, I couldn't really hear him, "Sup y'all, they call me Paul. Pauly G, baby that's me" But then I didn't really hear the rest. I didn't want to be rude and ignore Pauly so I nodded along but I sort of wanted to hear my Uncles band too. I swear Pauly never stopped moving his mouth the whole time he stood next to me. And he stood next to me for hours.

While Pauly G rapped my ear off, AJ Fresh started to hop around the break circle like a pumped up freak-a-zoid. He was skipping, up rocking, jumping, and top rockin' like a kid splashing in a puddle. Then he did this thing that made him look like a heavy weight boxer about to enter the ring with all of his jaunty jumping. Then AJ Fresh threw himself into a twist and onto the ground and did a move very similar to Brocks' beach ball, only he dove to the ground, spun about 5 times, and then popped back up to his feet. Blazin's beach ball was more of a dive, one spin and then back to his feet.

Another cat that I had seen at McCollum Park but had never learned his name had just arrived at the fest. Braun Drix went over to him and I heard him say, "Blake! You're late dude – your watch is always a minute past 420." And that told me volumes about Blake and why he was late. But I'm not into that sort of thing.

I later learned his name was Blake Kleinfeld. Right when he had arrived, the dude Blake wasted no time, and dove into the cypher. He rocked out lightning quick helicopters into pennies and then he popped into a freeze. Many of us had copters but Blakes' were twice the rate of speed as anyone else in our crew had ever rocked, which really caught Dan the man's attention, "Old boy izz going izz-off," he said boisterously over Uncles music.

"Word, he's got speed," I agreed.

Dan leaned over and told me, "You ought to ask those guys to join our crew. They are straight up going bonkers … berserk I say - berserk. Hit them up. We could use a few more B-boys for next weekend."

"Word, you might be right," I told Bruiser.

While Blake was wind milling, down rocking, and attempting to do air tracks in the break circle, Dan was still chatting me up but so was Pauly. Pauly G was talking about how he was going to be the next big rap star. It's funny how Pauly didn't stop talking to me, even though he knew Dan had started talking to me too. They both were talking to me at a million miles per hour and I wasn't very good at listening to two people talk at once, if you know what I mean, jellybean? But I tried.

When Braun Drix took another turn in the cypher I told Dan, "Braun is always boasting of his elbow spins, so check this out."

Braun spent most of his time attempting elbow spins whenever I had seen him. That was his signature move. I had never seen him try any other move. He was Drix the elbow spinner and that's all you've got to know about his breakin'; that's all I know. But just as soon as I told Dan to watch, Braun was already done.

"Well, he did one that time, but he is always talking about how he can do more," I told Dan.

"You should have seen the fish I caught last year," Dan mocked, "It was this big" he said while stretching his arms crazy far apart.

At the end of Uncle Wes's set, the music stopped and we could finally hear each other talk.

"Yo Phil, we ought to join up with you guys – you NSR's … we heard about your guys get together at McCollum last week, and we want in your break crew," AJ said.

"Absolutely my man," I said out of surprise, "I was going to ask you guys if you wanted to join our crew."

Pauly G said, "Yay man, that's the plan, we want in your crew – add us and the rest of the crews are through, we will be the proud few; NEIGHBORHOOD STREET ROCKERS, "he screamed boldly as if he was already one of us.

Braun nodded in agreement.

"Yep, I'm in," Blake said.

"Let's do it! Lets become one big super crew. Welcome aboard," I said to the four of them.

Then I yelled out, "Yo Bruiser meet the newest members of the Neighborhood Street Rockers."

Dan Bruiser nodded and gave a thumb up.

I looked at my new crew mates and said, "The Neighborhood Street Rockers are battling next Saturday at Chicagoland Rink at 11pm sharp against the Hip Hop Breakers."

"Cool bro, I'm in," AJ said.

"Killa, that's hella-cool," Blake agreed with his California parlance.

"I'll be there like Sab wah faire without a care, this aint no truth or dare," Pauly G. said.

"Sounds awesome," Braun said with glee.

"I'm glad you're all in! However, there's something I haven't told you yet," I said.

"Convenient," Hazy said smart ass-ed-ly to stir up the pot. It's funny too. I felt Hazy's smug eyes on me the whole time they talked about wanting to join our crew.

"… The ante for the battle is 50 bucks a guy and your shoes are a part of the ante. Each winning crew member will get 50 bucks and a pair of shoes from the losing team," I said.

"And vice versa," Hazy added snippily.

Blake, Braun, Pauly, and AJ started looking around at each other after I had filled them in on the news and none of them had said a word. It felt like they were all going to change their minds about joining up with us (NSR's) until Blake broke the uncomfortable silence and said, "Sound good to me, I'm not afraid."

Then, one by one, each of them had confirmed that they were "in" and that they would be there on Saturday night at Chicagoland Rink to battle as one big super crew; the Neighborhood Street Rockers versus the Hip Hop Breakers. We had grown by four more, just like that. It was on; on like James Bond.

We breakers said our "au revoirs" to each other and gave our BRUGS, and then I found my uncle and threw him mad props about his band and all, and told him, "It was a stone gas to break to hard rock Uncle."

My uncle laughed and said, "I've had some wild rockers start a mosh pit before at my concerts but I've never had a bunch of breakers doing their thing and getting all excited like that before. I loved it. It was cool watching you break, nephew.

I've got to finish putting my guitar and amps away, come back in a few minutes," Uncles Wes said.

"Rock on," I said.

Then, I darted over and caught Drix, AJ, and Pauly who were getting ready to leave.

"We're starvin' like Marvin ... give me some skin!" Pauly said.

I shook his hand (or gave him some skin) and asked, "Where are y'all eatin?"

"The dog stand at the end of the mall," Pauly said.

"Did you say dog?" AJ asked and then started barking.

"See ya B boy, were going to grab a bite. Do you want to come with?" Braun asked with a gay smile.

"I've got to get home and do chores and homework, but thanks bruh," I said.

"Catchya later," AJ said boldly.

"Did Blake bail already?" I asked.

"Blake had to go do his thing," Braun said as he feigned an inhalation sound while putting his thumb and index finger to his lips.

"Right on, it's not my thing but whatevvs," I said as they all started walking down to the other end of the mall where that Hot Dog stand was located.

"It's not my thing either," Braun said.

"If you knew what was in those things, you wouldn't even eat 'em," I yelled. (I was talking about hot dogs.)

This prompted Pauly and AJ to start barking like dogs again.

I went back over by my Uncle to tell him goodbye and he was already packed up, "Come on out with my band and me. We are going to grab some grub at the town diner; burgers, fries, and coffee -leaded; fully leaded; its rock n roll. I've got to get myself all leaded up on coffee nephew, you can't beat the natural pump it gives you," he said in his rocker voice. In fact, he always talked in a rocker voice. Real loud too. I mean, his loudness made it obvious that he was a leaded coffee drinker.

I regretfully told my Uncle Wes, "My parents told me I have to get home and do chores around the house, vacuuming, sweeping, and dusting ... all of that kind of stuff."

My Uncle scoffed, shook his head no, and then talked from his entire face, "Nephew, call them up and tell them: ITS ROCK N ROLL!"

"Rock n roll?" I questioned abashedly.

Uncle Wes repeated, "When they tell you that you've got to get home to do your chores, tell them: Mom ... Dad, I'll get home when I can. ... ITS ROCK N ROLL ... Every time they try to tell you to get home for chores tell 'em: ITS ROCK N ROLL!"

Uncle Wes had given this whole speech in his rockin' voice, so I really couldn't find a reason to say no. After all, he was Uncle Wes.

And so I did, I called up my parents from a payphone.

They told me to get home.

I told them, "ITS ROCK N ROLL!"

Then CLICK, Uncle Wes had hung up the phone before I could even hear a reply. It's funny though, he was laughing in the same coarse exaggerated way that he had laughed that time he had given me "whiskey" in his basement some ten years before.

I asked Bruiser if he wanted to come with but he said he had a girl that he was supposed to hang with later that night. So it was just my uncle, his band mates, and me that went for the grub. The one thing I learned while eating with Uncle Wes and his band mates was that coffee made my Uncle Wes even louder. Which I would have never thought was possible. However, I fit right in; I'm sort of a loud talker too. It must run in our family. And I wasn't even drinking coffee.

When I got home from hanging out with Uncles Wes, the P's informed me that I was going to get my chores done even if I had to stay up all night to get them done. When I told them that I'd be too tired for school the next day if I finished all of my chores before bed, they told me, "ITS ROCK N ROLL!"

If I hadn't been hanging out with my dads' brother; Uncles Wes that day, I'm sure I would have gotten in a lot more trouble for that whole ordeal. However, my Mom and Dad were well aware of the fact that Uncle Wes was a total Rock star crazy uncle, so they let it slide. Sort of, I did have to stay up until midnight to finish my chores. However, they didn't say much else about it.

On top of all of that I had left my homework for the last minute too; I didn't always do all of my homework on time but I eventually got it done. I thought about blowing off studying for my math test the next day, since it was already past midnight. However in my math class, there was this girl, Victoria Vanderbilt who sat right next to me and for whatever reason, she had it in her head that I was good at math. Ever since day one of class, she had always looked over at my paper to copy off me during test time. Now if this had been some dude I'd probably have covered up my answers and shiznit. But hot chicks, they've got it made, made in the shade – when it comes to that sort of thing. So I always let her copy off me, I'm not saying it's right. I'm just sayin' that's what I did.

Anyway, I didn't used to be all that great at math or anything but ever since this stone cold fox had been copying off me all semester long, it had made me study harder. So after I had finished my chores and I was lying in bed, I felt like I had to get out of bed and start studying, so I could do well on the test tomorrow because I didn't want her to get a bad grade on her test. Plus, I wanted her to keep looking my way. Hey, the way I saw it, having a hot chick staring at you for any reason is good, no matter what the reason. Well anyway, that's why I studied my butt off after the Wes Lee K concert and after I had finished my chores; all in effort to make sure Victoria Vanderbilt could get a good grade on her test tomorrow. Am I a sick puppy or what?

CHAPTER 18

Boogie Bobs shoes

I had been talking to Boogie Bob on the phone every day after school about our newest NSR b-boys and other shiznit like that. We'd shoot the old crap around for a good old hour, just about every day. The tone of his voice was strangely optimistic, yet vague, I couldn't quite put my finger on it. Whenever I asked him if he was coming on Saturday to the battle he would start to say yes but then he'd say, "well I hope so," or "Yep I'll be there … Lord willing," and he was still insisting that I visit him in the hospital ASAP; he wanted to, "Hang out before the battle" he would tell me.

The soonest I could get a ride to the hospital was on Friday (the day before the battle.) So Friday after school, Fandango picked me up in his newly acquired beater of a car. (He just got his drivers licence.) He dropped me off and squealed out of the parking lot to go pick up his girl du jour.

Even though Bob had stopped his chemotherapy, I still had to cover myself in the hospital scrubs, mostly because of the other patients on the unit and their immunities. I walked into his room and he said, "Hey Philip, I'm glad you're here!"

Bob had never called me "Philip" before so it sounded strange coming from his mouth. Then Bob told me, "My doctor told me: that my immunity is too low and my red blood cell count is too low, so I probably won't be leaving the hospital this weekend after all. I'm going to be here for a little longer Philip kid," Bob had said as he breathed kind of heavy; asthma sounding heavy, with pale and tired looking eyelids.

"I'm getting a blood transfusion on Saturday and then I'll be released Sunday or Monday … oh yay kid – I told my mom about the break battle that we are in on Saturday and she brought my 50 buck ante for me, here you go kid," he said as he handed me the dough. "And Phil, I want you to take my shoes with you. These are my favorite pair of breakin' shoes. I want you to wear these on Saturday night for me. It will make me feel like I am there at the battle. Can you do that for me brother?" he asked with begging and tired eyes.

"Absolutely, that's cool as all heck … You will be there with us brother," I said with joy, hoping to make him happy. But at the same time I was worried about not having his head spins for the battle.

"Make sure you put them on when you are about to do head spins, that's my move kid! That way, I'll be there! I will be there in high spirits," he said as he gave me a BRUG.

"After we serve those Hip Hop Breakers, I will come back the next day and you will have doubled your dough and added another pair of shoes to your collection," I said cocksure.

Bob started wincing like he was in pain, and then hit the "nurse button," which was unusual for him. Usually he was shouting for Nurse Mary.

"Hi Bob, can I help you?" Mary asked over the intercom system.

"I have a headache," he told her.

"Be there shortly," she replied.

Bob warned me, "Don't pay any attention to Mary today, she is acting all weird."

"What do you mean by weird?" I asked.

Bob explained, "… there were only 2 of us this morning on the treadmills; 'Cindy went home to be with the lord' was how Mary had phrased it while sniffing her nose off. Anywho, Nurse Mary kept looking at the darn treadmill today like a big weirdo. Every time she looked at the treadmill, she would start crying, balling her eyes out like a sissy. It's like: come on! She is all teary eyed over an empty treadmill; a dang treadmill is an item with no feelings. It's just a treadmill, not a person. It's just an empty treadmill. And crazy Nurse Mary is getting all teary eyes because that treadmill isn't getting any use," Bob laughed with ridicule.

"I even told the nut, I said: Mary, it's all good baby -I called her baby, she really got a kick out of that - but anywho kid, I told her not to worry because someone will be back here on that treadmill within the week. It happens every week, some new kid comes here with cancer and then Bamm, no more empty beds and no more empty treadmills. This made her cry even more, which was ridiculous because after all, we cancer patients are keeping her in business. Heck she should even thank me for having cancer," Bob laughed sarcastically

as he winked. (It was clear that he was only kidding about that last comment).
"But don't be surprised if she is acting all nuts," Bob said with disgust.

Another nurse came in to bring Bob a headache pill; she told us that Mary was giving med's to a new patient and that she would be in later to check on Bob.

"See! I told you! A new patient," Bob said and continued to rant and rave.

After that big rant, I could see that Bob was getting tired because one minute he was ranting like a madman and the next minute he'd be snoring, unless I spoke loudly and woke him up. Which I did a few times, but I started to feel rude.

I hung out in Bob's room for a bit anyway, while he slept. Soul Train was on the TV and they had some breakers on the show that day as special guests, so I woke Bob up for that, "Yo Bob! Dude! There are breakers on Soul Train today, chiggity check, check it out," I said

He shook his head and sat up quickly, "Oh yay, Phil, kid … don't forget to wear my shoes on Saturday night, it will mean a lot to me, that way; I'm there! … Can you get me some water? And none of that foo-foo water kid," Bob said with disgust, almost angry.

I rang the 'nurse' button on Bobs remote which was on his chest, that didn't even make him stir. Nurse Mary came in the room with red wet eyes and a cheerful smile and nodded at me. It was rather opposite emotions she had; happy and sad, all at once, I thought, but I understood her disguise, unlike Bob who did not. "Mary, can you get Bob some non foo-foo water please?" I asked as I smiled about Bob's choice of words that I had just borrowed.

Mary slipped out a half a second of a cry and then laughed, genuinely laughed, "Yep, sounds about right, Bob doesn't want any of that hoity-toity designer water crap. He's told me that before. He just wants cold wet water," she laughed, "As if water couldn't be wet or something? One time Bob told me: don't give me any of that sissy, complicated, metro sexual water, just give me some H 2 O," she said as she laughed with friendship for Bob in her face and then walked away.

Since Bob was sound asleep, I picked up Bobs shoes and started walking towards the door. I told Mary goodbye and I told her to tell him that I would see him on Sunday.

Mary said, "After your big break dance battle right?"

I held Bobs shoes up in the air and said, "Yep and I am bringing Bobs' spirit with me to the battle, he will be rockin' some head spins Saturday night. That's why I have his shoes with me- Bob's shoes will be revolving in head spins tomorrow night!"

As I exited Bob's room I walked past the treadmill room, it was empty, nobody was on the treadmills. I agreed with Bob, there was nothing sad about a bunch of empty treadmills. It was just an empty room.

When I got home from the hospital I immediately went right down to my gray cobwebbed basement. I threw on some B-Boy jams and Chicago House music. I kept alternating records from Hip Hop to House; I couldn't make up my mind. My vinyl record collection had really grown like mad. If you ask me, a vinyl record collection is a must for any true B-boy (or B-girl.) Everyone else is just posin', shakin', and fakin'. But that's if you ask me.

I began practicing head spins like a madman. I was already practicing head spins every day, but now that I knew Bob wasn't going to be able to be at the battle tomorrow, I stepped up my head spin practice sessions that much more. I wore three knit hats, layered on the top of my head because two was no longer enough to mask the pain. I had been practicing so much that I had a tender spot on the top of my head from forcing all of the weight on that tiny little two inch area of my head. I was the first and only to know that Bob would only be their spiritually at the battle and not physically and it was really weighing on my head in more ways than one.

CHAPTER 19

Let's go to Chicagoland

My phone was ringing off the hook on battle day. Every NSR, every hip cat from school (that wasn't afraid of the diversity at Chicagoland Rink) was hitting me up; some of them just to make sure that the battle was still on and others needed directions to the place. Apparently word had traveled around that we NSR's were battling some crew from "the city."

After I paced around my house and turned on and off the TV like 100 times that day, while waiting for 8pm to come, the doorbell finally rang. I told my P's, "See ya later!"

Dad yelled back, "Be home by midnight."

I yelled back, "Bruiser is dropping off like 6 of us at the end of the night, so I might be a couple of minutes late," I said as I closed the door shut before I could even hear my P's response. But they didn't worry about me too much when I was hanging out with Bruiser anyway, on account they knew, I knew him from church.

I hopped in the Stang and Bruiser said, "Sup Mr. Schlernious incorporated. (That's how I had answered my phone all day that day) Are you ready? - What's up with the extra pair of shoes?"

I told Bruiser what the dilly o was about the shoes and such, which kind of worried him but he didn't say anything at first. You see, Bruiser knew that sometimes I could rock a bunch of head spins and sometimes I couldn't. I'm not so sure that Bruiser believed in the power of Boogie Bobs shoes in the same way that I did because he eventually said, "Well dude, you should probably wear the shoes that you always wear when you're breakin' since you're used to them. You don't want to screw yourself up, is all I'm saying. It's not what's in the shoes; it's what's between your ears that counts," he said seriously with tight lips.

"But I've also got confidence around my neck," I told him as I clung to my NSR nameplate, while trying to seem relaxed but really Bruiser had started to make me a little nervous. I had convinced myself that Bobs' shoes would make up the difference, but now I was starting to worry that Bobs shoes were going to throw off my balance, since I wasn't used to them.

All in all, I had made a promise to Bob and I decided to keep my promise. I had once and for all decided that Bobs' shoes would make a difference – even though I knew that sounded crazy and superstitious. But I believed it anyway.

We pulled up at Blazin's crib and saw him pacing around his garage and checking out his shoes with each stride; he looked nervous; he always looked nervous.

Blazin' entered the car with concern on his face. On our way to pick up Miguel and Fandango, Blazin' told us, "Did you hear about Binny from school?"

"No, wazup?" We both said.

Blazin' in his most seriously toned voice said, "Dude, he was at a keg party last night at Alicia Vandykes house, hundreds of people were there. I guess he drank tons of shots of alcohol …well I didn't really hear how much he really drank but … He died of an overdose … It was supposedly his first time even drinking, at least that was what his best friend Johnny had said, but now, he's gone … Dead."

"That's why I don't mess with any of that Bull Shee-ott! If you do illegal drugs or slam too many drinks - you can die. Not always, but I don't want to spin that roulette wheel, screw that," I said.

Then Blazin, who was clearly shaken asked with a question in his voice," But some of the dudes at the party were just smoking pot and cigarettes and that's okay, right?"

"It's okay if you want to get tar into your lungs and burn your mouth, throat, and lungs while slowly killing yourself day by day with carcinogens and then BAMM … one day you're dead! BAMM just like that," I said, as I thought about Boogie Bob laying there in the hospital room. But I was also in that moment thinking about the nurses at the hospital who were smoking cigarettes just outside of the hospital when I had left that day wearing the hospital scrubs and stuff. And I thought about that chump Randal VanderNorth and his bull shee-ott too – I had really grown to hate second hand devil wings in case you couldn't tell.

It was funny though, I was actually trying to rile up Brock -I had even screamed the word, "Bamm" just for the effect of it. Just to mess with him. But really I was just mad that people who smoked were increasing their chances of getting cancer, yet someone like Boogie Bob was trying to get rid of his cancer. The worst part of it all was that Bob had told me that he had never did drugs or smoked. It didn't seem fair.

Anyway, Blazin' winced, "Enough with the Bamm dude." I could tell he was still freaking out a bit about Binnys' demise.

This made me want to continue though, just so he'd remember and maybe he'd stay away from all of that crap, "It just sneaks up on you without you even knowing it and then one day - Bamm." I had whispered. I was whispering in this crazy annoying voice; like a "cookie monster" voice, only more scary. I had way too much fun doing it, "… First you'll get emphysema … and next you're on a breathing machine," then I made these ventilator-breathing machine noises with my mouth, " … and then one day you're DEAD," I yelled like a monster, "because you can't breathe anymore … all because you smoked."

Bruiser interjected, "Alright enough of the grim friggin' reaper Shiznit gents! You all got a battle to focus on. Now Focus!"

Everyone got quiet for a couple of minutes as Dan turned on the radio that was airing mix jams. I shook off the grim reaper stuff like Dan the man had said and I began to think about the fact that I had two pairs of shoes with me that night and what those shoes represented.

We arrived at Miguel 2 tough's and Fandango's crib and waited outside to see if they'd notice that we had pulled up. Nobody wanted to get outside in the cold if we didn't have to; it was colder than a nuns buns and the wind was howling like a wolf in a horror flick. Their front door was open and we thought someone was looking outside but after a while we realized it was just the way the steamed up glass on their storm door and the shadows played off each other, so Bruiser started honking his horn like a cab driver in traffic since neither of them had come out yet.

"Go ahead and get 'em Phil," Brock told me.

"It's colder than a bee-othces cree-otch," I said.

"You get 'em Brock," Dan said.

"The wind is blowing like a ..." Brock replied just as their Mom opened the glass storm door and held up one finger to let us know that they would be out in one minute.

This sparked Bruiser into asking, "Who's that girl? ... Dinna-mack!"

Blazin' and I in synchronicity exclaimed, "That's Miguel and Gio's Mom." We knew what he meant though. All of us boys knew what he had meant.

"Damn man, she is one hot mama," Bruiser said.

Blazin' jumped in, "Yeah, I know when all of us guys first met her we thought she was someone's sister or girlfriend or something."

Moments later, Miguel got into the ride and Bruiser said, "Miguel dude, that's your mom?"

He started smiling from ear to ear, "Yep," and because everyone always told him how hot his mom was, he knew why Dan had asked. He liked the compliment unlike his brother, who took offense to it.

"Your mom is smokin' hot!" Dan said.

Fandango had hopped in as Dan had said that, "Dudes! Don't be talking about my mom like that; you're all a bunch of sick ducks," Fandango said.

Then Dan turned on the mixes and we all began to groove to JM Silk, "Music is the Key."

I was glad to see that all of us were wearing our black and gray colors and we all had on our NSR nameplates; which made us all look taller than tall. Tall Chicago! That's all I cared about in the whole world at that point, nothing else; the fact that we all had on our break crews colors and NSR nameplates, somehow made me relax.

On the way to pick up Kid Mojo and Jet Drinkwater Miguel told us about how he had just scooped up some turntables and how he had been practicing how to DJ and Break all week. This kind of made me nervous again, because I didn't want anyone to be distracted; I wanted everyone focused on the task at hand which was to take out the Hip Hop Breakers. I guess I was worried that he had spent more time DJing than breakin'.

Miguel assured me that he was mainly practicing his breakin' and just putting records on the spinning platter to break to and just occasionally working on beat matching and blends.

Then Fandango jumped into the conversation, just to mess with me. He could tell that I was getting nervous. I really wore my emotions on my sleeve sometimes. And even though I knew he was just trying to razz me, it still razzed me anyway, when he said, "Dude, I've been practicing DJing and Salsa dancing for the ladies bro. Nobody told me to work on my breakin'?"

I tried to pretend he didn't say anything but I'm sure my face looked tense. I was tense; break battle tense.

Miguel tapped my arm, smiled, shook his head and said, "Gio's been practicing his breakin' all week long. He even has some new moves rockin', you'll see." I believed Miguel, yet it made me nervous and confident all at the same time. Between battling the HHB's and Boogie Bob being in the hospital and having to rock out the head spins for our crew that night – I was all atwitter.

Fandango kept trying to rattle me, "I've been working on the Mambo, Tango, and Salsa," he said in an annoying voice with irritating eyes.

Dan Bruiser jumped in as if to give us a pep talk or something, "You all should save your best moves for last. Let's see what these guys got first."

"What if these guys start bustin' out with flares right out of the gate?" Brock Blazin' asked.

"I'm not saying not to counter their moves. Counter whatever they throw at you but only counter in the beginning, don't show off your show stoppers until the end; save your energy. You don't want to be tired at the end. You dig?" Dan the man said.

"Yep,"

"Foe-shawl,"

"Right on." we all had said in our own variations.

"When do I start my Salsa dancing -right after their tracks or head glides?" Fandango said just to keep me on edge.

Good old Bruiser helped me snap out of it when he messed with Fandango in my defense and said, "Hey yeah, cool, can I Tango dance with your mom? Your mom is smokin' …. Smoking hot."

Bruiser was good like that, he knew how to loosen us guys up, well, we all laughed, save for Fandango – even Miguel closed mouth smirked.

It was already tight in the Stang with the 5 of us and I guess I didn't think it through when I gave Dan the list of people we had to pick up that night. When we pulled down Kid Mojos' street the jokes started back up again. Miguel asked, "Where are you going? The rink is the other way?"

Bruiser said, "Were getting two more of the boys … you guys are going to have to sit on each other's laps or something. It was Phil's' idea to pick all you cats up."

"No one is sitting on my lap," Fandango said.

"Don't worry Fandango, you can talk about those farts in your lap," Blazin' said tauntingly.

"I won't be talking about anything because they are going to be sitting on your lap my man," Fandango said to Brock.

We pulled into Kid Mojo's driveway, I opened up the passenger door, and Kid Mojo said, "Dude where are we supposed to sit?"

I smart ass-ed-ly said, "On Fandango's Salsa dancing fart cheeks."

Kid Mojo retorted, "Nahh, I'm good. That's cool man, my sister already said she would take us up there if I needed her to, I'm not sitting on anyone's fart cheeks," he laughed with a gross smile.

Bruiser jumped in and said," Yo guys there's plenty of room back there. Just don't go grabbing any of the handles on the back seat when you get in or out … because … there are no handles in the back seat…" Bruiser said wheezing with laughter and then added, "And don't go sitting on any poles." … "There are no poles," he could barely talk he was laughing so hard. This sent Dan and Brock into another round of wheezing laughter and tears.

When we had enough of the joking around, Kid Mojo went back into his crib to get his sister, and we pulled out of Kid Mojos driveway chanting, "NSR" loud as heck. Jet Drinkwater was jamming out a top rock and shadow practicing his up rock against the garage; Dan's car headlights had given Jet a shadow battle mate as we eased back onto the street.

Bruiser yelled to all of us, "One more stop fellas then we'll head straight to Chicagoland Rink."

"Who are we getting now?" Blazin' asked with discontent.

"We've got to pick up Geeta, did you forget?" Bruiser said to Brock while looking in his rear view mirror at him.

"Who's Geeta?" Brock asked.

Bruiser erupted with a wheezing laugh, "Geeta the Frigg outta here!"

And off to Chicagoland Rink we drove.

The last ten minutes of the ride to Chicagoland Rink became quiet, except Brock tried to keep the burns going, but no one was falling for his schlerniousness. I was getting my focus on and picturing my break moves in my head while Dan kept saying the word, "smokin'" over and over again, just to mess with Fandango. I was also a little quiet because I still hadn't broken the news to anybody that Boogie Bob couldn't physically make it to the battle; save for Bruiser who was quiet about it. I was a little worried that would freak people out, so I figured if I was quiet, then maybe, nobody would ask me about it, until I was good and ready to talk about it.

We parked in the rink parking lot, Bruiser turned off the car, and it was eerily quiet. We had remained quiet for way too long for my liking – it was starting to get me anxious again. It was probably only a whole 5 seconds of quiet but it seemed like longer if you know what I mean.

Bruiser could tell everyone was in deep thought, nervous, or just that something weird was going on inside our heads because he intentionally started clearing his throat. Bruiser shouted, "It's like a friggin' morgue around here. Snap out of it guys," he said as he began to cackle at our tense asses.

"Okay okay, I'm cool, I'm cool," Blazin said.

"I'm just getting my game face on," I said seriously and then I added, just to joke around, "and I don't even know what a game face is."

"I am just trying to remember my Salsa moves," Fandango said.

"What did you say about your mom?" Bruiser said to Gio with a wiseacre smile and then he reached into his trunk and pulled out a duffle bag and put the strap around his shoulder, then said to nobody in particular, "Let's do this, let's do this."

Miguel scratched his head and asked, "What's in the bag Dan?"

"I brought everyone's Nunnya's," Dan said with a stone face and unblinking eyes.

"What's a nunnya?" Miguel asked.

"Nunnya friggin' business," Dan laughed loudly sounding like a chain saw.

A little goofing around by our crew boss had lightened up the mood; everyone seemed to be loose and smiling again; especially Miguel with his large closed mouth smile that shined brightly as he began to jauntily top rock around the parking lot.

As we were about to enter inside the rink I could hear the DJ jammin', "It's like that" by Run DMC thumping through the outside of the rink walls. This really got my mood kicked up into high gear. I couldn't hear the lyrics but I knew the drum patterns and chimes. Bruiser opened the rink door and show nuf, "It's like that" was kickin' hard right into our friggin' ears.

After paying to get in, I looked around every nook and cranny of the rink and noticed that the HHB's were not there yet. I was glad they weren't to be honest with you, I sort of wanted to warm up without them being there, but another part of me was worried that they weren't going to show up. I can really be all over the place sometimes.

However, I did see a couple of my classmates hanging around the lit up dance floor. They had apparently gotten there earlier in the evening to skate because they were just taking their skates off right when I had walked in. It was still early, right around 9pm and the battle didn't start for a couple of hours yet, so I went over by them and just started chillin'.

I was sort of hanging with them but I was also sort of watching the skaters. I looked out onto the rink floor and saw a couple, maybe in their 20's or

30's all dressed up as if they were going to the prom or something. The dude was wearing bell bottomed black pants and expensive looking roller skates, which was something that I really used to know a lot about, in fact, I had really cared a whole bunch about kick ass roller skates just a few months ago.

Even though he was a good 50 feet away from me I could tell that he was rolling on fanjet jumbo hugger wheels with black leather skate boots. He was wearing this white ruffled collared shirt, you've seen the kind, it was the kind that you'd picture Beethoven wearing when he was putting on his piano concerts in the days of yore. It was that kind of a ruffled shirt. The thing that was annoying to me was that he had 3 buttons or so, unbuttoned, and he was showing off his harry bro boobs. The girl he was skating with was practically wearing a turtle neck. "They should at least swap shirts or something," I said to Brock out of nowhere when I saw that he had caught my eyes gawking at those two skate around.

"As long as her boobs aren't as hairy as his," he said jokingly.

The girl, his roller disco partner was wearing a long 50's style rippled white skirt – the kind you've seen girls wearing in old "sock hop" video footage or like in the movie "Grease." She was sportin' white leather skates, and a fancy headband, that made their outfits look cheesy. You could tell they really wanted to match. After I thought about it, it became clear that they probably entered couples roller skating contests. It looked like ballroom dancing on skates or disco dancing on skates – whatever it was called but they looked good, save for their ruffled clothing and his harry tits.

It was never my sort of thing (competitive skating) but I could tell that the two of them were having a stone gas of a time, so it was kind of fun to watch them smile and do their moves. They were really good at it too. It took my mind off the break battle for a few minutes but when I did worry, I mainly worried about those cats Angelo and Sylvester and the fact that they were gangbangers - and that sort of made me nervous, if you know what I mean; mean Joe Green.

Girls were starting to filter into Chicagoland Rink, but even though I took a quick gawk, I still kept my mind fixed on the upcoming battle. But without even trying to look, I saw a group of girls with poufy hair, thick lipstick, and caked on mascara on their lashes heading directly to the ladies room with switches in full effect. It's as if they all had practiced switching their butt cheeks from left to right and left to right again before they had come that night; they were that switcherific.

I knew those girls were only heading into the girls room to check out their makeup and hair, even though, I would bet you they had already checked their hair in their car sun visor mirrors, just before they walked in. I bet you they took another quick peek in their makeup compact mirrors while they were in the lobby, paying to get in too. They were that kind of sophisticated. I'd have bet a million dollars that they all had compact mirrors, full makeup kits, and perfume in their purses too. They were those kinds of skeezers. – Not that any of us guys minded that. That's guys for ya, we don't mind anything girls do, even if we make fun of it, you can bet some guy somewhere is digging whatever it is that some other guy is making fun of.

One of those girls' hairdos would have given Einstein a run for his money. And even though their makeup would have made an opera singer feel like she needed more makeup; they were still looking HOT – just a different kind of hot. As Isaac had put it last week, they were "Bimbo" hot. Too much makeup and very tight clothing can earn a girl that kind of tag sometimes, at least from some guys.

I tried not to gawk at those girls for too long though, because Kelly was supposed to be showing up soon and the last thing that I needed was for her to see me checking out some other girls. Girls can be funny like that. Never mind I'd be looking at some old lady wearing a babushka and using a walking cane, if she had just walked in too, just because I don't walk around with my eyes closed. But it would be just my luck to only get busted looking at the young girls and not the old ladies in their babushkas.

Blazin' nudged my ribs, "Look Swift, Kid Mojo and Jet Drinkwater just made it in here, let's go chat 'em up," he said. While we were heading towards the rinks entrance, a flurry of people walked inside. I excitedly blurted out, "NSR is in the house my man," as I saw more of our crew entering the rink. Chi Girl and her two buddies; Tabitha and Sabrina showed up. And Slim Jim was following immediately behind them. He was totally staring at them in this very "boys will be boys" sort of way, as he walked in.

"Busted," I said to him as I winked.

"Sup Chi and my favorite groupies?" I said to the girls. Everyone smiled.

Tabitha gasped, "I'm starving" and then the three of them quickly darted to the snack shop as if they hadn't eaten in years.

"Slim Jim in da house," I said - and just as I reached out to high five him, in came our newest NSR's.

"Why didn't you tell me you wanted these guys in the crew?" he said as he high fived me, "I was just talking to them in the parking lot. I grew up with them," Slim Jim said. He was talking about Braun Drix, AJ Fresh, Blake, and Pauly G who had just walked in.

"I didn't know they were from your neighborhood," I said.

"Yizz-eah brizzo, we went to the same elementary skizz-ool fizz-ool," Slim Jim said in his usual rhyming form.

"I didn't think about asking them to join our crew until I had met up with them last week, that's all," I said.

All of us breakers started heading over to the "Saturday night fever floor" where we had hung out last week which suddenly made me feel more relaxed. I was a rollercoaster ride of emotions all day, in case you couldn't tell. But now that everyone was showing up, I was chill. – well sort of.

"I heard at 10pm they are going to open up the entire rink floor for dancing again, just like they did last week towards the end of the night, "Slim Jim said.

"Good – we are going to need room when we take out these chumps tonight," I said as my toughness started to kick up.

Slim Jim high fived me, grabbed his NSR nameplate, gave it a kiss, and then said, "Word up!"

Chi Girl, Tabitha, and Sabrina passed out a few hugs and hellos and then they went to the ladies room to fix their already perfect hair. Which made Slim Jim sing the vocals from Klymaxx, "There's a meeting in the ladies room" as he started poppin' and waving, just straight up boogalooin' it to the DJ's unknown beat track that went, "Da da-doom koosh koosh koosh –Da da-doom koosh koosh koosh."

Kid Mojo trounced the floor violently as the DJ picked up the bass and threw an accapella vocal over the track, "You aint really down ..." the song sang as Mojo was getting all excited, power moving the floor like a breakin' machine with flares and swipes.

I became inspired and started to limber up with top rock, floor rock and windmills of my own while Brock and everybody else in our crew started to mess around with their moves too.

Bruiser was hanging around the DJ booth, chatting up the DJ booth entourage, which included the four poufy haired, smoky eye-shadowed Chicas I had just told you about. Bruiser had this serious as a heart attack look on his face as he talked to the entourage that included the MC, DJ, lighting guy, and whoever else it was that was in there. I didn't have a clear view of the entire DJ booth from where I was standing but I could tell it was a crwth inside the booth.

My eyes were drawn back to the rink entrance where I saw these two cats from school; Logan Gelderring and Mickey Jumbo. Logan was that punk at school that called me "queer" at lunch time. Remember that butt wipe? He was one of those guys that was always talking shee-ott. When I wore designer jeans, his were better. When I wore Drakkar Noir cologne, he'd tell me his Cool Water got more ladies. When I told him our crew was the baddest break crew around, he told me that he was from Chicago and any crew from Chicago could beat a suburbanite crew like ours – even though he had never seen our crew break before. He was that kind of a jackass. He had told me that he was going to show up at the rink just so he could, "Watch a real Chicago b-boy crew take out yous wanna be suburbanites" was how he had said it. I didn't think he was really going to show up but there he was standing right in front of me, picking his teeth with his keys.

Just over by the popcorn machine that had finally finished popping. AJ Fresh and Slim Jim were chatting it up like two long lost pals, I could see their mouths' flapping and arms flailing and torso's bending with every laugh. I knew they were talking about graffiti artwork by the way Slim Jim took off his jacket and started pointing out his work to AJ. I guarantee that one of them, if not both of them had brought their sketch pads with them of their graffiti work. Slim Jim brought his everywhere he went, even though he usually left it in the car. The popcorn machine was by that wall mural of the afro headed guy on skates with the big gold rings I had told you about, so AJ and Jim hung out there for a while "oohing" and "ahhing" while pointing out every detail of the graffiti to each other.

"Oh snap Swift, you're about to be shown what's up tonight for real," that punk ice Logan said as he greeted me with a condescending tone in his voice and an equally annoying look in his beady eyes.

Blazin' walked up before I could even say anything and engaged Logan with a slap on the back, "Hey wazup Logan? You're here … cool man, I didn't know you hung out here?"

Logan replied, "I don't, I came here to watch Phil K Swift get blown out of the water tonight by the Hip Hop Breakers." (Logan and Brock were classmates and Logan obviously didn't know that Brock and I were friends)

"What are you talking about dude? We Neighborhood Street Rockers are going to take out the Hip Hoppers, you'll see dude. And you know why we are going to win?" Blazin' asked Logan, "Because we've got geeta on our crew!"

"Who's Geeta?" Logan asked.

"Geeta frig outta here! Now beat it," Brock said with emphasis. Blazin' finally was the burner instead of being the burn-ee. I high fived Brock while Logan just stood there and gave us a narrow glare.

"It seems like people like to mess with me, "I said quietly to Brock as we inched away from them.

Blazin' responded, "That's because you let people know it bothers you, if you just acted like nothing bothered you, people would eventually shut up, but with some people, especially people like Logan, you have to stand up to them and give them a taste of their own medicine or they will just keep doing it. I always talk like a punk to him, even when I'm joking around and being cool with him, because that's the kind of guy he is, he's a bully and bullies have to be talked to like they're punks, because they are," Brock told me.

We walked further away from them and Blazin' told me, "Dude, Logan and I are usually cool, even though he is a smart ass, we have study hall together but now he's talking all that shiznit, What's up with that?"

"Logan was talking crap all week at school," I said.

Blazin' nodded his head a few times and said, "Logan grew up in Chicago, so he thinks he's cooler and tougher than us suburbanites … whatever."

I responded, "Ok, I get it, that's why he is convinced that the half suburbanite half Chicagoan Hip Hop Breakers are going to take us out tonight because Logan grew up in Chi Town, so he thinks Chi town cats are hipper than suburbanites. I guess tonight is our chance to show the Chicago boys –

including Logan, what's up. It's funny though, when I go on vacation and people ask me: where are you from?; I always say I'm from Chicago …after all they call it Chicagoland," I told Blazin'.

"Word, Swift! We are from Chicago, or Chicagoland … whatever," Brock said.

I bellowed, "I'm Chicago, Tall Chicago … It's all Chicago … Chee Caw Go!" which made me feel like top rockin' as we walked.

While Blazin' and I were strolling around the B-boy turf, mingling with our friends, I spotted Angelo and Sylvester walk into the rink. They were easy to spot with their dark green and black colors; all of their boys were also dressed in colors; every single one of them. They snuck a peak over in our direction as they were heading inside; their eyeballs looked our way but their heads looked in the same direction as they were walking. They were heading to the same place they had hung out last week by the DJ booth and restrooms.

Bruiser was still chatting up the MC like the long winded cat that he was, and as the HHB's drew closer to the DJ booth, Bruiser spotted them and began pointing right at them; our nemesis. The group of about 12 or 13 Hip Hop Breakers that had just walked in were all starting to top rock and down rock and other Bboy moves as they neared the DJ booth.

The MC motioned one of the Hip Hop Breakers over to the DJ booth and it wasn't Angelo or Sylvester but I knew nonetheless that it was one of them. Bruiser, the MC, and the Hip Hop Breaker became engaged into a deep conversation of some sort – most likely about our battle tonight.

"Sup Phil K Swift?" AJ Fresh said to me out of the blue. I didn't even see him coming; I was so fixed on Bruiser's conversation.

"Sup AJ, I'm just Chillaxxin' my brother," I said but I wasn't really chill. I was anxious and excited about the upcoming battle, but mainly I was nervous about telling everybody that I was the head spin specialist for the night.

AJ asked me, "Where are these guys that we are supposed to be battling tonight? Do you think they are going to show up or what?"

"They just walked in, look by the DJ booth, they are the guys that are wearing the black and dark green," I said.

AJ stiffened his upper lip and waved his hand down towards the ground and said, "We can take those guys."

I appreciated AJ's confidence but I knew that he had never even seen the HHB' break before, so it kind of came across as false bravado. However, it was still nice to hear it anyway. I like false bravado rather than a negative Nancy or a nervous Nelly.

"Yo Philly Phil, Phil," Pauly G chanted as he cut into our conversation and then he did this crazy Shiznit that he always did, which I still have no idea what the heck he was even doing, when he yelled, "Scroooompt!" He would say it and then he would reach out, touch my chin, then pretend to throw it to the ground, and then he laughed to himself. But that was Pauly for ya.

"Yo Pauly, Paul, Paul – what izzz doing bruh," I said, while he offered me his complicated handshake that he called "giving him some skin." Then, just for the fun of it, I rubbed his chin right back and said, "You're being all schlernious, my schlerniouslness." - Do you want to know what was funny? After I had rubbed his chin, he actually looked at me as if I was nuts. This really got him going with laughter though. It is funny what happens when you give someone a taste of their own medicine.

Pauly G laughed, "Ohhh mannn, what the shiznit?" Pauly threw me a BRUG and then started rhyming like the opposite of miming while the bells from; "Lookout Weekend" were chiming.

I saw Bruiser zig zaggin' his way back towards us. Blake and Drix approached me to ask, "When are we battling?"

"Who's holding onto the cash during the battle? …"

I cut them off and I pointed over towards Bruiser and said, "Just hang tight a bit, Bruiser was just talking to the MC, DJ, and one of the Hip Hop Breakers, he's making his way back now. Don't speak shrill, chill for rill like me Phil the pill … in a bit, we will all know what's up that's the deal! –We'll all know WAZUP instead of nil," I said emphatically as I started to feel the pump circulating through my bones. When you hang out with someone that rhymes all of their conversations, it sort of rubs off on you.

"Oh straight," Blake said.

"Right on," Braun agreed. As they both started following Bruiser with their eyes.

The party people were starting to pour in, dressed all ghetto fabulous, thrift store chic, and sporting nice clothes to add to their mystique. Some of them were donning shimmery disco delighted clothing that was adorning their torsos, yet some of them were showing more so of their torso.

Some girls dressed pure and were chaste for sure while some girls had their makeup overdone, along with hair that was stormin', poufed, and flared out.

It was fun to watch the guys who were trying to throw down the mack like Romeos but what made it funny was the girls who let the guys know that they were really just wack and not the mack. - I thought - as I watched a nearby player, who was told to, "Take a hike Jack."

The banters and dares were forming, the laughter's were echoing in the rafters, and the dappers were enjoying the flappers. And we Bboys were waiting to hear rappers so we could pounce the floor with breakin' zappers.

Chi Girl, Tabitha, and Sabrina were done making themselves divaliscous in the "ladies room." They headed over to me straight quick, and Sabrina asked, "Are you guys really battling for shoes and money? She is really nervous about this," she said while looking at Chi Girl and me.

"Yep, I really put my foot in my mouth when it came to making these battle plans. I got a little cocky … but sometimes, you've just got to … talk it like you walk it … and that is the deal for real!

I made these battle arrangements when I thought Boogie Bob was going to be able to join us …" I was telling all of them. I accidentally blurted it out.

Sabrina jumped in, "YOU MEAN HE IS NOT GOING TO BE HERE TONIGHT?" she shouted. "Isn't he your 'head spins for days' guy?" she added.

"Not so loud, I didn't have a chance to tell everyone yet, besides … he is here … well, kind of … he gave me his shoes that he uses when he does his head spins and he told me to wear them when it was time to do head spins. I will be wearing his shoes during my head spin routine," I said – hoping it would mean something. I tried to make her feel better but she basically gave me this look as if I was coo coo.

"Boogie Bob our head spin guy isn't coming tonight?" Chi Girl asked with angry nervousness.

I quickly responded, "What I was trying to say is that Bob had given me his shoes that he rocks out his head spins with, and I will be doing the head spins tonight while wearing his shoes."

Chi Girl shook her head, then faked a smile, and said, "You better rock 'em Swifty or you're buying me a new pair of shoes. My mom's going to kill me, these are brand new shoes but I didn't have any old shoes I could wear here tonight without looking like a total fashion disaster, understand Swifty?" Chi Girl had told me with serious eyes. Her eyes were so serious; I swear I felt her mother's eyes peering at me.

Bruiser stepped into the middle of the jam circle and began talking to us as if we were a football team and he was our coach and said, "Listen guys and Chi Girl, I just talked to the MC Scott Shadows, the DJ Sweet Sammy T, and the lighting guy Trevor. Here's the deal YO: Lenny Poindexter, who is the captain of the Hip Hop Breakers …" then Bruiser cleared his throat, "… and I decided on everyone's behalf, that MC Scott Shadows would hold onto the dough, the ante, the purse, whatever … so on and so forth."

"Dude, what if he takes off with our dough?" AJ asked.

"Does anyone know this MC Scott character?" Blake questioned.

Bruiser replied, "Well, Lenny Poindexter … the HHB's captain, had the idea to have this girl Kelly, who is Lennys' sister, hold the money. However, I wasn't going to let that fly. Besides I know the MC, Scott from school, he's a good guy, his parents are rich – they just bought him a recording studio for his birthday, it cost 10 grand, so he doesn't need to swipe everyone's dough. He's rolling in dough. Besides, he's never even read cliff notes before, that's how honest he is," Bruiser told us with convincing eyes.

This seemed to allay most of our crews concerns. Except mine, I was now feeling betrayed, freaked out, and angry; not about Scott holding the money but about Kelly being the sister of Lenny of the Hip Hop Breakers.

Everyone started diggin' into his or her pockets while Dan held out his hand for everyone's "antes." Some were reluctant while some gave him the dough easily. As I handed over Boogie Bob's and my dough to Bruiser it started to seem all the more real, as my heart rate and sweat picked up the pace.

After Bruiser collected everyone's 50 bucks and stepped outside of the huddle. I approached him. Did you say Lenny's sisters name is Kelly?"

Bruiser confirmed, "Yeah dude, what's up?"

"I was here last week, I met this chick named Kelly, and she was all pretending to like me, and talking all that smack about how she wanted us NSR's to beat the Hip Hop Breakers in the battle and such. Now - I guess she was just false flaggin'. She was just hanging out with us NSR's last week just to be a spy or some shiznit, so she could report back to her brother and all of the HHB's about what we were all about, like what are moves were like or whatever," I said.

In the middle of my conversation with Bruiser, out of nowhere, I was greeted with sweet sensitive hands over my eyes, "Guess who?" I heard from the sweet smelling girl. It took me a second to realize, but the quiet girly voice was unmistakable. I knew whose voice it was.

I answered in a gruff sarcastic voice, "I was just talking about you!" It was Kelly by sheer coincidence.

"How did you know it was me?" she asked with a sweet smile.

"I just knew," I said shortly. I was still shaking off the shock of finding out that she was Lenny's sister. In that instant of feeling like a chump, I said, "So what's this I hear that you are Lenny Poindexter's sister?"

Kelly stepped back from me and scrunched her face, "Well you heard wrong!"

Bruiser was still standing next to me and said, "This isn't the Kelly that was by the DJ booth with Lenny and me, The Kelly I was talking about was hanging out with 3 other girls that had really big hair and very painted on faces."

"Ohh, those girls, I remember those girls!" I said –as I sort of felt like a jerk for speaking gruff to Kelly.

"Ohh, you remember THOSE GIRLS," she said sort of snotty and sort of jealously. Then Kelly explained, "I do know Lenny though … He used to ask me out all of the time, but he's not my type, so I wouldn't give him the time of day. But his sister KAYLEE," Kelly said loudly, "… is really nice and pretty cool. I hang out with her once in a while here at the rink."

"Oh yeah, she did say Kay-lee, didn't she?" Bruiser said sheepishly.

"Okay Bruiser thanks for freaking me out about this girl that I like KELLY … for a minute there I thought you were a sister of the enemy," I said while looking right at her.

Bruiser grinned, shrugged his shoulders and walked away.

"Oh, so you like me, do ya?" Kelly said with a flirty smile.

"So tell me, who is your type?" I said, "Walk with me, talk with me, stalk me, gawk me, hawk me," I said playfully.

She laughed and grabbed my hand which made my heart race and thump like an unbalanced washing machine.

"Sup cutie, are you putting the moves on me or what?" I said while trying to sound smooth, but really I was nervous as heck. If the music wasn't so loud she would have heard my voice squeal.

She unassumingly smiled and said, "What do you mean?" as she clenched my hand even harder.

We walked past Bruiser, who winked at me when we passed by. Kelly continued to hold my hand hostage while we walked around the dance floor chatting up members from my crew.

It got a little interesting when we stopped by to talk to Chi Girl, Sabrina and Tabitha who were flagging me down and waving me over. When we went over by them, they were being extra flirty and stuff -right in front of Kelly. Which I'm sure is why Kelly had squeezed my hand even harder. Plus, I noticed that Kelly had also toughened up her sweet demeanor that she had once worn.

"I've got to get ready for this battle," I told her once I had realized we were only one hour away.

"You're ready," she said as she leaned in to give me a hug. Kelly walked away and I got down to the business of practicing my breakin'.

Over the Rinks' speakers all of us NSR's were suddenly standing to attention, "Okay house people, Hip Hoppers, Neighborhood Street Rockers, b-boys, and all of the rest of you party people in the house TONIGHT. The rink floor is now open for everybody to dance, step, break, boogaloo, and boogie!"

The crowd let out a scream and added an extra bop to their hop as they headed to the rinks hardwood floor, becoming a part of folklore. The party was now in full effect for sure.

However, we NSR's stayed put in our domain. A couple of guys namely, Blazin' and Drix were about to start heading out to the main floor but I cut them off and said, "We will join everyone on the big floor just before 11pm ... at battle time ... okay amigos?"

Blazin' smiled, "For shizzo my brizzo." Then he asked, "Where's Boogie Bob? He's coming right?"

While staring Blazin' down I reached into my backpack and I showed him Boogie Bobs shoes. "Bob is here in spirit," I told Brock with a smirk.

Blazin' became confused and concerned, "Is Bob doing okay?" he asked.

"As far as I know, he is fine. They stopped his chemotherapy treatments and were moving him into this hospice phase of his treatment, whatever that means– at least that's what I overheard the nurses talking about Friday when I was walking out of his room when I was done visiting him. I hope that he will be out of the hospital soon though, but for tonight my brother, I am the one rockin' out the head spins for the NSR's ... along with the spirit of Boogie Bob and his shoes. I know it sounds nuts, I know that these are not magical shoes or anything but at the same time - they are," I told Brock.

Blazin' had this worried look on his face but he smirked anyway and said, "You can do it Swift, I've seen you do it before, plus you've got Bobs shoes. You'll rock it Phil," he told me with a straight face. And he meant it.

MC Shadows got on the mic and rocked it like this, "Dan the man Bruiser and Lenny Poindexter have informed me that there is going to be a B-Boy battle to settle once and for all, which crew is the best in the Midwest. For those of you who don't know what I am talkin' bout; We have a break dance battle coming up at 11pm; the Neighborhood Street Breakers vs. the Hip Hop Breakers, so hang tight, fasten your seat belts, hang on to your Kangols, and don't lose your shoes out there gentlemen," the MC said with a giggle in his voice.

Chi girl yelled over the crowd, "and LADIES!" the MC didn't hear her though as we were too far from the booth.

The MC's announcement served as our warning to get ready. The NSR's that hadn't been stretching out or breakin' had begun to limber up. Everywhere I looked someone was either: stretching out, jogging in place, top rockin' floor rockin', power movin', and working on freezes.

Slim Jim and Pauly G were struttin' their boogaloo butts around; poppin', tickin' and wavin'. And even though Sabrina and Tabitha weren't officially NSR's, they were still joining in on the warm ups. The three girls were flipping around; doing aerial cartwheels, triple flips, and handsprings, and other shiznit like that to help get their buddy Chi Girl ready for the battle.

Occasionally I glanced over to the far corner by the vending machines and DJ booth, where the HHB's were camped out. But I couldn't see much through the packed crowd of party people, except for an occasional spinning swirl of green and black. And the only reason I could see that far away was because our "Billie Jean" dance floor was raised up about a foot or two higher than the rest of the rink. But even still, I couldn't really make out any of their moves, other than the fact that I knew they were warming up too.

Little by little the news had spread that Boogie Bob wasn't going to be able to make it to the battle. I was originally worried that everyone would be angry with me for getting them into this battle. Now that our head spinner was unable to make his physical appearance; I thought they would feel like I had sealed their doom or something. However, all the guys were more sympathetic to the fact that one of our friends wasn't able to attend due to his cancer. It was no longer a battle about shoes or money or us; we were now battling for Boogie Bob.

Kid Mojo and Jet Drinkwater asked me if I thought that I could rock out head spins as good as the other guy's from the HHB's that we had seen last weekend, and I told them with confidence, "I have been practicing like a mo fo – MOJO. I'm going to spin around as quick as a jet, JET. Besides, I have the spirit of Boogie Bob and his shoes with me. I can't miss," I said cocksure. I even went as far as to tell them that, "I've got head spins for days now," which was a stretch, but I sort of got caught up in the moment. It was raw bragging coming from my mouth and I couldn't think of a reason to stop it.

Bruiser passed by Kid Mojo, Jet Drinkwater and me and gave us thumbs up. He mouthed some words to us, but I suck at reading lips, so I had no idea what he had said, but it was apparent that he was going to drop off our ante with the MC.

My heart began pounding harder and my face felt flush as I watched Bruiser make his way over to the DJ booth.

From behind Slim Jim I heard voices coming at me, "Sup Phil K Swift ... Are you going to trounce those guys or what Dog ... Dang?" It was Rodd Get Down from school.

"Were goin' to see Mr. Phil K Swift show us what's up for realz," Rory Ragz said.

You remember Rory and Rodd, right? You know - the poppin' battle in the hallway at school; Rory versus Isaac; and Rodd was Rorys sidekick that was talking all of that trash.

Anyway, Rodd and Rory both started shakin' my hand all tricky like. "It's hard to keep up with everyone's cool, hip, and complicated handshakes," I uttered in confusion. But I faked it as much as I could, so they didn't think I was disrespecting them or anything. Some people can really get touchy about the darnedest things, I swear.

Speaking of that poppin' battle at school – Dustin, Isaac and Hazy were just about to come on through the Frisk line as I was talking to Rodd and Rory. All the while I was asking Rory if he was going to try to battle Isaac again, which I was more or less just kidding, I was just making conversation. Rory said, "It's all good man, we cool. Isaac doesn't like battling" and then Rory cockily laughed, "Isaac already knows I would school him anyway, so I don't blame him for not wanting to battle me. Heck I wouldn't want to battle me, so I get it," he cackled like a mad joker about his own bragging and then Rodd high fived Rory so hard that I could hear the smack of their hands over the music that was pumpin' freakin' loud.

"Sup Hazy ... Isaac," I yelled.

They nodded and mouthed: "Sup" and "Hey" and kept walking towards the snack bar.

Rory questioned, "Well, I think we're all good?"

"Dude, they're probably just hungry, CHILL for rill," I said.

Rodd and Rory smiled, nodded, and walked away. They made their way around the rink saying their "Sups" to other cats from our school.

I spotted Bruiser walking into the elevated DJ booth and it appeared that he had handed over the Grants to the MC.

Fandango tapped me on the shoulder, he was apparently one of the last to find out, he asked me about Bob, so I filled him in on the details. He was all cool about it. He was really just curious was all, nothing else. He didn't even seem worried. In addition, for a change, he asked me about Bobs cancer, instead of busting my chops about Salsa dancing and talking about his girls and stuff. But just when I thought Fandango was getting all emotional and caring on me, he said, "Wow Phil, you have been holding them for a while, that's awesome of you. Can you hold mine too?"

"Sure, hold what?" I thought he meant to hold his shoes for a minute, while he threw down with a break move because sometimes he took off his shoes when he windmilled. But no – it wasn't that.

"Hold One of THEEZ FART CHEEKS!" he yelled as he walked away with swag. The night was not complete on any given night, unless someone yelled, "THEEZ Fart Cheeks."

A few of my fellow NSR's were chillin' nearby when I felt compelled to chant, "Lets win this battle for Bob, the guy is fighting for his life and all we are doing is fighting for 50 bucks and a pair of shoes. What's there to worry about? If we lose - we lose our shoes, if Bob loses, he loses his life … TO BOB," I yelled.

Everyone within earshot yelled, "TO BOB!"

"Aint nothing to it but to do it," Pauly exclaimed.

"We're going to take these chumps out," Brock said.

Along with some random, "Heck yeahs,

"Hells yeahs" and

"Yeah boys," that sprang out from our crowd of NSR's and classmates.

By that point, there were about a dozen cats from our school that were hanging out with us NSR's, mostly offering us good cheer or just hanging tough as if they were our fans or something. Except for those punk ice bee-otches: Logan and Mickey, who were hanging out in our section - unwelcomed, I might add.

After we had all "toasted" Bob -It occurred to me: why the heck are those punks hanging out with us ? So I yelled out in their direction, "Logan! Mickey! Why don't you make like Geeta and Geeta Frig outta here!?"

The two of them walked over to me with jerky smiles on their faces and Logan said, "The Hip Hop Breakers are going to school you guys tonight and I'm glad I can watch all of you suburbanites get whipped."

"In case you haven't noticed yet Logan, you are one of those suburbanites too .You go to the same school as I do and you even live in the same city as I do, so what is all of this talkin' out of the side of your neck BS," I said smart ass-ed-ly.

"You can take a boy out of the city but you can't take the city out of the boy," Logan quipped.

Bruiser came strolling up to me while I was in the middle of talking to those chumps, so I said to Bruiser, "These guys want to grab one."

"Grab what?" Logan asked.

In synchronicity, Bruiser and I sang, "One of THEEZ fart cheeks."

This sent the two punks walking away with scowls as Dan and I high fived each other.

"The Hip Hop Breakers are in that far corner. Beat it! Go over there," I yelled at them as they walked away.

Brock who had overheard most of the exchange yelled, "Don't let the door hit ya on the ass on your way out."

Bruiser started motioning with his hands to get every NSR's attention. "Ok guys, I just anteed up our dough, dropped off the purse, gave the MC the moolah, if you will. Here's the dilly o: the crowd is basically going to be the judge and jury but I told Lenny of the HHB's and he agreed, that if one crew out breaks another crew and if you know that your crew just straight up lost; own it, be a man and own it," Bruiser explained.

"Chi Girl Be a woman! " I interjected playfully.

Bruiser laughed and said, "Yeah, I'm not trying to slight you Chi Girl, I'm just talking quick. Anyway, In the event that both crews think they've won … we will let the DJ and MC get on the mic to help us take a poll of the crowd, to see who won. Whichever crew the crowd cheers loudest for – WINS. If it is still not clear, then the DJ, the MC, the Laser light guy Trevor, and the owner of the rink Paul are going to try and come up with an unbiased vote and pick a winner. You all dig?" Bruiser asked while looking everyone in the eyes as to take a poll.

Most of us nodded in agreement.

Chapter 20

The Neighborhood Street Rockers

VS.

The Hip Hop Breakers

The rinks MC got on the mike once again, "Ahhh yeah, it's almost time to see which break crew is the best break crew! Hey B boys ... B girls in 10 minutes we are going to be getting straight up stone cold funky in this place," MC Shadows said.

The crowd screamed.

" ... Neighborhood Street Rockers and the Hip Hop Breakers Get Ready, we are soon going to see who is king of the mountain, the Lords of the floor, and the masters of the circle ... Please move away from the center of the rink floor, to clear some room for our B-boys," MC Shadows demanded.

Chi girl waited about 5 seconds and then yelled, "AND B-Girl!"

The MC continued, "... It's going to be a straight up funk fest, the funky festival is onnn! Rappers, housers, disco ducks, do it to it," MC Shadows said in a slow, deep and crystal clear MC voice, as he pointed his finger at each and every person in the crowd.

I started making my way around the crowd. I told my crew mates and friends one by one, "We should begin our trek to the center of the rink – let's do it to it."

With the crowd being as dense as it was, I figured that it would take us 10 minutes just to make it out there. I was ready like Freddy; it was on like Donkey Kong. There was nothing to it but to do it.

All of my crew mates started gathering their belongings, jackets, hats, knee pads, and such. I grabbed Boogie Bobs shoes out of my backpack and I draped them around my neck, they were tied together by the laces.

Slim Jim was carrying his graffiti art jean jacket high in the air and proud, just like a heavy weight boxing champion would have held his champion belt high in the air as he walked through the crowd and towards the boxing ring. It really started to get my swagger going, if you know what I mean.

I nodded over to Kidd Mojo, who was standing next to Slim Jim and Jet Drinkwater. And he nodded back. I could see that they had their game faces on as they moved towards me.

Then I motioned to AJ Fresh, Drix, and Fandango who were hanging out together. They seemed so chill and comfortable where they were, but after I had motioned them over, indicating it was battle time, they bowed their necks, crinkled their foreheads, and began their cool as a cucumber saunter towards my growing crowd and me. We were almost ready to march.

Miguel 2 tough had seen me trying to get everybody's attention so he was already walking towards our herd with a big tight lipped smile and raised eyebrows. He looked focused as all heck. A hard look focus and a sweet soft smile; Miguel's face was quite the contrast.

Blazin' and Bruiser came over and stood right next to me and after we had all done a quick head count, we then officially started our move to the cypher that was waiting to be formed. We strode like soldiers. Everyone looked Tall; Tall Chicago.

My headcount was: twelve b-boys, one b-girl, and with Boogie Bobs shoes; that made 14 – fourteen fellow soldiers zig zagin' through the rink crowd. We must have had an obvious look about ourselves; being a train of b-boys dressed in b-boy regalia and all, because every once in a while, people that I didn't even know, would throw us a shout out or even pat me on the back and wish me, "Good luck!" or say stuff like, "Show us what you've got B boy." You know that kind of stuff. It kind of made me feel like a celebrity to have total strangers paying attention to me like that. Seeing all of that genuine excitement on people's faces as we steam rolled towards the center of the rink made me feel even more focused. I had so much adrenaline by that point that my forehead was throbbing like mad. I was too pumped to be nervous anymore. I was more pumped than a hot air balloon.

Kid Mojo was taking on the roll of "Rockefeller" by shouting out boldly the way that Rockefeller had done at Suburbanite Rink just 8 days ago by chanting, "NSR ... Tall NSR ... Neighborhood Street Rockers are in the house!" I swear Mojo had even borrowed Rockefeller's voice box. It gave me goose bumps, he sounded just like him. Swag to the core.

This got the other half of our crews toughness going loudly too as they joined him in the chant. I kept my serious, focused, and very confident look on my face, yet I was still chanting my own thing, more so just to get myself amped. I was saying with passion: "We are going to trounce these punks ... for you Bob ... for you. This one's for you! We are going to TCHRROUNNCE EHMM," I said with energy and anger in my eyes. I started by saying it to myself, but after a while I started saying it louder so everybody could hear.

"Play that beat" was thumping through the sound system loudly with bass, so I could barely even hear my own self talk – but I did it anyway. Globe and Whizz kid was thumping so hard I could feel it beating on my chest, as we paraded ourselves to the center of our universe. It was the best feeling that I had ever felt in my entire wildest fantasy of a life.

As we approached, I saw the cypher had partially formed. Dark green and black were floating around, top rockin', b-boppin', and eagerly waiting for us. I scanned through them one by one and I saw that they had looked equally as focused, which sent a chill down my spine, if I've got to be honest with you.

The MC got on the mike, "Alright party people in the place to be. It looks like the Hip Hop Breakers are ready to rock ... And the Neighborhood Street Rockers have just joined center stage."

The DJ started busting out with a scratch, "whoot chit, whoot chit whoot chit whoot chit, wicki wicki wicki, shooowittzzz, shooowittzzz, shoooWooooooooo," - then he threw in the Break Dance Battle Jam of all time, "Al Naa Fyish" by Hashim. It was perfect timing too because as the song was making us breakers battle ready, we NSR's had just outlined the other half of the break circle that was right across from The Hip Hop Breakers.

Without waiting, my boy who was always in a big hurry to get somewhere fast, boldly started us off. He can be so care free, so it was all very fitting that he started it off.

Brock Blazin' started circling around the inside of the cypher while staring down our opponents. He began to rock out a funky fresh top rock, with random up rock moves thrown into the mix but not aimed at any of the breakers in particular – he was just showing off some style. Blazin' had more or less aimed his random up rocks at their entire crew. However, he backed off before any of them could enter the circle and up rock against him.

Then Bamm! Blazin' stopped rockin' his foot rock and spiral dove into his famous beach ball. He dove, spun, kipped up, then dove, then spun, then kipped up again. He had done five consecutive beach balls in a row; he really did look like a human bouncing spinning beach ball.

Without pause, the Hip Hop Breakers made their start in the battle. All of the Hip Hop Breakers had their names written in green cursive writing on their black sweatshirts. Angelo was their first breaker up; he was the boy with the mousy tough guy voice; finger flickers sidekick, (in case you forgot.)

He stared me down as he top rocked and then quickly dropped down to a floor rock, and soon switched into windmills. After a penny or two (or nutcrackers if you prefer to call them that) - Angelo leapt to his feet and then pointed me out. I'm sure he did that because I was the only one that he really knew on our crew. And for whatever reason, he still had it in for me. It was all over his face.

I skipped my top rock; I walked in a full 360 degree circle with swag and then I pounced the floor into fast windmills, which quickly evolved into nutcrackers 6, 7, 8 times, (It's hard to count when you're rotating.) In all of the excitement I had forgotten to throw on my knit hats. (I hated when I did that)

Thing is, I used my forehead to push off of the ground when I was nutcrackin', so with each twist and turn my forehead was bashing the floor with each time around. The section of flooring was extra clean too, so each time I rotated, my forehead was squeakin' and scrapin' off of the floor. It sounded like someone with wet rubber shoes on a dry floor only it was my forehead.

While I spun around I was even thinking about how I was going to have a nice red mark on my forehead when I was all done, but of course, I kept on spinning anyway, it would be a proud battle wound. But I'm just saying, I thought of the craziest things when I was in the middle of my breakin' routines.

Then in the midst of it all, I widened my legs and attempted to jerk myself around more forcefully, I reached my hands and arms around my back, and clasped my hands together and spun around in handcuffed windmills. I did at least four of them but as I felt myself losing momentum, I moved into backspins, which I then quickly grabbed my left knee with my left hand and rolled to my left and started to spin on my left knee for half a turn, ending with a pose facing the HHB's.

I was dizzy and wobbly, so I almost walked to the wrong side. But half way there, I realized that I was walking towards black and green. Once I had gotten back to my side of the cypher, I could really feel that my forehead had been scraped like a madman. But it was all good in the hood. I'm just telling you, so you can picture what my forehead had looked like after I had finished.

I was feeling good about my routine though. I knew I had just nailed no handed windmills and I could tell by the looks on my crew mate's faces, that it was straight. Kid Mojo and Slim Jim could tell how dizzy I was. Each of them stood next to me like statues so I could use them as leaning posts.

Sylvester was next. He attempted to up rock against me but I was still regaining my balance a little, so I wasn't even thinking about trying to up rock against him. But my boy had my back.

Kid Mojo jumped in and started up rocking against him, whom Sylvester wasn't diggin' with Mojo's stomp style of rockin'. I was never sure if Mojo had done it on purpose to him or anyone for that matter, but he stepped on your feet, anytime you up rocked against him. Sylvester backed away from Mojos stomp rock and pointed me out. (If you remember, he was the cat that had thumped me in the chest last week while asking me, "What you be about?")

Mojo backed away when Sylvester began to down rock and do his own thing. Sylvester rocked a similar routine as mine: windmills, nutcrackers, but no handcuffs - then he finished off with hydraulic penny's (windmills where you bounce a few inches off the ground with each rotation.) I had the handcuffs and he had the hydraulics. But that didn't stop him from saying, "I just took you out boy."

"I had the handcuffs bro," I said but it had fallen on deaf ears.

Kid Mojo whispered to me, "With a gang bangin' attitude like his … he'll be wearing handcuffs one day." I smirked but I was too focused to laugh.

As soon as he exited the circle our boy Miguel 2 tough dove into hydraulic pennies of his own. Miguel loved to rock power moves with style, so he threw in high shouldered spins on his back for an artistic transition in between his hydraulic nutcrackers. Then as if someone had flicked a reverse switch. Miguel reversed it all. Every single move, he did in reverse. He started spinning counterclockwise windmills, then abruptly stopped and reversed back into clockwise windmills; he could stop on a dime and resume full speed in the other direction in no time flat.

As Miguel was finishing up his routine, the girls in the crowd were going bonkers, "Woo hooing" and all of that kind of schlernious business, which was par for the course. This was how it always was. Girls were always screaming and yelling whenever he hit the break floor. He was quite the charmer with his big smile, mocha Latin skin, and all.

Drix moved next to me and mouthed into my ear, "Miguel nailed those windmills like a hammer!"

"His hydraulics were like a jack hammer," I said.

"Word up," Braun agreed.

The DJ played his next track "Egypt, Egypt" by the Egyptian lover and the cypher kept moving.

The name "Bennedicto" read across the next Bboys back in block letters. He started circling around us NSR's with taunting glares. Braun Drix whispered, "He must not have gotten the memo to have his name written in cursive letters like the rest of his crewmates."

I nodded with focus.

Then I heard the Hip Hop Breakers chanting, "Go Benny! Go Benny!"

"Get 'em Benny!"

After swaggering around the inside of the cypher, he took a few steps back, then he made his grand entrance. He started flipping the flips, hurling the hand springs, maneuvering the mule kicks, kicking the kip ups, slamming the suicides, and other acrobatic types of exercises that made me think of Chi Girl and everything that she brought to our side. He was clearly the HHB's gymnast of the bunch.

Their boy, "Benny," as they were calling him, rejoined his group to massive high fives and, "Heck yeahs" and "you showed them boyee," and stuff like that while I began to look towards Chi girl.

In fact all of us NSR's were staring at Chi Girl. She smiled and confidently entered the cypher; Chi Girl smirked like somebody who knew she had some tricks up her sleeve. She revolved around the circle with an exaggerated switch in her butt. She kept walking around the circle as if she was flirting with the opponents, but in this, "you can't have me sort of way" as she playfully shook her head no and waved her finger from side to side. Then she purposely fooled them with swift and smooth pirouettes; ballet type stuff, leaps and everything; very feminine and very soft.

Some of the Hip Hop Breakers were mocking her in that instant, not knowing that she was about to go Izz off! Then I remembered how she had told me over the phone the other day that she was going to toy with the HHB's, since she was a girl and all. She knew how "chauvinistic" most guys were, so she wanted to act at first as if she was only going to do ballet, and then,

"Bamm, hit 'em wit it," she had said. She usually didn't talk like that, you know, "Bamm hit 'em wit it" type of expressions, so it made me laugh. I probably laughed because I knew we NSR's had been rubbing off on her. She usually talked very vanilla, very suburbanite, and soft spoken too, so it was funny hearing her yell, "Bamm" on the phone the other day.

I eagerly waited for her big moves as I watched her ballet around. Knowing she was going to bust out with big tricks had put extra joy in me when I saw a couple of the HHB's bust out with golf claps to mock her. You know the kind - fingers tapping the palm ever so softly and successively, just to be a smarty pants.

Then Bizz – Bamm, Boom, Chi Girl started flippin', twisting, and doing Aerial cartwheels and some other acrobatic twists and turns in the air; tit for tat with that other guy. (Pun intended.) No doubt about it, she equaled all of their guy Bennys' moves. She busted out with handstands that rotated at 360 degrees and then she reversed her motion, and even added 2000's into the mix - just for the upmanship on him or is it (upwomanship)?

Chi girl impressed the heck out of the crowd when she ended her routine with what seemed to be about 3 no handed flips, high up in the air, with some twists in the midst of her flips, and she had stuck the landing to boot. Which is a big deal in the gymnastics world, you know. I wished you could have seen it. The way the HHB's jaws had dropped and all.

Having a girl equal and I'm going to say outdo their guy, really changed the tone of the whole battle. The HHB's mocking golf claps had stopped and they were no longer offering smug smiles; save for my two gang bangin' "buddies" that really seemed to have it in for me.

Their next boy had "Flip Tone" written on the front of his sweatshirt. He looked to be Filipino, hence the name: Flip tone. Flip Tone skipped the Top Rock and twisted to the ground into swipes, floor work, into an air swipe movement that failed to keep its momentum so he went back into regular swipes on the ground. He ended his assault with a contorted intricate freeze that had his head smashed to the ground, his body was balanced on one hand, and his torso and legs were twisted uncomfortably like a pretzel.

AJ yelled, "Ohhh, that's gotta hurt" then he added, "Isn't he racking his nuts being twisted up in a pretzel like that?"

AJ and I wore a split second cringe on our faces after he had said that "racking nuts business."

Drix laughed and said, "Pretzels and nuts – who's got the popcorn?"

This made AJ and Drix laugh like school girls for a while to the point where I had to stop AJ from stepping on me. He laughed with his whole body.

Jet Drinkwater entered the battle just as Flip Tone had made his exit, when I suddenly had realized that I needed to switch my shoes. I had worn "my" shoes during my no handed windmill routine for my turn, so while I was watching Jet Drinkwater rock it out, I started putting on Boogie Bobs shoes. I even started singing quietly to myself almost as a joke, "I'm going to rock these head spins … in my boogie shoes." I was singing it in the melody of this song called, "Boogie shoes "which is a disco song that I grew up with as a kid. I had changed the lyrics and was laughing to myself about it while I was un-knotting Bobs shoes, which made me relax. I swear I even laughed through my nose on accident, just like Boogie Bobs laugh. It must have been the shoes.

Jet Drinkwater had ended his routine just like his counterpart had; with a crazy contorted freeze, balancing on his left hand, left side, left foot, and then he reversed momentum and did the exact same freeze but used his right hand, right side, and right foot that time. Nobody from the Hip Hop Breakers wanted to openly admit it but you could see by the looks on their faces that they knew that our boy had just taken out their boy. Jet was that good.

I was still in the middle of the shoe change but I looked up to see the name of their next boy, "Steve Thailand" not only had cursive writing on his sweatshirt front and back but he also had, "Steve" written on one leg and, "Thailand" written on the other leg. It was the guy I had seen last Saturday jamming head spins from across the room; I recognized his pony tail coming out of his knit hat.

Steve Thailand approached and up rocked against Blazin', who countered him bold and tall. Then Steve from the HHB's returned to the middle of the cypher and began to hop, dance, his top rock like he was on a pogo stick. He was hopping, dancing, and top rocking as if he was a kangaroo. Then as if someone had said, "Hit the deck" He dropped to the floor into fast windmill nutcrackers into tabletops: (windmills transitioning into head spins back into windmills). Steve of the HHB's had rotated around about 5 times on his head with tap head spins and then rocked out about 3 or maybe 4 no handed fast head spins before falling down to the ground.

Everyone on his side was going nuts while everyone on my side was staring me down as I tried to untie my (Bobs) shoes. They had somehow knotted up when I was wearing them around my neck earlier; therefore I was unable to jump out after Steve. Another cat by the name of, "Joon Bug" from the Hip Hop Breakers yelled from across the cypher, "It's cool dude … you can wait to give me your shoes until after the battle."

But I just ignored him and kept unknotting. It would have been so much easier if Bob had used fat laces in his break shoes (because you don't tie or untie those), but Boogie Bob didn't have fat laces; he didn't like 'em. I betchya he'd have called 'em foo foo laces.

Kid Mojo looked over to me since he knew I was our head spin guy but he could see I was still tying my laces, so he strode out to the middle, looked back at me and us NSR's and said, "I'll show 'em wazup … We'll mess anybody up!"

Kid Mojo leapt into the air until gravity had bolted him into windmills and a couple of air flares that evolved into Thomas flairs aka Atomic Flares. He had rocked it in one fell swoop; continuous motion. He was tall Chicago. It was the move of the night up until that point. The crowd started going crazy. He had rocked out with his clock out but deep down, I knew, I needed to execute Bobs head spins before it was all said and done. So the battle, and its pressure, pressed on.

The Hip Hop Breakers sent out their next boy who had to be practically pushed out into the middle of the break circle. This boy, by the name of, "Matt Luther," had no Top Rock and no up rock. He just lowered himself to the ground looking all clumsy as he attempted his Flares. He did one complete revolution at best. Matt Luther's turn in the cypher was a clear example of them not being able to match our boys Flares.

Our crew started yelling, "NSR."

"We got you boys," AJ yelled.

"He can't counter … he can't counter," Slim Jim chanted.

In the midst of his failed attempt at a counter, another one of the HHB's bounced out into the circle, fearing we've one upped them. He did this move that was similar to flares but he held his legs together instead of apart as he circled around. He did 4 in a row at best, but I could tell that his legs were dragging on the floor as he revolved around, so it did not equal our boy Mojo's Atomic Flares, and that was for sure. But that's not how the HHB's saw it.

The Hip Hop Breakers started cheering their heads off as if they had just won the super bowl when in fact they didn't even counter Mojo's flares.

Angelo started shouting out to remind us, "You aint got no head spins on your side … you all aint got no head spins – what you be about now? What you know about now punks?" he asked tauntingly with cold eyes.

I had just finished unknotting and tying my shoes when suddenly I had felt the need to shut them up straight quick.

I was just about to jump into the cypher when our master floor gliding, waving machine; Slim Jim slithered smoothly into the center ring. Part of me was mad because I wanted to counter that dude Steve's head spins right there on the spot; Swifty on the spot – not Johnny on the spot. But I also knew this was a team sport and everybody should get his or her chance to rock rock.

I heard AJ Fresh yell, "Slim Jim is in the freakin' hiz-ous!"

He rocked out his usual faire of: floor gliding, moon walking, and doing his deceptive foot trickery, like only Slim Jim could. You would swear he was walking in zero gravity or wearing skates when you saw him floor gliding. Slim Jim had busted out with electrifying pulsating tick movements as he floor glided himself around the entire cypher, while looking every HHB squarely in the eyes.

Slim Jim's counterpart from the HHB's popped out onto the floor next. His name was "Lectro wave." Apparently Slim Jim didn't feel like leaving the floor though because the two of them kept on poppin' and moon gliding against each other in the middle of the cypher.

Slim Jim would execute a move and Lectro wave would counter. Lectro wave would bust out with a moonwalk floor glide and Slim Jim would follow suit.

They were both good but all I could think about was busting out with my (Boogie Bobs) head spins.

After the poppers were done battling against each other. AJ Fresh breached the cyphers human structured walls– someone had beaten me to the punch yet again. I swear everyone had jumped into the cypher before the other man was done. He started Top Rocking in a way that looked kind of awkward; he looked like a canine on ice, slipping and sliding like a mad dog that was running in place. When he finally felt just right, he dove to the ground on his hand while kicking his legs up high into the air, "1990's you go boy," I said loudly as he spun around. AJ Fresh had spiraled at least 10 consecutive 1990's (a one handed handstand while revolving around in continuous 360 degree circles.)

After he spiraled his 1990's, he landed on both of his hands (feet still up in the air), and then pushed off into a handspring that had him land on his feet. He landed facing our opponent and then pointed down to the ground as if to say 'beat that'. As quickly as AJ Fresh had flashed in, he had flashed out; Nuff said.

The next B-boy out for the Hip Hop Breakers was Rolly Lex, and just as I was expecting, he attempted to counter AJ's 1990's, and he did just that. Well truth be told; he did more than that - he whirl winded his feet up into the air while his hand drilled down to the ground. He was a human tornado of one handed spins. When his feet had landed onto the ground he continued spinning around on his feet like a figure skater revolving round and round. Then he reversed and leapt onto his left hand and began executing 1990's with his left hand in a clockwise direction about 4 or 5 times. Braun whispered to me, "Well, I think their guy Rolly has AJ beat on this one."

I agreed. After all, he did just execute AJ's move just as good; and then he reversed his move to top it off. "You've got to give credit where credit is due," I said.

The DJ changed the track on the ones and twos to, "Electric Kingdom" by Twilight 22. Our next man up was none other than, Blake Kleinfeld. He boldly walked into the break circle and got on down to business with "Buddha's." Buddha's are kind of like crabwalks. Picture Blake kneeling on the ground like he is praying but he has his hands on the ground in front of him. He begins to spin around in circles, with all of his body off of the ground, except for his hands, while keeping his legs and knees in the praying position.

While keeping his motion, Blake moved into serious crabwalks; superfast, lightning speed. He bounced his crabwalks at least 5 inches off the ground with hydraulics twice per revolution. Then with a burst of might, he twisted into mega speed superman windmills, (hands out like superman's are when he is flying) then freeze! He stopped the action on a dime and stared our opponents down.

Next up was their guy Jeff Jackin'. This Jeff Jackin' guy was pantomiming as if to say, "Kiss my butt" to Blake, who had just left the cypher. You see, Blake had ended in a freeze and this Jeff Jackin guy was "burning him" in the midst of his freeze. Jeff was putting his butt near Blake's face as he posed his break move; very boys will be boys humor. I think that kind of shiznit is corny; "burnin'" and crap, but I catch myself screwing around sometimes and burnin' people too, it's just a way we breakers can show a sense of humor or be juvenile when were breakin', I guess. It's a guy thing, and I think you need to see it to understand.

Other than that burnin' crap, Jeff rocked windmills and freezes but when you've got someone like Blake out there supermanin' at kryptonite speeds and you only answer the call with windmills, to me, you're basically saying: 'you can't hang.' Advantage NSR, you dig? At least that's what the talk was like on our side of the cypher after Jeff had made his exit.

Braun Drix stepped into the circle next. He circled around the break cypher with a serious face. I waited with anticipation because frankly I had only see him rock out his elbow spins with multiple revolutions once. The other 10 or 20 times I had "seen him" elbow spin he'd usually only revolve around about once. Not because I didn't want to watch, but because I was always so busy practicing my own moves.

It's funny though because at least 20 zillion times Braun had come up to me in between random jam sessions (when we were practicing our breakin' together at McCollumn) and said, "Dude, dude did you see it? Did you see 'em?"

And I'd say, "What?"

Then he'd say, "Ohh dude, you just missed it, I just spun around like 10 times on my elbow."

After the millionth time of missing it, it started to feel like I was missing out on seeing a Leprechaun or something. In addition, every time I did watch, I would only see one revolution – at most, which still aint bad, it still looked cool. But it wasn't the ten revolutions he had boasted of.

Anyway, that's what I thought about as Braun Drix circled around with this serious as a heart attack look on his face. Then he swirled onto his elbow and showed me his elusive trick; he spun around on his elbow 5 times with legs that were spread into a V shape. After Braun fell to the ground he stumbled his way over to me and said, "How many times did I spin? How many was that? 9, 10, 11?"

"It was about 4 or 5," I said."

"No … it had to have been at least 9 or 10 … it felt like the most I had ever done … EVER," he yelled with glee.

"Dude, you rocked out," I said with a smile.

Chi Girl inched closer, high fived Drix, and asked me, "Who do you think is winning so far?"

I could tell she was mostly worried about losing her shoes by the way she tensed her mouth and swallowed while staring at her shoe as if it were a dog that had just died.

"We've got it so far," I told her but actually I was thinking we were in a tie and that included me counting on my head spins that I hadn't rocked yet.

My attention was drawn to the next cat wearing black and green.

Oddy Kamm entered the cypher spinning, pirouetting and top rockin' in a style of dance I had never seen before; it was a cross between ballet, Brooklyn rock, and jazz dance. I almost got the impression that he was just messing around and tying to be goofy but the look on his face was serious, so I was not sure. Perhaps he was taking a page out of Chi Girls handbook.

Then Oddy dove to the ground into shoulder spins, and revolved with might into one legged helicopters; one leg bent and one leg straight out. And just as I thought he was done, their boy Oddy, eked out a couple of Halos, a move that our team hadn't done yet. However, every time he did "Halos" he would run out of steam, so he would transition back into windmills. This made me a little nervous though, because I wasn't sure if anyone in our crew could rock 'em. Oddy walked out of the circle, Fandango looked at me, banged on his chest with his fist, and began his entrance.

Just as our boy Fandango stepped inside of the circle a cheer came out from the crowd. Someone was streaking across the rinks hardwood floor wearing only underwear. He was shuffling his feet with his drawers on the ground, still around his ankles. He was laughing like a freak a zoid as he half nakedly shuffled, while some girl chased him with a mad look on her face. Braun tapped my shoulder and said, "That is why some people should not do drugs or drink alcohol …. Some people end up doing stupid things," he laughed. I noticed that Fandango had paused his routine, so he could check it out too.

"It's like someone put a say no to drugs and alcohol commercial right in the middle of our battle," I playfully replied to Braun as I watched the half lit, nit wit, shuffle his pants on the ground, across the floor.

The semi-streaker finally faded away into the dense crowd, and our boy Gio (Fandango) continued his rather casual and aloof romp rock; his own version of a top rock. I can't really even call it a top rock just yet, he was just dancing, but he was circling around the cypher, staring down all of the Hip Hop Breakers- meanwhile some random spectator chick tapped me on my shoulder and said all chipper, "Hey can you do the wave? … Do the wave!" and if she wasn't chipper enough, she picked up her chipperness and added, "… that'll show them, do a wave, and then you guys will win," she said with high eyebrows and an over bit-horse toothed smile, while moving her arms like a cheerleader would.

I shook my head NO - more or less to myself, and I ignored the goof balls comment, and refocused my attention on Fandango who wanted to taunt me with salsa, rumba, or cha cha, or whatever the Latin dance was really called. He gave me teasing eyes as he top rock and salsa danced around. He was messing with me because of the conversation we had earlier in the car.

When he was done taunting me, Fandango began looking at me with this confident look, while motioning: "one minute" with his index finger and mouthing the words, "Watch this" and "you'll see" as he pointed to his eye and winked with a sideways smile.

Suddenly Fandango fandango'd the night breaktastic and pounced the ground into fast Air Flares, (which are the same as atomic flares except your legs are higher up in the air.) Then he slowly lowered his head down and transitioned into the move that we later started to refer to as "tracks," "head glides" or "halos." Since it was 1985 when this battle at Chicagoland had taken place, it was a very brand new move to everyone around at that time. We had all sorts of names for that move but not many breakers could rock 'em just yet. Save for Fandango.

Drix was calling them "Supersonic windmills."

I had been hearing about them for weeks from Bruiser and he had always referred to them as "head glides" but it was only a legend until that night that Fandango had tracked them into the night fantastic. Their boy Oddy may have done a couple of them but our boy Gio had rocked out dozens of them continuously. "Gio's got Halos for days," I yelled as loud as I could to nobody in particular.

Here it was, right in front of my eyes, our very own boy Fandango, rockin' 'em out. By the way, Halos kind of look like windmills but instead of revolving around on your shoulders, chest, and back; you revolve around on your head. Think of it this way, with head spins you spin on the top of your head, but with Halos you spin around in circles on the front, sides, and back of your head while the rest of your body looks like a revolving windmill. It defies gravity.

Fandango had rocked out dozens of air flares and halos but for whatever reason, he never did straight up head spins. He once told me, "It's just not my move."

So I wasn't off the hook.

After Fandango was done, it was obvious that we were on top. He had rocked out, without a doubt, the best move of the night. Even the HHB's had widened eyes and opened mouths, along with looks of: oh shiznit ... we're screwed- all over their faces ... The HHB's couldn't hide their fear and despair. Fandango had rocked it too tough, too Chicago; Tall Chicago.

I yelled out to Fandango as he rejoined the sidelines, "You've got to teach me how to salsa bro." This drew an exhausted smile and nod from Gio, who was still out of breath.

From across the cypher Angelo from the HHB's yelled out, "That's cool guys – but we've got you on the head spins ...it's a tie so far ... So what we gonna do? Call it even?"

Then Oddy jumped back into the cypher and executed 2 halos in a row, then fell. He walked back to his crew and Angelo shouted, "I don't know man ... we've got the halos too ... I think we're one up on yous ... we've got the head spins and halos." ...

"My brother spun dozens of them .... Your guy did TWO," Miguel 2 tough roared.

"We've got the head spins brau," Angelo spat with cocky eyes.

Sylvester chimed in, "I wear a size 10 gents!"

I knew this was my moment to make my move. So I stepped into the cypher but so did Pauly G, a millisecond before me, he was boisterously making his presence known, "Neighborhood Street Rockers are in the house y'all ... NSR is in the hizz-ouse Y'all!"

Pauly G started: wavin', poppin', and tickin' something fierce whilst moon walking and floor gliding like an astronaut.

The chipper girl that I had blown off just minutes before, tapped my shoulder again, and said, "Now you guys are going to win." I had never seen such a chipper girl with a horse toothed smile before. I was so focused on wanting to get out there to do Bobs turn that I didn't even pay her a word.

Kid Mojo and Blazin' were both staring me down and making motions with their hands, which made it clear to me. They wanted me to get out there and counter the comments being yelled around by Angelo and Sylvester; and I agreed with them.

The music was too loud and the action was too intense for me to try to explain to them in that moment, that in fact I was about to enter the cypher but Pauly G had beaten me to it. I just nodded and mouthed the words; "I'm next."

Then we all watched Pauly G who was then countered by a cat by the name of "Shock La Rock" from the HHB's.

Shock La Rock took over the cypher in more ways than one. He was wearing flip flop –sandals which immediately drew the attention of our crew mate AJ Fresh who thought "flip flops for guys were girly." AJ yelled, putting him down, "Yo dude, flip flops? Sandals? Isn't that like wearing thongs on your feet?" AJ laughed in a taunting voice and then yelled in an even louder voice (and he was already yelling), "Nice thong man, nice thongs on your feet - Dude I don't even want to see your thong underwear or butt floss man, you're wearing thongs on your feet bro! ... toe floss," AJ cackled to the crowd. But that didn't stop "Thong boy" who dove into windmills despite AJ's taunts.

While Shock La Rock was twirling around, he executed a few helicopters into the mix of his windmills (helicopters are windmills where you bend one of your legs while keeping the other leg straight out.) Anyway, this cat Shock La Rock took off his flip flop sandals while helicoptering around, and was now wearing his flip flop-tongs on his hands while wind milling.

Suddenly the cypher started to smell like old tacos or feet or dirty socks, or something. Shock Rock transitioned into crabwalks and began walking on his sandals which were still on his hands. It was becoming obvious that the smell we were all sniffing was coming from Shock Rocks socks.

AJ Fresh, who was already lathered up from throwing out the name calling, started back in on Shock Rock again, "Yo dude … it smells like you dipped your socks in a SEWER bro! Yo thong boy! Did you dip your socks in a sewer?"

AJ tapped my shoulder with a wide mouthed smile and said, "Yo Phil, they ought to call him Shock Socks, cuz he's shocking the heck out of me with his sewer socks." AJ started snorting through his nose and convulsing so much I had to hold his back to stop him from accidentally stepping on two spectators who were very close behind us.

"I think I can see a green fog coming from his socks bro," I said to AJ which practically made him pee his pants.

Suddenly, the DJ lowered the music and the MC checked the mike with a: "Yo Yo YO …the Hip Hop Breakers got the head spins. … The Neighborhood Street Rockers got the Halos. -So it's a close call … we may have to call this one a tie boys. What do you all think? Is it a tie guys?"

Chi Girl yelled, "Hey, there aren't only Bboys here?!" and with the music being low enough the MC apparently heard her and said, "Sup B-Girl … I know you're out there, I aint trying to diss … you rocked them flips girl!"

The middle of the cypher was starting to get clogged up with some of the HHB's and some of my NSR's giving each other friendly handshakes that seemed to mean that they all thought the battle was a tie, which really started to get me mad. Some of the breakers from each side took that emcees comments to mean that we had ended in a draw. It seemed like everyone was all slobbering all over each other like it was a relief that the break battle was a tie.

I boldly jumped into the center of the break circle and started swaying from side to side. I circled around the cypher while staring everyone down – including my own crew, just to let them know that I meant business.

I started buckin' wildly and kickin' my up rock against some of my fellow NSR's in an intimidating way, to the point where they were all starting to back up and make room for me in the cypher. I wanted everyone to understand that I owned that cypher. Once the cypher had made its room for me, I started getting even crazier and I was top rockin' like a madman; all buck wild – I wanted to look awkward. Then the DJ threw in, "Boogie Down Bronx by Man Parrish. This was my jam of all Bboy jams. I mean Rocky Balboa had his theme song for boxing and yours truly Phil K Swift had his for breakin'.

As the vocals started on, "Boogie Down Bronx" I started gettin' all excited and was fixin' to create my disturbance. I started thinking about how this was Boogie Bobs turn - Not mine. I even felt like Bob was whispering in my ear or maybe he was staring at me from the ceiling. It's hard to explain but I felt Bob's presence at Chicagoland Rink that night. Maybe it was the shoes?

The cypher was now mine, I could tell by everyone's eyes. My top rock had turned into crazy top rock stomping. Nothing very flashy or stylistic just stomping like a soldier in a combat zone while swaying from side to side. After I had managed to create enough room to get on down to business, I took one last glance at my (Boogie Bobs) shoes. I found the eyes of many of my crew mates, I pointed up to the ceiling and I said loudly, "This is for Bob!" Then, as if I had been guided by a higher power, I pounced the floor with angry adrenaline; angry for Bobs' struggle. With a burst of might I began revolving into windmills. My adrenaline was flowing and my toughness was growing. I pushed fiercely onto my head and began tapping myself around into tap head spins. Even though I was in the midst of breakin', even though I was spinning around on my head, I was clearly thinking to myself as I revolved around: I did it! I made it! I transitioned into head spins from windmills! Something I had only done but a couple of times before in my basement during practice sessions.

I kept spinning and tapping, I could hear the roar of the crowd. I knew that I had already done enough to equal the other guy from the HHB's, so I began to close my legs tighter and stiffen up my entire body. My legs were now together pointing upwards to the sky; my body became completely vertical to the ground. I stopped tapping with my hands; I put my arms out horizontally and made them parallel with the ground and I continued revolving around at least another 10 or 15 no handed head spins – it's really hard to count when you're spinning that fast, you know. I could no longer hear the cheers of the crowd while I was spinning around no handed; time had sort of froze. However, when I fell to the ground and ended my routine, I heard the crowd again, louder than I had heard them all night – thanks Boogie Bob, I thought to myself as I began to gather my bearings.

Slim Jim knelt down, leaned in, offered me a hand up, picked me off of the ground, and guided me back to our crew. I was dizzy after doing Bobs head spins. It was the most I had ever done before, so it's hard to prepare for that kind of dizziness, you know?

I was relieved that I had pulled it off, because honestly, I wasn't really sure what was going to happen until it had happened. I may have talked up a good storm about how I was going to rock those head spins and everything, but that was just talk.

… Now I had done the walk.

I was too busy to catch it all because I was still recovering from the dizziness but Slim Jim told me that their guy Steve Thailand jumped back out into the break circle immediately after I was done and attempted his windmills into head spins again. Slim Jim said, "He failed to get on top of his head the first time, and then he attempted it again and was only able to do two head spins before falling again … and everyone started to BOO when he fell," Jim said.

"I heard the boos," I told him. In fact, as I heard the "boos," it made the hair stand up on the back of my neck.

Then, Blazin' came over to high five me, so I asked him, "How many times did I spin around?" It was the only thing I could think about at that moment.

"Dude … you did a lot, I don't know but you schooled their guy, he just went out there and couldn't do Shee-ott! He was bunk! You schooled him Phil," Blazin' said.

"Boogie Bob schooled him, I was just the dude wearing his shoes," I said.

Blazin' smiled, rolled his eyes, and gave me this look as if I was coo coo and said, "Yeah, Bob schooled him." But I could tell by Blazin's face that he didn't really think that Bob had much to do with anything. However, I still did. I really did.

Fandango took liberties, reentered the cypher, and began to do our decisive winning move again. That's right, our decisive winning move. In my opinion Fandango's Halos, head glides, tracks or air flares – whatever you want to call them, had stolen the show. And his second round was even better than his first. The head spins were important, but that was just to match Steve Thailand. It was Fandangos "Salsa dancing" that had won it for us.

Everybody played their parts but hands down, when Fandango jumped back out there and revolved a million more air flares, Halos, and head glides without falling and then leaping to his feet with might for his ending, we all knew we had won. Fandangos' pointing at all of the HHB's with a taunting and playful look on his face was just the icing on the cake. You could see, one by one, the Hip Hop Breakers had started to deflate. The roar of the crowd and the random slaps on our backs and high fives from spectators had said it all. We knew and the crowd knew that we had won.

Everybody at Chicagoland Rink knew what was up. There was no denying it. The Neighborhood street Rockers had won the battle.

Bruiser approached me and said, "Dude you did about 10 tappers and about 10 no handers ... dude you won us the battle."

I was really thinking that Fandango had won us the battle but I ended up saying to Bruiser, "Yo dude ... Boogie Bob won us the battle, if it wasn't for his shoes, I never would have done 20 head spins. - Did I really do 20 head spins?"

Bruiser nodded a decisive yes.

I paused, thought for a moment, and then I asked Bruiser, "We won? ... Officially or in your opinion? ... Or what?"

"Look across the circle Mr. Swift," Bruiser said.

I looked across the cypher and I saw all of the Hip Hop Breakers taking off their shoes, except for Angelo and Sylvester, they were still staring in disbelief with angry gangbanger scowls. One by one the Hip Hop Breakers started sliding away in their socks, disappearing into the jacking and housing crowd while we NSR's were jumping up and down with grins on our entire faces.

Now that the cypher had disappeared and the break battle had ended, the DJ immediately switched gears back into house music and started playing this song called, "Deputy of love."

"Straight up deep house," Bruiser said as the song came on.

The shoes were just left on the floor for everyone to trip on but their captain Lenny Poindexter was gathering the shoes and being a good sport of it all. I guess sticking around to shake our hands wasn't in the Hip Hop Breakers plans but at least they were good enough sports to concede defeat.

I watched Lenny talk to Angelo and Sylvester who then finally and reluctantly took off their shoes. They handed their shoes over to Lenny and angrily walked away. You could feel the anger in their eyes. They both made sure to look at me with cold looks on their faces as they disappeared into the sea of Bboys, Bgirls, house people, and party people.

Lenny who had gathered the 10 or 12 pairs of shoes was trying his best to hold them against his chest. A few shoes had fallen as he had walked over towards us when some chick who had been hanging with the HHB's all night, helped pick up the fallen shoes. It was one of those big puffy haired, smoky eye shadowed girls I was telling you about when I had first arrived at the rink that night but it wasn't his sister Kaylee. I heard Lenny say, "Thanks for picking those up Gertrude. You are always in the thick of it all."

"I know everything about everything for a reason," Gertrude said randomly.

The two of them handed over the shoe trophies to Bruiser who then handed me half of his half. But I had noticed that Lenny had kept one pair in his hands.

I overheard Lenny say to Dan, "I guess you can get the money from Scott Shadows."

Dan Bruiser nodded and shook his hand.

After that, Lenny came over and congratulated some of us Neighborhood Street Rockers. He was a pretty good sport about it all. He was obviously let down, but he was cool about it at least. He probably would have shaken all of our hands but some of us NSR's were too busy jumping up and down in victory. I could tell that kind of made Lenny want to beat it sooner rather than later. So I piped in, before he bailed, "Can I have that last pair of shoes?"

He looked at me as if I was crazy for wanting the other pair of shoes.

It was the smelly sewer tongs – flip flops. He just shrugged and said, "If you really want these, you can have 'em. I was just going to throw them away."

Then, I asked Lenny about that, "What you be about business? – from his crew mate."

And he told me that Angelo and Sylvester were the only ones like that on their crew. (He meant gangbangers.) And the only reason they had them on their crew was because Chicagoland Rink was their turf and it was easier to let them break with them than to not.

After Lenny was done talking to me, he slowly slid away in his green socks and into the dancing crowd of jackers not to be seen again.

I watched Bruiser start to shuffle his way through the crowd towards the DJ booth. He is so easy to pick out with his Jesus beard and all. Minutes earlier I had heard some of the guys busting his butt about getting their 50 bucks back. Some of the guys weren't even asking for their winnings, they were just worried about getting suckered out of their ante.

You see, immediately after the battle, we saw some cats in black and green chewing off the ear of the DJ, MC, and others that were hanging in the DJ booth which prompted a couple of my fellow NSR's to come up to me and stress about the whole money thing.

"How come the MC didn't get back on the mic and tell everyone we had won?" Braun asked with concern.

"I don't know, but we'll get our dough," I said.

I assured them we were going to get our 50 bucks back and 50 bucks in winnings, but really their concerns had started to worry me too.

"I'll believe it when I see it," Slim Jim said.

"They probably didn't even ante up," AJ Fresh said with doubt.

I told them both, "Bruiser told me that everyone paid in before the battle had even started and old boy is on his way right now to collect our dough, yo."

For the next million minutes everyone watched "Jesus" walk through the crowd and towards the DJ booth while we all tripped off the battle we had just won. I started to feel a little devilish. I had the sewer tongs in my hands, but I was sort of hiding them. Every chance I got, I would quietly put them very close to someone's nose, when they weren't paying attention; kind of by their ear, just out of their side vision. I sort of tried to do it on the Down low, and once I saw them make a vomit face or gag from the shoes green fumes –Bamm, I would smash that shoe right into their face. This forced out a few dry heaves from a couple of my crew mates. I got a pretty big bang out of it to be honest with you. But after a while, they all started avoiding me like the plague; a sewer shoe plague. I stopped after Slim Jim had given me a stink face but not before I got Brock Blazin'. "Paybacks a bee-otch," Brock said after I had smothered the smelly tong right in his nose.

The DJ started to play some straight up Chicago house music. "Music is the key," by JM Silk was pulsating throughout the rinks speakers. Most of us NSR's were still jumping up and down and gloating about our victory but I was more relieved and serious than anything.

When Kelly came over and hugged me, I thought about how she was in the thick of it all when Angelo and Sylvester had first challenged me. She hung out for a while and I did my best impersonation of James Dean; you know, I tried to be a sexy-cool cat. Although, I wasn't really sure if I was coming across as a sexy-cool cat or a dude with crazy tight britches? But I had just rocked out a million head spins, so I wasn't too worried about it. Mainly, I was really excited to see Kelly again.

However Kelly warned me, "Those guys may have given up their shoes and money ... but they are not really good sports. Most of the Hip Hop Breakers play fair because most of them are just breakers. However, Angelo and Sylvester are gang bangin' breakers so watch out for them. You can't trust those guys as far as you can throw them, I know they gang up on people and box out sucker punches," Kelly warned. "They are always getting kicked out of school," she added.

"I'm not worried about it. I've got my boys up here." That's what I said at least, but really, deep down inside, her warnings had made me into a nervous Nelly. Yet, I tried to keep my face cool, if you know what I mean, fool?

"Just make sure they don't catch you up here alone or anything. I know them and they don't play fair," Kelly told me as she hugged me in a strong embrace before walking away. After she had left, I really wanted to bail, I didn't even care about the money anymore -but I didn't bail. Dan was my ride, so I couldn't; he was still at the DJ booth.

It took forever because Dan can really be a chatty Kathy sometimes. He was chattin' up the DJ booth entourage like mad while all of us NSR's chilled by our side; the Billie jean-Saturday night fever dance floor side. I swear every last one of us had watched Dan the whole time he was over there.

Eventually Bruiser came back and passed out our cash, which really lifted the spirits of all of us NSR's. Money may not be everything but it sure doesn't suck having some.

I could still feel Angelo and Sylvester's eyes on me as Bruiser handed me Bobs' and my cash. I could also tell they were trying to act as if they weren't watching me. Every time I looked over towards them, they would quickly look away; they were trying to be on the DL but it was as obvious as a freshly popped red zit on a bright white cheek, that they were keeping tabs on me.

Kelly came back over by me one last time, gave me her number, a hug, and said good bye and then right when she had walked away, Angelo and Sylvester came up to me with big friendly smiles. They were acting as if they were my new best buddies in the whole wide world. Telling me, "You really rocked out on the head spins bro!" They even started telling me how great my crew was and schlerniousness like that. It felt fake. I wasn't buying any of their friendly compliments. I kept thinking about how Kelly had just warned me that they couldn't be trusted.

They went from being punk gangbangers that had thumped me in the chest last week and sore losers that had also given me angry scowls right after the battle had finished - to suddenly acting as if they were my new best buddy old pals in the whole world. That did not make any sense.

Angelo said, "Dude, do you smoke?"

"No ways bro, I've got asthma," I said with a fake smile; I was wearing my best poker face.

"Ahh snap, I was going to ask you to come out to our car and we'd smoke one up with you," Angelo said.

I knew they were talking about 420 but either way, it was not my thing.

Then Sylvester said, "Yeah dude, come on out to smoke one up with us- A victory smoke dude!" This was the friendliest voice I had ever heard Sylvester use. It seemed eerie, if you know what I mean.

I repeated, "I don't smoke at all my man, it screws up my lungs. I don't mess with it, I've got Asthma bro, and the doctor won't let me."

"Hey cool, I feel ya, I feel ya, but yo, check it, we have this cool bangin' stereo in our car, we want to show it to you," Sylvester said in this sly voice.

"Yeah bro come out with us and we'll thump some breakin' jams and shoot the shiznit for a bit. Maybe you can teach me how to do some of those head spins? You're alright with us Phil," Angelo said in this strangely nice tone as he shook my hand. I didn't really want to shake his hand but I did. I bet my arm had looked like a wet noodle as he shook it but I didn't care. I wasn't about to act as if I was his friend all of a sudden.

I was starting to get a little nervous though, if I've got to be honest with you because the more I had held my ground and said, "no," the more they had started to shed their "nice guy" and friendly acts towards me. In fact, as it became clear I wasn't going to go outside with them, they really started to show their true colors.

"Yo bro, are you really going to make us go home without our shoes dude?" Angelo asked.

Then Sylvester sounded angrier, "I really need that fifty bucks back man. I think you should give it back to me."

"Yeah, you have a hundred bucks on you, fifty for him and fifty for me" Angelo said as he pointed at Sly and himself.

As the seconds ticked away, that felt like minutes, he had inched closer to me and was no longer that "nice guy" that had wanted to smoke me out and show me his bangin' stereo.

"Ask my boy Slim Jim or Bruiser about that money," I said to them as I tried to inch my way away from them.

When a random group of guys had walked by and got in between us, I took that as my chance to bail. I walked away in fierce search of my crew mates. I tried to act cool as I bailed by saying, "I'll see you guys later." But I didn't even listen for their response as I made my cool, speed walking getaway towards my friends.

I could sense Angelo and Sylvester on my heels. I swear I had heard their voices the whole time I had made my obvious escape. Their thick gang bangin' style of talkin' was unmistakable. However, I didn't look back. I didn't want to know for real if they were following me or not. I didn't want to run either, that would look pansy, plus I thought that would make them want to chase me even more – if they knew for sure, I was trying to get away that would show I was afraid; and you know how they say, never show a dog fear – Well, I wasn't exactly walking slowly either. All I knew was that I didn't want to get caught by those cats again while I was still alone.

I felt a hand grab the back of my shoulder, "What's your big hurry? ..." was said in a deep voice.

"Where are you going?" was said by the other tough voice.

They had said it in purposefully loud and threatening voices too - just to mess with me.

It was Brock Blazin' and Kid Mojo. I had recognized their voices right away but it's funny, even though I had recognized their voices in that instant, my heart had still skipped a million beats.

"What's up dude, you look stressed?" Blazin' asked.

Neither one of them knew what had been going on with those two HHB punks just a few seconds before. It was just coincidence and perfect timing that they had messed with me in those scary voices. Brock was always pulling that gag. It was one of his things; he usually did it to me in the hallways at school when he saw me running. "No running in the halls young man," he'd say in this teacher-esque voice. He'd get me every time too. Only this time, I had recognized his fake grown up voice.

"I knew it was you," I said.

"Then why'd you jump," Brock said laughing.

I finally decided to look. I spotted Angelo and Sylvester staring me down from a few dozen feet away. They must have stopped following me when they saw my homies approaching me. Neither "Sly" nor Angelo were looking away any more. They both looked at me with cold unblinking eyes as I talked with my crew mates.

I told Kid Mojo what had just happened and he just shrugged and said, "We'll mess anybody up."

"Dude, let's just go back over by our crew," Blazin said as he looked at Angelo and Sylvester and then scoped the scene for our "backup." Brock was always like that, if there was ever any type of danger around, Brock would immediately start scoping around for possible back up. He was good about having animal instincts like that. Sometimes I needed back up and sometimes I was the back up. Sometimes you are the hydrant and sometimes you are the dog.

We walked back by the rest of the NSR's and chilled amongst each other for a while. Other friends and classmates from our neck of the woods were still hanging around. Hazy, Isaac, Rory, Rodd and a few others that I didn't really know, they were friends of friends that I knew only by their faces.

Do you want to know what was really starting to annoy the heck out of me though? - Punk ice Bee-otch Logan the key-tooth picker was chillin' by us NSR's for some unknown reason. He started being all fake too; he actually started to bow and salute me when he saw me coming; phony holder crap like that bugs me.

Ever since we had won, Logan began to act like he was cool with everyone that was in our crew, for the rest of the night. It was as if he was trying to be one of us. It really annoyed the crap out of me; I hate a bandwagon jumper like that. I was too stressed to say anything to him though; except to accept his apology, which was a backhanded apology at best, "You all didn't suck as bad as I thought you would." and "You're lucky their boy Oddy was off on his Halos tonight, otherwise it would have been a different story," is what Logan had said. Which I guess was a compliment coming from the likes of a cat like Logan.

I was only half paying attention to Logan though, in fact I was only half paying attention to anybody; I couldn't get Angelo and Sylvester off of my mind. I was supposed to be enjoying this victory but somebody always has to spike my pleasure with stress.

Every time I looked around the joint, I saw 2 black and green ghostly figures in the shadows; there was no doubt that they were planning and plotting something against me. I knew they weren't done. I could feel it in the air.

After a while, most of my friends from school started bailing and bragging loudly about our winning the battle as they were on their way out of the rink. Rory said, "NSR owns this joint!"

And Rodd said, "You all whipped those boys, they were stuck!" which made me proud and nervous all at once. I knew "they" could hear the bragging.

I knew it was being said so loudly that it was undoubtedly irritating Angelo and Sylvester; I could feel their psychopathic frigid eyes coming from the shadows. Bragging around sore gangbangers is like peeing on a bee's nest, if you know what I mean. Everyone was laughing and high fiving all of us NSR's as they left the joint but every time someone bragged on us loudly, I shrieked to myself, just knowing that it was making my enemies blood boil.

There was a change in the action. A new guest DJ took over the turntables; it was the Chicago mix master from WMIX FM named "Radd Kidd Sidd." He was kind of a big deal because of his mean scratch, tricks, and stuff. Normally I would have been interested in that sort of thing but because of Angelo and Sylvester, I mainly just wanted to get the flip out of there and go home.

Half of the people in the joint, which was now half empty, were standing around the DJ booth checking out Radd Kidd but I kept trying to tell Bruiser, "I want to get the heck out of here while the getting is good." ... which he blew off, so then I said, "Angelo and Sylvester were messing with me and asking for their shoes and money back."

But Bruiser was only half listening to me because he was busy talking to the DJ, the MC, the lighting guy, and Braun Drix, who was now getting along famously with the smiley, pink scarfed, and soft spoken, lighting guy.

I'm not sure which scared me more. Those guys lurking in the shadows or when those cold hearted cats had made their exit. I watched Angelo and Sylvester walk out of the rink staring me down with unblinking eyes. They probably didn't walk over by me because I had numbers with me and there were bouncers on the inside. However, in the parking lot, there were no bouncers. So now I was stressed that they were going to be waiting outside in the parking lot for me. I hate to sound like such a chicken but I've never really had to get into "fisticuffs" all that much before. I mean come on; do you think someone who refers to fighting as "fisticuffs" really gets into fights all that much?

Finally Bruiser was ready to go; we walked outside with Blazin' and Miguel who were riding home with us. Fandango, of course, found a ride home with a girl; he was always meeting a girl wherever we went. – and those girls always thought they were the only one (but Gio had many.)

Everybody else I knew in the world that night had already bailed. Except for Braun, who hung back to hang with Trevor Pink, it looked like they were making their way to the dance floor, that was still going strong with deep house people as we had walked out of the rinks doors.

Dan half regretted leaving, "Aw shiznit bee-otches. Why do we gotta leave when they are playing "Pam Todd and Love Exchange?" he said as the DJ got even deeper into his house music set.

When we walked out, I spotted the two thugs standing by their car. One of them called out, "Phil ... hey dude ... come here for a minute." I think it was Angelo; he used the nicest voice you had ever heard in your whole life. Real phony, very charming.

"Yeah dude you're awesome at breakin' come over for a quick sec," the other banger said as if we were buddy old pals.

I was thinking: What the Flip? Are you guys really going to try and sweet talk me over there? But I just ignored them. Bruiser, who was apparently confused, even though I had just told him the whole story just minutes ago, asked me, "Aren't you going to go over there and see what those guys want?"

"Didn't you hear a word I had said to you just about 15 minutes ago, about how those guys were trying to get their money back from me?" I asked.

"Really? No," Bruiser said with surprise.

"Can we just get in the car and bail?" I asked.

Bruiser laughed, "I'll go over there and talk to those guys."

I told him, "No!" but it was too late he was already half way heading over to them as I spoke.

When Dan got over there, Angelo and Sylvester acted as if Bruiser wasn't even over by them; they looked through him with their antisocial eyes and said, "Yo Phil … come over here and talk to us." Even though they were half of a parking lot away, I had never seen such cold "friendly" eyes before.

The wind was dead, so I could hear Bruiser tell them, "Anything you want to say to Phil you can say to me right here and now."

"We don't have anything to say to you," Angelo said to Dan.

Bruiser turned around and started walking back over to me when I heard Sylvester say, "Don't ever come back here alone PUNK … you don't belong here." And the way he said "Punk" I wondered if Bruiser felt spray on the back of his neck from it.

"What sore losers," I said quietly to Brock and Miguel but I mainly kept my mouth shut, even though I had numbers.

"What's that PUNK?" Sylvester asked.

I knew he didn't hear me, I had said it that quietly but because he saw my lips move he had to ask.

We could all feel the tension in the air, so we all just piled into Bruiser's blue Stang and drove away swiftly.

Mouthing off is a great way to get yourself into trouble and you won't always have the numbers to back you up. Sometimes the smartest thing you can say is said, with your mouth closed.

I was finally able to enjoy our victory now that I wasn't worried about looking over my shoulder anymore. I counted Boogie Bobs Cash, my cash, and checked out our winning shoes. We pulled over after a few minutes though. Dan made me put the "sewer tong-flip flops" in the trunk; they really did smell like butt; it smelled up the whole car, no kidding. Nobody on the HHB's side had worn their good shoes that night. And maybe that's why we had won. I noticed that every single one of us Neighborhood Street Rockers had worn the same shoes that we had always worn. We all wore our new bad to the bone breakin' shoes, not some second hand bull Shee-ott. We had the stronger will to win;

the other crew knew deep down inside that if they lost, they would only be losing their crappy pair of second hand shoes. They had less to fight for and it showed.

The fact that I got stuck with Shock Rocks "smelly sock thongs" or "sewer socks tongs," or "flip flop fart shoes," as AJ had called them on different occasions - didn't matter. I would always know that those "flip flops" were my trophy for winning the break battle against the Hip Hop Breakers.

The whole ride home we were jamming out to Chicago house music; deep house, jackin' tracks, and the like that came from a mix tape that Dan had recorded off the radio from the famous WMIX FM a few weeks prior. Dan was always recording mixes off of the radio and playing them for us on his cassette deck.

Blazin' started ranting and raving to us that hip hop was the music that defined us B-boys.

So I jumped in with my two cents, "To me a B Boy means someone who spins around, up rocks, top rocks, down rocks, and power moves -TO BREAK BEAT MUSIC ... all styles of music have breaks. Maybe it's just me, but I like to get on down with breakin' to: House, Italo, Disco, Funk, Techno, Hip Hop, Freestyle, and heck I was even getting on down with breakin' to some Rock n Roll last week.

What is a b boy, a breaker, or a break dancer? It's someone who likes to have fun with the sport of breakin'. Some people can really be touchy about the proper way to refer to us breakers. But I say, as long as you're having fun with breakin' or poppin' or any kind of acrobatic dancing, and you dress like a hipster, and you listen to hip cat funky dance music; then I think, you are down! You are a part of the down crowd –you're in baby," I said to Miguel, Blazin', and Bruiser as I ended my rant.

But by the time I was done with my rant I had realized that Blazin' and Miguel were both starting to doze off in the back seat of the car. It was quite a long night and we had practiced, jammed, battled, and rocked out like mad cats all night, so I understood. The only reason I was probably so wide awake was because my adrenaline was still pumping like mad because of those two gang bangin' thugs.

But Bruiser had finally heard me this time, "Word Swift, Word!" he said. Which was the best compliment a Bboy could ever give another Bboy.

Chapter 21

Niagara Falls

I woke up unusually early on Sunday morning feeling ecstatic and anxious. I was excited that we had won last night but I also felt deep down inside that the victory celebration wasn't complete until I got to see Bob that morning at the hospital and hand him his winning 50 bucks, his ante, and his raggedy winning shoe trophy. The shoes were nothing to write home about but at least I wasn't going to stick him with the smelly flip flops; but a trophy was a trophy, no matter what it was – is what I say. I'm not complaining, I'm just saying.

I got dropped off at the hospital at 10am that morning with my shoe trophies in hand. I walked as slowly as I could because I knew that Bob usually did his morning treadmill run around 10am. I tried calling him a few times over the past few weeks at that time, his phone would ring off the hook, and I'd always get nervous. But like clockwork, around 1030am, I'd finally get a hold of him and he'd tell me over the phone that he had just finished working out on, "that darn treadmill', and then he would say, "we wouldn't want Mary crying her eyes out over an empty treadmill." He would always say that, every time I had called, right after his treadmill run. He really hated how she cried over empty treadmills. He thought she was nuts to cry over such weird things. He really did.

You would think that I would have learned to not keep calling him at 10am. But I never did. I always forgot and I kept calling him at 10am every day. It was right after morning cartoons, so that was just when I sort of felt like calling him, that's all.

And there I was, at the hospital at 10am but that was more or less because that was the only time I could get a ride that morning.

One can only walk so slowly when you can't wait to deliver awesome news. It was only 1005AM when I finally got to his floor. I was the most chipper cat that I had ever been while visiting at the cancer unit. It's not really a place that one can really be all that chipper all of the time; heck being chipper part of the time when I was on the cancer unit was kind of hard to do, if you really must know. I was so chipper that morning that I'm using the word chipper to describe how I felt, and I hate the word chipper.

Anyway, I started putting on all of the cancer unit "scrubs" garb in record time, I couldn't wait to see the look on Bob's face when I handed him his dough. I had walked to the cancer unit slowly but now that I was on his floor, I couldn't wait to tell him, even if that meant I would have to watch Bob run his bald and boney legs up and down on that, "Darn treadmill."

I got buzzed in after getting dressed and I entered the cancer unit. I walked past the treadmill room, once I saw Bob wasn't in there. There was only one person using the treadmill, so I figured that Bob must have finished early. I knew that he had been sharing his treadmill time with "Purple Bandana Girl" over the last week or so – who was on the treadmill that morning. Purple bandana girl, which is what Bob had always called her, was running on the treadmill as fast as she could – she was sprinting like a swarm of bees were chasing her –and that's pretty freakin' fast in my book. It was impressive; she was sprinting so fast she looked mad – that's how serious her face had looked. And honestly, cancer or not, I don't think I had ever seen someone run so fast on a treadmill before.

I think I may have told you about her before; she's the girl that Bob referred to as "The hottest bald chick you've ever seen in your life." He even went as far as to say, "When she gets done with her chemo, she should consider just rockin' the bald look from now on – even if her hair grows back, she should just shave it all off; just shave it bald, she looks hot that way, cue ball scalp and all," he said. That's how fond of bald purple bandana girl he was. He really did like her – purple bandana, bald head, and all. And he meant it, he really did. I saw it in his eyes.

I kept on walking towards Bob's room and I kept thinking about how I must have timed everything perfectly because he had probably just gotten done with his work out, and since he knew I was coming first thing in the morning, he'd have the hook up. He always had a Popsicle right after his treadmill run and I knew he would have a Popsicle sitting there waiting for me in his bucket of ice. He used one of those "puke" plastic buckets that hospitals give their chemo patients, (in case you needed to puke from the chemo.) But of course he never puked in it before, he only used it for ice to keep his popsicles cold or to make his non foo foo water cold. Popsicles were the highlight of his day at the hospital. I smiled as I walked to his room. I couldn't wait to clang popsicles with Bob and say, "Cheers" in victory about our break battle win. I kept picturing his brow-less brows raised as he laughed with joy through his nose about our victory.

I felt like the nurses at the front desk of the cancer unit were looking at me strange but that was because they were probably wondering why the heck I was carrying two pairs of shoes in see-through bags and all. They smelled so bad I had to bag 'em. Of course I was going to give Bob his shoes but I also wanted to show Bob the flip flops, so he could see them as I told him the sewer sock story. Kind of crazy, I know but I like to have props when I'm telling a story or maybe it's that I looked at them as a trophy or something and I wanted to show him my trophy.

I rounded the corner of the nurse's station and I entered Bob unusually dark room. He usually had the blinds open, the lights on, and the heat cranking since it was winter. However, it was cold. Colder than I even knew. I saw Nurse Mary taking the bed sheets off Bob's bed. Mary seemed Maudlin. "You're cleaning Bob's sheets?" I asked.

The dark, cold, and quiet room seemed very empty. Bobs bed was empty, Maudlin Mary's expression was empty, and my stomach suddenly felt empty as I read Mary's sullen emotions like a book. I had seen that look on her face before and I didn't like it. I was hoping that Bob was going to walk out of his rooms' private bathroom, even though I had this feeling that he was not in there. A blip ran through my mind that Bob and I would have a good laugh about Mary's sniffling and crying over empty beds and empty treadmills and such, just as soon as he got back in the room.

To combat Maudlin Mary's teary sniffled mood I ramped up the chipperness and I asked Mary, "I didn't see Bob on the treadmill? Is he in the bathroom? Or is he walking the halls like he sometimes does? ... Trying to find some non foo foo water, I bet you he's harassing the Popsicle delivery person ... isn't he?" I laughed like a madman with nervous fluctuations in my voice as Mary remained Maudlin.

Mary quietly whispered, "He passed ..." Then she sniffed and laughed, so I thought that I had missed a joke or something but really my nervous fake laughter was just contagious. Then she spoke again but it was so quiet that I could barely hear her, "He always made fun of me for crying over empty treadmills ... and ... and ... now his treadmill and bed are empty this morning," she said sort of laughing and sort of crying at the same time.

"I'm sorry Mary, I didn't hear you," I said, even though I knew I had. My mind and soul didn't believe it but my body had heard her, my body felt like it had plunged to the floor even though I was still standing. My hands started to feel like needles, my head felt light, and I fought back tears. I didn't want to be what Bob hated, someone who cried over a darn empty bed or a darned empty treadmill.

Mary cleared her throat, faked a smile, and said, "Boogie Bob went to enter a break dance battle in the sky last night."

I said, "Yeah, I know he battled last night, well his shoes did, of course, but you're right, he battled last night and we won! We won the battle! I can't wait to tell him," I said while still not fully accepting her talk about that sky business.

Mary responded, "You just did tell him, I'm sure he heard you." Even though I already knew the answer I guess I just couldn't grab on to it until I had heard it in clear terms.

"Where is Bob?" I asked point blank.

Maudlin Mary said, "He went to be with Jesus last night at 11:45pm."

I started thinking out loud, "The battle started at 11pm and I probably was head spinning around 1145pm ... thanks Bob," I said in a cheerful cry.

Mary's eyes became wet.

And my eyes became wet. I couldn't stop staring at his empty bed. It made me realize that there were two kinds of empty beds.

I told Mary about the battle as we both stared at his empty bed. I could tell that it made her very happy to know that Bob's shoes had won the battle for us that night.

272

Just before I left the hospital room, I told her, "I'm going to take Bob's shoes home with me, if that's okay? However, you can tell his parents that they can have them if they want them. I am going to give you these shoes from our opponent," I told her as I handed her the bag of tattered shoes. "You can tell his parents that Bob won these shoes in the battle last night and they should act as if these shoes are Bob's last trophy he won here on planet earth," I said, which felt really weird to say it like that. It's like, if someone ever comes up to you and says, "Hey, where are you from?" and if you respond, "Earth" they are going to look at you like your nuts. So I felt nuts.

But she knew what I meant because she said, "Yep, he is in a better place right now, no more earthly problems; he's break dancing on streets paved with gold. ... Bobs parents knew all about the break dance battle last night and they will be very happy to hear that you guys had won ...

Bob had said to me a few times over the past few weeks: I'm not a cancer patient, I'm a Neighborhood Street Rocker," Nurse Mary said.

I handed her Bobs 100 bucks and my winnings and said, "Can you donate fifty bucks in the name of Robert Charles aka Boogie Bob to a charity for: A,L,L; Acute Lymphocytic Leukemia and give the other hundred to his P.s."

"Peace?" Mary asked.

"P.s .... Parents," I said.

Then, to cover my tracks, since I was the king of denial, I said, "Is someone chopping an onion around here?" But that only got Mary's' eyes going like Niagara Falls again.

Mary nodded and said, "We will donate Bob's winnings to a charity for Acute Lymphocytic Leukemia."

"We lost a really cool dude, way too early," I said sadly as I walked out of Bob's room.

I exited Bob's room and I slowly walked past the exercise room and peered in there with this feeling of contempt and hate at the vision of empty bikes and treadmills. But I snapped out of it quickly because I could picture Bob saying to me, "Listen kid, they're just treadmills – just empty treadmills. But don't worry; someone will be here to fill them up before you know it. There is no use in crying over an empty treadmill." I could remember his voice so well in my mind's eye it was surreal.

I took off all of my cancer unit clothes and headed towards the hospital exit. I had purposely used the same exit where I had first seen those two nurses smoking cigarettes on that day that I had walked to McCollum Park in my scrubs with the mask on and all. I was hoping and begging with anger that the smokers would be out there smoking again. I wanted someone to yell at. I wanted to call them morons for smoking cigarettes.

I was so mad that I even muttered out loud to myself, "It says it right there on the damn box that it causes cancer you friggin' idiots!"

But they weren't there. Nobody was out there. It was empty outside. The most empty outside I had ever seen.

Then I screamed in anger, "Smoking sucks, Leukemia sucks, Cancer Sucks, Empty beds and empty treadmills SUCK!!"

ABOUT THE AUTHOR

Philip Kochan a.k.a. Phil K Swift™ (that's me) grew up in the suburbs of Chicago, Illinois U.S.A. during the Atari, Pac Man, Donkey Kong, and original wave of "breakers" generation.

In the early 1980's, It was at the roller rink that I learned about Disco/Soul and R n B, (now they call it house music), the DJ mixes, Cool cat fashion, and Breakin'; it was a place where I turned from a kid to a cat; a hip-cat.

When Break-dancing took over Chicago and the USA during the early 1980's, it was all I did 6th thru 9th grades (when I wasn't busy messing up puppy love.) My break crew and I hit up the malls, parks, street corners, and roller rinks and threw down with breakin' every freakin' day. It wasn't just a hobby, it was and IS a way of life. A B-boy way of life.

As a young B-boy, I began collecting 12-inch dance records, which is a must for any true B-boy/girl. This vinyl addiction sparked my main path in life; a real deal turntable DJ.

In the mid 1980's, Breakin' was growing overseas and as House music and DJ-ing became de rigueur, the tables began to turn - literally. While I still vowed to remain a B-boy and keep on breakin' for the rest of my life, I bought my first pair of Technic 1200 turntables during the summer of 1985 and I have been DJ-ing and Breakin' ever since.

In 1986, I started mixing at dance parties (now they call them raves) where I played House music, Freestyle, Italo, Disco, Hip-Hop, Hip-House, and Techno music and was sure to be seen mixing, tricking, scratching, beat juggling, and Breakin' every weekend.

Ultimately, it wasn't enough for me to just spin at parties and clubs, the competitive B boy in me had to prove that I was the best DJ around. I entered numerous DJ battles throughout the years: DMC DJ battles, A Chicago radio-station mixer search, Nightclub DJ competitions, and "One-off" dance parties were among the places that I had entered and won many DJ battles.

I have held top nightclub and teen club residencies and have DJ-ed nationwide but now I'll give it to you straight. The one thing that has always stood out about me is that I can Trick, Scratch, Mix and Funk the heck out of any set of turntable decks with a DJ ear that was developed in Chicago during the original wave of breakin' and house music.

When you come watch me mix live, you might even catch me jump away from the decks for a minute and throw down with breakin' right on the stage or on the dance floor with the crowd, this is why many B-boys/girls like to follow my DJ sets.

Even though many "DJs" have abandoned turntables, I have remained a staunch devotee to the turntable. Phil K Swift is a turntable DJ for life. I sleep with records under my pillow. If you want to book this "real deal DJ" for a gig, you best be sure to have turntables on your stage or in your DJ booth. And my crowd loves it, they always know that I am really mixing live, aint no jive.

I have finished writing other "Phil K Swift" novels that will be released soon. However, I am waiting for you, the reader, to make your comments and reviews for this novel before I release the next.

Go to Philkswift.com, Facebook.com/djphilkswift, philkswiftassemblesanincrediblebreakdancecrew.com

Philip Kochan a.k.a. Phil K Swift is married with five kids, has two dogs, and lives in Chicagoland USA and is coming to a store, library, nightclub, festival, event, and a movie theater near you soon.

GET READY! It is On – On like Donkey Kong!